I0561115

Sign up for our newsletter to hear
about new and upcoming releases.

www.ylva-publishing.com

Language of Love

A Flirty, Festive Anthology

Edited by
Astrid Ohletz and Lee Winter

Introduction

Language of Love is a diverse, festive collection of fun short stories that shows laughs, loves, and lives are universal.

Eleven lesbian fiction authors, many of whom are award winners, offer diverse tales of romance, adventure, humor, and whimsy, set against the holiday season in South Africa, Australia, England, Wales, Scotland, Germany, India, Jamaica, and the US.

Whether Christmas or Chanukah or something else is being celebrated, this disarming book offers a wonderful glimpse into women's festive experiences all over the world. The touch, taste, and smell of celebrations burst into life.

We hope you enjoy reading *Language of Love* as much as we enjoyed bringing it to you.

Astrid Ohletz
Lee Winter

Table of Contents

The Friend

BY LEE WINTER

NUMBER NINE MAXWELL BROWN DRIVE, Southport, Queensland was, unfortunately, exactly how Dani Sullivan remembered it.

She turned off the ignition to her beat-up mustard Datsun 120Y and stared up at the two-storey building in front of her. Developers had been trying to get her eighty-four-year-old great-aunt to sell it for years as it was a five-minute drive from one of the best beaches on the Gold Coast. But like most things related to the formidable Jean Thirkhill, the answer was a firm no.

"This is it, huh?" Ro asked. "Hon, it doesn't look *that* scary. Yeah, it could use something to bring it out of the seventies, but still…"

Dani eyed the yawning concrete drive and, to the right, a pool of white, jagged pebbles that caught the glare of sun every afternoon. Not a tree, bush, or skerrick of life was allowed to flourish. Jean didn't lean towards warm, soft, or living things.

Perspiration slicked Dani's palms at the reminder of two years of her childhood spent inside this precisely ordered house. She'd never called it home. Her sister had.

Ground floor had a pair of brown garage doors at the left of it; a line of curtained windows to the right. The floor above was lined with large, square windows. No curtains there. All the better to size up interlopers from. Above that, at the top right, sat a box-shaped room with a tall aerial on it. The ham-radio operator's nest that Fred, Jean's husband, inhabited.

Each storey was delineated by a fat strip of brown paint, like a layer of fig jam on a double sponge cake.

Ro nudged her. "Shake a leg. We can't sit here forever."

"But it *is* tempting." Dani shot her girlfriend a pained glance.

Today marked her first Christmas with Ro—the first of many, she hoped. Dani prayed her oddball family wouldn't scare off her girlfriend too much, but then Ro Tapu was tougher than most. You didn't go from a sprawling family of Samoan immigrants in a poor outer suburb to captaining the elite national netball squad without a lot of stern stuff shooting around your bloodstream.

Ro's light-brown skin glowed from her lean athlete's diet. Her pixie-cut black hair was sculpted around her high cheek bones and ended in wisps at the back of her sensuous neck.

Dani sighed. They could be seeing in Christmas in the cosy Brisbane townhouse they'd shared for five months, and teasing each other while wearing nothing but Santa hats. Instead, they were here, where even Santa would fear to tread.

A squawk of chickens echoed from somewhere nearby. A car honked a few streets away. The anxious pattering of Dani's racing heart almost drowned it all out.

I can do this. I can.

Ro placed a comforting hand on her thigh. "Come on, hon, stop freaking out. It'll be fine. So you brought a friend for Christmas for the first time. No big deal. Jean's what, mid-eighties? And her husband? Ninety-something? They won't know what it means."

"No, I know." Dani fidgeted. "Although younger-me was convinced she was a mind reader."

Ro laughed.

With an aggrieved sigh, Dani slid out, locked up, and peered over the expanse of mustard-yellow metal. Ro parked a round food container on the roof as she gathered their bags.

Dani had spent half the night trying to make the perfect trifle. This one was her third effort. She knew her dessert choice was about as cool as a purple mohair sweater, but for some reason Jean enjoyed the concoction of jelly, custard, and sponge all soaked in sherry.

Dani had balanced the alcohol content as best she could to meet her great aunt's exacting standards—more than enough to daze a koala, not enough to sink a croc. So…'tipsy lizard' for the win. Not that she held any delusions the gift would be appreciated. But at least she could tell herself she'd tried.

Collecting the trifle box from where Ro had placed it, Dani inhaled deeply, and looked back up at the house. "Right. We're going in. I'm sorry in advance."

"It'll be fine. I have a hundred percent track record on meeting parents, in-laws, and outlaws. It's universally accepted I'm awesome." She gave her eyebrows a teasing waggle.

"So you keep reminding me," Dani said. "But you're not the issue. It's me they don't love."

"Now I know you're exaggerating. You're so adorable and sweet. Who could hate you?"

"Fine. It's mainly Jean. She looks at me like I'm beneath her. She's been like that since I was twelve and lacked all my sister's lady-like decorum. I loved running, jumping, climbing trees, being loud. She called me an undisciplined wild child. It was death by a thousand nit-picks living here."

"Well, to be fair, you are kind of wild."

At Dani's huff, Ro added hastily, "But I love that about you." She waved their bags of wine and gifts. "Now, stop stalling, and let's crush this Christmas lunch."

Dani nudged the outer white door with her elbow, trifle carefully balanced in her hands, and it swung open. She led the way up the inside polished wooden stairs, dodging two freckled blurs of nephews playing tag amidst a mountain of boxes of wools and fabrics. These teetering cardboard piles were leftovers from Jean's former life running her beloved haberdashery shop.

There was a solemn bass beat coming from above. "Little Drummer Boy," a staple of Jean's Christmas mix tape. Her battered, old-style cassette came with a faded name from a felt-tip pen. If you held it just so, you could almost make out "Xmas 1998" on it.

They reached the second level and stepped onto a flecked white carpet. Dani turned to explain that her aunt loved everything hospital-grade clean, so spill something on that carpet at her peril, when she noticed Ro was frozen, looking transfixed.

Ah. *That*. Down the left wall was an enormous glass display case that contained thousands of little glass and crystal animal figurines. Tiny dogs, cats, mice, and birds were neatly corralled inside.

As a child, Dani had longed to be able to take them out and inspect them, name them, befriend them, give them little stories, but Jean's bony fingers held the key to the cabinet. She'd been very clear: pretty things were for looking at, not touching with clumsy children's hands.

A white-haired Fred roamed by, in his trademark singlet, blue shorts, white knee-length socks, and leather sandals, clearly on a mission of some sort. He'd obviously shucked his shirt, most likely despite Jean's best hopes. When her husband wasn't in the mood to stay fully dressed, Jean had never successfully kept him that way.

Dani called out a greeting, but the old man's focus was complete.

Fred was always like this. He spent most of his life upstairs in his hidey-hole talking to ham-radio friends. His constant companion was a Huntsman spider the size of a tea plate. The terrifying arachnid kept the mice away, he told everyone. It also kept Jean away, and Dani had long suspected that's what he enjoyed most about it.

Fred and his wife of sixty years had little in common beyond their marriage. Jean was an imposing woman, held together by sinew, subtle sneers, and plumes of hairspray on her stiff, coiled grey bun.

Fred, by contrast, was fuelled by a childlike fascination for anyone on the other side of the world. Or just anyone not in the room. The pair didn't share beds, conversations, or philosophies. Dani had never seen them even touch in her entire life.

It was a little sad, now she thought about it. Apparently, Jean's rules for figurines also applied to husbands. Both were for display purposes only.

"That was Fred," she murmured, as he reappeared, crossing their path again, now bearing a glass jar.

"Hey, Fred," Dani called out.

He ignored her, but then his hearing wasn't the best.

"What on earth is he holding?" Ro whispered as he disappeared again.

"Curds?" Dani shrugged. "Or it could be whey. I forget which he prefers from week to week. So does he. On that note, don't be alarmed if he calls me Edith. It's his best friend's late wife. They were all really close mates."

"He's senile?"

"Shh! We do not speculate on that around here no matter what."

"Doesn't Jean notice?"

"We think she's in denial. But this is not a safe topic. Okay?"

Ro nodded, for the first time looking a little less confident at winning over Dani's family.

Dani glanced around the small front room. There were wide windows on opposite walls, an arched doorway in front, and against one wall, facing an ancient TV, were a pair of green armchairs with faded crocheted armrest protectors. Nothing had changed in the three decades she'd been coming here each Christmas.

From outside came a loud, indignant squawk. Ro's face lit up, and she rushed to the windows facing the backyard. "Chickens! We had a chook pen when I was a girl." Ro squinted down and tapped the window. "Whoa. Those chooks look like they've put their claws in a power socket."

"Because they are not *chooks*." The angular, whippet-thin form of Jean Thirkhill swept in and stepped up beside Ro at the window. A maroon knit-dress clung to her lean body.

Dani blanched. Damn, Jean was still fast and silent. A greyhound came to mind. She wished she could warn Ro to change topics, because no one dissed Jean's fancy-pants chickens and lived.

"Well, they sure cluck like chooks!" Ro grinned, heedless to the danger.

Jean's expression became pure disdain. "Young lady, you are looking at prize-winning *show* chickens."

"People put chooks on show?" Ro blinked. "Seriously? What type are they?"

"Bantam frizzled Cochin. Less accurately dubbed *frizzles*."

"Frizzles?" Ro gave her a sceptical look.

"It denotes the outward curl of the feather." Jean tapped the window with her clear-lacquered nail, pointing at one. Her tone warmed slightly to her pet topic. "I also keep Plymouth Rocks and Silkies. Silkies are sometimes called sizzles."

"Okay, now I know you're pulling my leg." Ro laughed.

Dani groaned inwardly. At least Ro hadn't nudged Jean in the ribs, too.

"I'm entirely serious. See that white one? That's Leonora. She won the Grand Champion Soft Feather Fowl of the Queensland Royal Show last year. She also won Grand Champion Fowl of the show, and would have won Supreme Grand Champion if not for some skulduggery on the part of Mrs Rutledge."

"Ooh, a show scandal?" Ro's eyebrows shot up. "What'd evil Mrs Rutledge do?"

"*She* knows." Jean huffed. She turned and sized up Ro. "So, I take it you are the *friend* Danielle was so intent on inviting to our *family* Christmas?"

Her voice was cool and polite, but her emphasis was damn rude, as if Ro was some interloper they'd allowed in.

"Yep. I'm the friend." Ro ignored the subtext and gave her a friendly smile. "And you must be Dani's Great-Aunty Jean. I'm Ro Tapu."

"How nice for you." Not a hint of warmth flickered across Jean's features. "I trust you play netball better than you identify chickens?"

Ro laughed and shrugged. "Well, you gotta admit that wouldn't be hard."

Astounding. Dani stared at her girlfriend in amazement. It was like the barbs just bounced off her. Yet they'd always stuck to Danni like bindii prickles to her bare feet.

Jean glanced to Dani and the box in her hands. "And what have you there?"

"Trifle," Dani said. "I, ah, tried to make it the way you like it."

Ro darted her a curious look.

Dani didn't blame her. She sounded all kinds of pathetic.

"We may not have room for trifle as I've prepared pavlova as well as fruit mince pies." Jean waved at the archway. "Put it in the kitchen. Mind Harriet. She's attempting to become one with the kitchen rug today. I've lost count of how many times I've shooed her out and she's ignored instruction."

Dani, smarting at the trifle dismissal, turned to Ro. "Harriet's the cat."

"I'm sure even your *sporty friend* could have worked that out," Jean said.

Wow. Only Jean could make "sporty" sound like an insult. Dani reddened. What must Ro think of her family?

There was a bellow of laughter down the hall—one of her uncles—then a giggle that was far higher and louder. Aunt Rhoda. Sloshed already. Dani glanced at the antique wooden wall clock. Barely eleven.

Jean's eyes narrowed, and without another word, she ghosted down the hallway towards Rhoda, with a look that did not bode well for Dani's merry aunt.

"You lived with her for two years?" Ro whispered.

Dani nodded. "My parents were out of work, and she let us all move in downstairs while they looked for jobs. Problem was it took them ages."

Of course, there was way more mess, stress, and anger to it than that. Jean had used the situation as an excuse to slowly dissect Dani's awkward pre-teenage existence and dismantle her budding self-esteem.

Her sister Sally's beauty and deportment had been held up as an example. But Dani just didn't have that gene. She'd felt like a bull in a china shop most days as she grew into her broad shoulders, five-foot-ten height, and tangle of solid, strong limbs.

The day Dani's mother had finally noticed Jean's sly, usually subtle, ridicule was the day Dani's parents packed up and moved to live in a tiny, mouldy-smelling, second-hand caravan in the middle of nowhere. As bad as living on the outer reaches of Hell had been, it still beat enduring a clipped daily diatribe listing Dani's many failings.

Not everyone agreed. Sally had forever resented that their living conditions had been downgraded just to spare Dani from Jean's cruel tongue. They hadn't been close since.

Ro leaned against the window, watching the frizzles peck at grain. "I've never heard someone make my athleticism sound like I must be stupid." She sounded awed. "I'm sorry, hon. It musta been hell living here."

Dani grunted in agreement, not wanting to get into it. Her stomach was churning enough. "Come on. Let's drop the food in the kitchen so we can do the round of rellies. Mum and Sally are much friendlier. Which wouldn't be hard. Don't be alarmed if Mum doesn't say much—she's shy—and Sally's a bit of a snob. On the plus side, there's Rhoda's rum balls if you need a pick-me-up. Just don't operate heavy machinery after them."

"No probs." Ro looked back on solid footing.

The saying that a table was groaning with food was clearly invented for Great Aunt Jean. At the centre, atop the white linen tablecloth, was an enormous roast chicken, its orange-brown skin sticky from marinade. Beside that sat a roast lamb beneath an aromatic crown of rosemary, lemon, and garlic. Next to that were fat turkey slices, the skin studded with peppercorns.

Little pots of gravy, mint sauce, and cranberry sauce were dotted up and down the table, along with giant blue-and-white bowls of potato, green-leaf, and tomato salads, freshly cooked prawns, and mounded platters of roast vegetables. The smell was incredible. And so was the heat generated by all the dishes.

As if the day wasn't hot enough. The days of slavishly paying tribute to Australia's English roots had been fading for decades across the country, in favour of cold dishes and barbecues or picnics at the beach. Not here, though. Jean always opted for the full, glorious hot English spread because that's what she'd had as a girl.

The matriarch in question was seated at one end of the long table, along with uncles, aunts, and random cousins, facing Fred. Three along from her, Dani and Ro were positioned under Jean's watchful eye. Dani's mother sat opposite them both, nibbling on finger foods, sipping wine, and saying little.

Ro's eyes were wide as garbage can lids. "There's so much." She patted her stomach. "Thank God it's the off-season."

Dani laughed. She lowered her voice. "Please, with your metabolism, you'd burn all this off in one training session. Well, unless you have the plum pud with brandy sauce—that's ten sessions easy. So maybe skip that."

"I can't have *any* dessert," Ro whispered. "I'll be full just on this. And I haven't had processed sugar since I made the national squad."

"You have to," Dani said with a worried gulp. "The pavlova and fruit mince pies are Jean's pride and joy. If you skip either one, it's like spitting in her eye."

"Oh hell." Ro swallowed. She stared at her plate. "Um, I better pace myself."

"Thanks." Dani glanced at her aunt and saw her immersed in conversation. "It'd be impossible to claw your way back into her good graces if you turned that down."

Ro laughed and leaned into her ear. "Wait, she has good graces?"

Biting back a snort of laughter, Dani refocused on the rest of the table. Her uncle Stephen, at her left elbow, was watching them both curiously.

Dani braced herself for awkward questions. Her sexuality was firmly in the "don't ask-don't tell" category with her extended family. Bringing Ro today meant some of her more aware relatives might join the dots.

"You two," Stephen began, waggling his finger to and fro between them. Dani tensed.

"Any interest in real estate? Have I told you about my new business?"

Ugh. No. He always had some get-rich scheme underway.

"See, it's all about leveraging. Negative gearing. Right?"

Right. Dani glanced across the table to find her mother's gentle smile.

Jean glanced at her, too, and cleared her throat. "Clarice, where is your husband? Why would he drive that truck on Christmas day?"

Her mother's smile faltered. "He volunteered. He's transporting toys this run. For the January sales."

"Consumerism. How lovely." Jean lifted her wine glass and tapped on it, quietening the room.

"Before we continue…" She paused and eyed Rhoda sharply until she put down her utensils with a clatter. "…a few words. We come together as one to share these bountiful gifts from God."

Dani's eyebrows shot up. This was new. Her great aunt was not a religious woman. Probably couldn't stand the thought anyone was higher up than she was.

"That means we're grateful not only for what we have in our lives, but whom."

Ro's warm hand snuck under the table and found Dani's fingers, giving them a squeeze of agreement.

Dani sighed with contentment.

"We celebrate the people we have known and the ones we have lost."

She sounded so sad. Frowning, Dani sifted through the family gossip from the year. Who had Jean lost? Her eyes followed her aunt's gaze and landed on Fred who was humming softly to himself. Oh. So they *were* going to mention it?

"Never forget the privilege you all have. You enjoy lives of opportunity previous generations never had. You are lucky. Spoilt even." Her eyes settled on Dani.

The hell? Was that how Jean saw her? Some lazy wild child swanning around?

Her mother's brow knotted together in confusion.

Dani clenched her paper napkin into a ball.

"You should appreciate what you have, as others have considerably less." Jean's lips bared.

What might be an uplifting sentiment was now sounding a lot like a threat.

"Come on, Jean," Dani's oldest uncle whined. "Lunch is getting cold."

Rhoda took that as the go-ahead and reached for the potato salad. Everyone else swallowed their drinks, called a polite "Cheers," and it was a free-for-all.

Jean sat back with a discontented sigh at the unceremonious end to her speech. "Decorum is dead," she muttered.

Dani smirked at how aggrieved her great-aunt sounded at the mutiny. It fell away when Jean's cool gaze fixed on her.

Every. Time. That damn woman could sour a plate of milk with that look. Dani was suddenly beyond grateful that Jean obviously didn't know the true nature of her relationship with Ro. There's no way she'd have missed the chance to toss something vicious into her speech to embarrass them both.

"So, girls," Uncle Stephen continued as he forked some lamb and dragged it through a gravy puddle on his plate. "Have you two thought about what I was saying? Negative gearing? I could help."

The Christmas mix tape had been flipped three more times and was back to "Little Drummer Boy." Dani had by now sat through numerous anecdotes about how perfect, accomplished, and smart her sister's kids were. She'd tuned out at the trombone classes.

"And Ted is doing so well at learning Polish."

That woke her up. Dani glanced at her sister. "*Polish*? Who's he going to talk to in Polish around here?"

Sally shot her a condescending look. "Knowledge for the sake of it is never a bad thing."

"Quite right," Jean said. "Not everyone has aspirations to sell shoes at Athlete's Kit. I'm sure my great-grand-nephew will go on to great things with that fine mind of his."

"Hey, I don't sell stuff at Athlete's Kit." Dani put down her knife and fork.

"Well, you did." Acid dripped from Jean's tongue. "I recall how excited you were. You felt the need to share with everyone."

"When I was twenty. Now I'm the assistant manager."

"In a *sports shoe* store. How…impressive."

Right. Like selling haberdashery was such a step up to greatness. Dani tried to keep a mutinous glare off her face.

"Well," Ro said, spearing a prawn and eying it for a moment before looking around at the faces watching her, "I'm glad she works at Athlete's Kit. I met her there. We bonded over sneakers for people with narrow feet."

Dani had a sudden flash of memory of how Ro had flirted with her so shamelessly that she'd been a wreck. She hoped her blush would be blamed on the room's rising temperature.

"So is that your crowning career achievement?" Jean asked Dani, eyebrow sky high. "Befriending a sports star?"

Sally laughed. "Probably."

Fury slashed through her.

The table fell silent, as if expecting more of the fireworks that had punctuated their teen years. Even Jean's eye took on a vague gleam of interest.

Dani inhaled sharply. The carols tape started a cheery version of Dean Martin's "Let It Snow." The ceiling fan was making lazy *whumpf, whumpf* noises as it circulated the stifling air.

Out of nowhere, a chipper voice from the end of the table shattered the icy silence. "I remembered to flush today."

All eyes turned.

Fred. Looking so damned proud.

"What was that, Fred?" Rhoda asked, looking confused.

Jean blanched. "Who'd like seconds?" she asked loudly. "If anyone…"

"I remembered to flush today," Fred repeated helpfully. "The toilet. After a poo."

Several of Dani's smaller nephews and nieces at the small children's table nearby tittered. Teddy, Sally's Polish-mastering, trombone genius son, didn't. He was too busy putting a pea up his nose.

Jean's lips thinned. "Yes, well, thank you for that update, Fred, but that's not appropriate for the table."

His enthusiasm seemed undimmed. "I don't always remember," he explained to everyone. Spying a piece of tinsel on the Christmas tree behind him, he reached for it, yanking hard. Baubles and fake snow sprayed off it.

Fred beamed at his prize and wrapped it around his head like a bandana. The excess tinsel hung down one ear like a possum's tail.

"Very cool, Uncle F." Dani shot him a thumbs up. "Could spark a whole new trend."

He beamed back at her and chuckled. "Zactly."

Jean hissed at her under her breath, "Don't you dare mock him. I will not tolerate that."

Dani's jaw clenched. "I would *never* do that."

"Soooo," Rhoda called from Fred's end of the table, "if we're talking embarrassing stuff, I have news. Got a *vicious* urinary tract infection. Like, Jesus H. Christ, the itchiness. You got no idea. But don't worry, not catching."

"What's a yinary track affection?" Teddy piped up. A pea popped out of his nose.

Ro laughed, and Jean shot her and the boy an appalled look.

Rhoda picked up her glass and waved it about. "It's as fun as pissing staples, young man, thanks for asking. Thank Christ I got it fixed. The doc says I have to remember to stay hydrated. So, on that note, cheers!" She skulled her wine, finishing it with a satisfied smack of lips.

"Really?" Fred sounded intrigued. "That's good to know." He reached for a glass in front of him.

Dani squinted. Definitely whey. She shuddered. He really loved his health kicks.

Unfortunately, Fred's bid for rehydration failed as he missed his mouth by a wide margin and wound up with an expanding yellow stain on his shirt. He blinked at it in confusion. "What?" His look was heartbreaking. He glanced around the table, as if seeking answers.

You could have heard a pin drop. Even the music fell silent between songs. The fan continued its slow whumping sound. Nobody met Fred's eye.

Dani gave her plate her fullest attention.

Jean was out of her seat in an instant, striding to her husband's end of the table. "You must be more careful, Fred." She hauled him to his feet by his elbow. "We're getting cleaned up," she added, with a look so fierce it dared anyone to mention what had just happened. Then she frogmarched her husband out of the room and down the hall.

The moment she was gone, the table broke into chatter.

"Oh boy," Uncle Stephen said. "I thought we were finally going to discuss the elephant in the room."

"Not likely," Sally snorted. "He'd have forgotten his own name and Jean still wouldn't notice."

"I'd have thought my UTI would merit some support," Rhoda called out. "More important than genius Teddy updates. Jesus, Sally, does your kid suck at *anything*?"

"You're just jealous, Rhoda," Sally snapped. "I have a wonderful family and you have a series of failed AA meetings."

Dani winced. "Shit, Sally, lay off."

"What do you care?" Sally's blonde hair swirled as she spun back to glare at her. "Look at your life, little sister."

"What's wrong with it?"

"Where to start? The pathetic job or inability to find a boyfriend."

Seriously? She still hasn't worked it out?

Ro snorted.

"Girls," their mother cut in. "Please don't start."

"Does no one want to talk about property investments?" Uncle Stephen asked no one in particular.

"Ha!" Rhoda cackled. "Get Genius Ted to sell it to me, since he's perfect at everything. Including peas up noses."

"Not really good at *everything*," Mike, Sally's husband, inserted. His tone was placating. "I mean, he's only had two lessons in Polish. On YouTube."

"I hate Powish! Powish sucks!" Teddy called out.

Rhoda cackled. "Now it all comes out."

"Michael!" Sally looked askance. "Would it be too much for you to support me?"

Her husband shrugged and reached for the roast vegetable serving spoon.

Dani cast a glance at Ro, wondering if she'd ever be forgiven for bringing her into this madhouse. Would explaining they weren't ordinarily like this be believable?

Ro merely shot her a grin. "Hey, have you tried those garlic prawns? They're wicked."

Shaking her head, Dani rose. "I need a loo break. Will you be okay alone with the rabble?" She leaned closer and whispered in Ro's ear, "You have my permission to poke my sister in the eye with the salad spoon if she badmouths either you, me, or the high-octane world of sneakers sales."

"Leave 'em to me," Ro said. "No spoons of doom will be required."

As Dani padded softly down the hall to the bathroom, she heard low voices from the master bedroom. Nearing it, she paused, unable to resist peeking through the ajar door.

Fred was sitting on the bed, his bared chest on display, which was covered in liver-spots and white-hair.

Jean bent over him, using a flannel to wipe his torso of splashes of liquid, and murmuring to him softly. Her face was no longer disapproving or austere. She looked...sad.

"Silly duffer," she said with a voice so tender that shock flooded Dani. "Always making a mess and a fuss." She drew the cloth with gentle slowness across his skin. "What am I going to do with you? Hmm?"

"Anything you want, love," he said with the roguishness of a man who still believes himself young...or young enough.

"Incorrigible, too," she said with a fond tsk. She slipped a clean shirt over his head and straightened it, tugging the hem and collar into place. Jean smiled. Her thumb whisked over his cheek. "There now, good as new."

There was so much love in that statement. So much ache and despair, too. Like she was saying good-bye to the man she loved, with the dusting of her fingertips, memorizing his skin.

Jean's head turned slightly, just enough for Dani to see the gleam of a tear in her eye. She inhaled in surprise.

Jean's head snapped around.

Dani held her breath as suddenly cold, fierce eyes met hers in challenge.

Twisting around past his wife, Fred turned to see what had her attention. His face broke into a wide grin. "Why hello, Edith." He waved. "It's been such a long time. I'm so happy you came."

Jean strode towards Dani in four sharp steps and glowered at her. "Spying on me?" she asked, her voice a low snarl. "To what end? Will you mock Fred? Share what you saw with the rest of them? Laugh to your friend about your confused uncle who needs help to get cleaned and dressed? Are you so cruel?"

Dani sucked in a startled breath. "No! I was just..." She jerked her thumb behind her. "I needed the loo."

"Then why are you standing here, pressing your ear to my door? It's sly and rude." Her eyes flashed. "Leave!"

With enormous restraint, Dani only just avoided slamming shut the door of the bathroom behind her. Slumping against it, she took stock of how angry and embarrassed she felt. She was tired of being treated like the idiot toddler. Her irritation soon began to ebb as she processed what she'd seen. Jean's aching sadness began to settle around her.

As she finished and washed up, Dani mused on how strange it felt to discover Jean cared deeply about anyone—even if she hid it behind layers of disapproval as thick as winter clothes.

How must it feel to be losing a loved one, piece by piece, as their brain slowly forgot itself?

And Jean hadn't been oblivious after all, instead carefully hiding his secret to protect Fred's dignity. How long had this been going on? Months? Years? Longer?

The sticky air hit her the moment she arrived back at the dining room. Sweat was prickling down the back of her shirt. She glanced at the clock. It wasn't even the hottest part of the day. Was it forty degrees yet? At times like these, she wished Australia used the American scale. A hundred and four sounded much closer to the furnace this was.

Ro was telling her famous netball grand final story about their glorious come-from-behind victory against England that had her family agog. Even Rhoda had forgotten to drink.

Holy shit. Ro really was the in-laws whisperer.

Dessert usually signalled the beginning of the end.

They had survived Rhoda's additional proclamations about her medical issues, which had been brought to an abrupt end after Jean pointedly turned up "Little Drummer Boy" when it came around again.

Fred settled back into his seat with a fresh shirt on and was popping rum balls like grapes.

They all pulled the paper crackers and read out the terrible jokes and squeezed on paper hats.

"I like my joke," Dani said, examining the white rectangle of paper. *"Why did the hedgehog cross the road? To see his flat mate."*

Ro pouted adorably. "Nooo. You gotta feel so bad for the little guy. His mourning is for our amusement."

"Oh damn, now how can I unsee that?" Dani smirked.

Jean shot Dani an icy look. "If you're quite finished talking nonsense, it's time for dessert." Her mood had become progressively worse since Dani had caught her with Fred.

A burble of approval went around the table. It was impossible not to salivate at the thought of Jean's gooey pavlova and crispy fruit mince pies.

Jean headed towards the kitchen, waving off any offers to help.

"Right," Dani stood the moment she was gone. "I'm gonna make sure my trifle is at least on the menu." Making that concoction had taken half the night after all.

"I love trifle!" Fred called from the far end of the table. He beamed. "Thank you, Edith."

In the kitchen, Dani found Jean pulling the tray of fruit mince pies out of the oven with thick oven mitts. Her pavlova was already on the counter, artfully drizzled with passionfruit. It looked as though a food stylist had slaved over it for hours.

Dani stepped over the ginger cat curled in the centre of the room and flipped the lid on the trifle box.

"There's no room for that," Jean snapped. "Don't bother plating it up."

Up all night. She reminded herself. Up all night. She ignored her and reached for a large plate from the shelf.

"Did you not hear?"

"I heard. But I spent ages on this. Uncle Fred seemed keen."

"He prefers my pavlova. And this is my kitchen, in my home. Even though you apparently feel you have the right to invade any space you wish."

"I'm sorry I upset you before. And I'm bringing it out anyway." Dani bit her lip, heart thudding at her uncharacteristic show of defiance, and slid her fingers into the container to carefully remove her trifle.

"Absolutely not. I—" The rest of Jean's sentence turned into a startled half shriek.

Dani spun around to see Harriet darting through Jean's legs and the tray of mini fruit pies flying across the kitchen. Jean was falling. Her arms flailed as she sought her balance, her left arm catching the edge of the pavlova. It flew off the counter.

Time slowed for Dani as she saw her choices. Save Jean, save the nearby pavlova, or fling herself at that airborne tray hurtling toward the door.

Her hand shot out to catch the dropping pavlova from underneath as she slid her other arm around her aunt's waist, controlling her fall to the floor. She lay the pavlova beside Jean just as a loud grunt sounded at the door.

Dani's head snapped up.

Ro, at full stretch, had somehow managed to catch the tray of fruit tarts. It was a spectacular save—well, until her fingers closed fully around the scalding metal.

Her agonised yelp was sickening.

Ro tossed the tray on the oven top with a hiss. The little tarts played dodgem cars but somehow stayed on the metal. Tears streamed down Ro's cheeks.

"Ro!" Dani jumped up and ran to her side, grabbing her wrists. Two parallel lines of angry red welts ran across her fingers. "Oh my God! Your hands!"

"I'll live," Ro ground out. "Ow, ow, ow. Really glad it's off-season now though. Shit."

"Get OUT!" Jean bellowed.

Dani saw red. She whipped around, a sharp barb on her tongue to unleash at her ungrateful aunt. It was one thing for her to belittle Dani her whole life, but that gave her no rights to insult her girlfriend.

Jean, however, was flapping at the sulking cat, whose ginger fur was on its end like a toilet brush.

Harriet bolted.

Jean gingerly rose, and returned the battered but saved pavlova to the counter.

"Are you okay?" Ro asked, her voice a rasp.

"You're asking me that?" Jean's lips were white and her hands seemed than less steady as she wiped them on a dish towel.

"Yeah." Ro flapped her hands as if to get a breeze on them. "I mean, people don't bounce so well when they get older. Y'know?"

Dani winced at the reference to Jean's age. Her great aunt deeply resented being retired.

"I'm...unhurt." Jean's gaze fell to Ro's welts, eyes wide. "Your hands though!" She turned to the sink and flicked on the cold water. "Quickly! Under the water now. Danielle, the aloe vera lotion is in the bathroom cupboard, top shelf. Go!"

Dani sprinted for the bathroom. She flung things aside in the cabinet. God, if this stupid lunch had hurt Ro's career, she'd never forgive herself. Would Ro forgive her? Her gut twisted.

She raced back to find Jean holding Ro's hands under the water and murmuring to her.

Jean snatched the lotion from Dani's outstretched fingers and pulled Ro's blistered hands from the flow.

Ro stared at them and glanced at Dani. "I know it looks a mess, but I heal fast. And I'm sure..." She bit her lip, "...I'll be fine."

"You have superb reflexes," Jean dolloped lotion onto Ro's hands. "I've never seen anyone move that fast."

"Well, it is my job," Ro said with a grimace as Jean worked the ointment in. "They train us to react, not think. Which, as you can see, isn't always a good thing." She gave a wry chuckle. "I was just coming to see if Dani needed a hand and saw a tray coming right at me and reached for it. Pure instinct."

"Your job," Jean repeated. "Yes, I can see you're a professional." She glanced at Dani. "So what's your excuse?"

"Huh?" Dani asked cleverly.

"Your friend is trained to react in an instant. You are not. Your quick thinking was...most unexpected."

"Unexpected?" Dani hid her annoyance. Would it kill Jean to say thanks? Even her compliments sounded like accusations.

"Oh, Dani's always been pretty quick," Ro said. "She trains with me at the local park some weekends. I guess something stuck." She grinned.

"So it seems," Jean said. "Well"—she shook her head—"enough of the dramatics. Everyone will be wondering where dessert is." She waved at the pavlova. "I'll take this out. Danielle, plate up those fruit pies. We can't have Ro's sacrifice being in vain, now can we?"

Dramatics? Oh, and you're welcome.

Jean paused and added, "And plate up that trifle. Fred always enjoys it."

Her face was implacable as she swept from the room, leaving Dani speechless.

"Well, there you go," Ro said. "Your trifle is officially a welcome addition to the feast."

"Until anyone eats it," Dani joked, but her delivery was strained. "Are you really all right? I'm so sorry."

"The aloe's working. It's already hurting less. Can you get me a bandage to cover the blisters, and we can go and try that pav she's so proud of? I won't put myself on Jean's blacklist by knocking it back."

Rhoda was snoring in an armchair. Torn festive paper lay all around from gift wrappings. Dani stared at her present from Jean. A scarf. Tartan. She'd knitted them for everyone. Had it ever snowed in Brisbane once in its entire history?

Peak heat had hit, and the old ceiling fan was now just swirling sweltering air around the room. All the leftover hot food on the table just added to the stifling warmth.

No one could move. The paper party hats affixed earlier on sweaty heads (except Jean's brow, which neither sweated nor permitted party hats) had begun to disintegrate on foreheads.

Mike's red hat stain looked like someone had attempted to lobotomise him.

The conversation had moved on to next to nothing. Occasional spurts and starts of half-remembered things to share. Even Sally had dropped Teddy as a topic and was bitching about her boss.

Jean, however, sat, ramrod straight in her seat at the head of the table, saying little but watching everything through half-lidded eyes.

Dani's nephews and nieces had been roped into dishes duty. They were making a loud, sudsy game of it in the kitchen—usually grounds for an intervention. For once, Jean had not so much as twitched.

Stephen seemed to think he was closing a real estate deal with his brother, John, who actually seemed to be agreeing to everything just to get him to shut up.

The mix tape came to an end and Rhoda flipped it over on her way out the door while hauling her husband in her slipstream. She gave everyone a breezy wave and promised to furnish them all with updates on her ailments. "Check your emails!"

Dani's mother came around to give her a quick hug good-bye. She whispered in her ear, "She's lovely. We'll talk properly later. I'm happy for you."

Dani smiled. Her mother loved all her girlfriends.

Sally's hug was harder, more bruising. "Merry Christmas, sis," was all she said.

Mike's hug followed. "I like your friend." He smiled, then murmured, "And so does my stubborn wife. Not that Sally'd admit how cool Ro is. I hope you're really happy together."

Dani grinned at him. He was one of the good ones. And he obviously had better gaydar than his wife.

Soon only Dani was left, along with Ro, who had disappeared to use the bathroom.

Jean regarded her in a strained silence. It was unsettling. Dani was pinned to her chair by Jean's considering stare.

"Your friend has discipline," Jean suddenly said. "She'd have to, to do what she does."

"I guess."

"A pity it hasn't rubbed off on you."

Dani's eyes narrowed. "You think I'm undisciplined."

"I don't think, I know. Your mother let you get away with far too much. Let you run wild."

"Great..." Dani licked her lips. *Come on, Ro...*

"When I was a young woman, we were taught self-control and restraint. There was little freedom. Ladies were taught to dress and behave correctly. We did not climb trees, ride bicycles, or run riot the way you did."

Awesome. Another etiquette lesson. Just what she needed. She'd value it as much as the scarf. "Well," Dani said, with a tired wave, "I'm sure you aced those lessons as a girl."

"No." Jean studied her. "I did not. It was stifling."

Dani blinked. "I don't understand."

"No, I don't imagine you do." Jean flicked lint off her dress. She appeared to be debating whether to continue. "You've had quite the life, Danielle. Freedom. Possibilities. Opportunities."

"I suppose."

"Even if you've wasted them all. I can't imagine the thrill in shoe sales."

"And I can't imagine the thrill in selling wool and fabric." *Oh crap.* Dani bit her lip. She couldn't believe that had slipped out.

Jean regarded her evenly. "The difference is it was *my* store. I owned it. It was one of few options available to me in the fifties when I arrived in this godforsaken place. I can't say the same for you, who had options galore at your feet."

"Wait, you didn't want to move to Australia?" Since when?

"When I was eighteen, all I ever wanted to do was travel. I wanted to choose my own path in all things, including matters of matrimony."

Dani stared at her in surprise.

"I got a job, over my mother's objections, working in a respectable dressmaking shop and saved up all year. Finally I had the money I needed. I had the tickets booked. My best friend, Maggie, and I were off to see the world. We had organized a chaperone, of course—Maggie's aunt from France. It was terribly exciting. France would be our first stop. Then Italy, Spain, over to Portugal, on to Scandinavia, home to England. The following year, we planned we would save up again and then take on America. North and south."

"Wow." Dani couldn't imagine that. She'd never left Brisbane, let alone Australia. But seeing Europe in mid-last century? She tried to imagine that. It'd still be rebuilding after the war. New stores would be springing up, tourists would be returning to the historic sights. "Was it amazing?"

"Oh yes. Thrilling." Her tone contained a biting edge. "Or so my brother told me."

"Peter?"

"Just before I was due to leave, my mother suddenly took ill. In my day, the daughters were always the ones to tend their parents. It wasn't an option. I was tersely instructed to give Peter my ticket that I'd saved up all year for. He would go in my stead. No arguments."

"That's awful."

"Actually, the particularly awful part was when I discovered, after Maggie and Peter were abroad, that my mother wasn't really ill. She simply didn't wish me to go. She decided she'd be lonely without me tending her. And, again, being the times they were, I was not able to say one thing." Her eyes narrowed.

"Did you get to go to America the next year?"

"No." Jean tilted her head. "I am not a fool. I knew my mother's health would suddenly take a perilous turn then, too. Or perhaps my passport would mysteriously go missing. Or something else. So I made other plans."

"What happened?"

"I chose a husband."

"Chose? You mean you fell in love with Uncle Fred and—"

"No. Listen to what I'm saying: I chose one. Very carefully. I found the first man I determined had the means to move me far from my parents' control. On our first date, Fred expressed an interest in emigrating to Australia, and that's how I knew he was suitable."

"Did your mother approve of you leaving England?"

Jean smiled. It was not pleasant. "Oh no, but she couldn't do a thing to stop me. After all, she had trained me to obey my husband. And if my husband wanted to go to Australia, that's what one did."

Hesitating, Dani was unsure if she was about to cross a line. "Was Uncle Fred good to you?"

"I chose correctly." A hint of steel crept into her voice.

Dani wondered if she dared ask the next question. "Did you...love him?"

"He has been exactly what I thought he'd be."

That didn't answer anything. Dani caught Jean's even gaze. *Actually, it did.* A whole life, sixty years, without any romantic love.

"It is what it is," Jean said, her expression stony. "Every time I look at him, I'm reminded of the scarcity of choices women had in my day. Choices you seem to blithely take for granted."

"You think I take my life for granted?"

"Yes. It's appalling to watch."

Dani frowned. "Why?"

"Your sister is tolerable. Sally never aspires to anything more than the mundane. She doesn't have a spirited bone in her body, an inquisitive thought, a curious nature. You, though…you have all three, and I had to tolerate the unendurable. Watching you grow up without an ounce of discipline or ambition to make the most of your life. You just…" She waved her hand.

"What?"

"Take it all for granted and do nothing with it."

"You're jealous of the opportunities I had that you were denied?" Dani couldn't believe her ears. "Are you saying you are jealous of *me*?"

"I suppose you'd like to believe that. Would it help you make sense of things between us?" Jean's eyebrow cocked in challenge. Taunting her.

"Yes," Dani whispered.

"I'm not jealous of you, Danielle. You are *enraging*. Your life is just so easy."

"So that's why you decided to make it hard?"

"I was teaching you discipline. Your mother never pulled you into line. Your father was never home. What hope was there for you to excel at anything?"

"My parents did the best they could." Dani squared her jaw. "And for the record, you don't have to grind someone under heel to teach them something."

Jean's mouth twisted into cruelty. "Suffered *so* much, have we?"

"Oh, I get it." Dani couldn't believe she'd never seen it before. "You've been punishing me. You had it hard, so I should, too? Otherwise it's not fair." She gave her a bitter look. "Charming philosophy."

"How dare you! You have no idea what my life has been like." Jean rose halfway out of her seat, her twisted arthritic fingers curling into fists.

"I know you were a young woman who felt trapped and so used a husband as a means of escape."

Eyes still mutinous, Jean opened her mouth to speak but instead clamped her mouth shut and resumed her seat.

"But then you got stuck in a loveless marriage," Dani continued. "However, you had discipline. And hard work. Ambition. So you flung yourself into your shop so you didn't have to think about your lonely, sad life."

Jean's nostrils flared. "You are *intolerable*."

"I guess I am. And you're exactly like those glass figurines in your display case that you never let me look at. Perfect, cold, and untouchable."

For a long moment, there was no answer. Jean glared at her, rolling her wedding ring around her finger.

"I'm sorry for what you had to go through," Dani said more kindly, "but how is forcing me to be someone else, someone you approve of, a good thing?"

"Silly girl," Jean said, her voice harsh. "You think I'm taking from your path? I was the only one who truly saw *you*."

"You saw me? Then based on all that disciplining, you clearly hated what you saw." Dani inhaled, dreading the answer but knowing it all the same. "Right?"

"Of course. Mirrors are the ugliest implements to endure."

"What?" Astonishment flooded Dani. She couldn't seriously mean…

"Do you know what my mother called me?" Jean demanded. "Over and over, it's all I heard. An undisciplined *wild child*."

Dani gasped.

"Now do you see?" Jean snapped.

Wait, Jean hated her because Dani reminded her of herself? All these years she'd just seen Dani as a bitter reminder of dreams lost and wasted? But why didn't Jean reclaim her dreams? "Why didn't you ever travel? Later?"

"Fred didn't want to." She gave a faint eye roll. "I follow my husband's wishes."

Screw that. "I don't obey anyone," Dani blurted out.

"I am well aware."

"Do you really resent me, Jean?"

The older woman leaned forward and cupped Dani's cheek, angling her face to the light. Jean's eyes locked on Dani's. Her fingertips bit in. "With every fibre of my being."

Dani flinched, trying to pull away.

Those old, claw-like fingers tightened their grip.

"And I'm self-aware enough to know my resentment of my own circumstances is far greater than my resentment of yours," Jean's eyes bored into Dani's. "This bland existence is my life. You have your own. So my point in telling you all this is whatever you do, don't waste it."

"I don't plan to."

"Then go to England with her," Jean said abruptly.

"What?"

"At lunch, your friend mentioned her team is competing in the netball world cup next year in England. Go with her. See the world. Live. Get out of Brisbane. Do something, *anything* with the opportunities you have. My God, it's physically painful watching someone with the zest for life I once had just scratch away at sneaker sales and little else."

Dani's hand lifted to claw Jean's fingers from her chin, annoyed, yet again, that her choices were being mocked. She met Jean's eyes. Instead of the censure she expected to see, she saw only deep loss.

Against her will, Dani's fingers curled into Jean's, cupping them against her face. "I'm sorry for all you went through," she said honestly.

"One makes do." Jean dropped her hand. "All over the globe are women like me, still dutifully obeying rules the world no longer seems to follow."

"You don't have to keep following them."

"Of course I do. I made vows. Love, honour, obey. Though I know you'll never understand my life."

"No. My world's not the same as yours."

"Finally, something we agree on." Jean's lips curled into the faintest of smiles.

"Yeah." Dani offered a tiny grin back at her concession.

Ro returned. "Sorry I took so long," she said with a hefty sigh. "Figuring out button-flies with bandaged hands is the pits. We ready to go?"

"Yes." Dani looked to Jean. "Um…I guess…until next year."

Ro grinned at Jean and lifted a bandaged hand in farewell. "Yep. Until then."

The suggestion they'd still be together to do it all again in a year's time filled Dani with joy.

"Next year?" Jean queried.

Dani braced herself, wondering if Jean was about to say something hideous. Point out all the ways Ro wasn't family and she was lucky she'd even been invited this year.

Instead her aunt's voice contained the faintest hint of warmth. "But of course. What would Christmas be without *the friend*?"

There was no mistaking that particular emphasis.

Oh shit! She knows. Dani swallowed.

Ro laughed and softly elbowed Jean. *Actually elbowed her.* "Damn straight. This friend will be back, ready to stare at your frizzles and catch whatever desserts Harriet scares my way. Thanks for lunch. It was great meeting everyone."

Jean arched an eyebrow. "Not *frizzles.*"

"I know, I know." Ro grinned. "It was crazy of me to call them that. I don't know why you put up with me."

"Your dessert-catching skills, perhaps." Jean's lips were pressed together as if desperately preventing a laugh. Her eyes were bright.

Dani stared in disbelief. Jean did not tell jokes, and certainly not with Dani's girlfriend. A familiar form shuffling down the hall caught her eye. "Bye, Fred!" she called.

He turned, his face wreathed in delight. "Bye-bye, Edith. Lovely seeing you again."

With a faint sigh, Jean shook her head and that ever-pressing sadness seemed to settle back over her. She began closing the door, shooing them out. "Good-bye, Danielle." Then she paused, her eyebrow lifting. Her smile became full and real. *"And friend."*

The click of the door ended the conversation with finality.

"Little Drummer Boy" played on.

Deck the Halls with Bullets and Holly

BY ALEX K. THORNE

LERATO LIKED LISTS. SHE LIKED bullet points, and pros and cons. She liked ticking things off and the satisfaction of pushing down on her pen and dragging thin lines over accomplished tasks. So, when she was offered the job two weeks before Christmas, she made a neat, numbered list of pros and cons below the underlined heading "Hired Assassin".

The list looked like this:

Cons:
have to commit to gym
weird hours
illegal
can't tell the family what I really do
murder??
two-year contract

Pros:
better pay than Bargain Books
no annoying co-workers
tools to murder previous annoying co-workers
travel opportunities

In the end, it was that last one that decided it, despite the fact that there were more cons on her list. She was twenty-five and had never even left the country. What kind of artist would she make if she never actually saw the world? It wasn't only lack of opportunity—Lerato had her family, her friends, and her student loan, all of which seemed to take priority. And so, with the eventual promise of travel, she signed on for the three-week trial as an official employee of Adams and Locke Investment Banking, or at least, that was what her South African Revenue Service tax return would say.

Lerato's thighs ached from crouching, and the backs of her knees were beginning to sweat against the creases of her pants. In retrospect, wearing fake leather on a summer evening in late December probably wasn't her best idea, but it made her look the part and they'd never explicitly told her how to dress except to remain "dark and inconspicuous". In her black T-shirt and pleather pants, she definitely had the dark thing down. Remaining inconspicuous on the rooftop of an apartment building at 10:40 p.m. on Christmas Eve was a little harder, but she'd been keeping low, and as far as she could tell, she was successful.

She reached for the small pair of binoculars around her neck, and her stomach grumbled loudly. First lesson learned: pack more than one snack. The apple she'd brought was now just a browning hourglass at her feet. To be fair, she hadn't anticipated a five-hour-long surveillance mission.

She'd already received three texts from her sisters berating her for missing their annual Christmas Eve ritual of hate-watching *How the Grinch Stole Christmas* and eating too many gingerbread biscuits.

Lerato's instructions, delivered via encrypted text message onto her new phone that looked like something out of a Tom Cruise sci-fi movie, had only said, "Recon target until lights out. Report. Do not engage."

The target in question was a young woman, a little older than Lerato herself. The file called her "Shikari Singh", but Lerato was pretty sure that was fake. No one was *born* with a name that cool. The file didn't say much else, except to list Singh's address and physical description, which was mostly spot on. Tall, slim, dark-haired woman who lived in a cool, expensive apartment block just steps away from one of Cape Town's most popular beaches.

The file hadn't referred to her as a knock-out though, and thanks to her awesome new binoculars, which might or might not have been tech from the distant future, Lerato was pleasantly surprised that her first target was so pretty. It would be a good first memory. Even as she thought it, she knew she was breaking some sort of rule. Targets were targets. Their gender, ethnicity, and general level of hotness was irrelevant. This was one of the first things she'd learnt at orientation. Still, she supposed there were worse faces to be looking at for five hours.

Five particularly boring hours.

The first hour was okay. Lerato got a glimpse into the lives of the rich and famous. Well, rich at least. Lerato had certainly never heard of her target before now. Shikari Singh had had groceries delivered (because why would anyone brave the shops on Christmas Eve if they didn't have to?). Lerato got a comfortable spot from her vantage point, adjusted her binoculars, and watched her put them away. Quinoa, kale, coffee that looked about as expensive as Lerato's rent.

Hour two literally consisted of Lerato watching Singh watch Netflix, which was mildly annoying since it seemed her target was already on season two of *The Crown* and Lerato still had to catch up. For a show about rich white people, it was surprisingly good. At least Singh had decent taste.

What followed was a montage reel of watching Shikari Singh mill about her apartment (it was a rather big apartment), speak to someone on the phone who seemed to make her laugh (she developed two little dimples on either cheek when she laughed), heat up dinner (what looked like a curry of some sort), and finally, mosey on back to the couch. Typical, boring, and sort of lonely.

She was mulling over this when the bathroom light flickered on. Lerato supposed this might be a good time to text her sister back and ask if there were any last-minute items she needed to bring for their big lunch the next day. She wasn't about to watch the woman use the bathroom—she was an assassin, not a pervert—so it was complete coincidence that she happened to look up at the very same moment Shikari Singh was stepping into the bathtub. Fully clothed.

Lerato brought the binoculars back to her face and squinted through them. She watched her target slide further and further into a bathtub full of water, until the very top of her head disappeared.

What?

Lerato waited a beat, and then another, and then stood up.

Shit.

She sprinted down the fire escape and ended up jumping off someone's balcony on the second floor, scraping her knee in the process. She made it across the road, almost getting hit by a car, and managed to yell at the driver as if she was not a crazy lady running across the road in the middle of the night.

Of course Shikari Singh lived on the fifth floor, and of course the elevator was occupied. Lerato took the stairs, two at a time, and was panting hard when she finally made it to the apartment door, finagling her lock pick into the latch like she had learnt at breaking-and-entering orientation. It was a lot harder to do when you were out of breath and trembling from nerves.

Lerato thought back to the apartment layout, as seen from across the street, and figured out how to get to the bathroom. She half-expected the door to be locked and was already reaching for her lock pick, but the knob turned and she crashed inside the room.

The woman in the bath shot up, getting water all over the floor.

"What the hell?"

Lerato approached carefully, the soles of her boots squelching in the puddles. "Are you okay?"

Shikari Singh looked around, appearing disoriented. Her long hair hung around her face in thick, wet clumps. Her T-shirt (printed with tiny multi-coloured cacti) clung to her like a second skin. "What!"

"You were...you were trying to drown yourself," Lerato began, taking another tentative step towards the tub. "I saved you. You're okay now."

Shikari Singh frowned. "I wasn't going to stay under."

"You looked like you were in trouble," Lerato countered, suddenly feeling more than a little foolish as she stood in the middle of a stranger's bathroom, a stranger that she was supposed to be stalking. Professionally. For professional reasons.

"Well... I wasn't. I...knew what I was doing." Shikari Singh stood up, splashing more water over the edge, and Lerato winced, thinking of

Cape Town's stringent water restrictions since the drought. Singh's jeans, supposedly blue, were now black and sodden against her thighs. "But more importantly, what are you doing in my bathroom?" She climbed out of the tub, and for some bizarre reason, Lerato noticed the colour of her toenails, painted a deep purple.

"I...um," Lerato faltered, still distracted by those eggplant-coloured toes. "I was passing by."

Shikari Singh crossed her arms over her chest, managing to look surprisingly intimidating despite resembling a drowned rat. "You were passing by my bathroom?"

"Look." Lerato started to back away slowly. "You've been through a traumatic event. You're obviously not thinking clearly. Maybe we should just call it a night."

"Call it a—" Shikari Singh's expression turned incredulous, and then a look of understanding took over. "Wait. You're here to kill me, aren't you?"

"What? Kill? Why—I...no!" Lerato Mnguni—assassin extraordinaire, at her most eloquent.

"I should have guessed sooner." Shikari Singh proceeded to pull off her drenched T-shirt as if this was a completely normal interaction. "Do you mind?" she asked as she began to unbutton her jeans, and Lerato turned around, blushing despite the utter absurdness of the situation.

"I—sorry." She waited while Shikari Singh shuffled around behind her, a million thoughts racing through Lerato's head. She had messed up. Not only had she made contact with the mark, but she was now standing in said mark's bathroom, as said mark got undressed. This was definitely not in the handbook.

"It's just that you're nothing like the others," Shikari Singh was saying. "You're pretty wimpy looking for an assassin."

"I'm not an—wait, wimpy looking?" Lerato automatically turned around and found Singh now in a fresh, dry pair of jeans and a black tank top. She was towelling off her wet hair, head cocked to one side as she appraised Lerato with a perfectly arched eyebrow.

"I mean..." She gestured to all of Lerato with one hand.

"Well, anyway." Lerato put her hands on her hips and puffed out her chest, trying to seem more threatening. "I'm not here to kill you. Not exactly."

"Then why are you here?" Shikari Singh tossed the towel she was holding onto the clothes she had piled on top of the washing machine. She walked out of the bathroom, her bare feet leaving wet footprints as she went.

"Reconnaissance," Lerato replied, following her down the corridor. The apartment was huge. "The hit was arranged for Saturday."

"So…what?" Shikari Singh stood on her tiptoes to reach for a mug, then seemed to think about it and retrieved two. "You're just watching me from afar like some creepy stalker?"

"I know, it's weird." Lerato sighed. "It's my least favourite part of the job." And it really was. "I'd rather just get it over with, you know? But they like to have details, routines, habits."

"They?"

"My employers."

"Ah." Shikari Singh opened the refrigerator and stared into its depths. In the florescent light of the fridge, the reddish highlights in her hair seemed to glow. "So, who are your employers? Neeman and Jurgens? The Black Hood? Adams and Locke? The Ivancic Brothers?" She pulled out a jug of milk.

"Sorry," Lerato replied. "It's confidential."

"Of course." She held up the milk and jiggled it in the air. "Tea?"

"Why not?"

Shikari Singh filled up the kettle and flipped it on. "So, you do this a lot then? Breaking into homes, saving your future targets from fake suicides?"

"Actually, it's my first time." Lerato took a seat on one of the high bar stools. The kitchen was all dark marble and shiny red appliances. Very neo-modern. Lerato liked it. She could imagine living here, if she ever won the lottery and finally managed to pay off her student loans.

"Hmm. I guess they discourage interacting with the prey."

"No. Well, yes." Lerato watched as Shikari Singh moved around the kitchen—her hair was curling at her back. It was pretty. Lerato's own braided hair was piled up atop her head in a neat bun. "I meant it's my first job. You're my first assignment."

"Well. I guess I'm honoured."

Shikari smiled, the kettle clicked, and Lerato's heart skipped a beat.

Uh-oh.

"I'm not yours, though." Lerato cleared her throat. "Your first, I mean. You said I wasn't like the others? You've been a target before?"

Shikari Singh looked amused. "You don't know who I am, do you?"

"We get a file." Lerato felt suddenly defensive, as if she needed to justify her ignorance. "Everything I need to know is in there."

"And what does this file tell you?"

Lerato listed facts off her fingers. "Shikari Singh, twenty-six, vegetarian, Virgo."

"They don't tell you *why* I'm a target?"

"Nope. That's need to know."

"Okay, then you need to know that I prefer to be called Kari. Singh is my mother's surname." The edge of her mouth curled up in a bitter smile. "My father's is Bojović."

Lerato's eyebrows shot up. The name had been dominating the headlines for the past few months. "So you're—"

"A blood member of the Serbian Bojovićs."

"And your father is…"

"Was. A mafia kingpin, yeah. He died last year."

"I remember reading about that. I'm…sorry?"

Kari gave a little nonchalant shrug. "It is what it is."

"So… How come you're still alive? I mean, why haven't any of the attempts been successful?

"I've got a very competent bodyguard. Milk?"

Lerato nodded. "And two sugars, please. Where is he?"

"*She* is home for Christmas." Kari placed the mug of tea in front of Lerato. "Michelle's parents live in Bloemfontein. I suspect your employers know this, which is why they've sent you, a rookie, while I'm vulnerable."

"Hey." Lerato swallowed a sip of her tea. It was really good. "I'm competent."

"How do you know? You haven't done it yet."

"I…I did really well in orientation."

Kari hid her laugh as she brought her mug to her lips. "Good for you. Still, making contact with your mark, that can't be great."

"No." Lerato sighed and tugged at the string of her teabag as visions of her university loan flashed through her head. "I guess not."

Kari leaned back against the kitchen counter and fixed Lerato with a pointed expression. "You could have let me drown, you know?"

Lerato looked up sharply. "You said you weren't trying to kill yourself."

"You didn't know that. You could have let me do it and your job would have been done."

"But that's like cheating, isn't it?"

"A hired killer with a conscience." Kari smiled. It was disarming. It was… "Cute."

Lerato blinked and mentally shook herself out of it. "I think the word you're looking for is *terrifying*."

"Yeeeeah." Kari didn't look convinced.

"The tea is good," Lerato offered, trying to fill up the silence.

"It was a gift from my ex." Kari shrugged. "She got it in Nepal. Apparently, it clears the chakras or something. I don't know, she was into all of that stuff."

Well, that answers *that* question.

"I don't know if my chakras are cleared, but this is great tea."

Kari's smile was a little distracted, and Lerato wondered if she was thinking about the ex. For some reason, she now wanted to know more. Was it a painful break-up? How long ago was it? Were they still friends? Before she could ask any of these questions, Kari dropped her mug into the sink and said, "Come on, let's go sit on the balcony." She started walking, leaving Lerato to follow.

This was very much not how the night was supposed to go. She wondered if there was someone doing reconnaissance on *her*, if this was some sort of test that she'd already failed horribly. "It's, um…getting late," Lerato protested.

She surreptitiously pulled her phone out of her pocket. No calls, no angry work texts, only one from her sister replying to her previous message. *Bring cranberries for salad. Also wine. Ma's already gotten into the sherry.* Laughing face emoji, wine bottle emoji, laughing face emoji. Lerato shoved her phone into her back pocket and found that Kari was already opening the glass sliding door to the balcony.

Lerato started towards her and then hesitated. What the hell was she doing?

"Oh, come on!" Kari called from outside. "You've already had tea with your mark. You might as well keep me company a bit longer."

She wasn't wrong, and it did seem like a nice night to spend on a rich person's balcony.

It was warm outside, a little windy, but not unpleasant. For the past month, bad made-for-TV movies and holiday specials depicted frosty Christmases—scarves, fireplaces, and snowball fights—but Lerato couldn't imagine anything better than the hot December days and balmy nights leading up to a Christmas lunch outside, when the sun was bright and their drinks cold.

Kari's apartment overlooked a main road, and just beyond it was a beach that Lerato and her friends had often come to. It was weird to think just a few weeks ago, she was sunning herself just metres away from Kari's place.

It was fairly quiet by the time they stepped out, as most people settled in for Christmas Eve. The crash of waves against surf could be heard from the balcony. The air smelled like salt and summer. It was beautiful, Lerato thought, leaning against the railing, her back to the ocean.

Kari crossed her legs as she sat back in a patio chair. Her hair, now mostly dried, played gently against her face in the wind. She really was ridiculously pretty. Lerato guessed she had her mother's complexion and her father's strong features. If Wonder Woman was half-Indian, she'd look something like Shikari Singh.

"So why an assassin?"

The question startled her, and Lerato blinked, trying to find an answer. "The money seemed good and I like shooting things, and to be honest, my art history degree isn't exactly in high demand. The gallery scene here is a joke. I'm tired of trying to sell my paintings."

"You're preaching to the choir."

Lerato squinted, appraising Kari. "Drama major?"

Kari snorted back a laugh. "Is it that obvious? I'm a performance artist. What you saw, the stunt in the bath, was part of my piece."

"Well, why didn't you just say so?"

"I don't know. I was embarrassed? Everyone expects me to go into the family business, now that my father's gone. But my heart just isn't in organized crime. I'd much rather leave all of that to the extended family."

"So, they're still in Serbia?"

"They're all over," Kari replied. "We're not exactly close." She pointed to her cheek by way of explanation. "They weren't thrilled about my father marrying a South African Indian woman."

Lerato thought of her Zulu parents and her Zulu grandparents and her great-grandparents who were Zulu as well. "My family history is so boring in comparison."

Kari rolled her eyes, but not unkindly. "Right now, I'd much rather be boring than a target."

"Hey, um," Lerato started awkwardly. "Sorry that this whole thing is on Christmas Eve."

"Oh, don't worry about it." Kari drew her legs up under her. She reminded Lerato of a sleek jungle cat. "I don't really celebrate. My mum's in Durban and all about celebrating Diwali and my father's family is Greek Orthodox, so they celebrate Christmas in January. I don't really get the big deal."

Lerato sat up straight. "Wait, wait, wait. You don't get the big deal about Christmas?! It's Christmas!" She felt personally offended.

"I take it you're a fan?"

"Yes, but not because of the religion stuff. I mean, my mother forces my sisters and I to go to church sometimes and she's really into the whole thing, but even if you're not, Christmas is magical."

"Are you sponsored by Father Christmas? Is this a paid advertisement for the Christmas spirit?"

Lerato laughed. "No. I just really like this time of year."

Kari looked unconvinced.

"Okay, so at my house, we get a real tree every year," Lerato continued. "None of that fake plastic nonsense. We've been buying it on the side of the road from the same random sketchy man since I was young. We decorate it with all of our ancient trimmings and crafts my mother's collected over the years. There's always an argument over where to put this little figurine of baby Jesus, because my sisters and I think it looks like a naked mole-rat in a towel, and my mother insists on giving it centre stage on the tree. Its eyes follow you around the room, as if baby Jesus mole-rat knows we wanted to hide him away."

Kari chuckled. "You sound close to your family."

"Well, it's just my mother and my two sisters. So..." Lerato thought about it. "But yeah. I am."

"Tell me about the food."

Lerato's nose crinkled in confusion. "The food?"

Kari nodded enthusiastically. "I love food. A trait I picked up from my mother. She grew up in her parents' restaurant. I'm obsessed with trying everything. Everything I can eat as a vegetarian. I don't think I've ever had an actual Christmas meal."

Lerato opened her mouth, then shut it quickly before she could propose something really, really stupid.

"What?"

"Nothing. Um, the food. Okay, so there's lots of meat. Turkey, gammon, roast beef."

Kari made a face.

"I know, but you asked!"

"Sorry, go on." She drew her fingers across her mouth in a zipping motion.

"Okay, so lots of meat. Phutu is a staple."

"Phutu?"

"Pap," Lerato answered. "You know, like maize porridge. And not that rubbish you get from the shops. My mother cooks the maize over the cast-iron pot in the back. Then potatoes, a salad of some kind. This year, I think my sister's making something with grapefruit, which honestly sounds disgusting. For dessert, there's always trifle. Cream, jelly, sponge cake, and fruit." Lerato closed her eyes and hummed wistfully. "Ah, trifle."

Kari grinned at her. "It sounds lovely."

"I'm not sure if lovely is the word for it, but by the end, we're always stuffed and happy."

"You're lucky."

Lerato nodded. "I know."

They were quiet for a while, as around them the night buzzed. String lights lined the street, specifically set up for the holidays. Shapes of reindeer, bells, and trees twinkled between lampposts.

Lerato knew she should have left already, and she certainly couldn't justify staying. Except that Kari was looking out at the sea, her expression sad and wistful, and Lerato knew with sudden clarity that come morning, she'd be out of a job.

"What is your art like?"

Kari turned from the dark, frothy ocean to look at Lerato. "It's…" She seemed to think for a moment. "It's performance, so it's a little out there."

"Out there can be good."

"It focuses on themes of birth and death. Sort of a Frida Kahlo come to life. Lots of, uh, fake blood and water. The thing in the bath was me trying to figure out if I'll be able to hear my cues when completely submerged. It's…weird."

"No, it sounds really cool. I'm a big Kahlo fan. She's really influenced my painting. My mother is less thrilled by the direction my art has taken. Lots of vaginas."

Kari guffawed. "Frida did like her vaginas."

"I think your work sounds cool," Lerato said quickly. "I'm not just saying that."

Kari smiled. It was a soft, shy smile. "I have a show next Monday. Maybe."

Lerato leaned forward, desperate to see that smile again. "Why maybe?"

"Well, they're supposed to kill me some time, right?"

"Oh." Lerato's heart sank. "Right."

"I can get you tickets," Kari offered. "If you want. I don't want to assume…"

"No, I want," Lerato replied quickly. "I mean, it sounds good." She thought for a second and then said, "Can I tell you a secret?"

"Seems the night for it."

"It's not just the money." Lerato basically whispered it. "I took the job because after a few months you get to travel. Like, all over. And right now, I can't really afford it, but…if it was for work…" She sighed. "My family doesn't get it."

"They don't want you to travel?"

"More like they don't feel the need to, so don't understand why I want to so badly."

"Where would you go?"

"Paris," Lerato answered immediately, and then felt a little foolish. "Maybe Rome, possibly Berlin, but before anywhere else, it's got to be

Paris. And I know, I know, it's trite and—and obvious, but I wanted to see the Louvre and Versailles." She rolled her eyes at herself. "I want to take stupid pictures in front of the Eiffel Tower."

"It's not trite. Paris is one of the few places that's exactly how you imagine it to be."

"You've been?"

Kari nodded. "A few times. Though I suppose my last time really was my last time." She looked at Lerato meaningfully.

"I don't think I can go through with it," Lerato admitted. "You make really good tea and it's Christmas Eve, and…I suppose I'm not as good at this as I thought I'd be."

"Hey," Kari leaned forward and tapped the back of her hand against Lerato's knee. "Don't be so hard on yourself. I'm sure it would have been easier if I was some megalomaniac CEO white dude with a comb-over. You'd totally be able to go through with it then."

Lerato looked hopeful. "You really think so?"

Kari smiled, that soft, shy smile. "I really do."

Lerato smiled back. "Thanks."

"And look." Kari sat up and flicked her hair off her shoulders in an exaggerated gesture. "It's not your fault I'm this kind and smart and attractive."

"Yes, and modest too."

They both laughed, and Lerato wondered why her heart was threatening to beat out of her chest.

"You're wrong though," Kari said, pulling Lerato out of her momentary panic. "It's not Christmas Eve anymore." She lifted her phone to show Lerato the time. *12:07.*

"Oh. I should probably…" She jabbed her thumb over her shoulder. "I've got to help cook in the morning."

Lerato found she was not as eager to leave as she would have thought.

They walked to the door, and Kari chose not to comment on the fact that it was still unlocked from when Lerato had picked it. Instead, she leaned against the door frame as Lerato stepped into the hallway.

There was an unmistakable date-like quality to the moment, the two of them standing facing each other under dim lights. It was almost romantic.

"Thanks for this evening. The, uh, company part, not the attempted-murder part." Kari's expression was both wry and sincere.

"It wasn't really…" But then Lerato gave up. "You're welcome. I had a good time. A better time than I expected." Lerato was no longer surprised to find that she meant it.

"So, will I see you again?" Kari's eyelashes fluttered down before she looked back up. "I mean…you're sure you won't try again?"

"Probably not. But you know if I don't they'll just send somebody else."

"Michelle comes back in a few days. I'll be okay. What about you though? You'll be out of a job."

"Eh." Lerato shrugged. "There are other jobs."

Kari didn't say anything for the longest time, but watched Lerato with a soft, unreadable expression.

"What?"

Kari's lips tugged into a smile. "You're cute."

"Pfft." Lerato could feel her cheeks getting hot. "I'm not. I'm terrifying."

And then Kari was leaning in, and her lips were warm against Lerato's cheek.

"Merry Christmas, Lerato."

The kiss was brief and sweet, and much like the Grinch, it made Lerato's heart grow three sizes.

"Merry Christmas, Kari."

Christmas Day was predictable. Lerato's family ate too much, drank too much, and by four p.m., everyone was half asleep. It was the perfect day.

Lerato was sprawled out on the couch, considering a second helping of trifle, when the doorbell rang. They weren't expecting anyone, so she assumed it was one of her sister's friends and continued to revel in doing absolutely nothing at all.

"Hey, Rara! There's something here for you!" Lerato's youngest sister, Thando, bounced into the room with all the enthusiasm of a fourteen-year-old on Christmas. "A weird man in a suit dropped it off." She handed Lerato a thin, A4-sized envelope. There was no return address.

"Is it a Christmas present?"

Lerato held the letter to her ear as if it were a bomb. She was ninety percent sure her employers wouldn't send her a bomb in the mail, but she kept expecting some sort of slap on the knuckles for the previous night's transgression.

"Who is it from?" Thando asked, hovering.

Lerato swatted her away. "None of your business. Go get me another spoonful of pudding."

"Only if I can get one too."

"Okay," Lerato answered, distracted. "Don't let Ma hear you."

Thando bounded off to the kitchen, and Lerato tore open the envelope.

Inside was an itinerary for a flight with her name, Lerato Patricia Mnguni, clearly printed at the top.

The flight was in a week, and—she frowned at the page—apparently, she was flying first class. She was too confused to be even remotely excited. There was no way this was real. She was fully prepared to get an email in the next few minutes from a Nigerian "prince" asking for $5,000 in cash to help him get out of the country in exchange for something equally implausible. It was the oldest scam in the...

And then it clicked. Surely not. No one was that generous, or crazy. Unless...

Kari?

The phone rang for so long Lerato was convinced she wasn't going to answer. And then finally, in that specific tone that millennials have come to adopt when having to actually speak on a phone, Kari said, "H-hello?"

"Hi." Lerato's heart was going crazy.

"Oh." A beat, and then Lerato could almost see Kari smiling. "Hi. How did you get my number?"

"Oh, they give you all sorts of details before you set out to assassinate someone."

"Makes sense."

"So," Lerato began nervously. "Um, you're insane."

"You got my Christmas present, huh?"

"I know you're new to this, but around here, we give each other socks and mugs, not first-class tickets to Paris."

"You said you wanted to see my show." Kari's voice was slightly muffled, as if she had just taken a bite of something and Lerato marvelled at how she could be so cavalier about this.

"Yeah. I thought it was, like, at the Fugard Theatre, down the road."

"If it makes you feel any better, I am doing a show here in March. But Europe comes first. And…" Kari paused for a moment. "I'd really like you to see it."

"The show or Europe?"

"Both."

Lerato let out a disbelieving laugh. "We barely know each other."

"Think of it as a business arrangement. You're currently out of a job. I'm out of a bodyguard." Kari's reply came quickly, as if she'd been thinking about it.

"You want me to be your bodyguard?"

"Just for this trip. Michelle is still with her family."

Lerato was quiet, letting the absurdity of the situation wash over her. Allowing herself to finally acknowledge how exciting a prospect this was.

"You bought me a ticket to Paris."

"I know."

"This is nuts."

"I know."

"I'll be in Paris on New Year's Eve."

"Okay, you're just stating facts now."

"I'm sorry," Lerato took a breath. "I'm just…."

"You're freaked out. It's too much, isn't it? See, I told you. I don't get this Christmas thing."

"I think"—Lerato tried to choose her words carefully—"I think it's less of an inappropriate Christmas gift thing and more of an inappropriate 'I just met you last night when you were spying on me' gift thing."

"I…" Kari was quiet for a long time, and Lerato was worried she'd hung up. "I wanted a friend," she finally said softly. "You know, to be there. You seemed like you got it. I didn't mean to make it weird."

Lerato exhaled, wondering if she was going to make it better or a hundred times worse, but she took the plunge anyway. "You, you didn't make it weird. I guess I just wasn't expecting to fly 7,000 miles for a date."

Kari's laugh was a mixture of delight and anticipation.

The day after Christmas, traditionally called Boxing Day but changed sometime in the nineties to Family Day in South Africa, found Lerato at the "offices" of Adams and Locke, which she was sure was just a rented office space with a fancy front desk and a leggy blonde "receptionist". The building itself might as well have existed in perpetual quotation marks.

Still, it was the best way of getting to them directly, so Lerato arrived at the office with her security card, gun, and duffle bag full of poisons, her space-binoculars, and rope—the basics. A flash of the card got her entry to the waiting area, where a middle-aged woman, who looked like someone's nice librarian grandmother, came down to meet her.

"Hello, dear. I'm Virginia." The woman smiled and sat in the plush leather armchair opposite Lerato. "I hear you've come to turn in your items."

"I'm sorry," Lerato replied, and found that she meant it. "I completely failed my recon mission."

"No worries, dear." She smiled. "It isn't for everyone. That's why we give you the three-week trial period."

"So…" Lerato shrugged. "That's it? I just turn this stuff back to you guys?"

"That's it." Virginia stood up and reached for the card Lerato handed her. "Of course, the non-disclosure agreement is binding, and if you bring any publicity to our little firm, we will find you, torture you, and have your limbs torn off your body and buried in different parts of the world, so no one will ever find you."

Lerato swallowed. "Of-of course."

Virginia's smile widened, her wrinkled cheeks broadening. "Well, then. I think that's good. Thank you for stopping by, dear. You have a wonderful festive season now."

"Thanks." Lerato smiled back. "I think I will."

Lerato stood in the airport, small carry-on suitcase in hand. "I'm sorry. I've changed my mind. Is it too late to cancel?"

The barista at the other end of the counter looked annoyed but resigned, as if this was his daily struggle. "The latte or the entire order?"

"All of it." Lerato apologised again and walked away, her stomach already twisting with nerves.

"You're not hungry?" Kari asked, trailing behind her, eyes down as she sent off a text. Seeing her again, almost a week after their first meeting was…jarring. Not because it was awkward, but because it felt so familiar. It felt as though they'd known each other for decades. It was easy and exciting and completely unexpected.

Lerato stopped and turned to her. "Now is probably a good time to tell you now that I flew to Johannesburg when I was ten and threw up all over the aisle. The flight attendant was not impressed."

Kari shook her head and reached out to tap the tip of her finger against Lerato's nose. "You know, for an assassin, you're kind of wimpy."

Lerato huffed. "Ex-assassin."

"Huh. Got any new job prospects lined up?" Kari asked as they began to walk towards their gate.

A departures board nearby indicated that their flight was about to start boarding. Kari opened the ticket on her phone, double-checking as if out of habit and then closing it again.

"You know, I'm thinking of personal security."

"Really?" Kari stopped walking and closed her fingers over Lerato's shoulder. Her touch sent little tingles down Lerato's spine. Good tingles. Happy tingles. "I happen to know of a great opportunity in Paris."

"Does it happen to involve stupid pictures in front of the Eiffel Tower?"

"If you play your cards right."

"I don't know if I'll have time." Lerato dropped her voice to a conspiratorial whisper. "I'm meeting a girl there."

"Oh? Who is she?"

"You wouldn't know her." Lerato pursed her lips together to keep from grinning. "She's one of those rich, artsy types. Really hot, makes a great cup of tea, sadly ignorant of most Christmas traditions, but she's learning."

"Ugh." Kari winced. "She sounds like a handful."

"Yeah." Those butterflies did jumping jacks inside Lerato's stomach. "I'm quite into her, though. I'm not really sure if she knows it."

Kari reached for Lerato's hand and pulled her forward with a quick tug. She kissed her softly, just once—more of a promise, really. "She knows." Kari's mouth was warm and sweet.

Lerato sighed, filled to the brim with all kinds of fluttery, squishy feelings. "I think almost killing you was the best thing I've done all year."

Kari laughed, and the sound of it rang through the airport lounge.

"Best Christmas present ever."

Mask

BY SHERYN MUNIR

PEOPLE IN MY FAMILY OFTEN joke that my grandmother loves Shashi Kapoor more than she loves the rest of us. When I was younger, she would boast that she's seen every one of the veteran Bollywood actor's movies, many more than once. Legend has it that when the news of his character's plane going down was announced on the radio in *Silsila*, she walked out of the movie theatre in a huff. Another story goes that she ironed a hole in my mother's school pinafore while watching Shashi Kapoor for the first time in colour in *Do Aur Do Paanch* in her home in Kottayam in the 1980s. There are various tales of rice being burnt to cinder and my grandfather's lunch not being delivered to his office in time. We have no way of verifying those stories. But the family is unanimous on one thing—that Ammachi's decline started just before Christmas last year, when Shashi Kapoor died of liver disease in Mumbai at the age of seventy-nine.

Thinking of my grandmother and Alzheimer's in the same sentence turns my bones to dread. I'm a medical student, so I know what dementia does to the mind and body. I don't want to dwell on it. I want to remember the grandmother who sneaked out of the house with me on hot, sultry summer-holiday afternoons to catch the latest Bollywood releases. I want to remember her famous fish curry, so spicy that tears ran down our faces; I want to remember the stories she read out from Malayalam magazines, complete with voices and sound effects; I want to remember her Christmas cakes that I can still taste in my imagination.

Most of all, I don't want to come home for Christmas and look at Ammachi and have her look back at me with twinkling incomprehension. But I'm here, and Ammachi is going to be here tomorrow.

There's no place to run. Or maybe there is.

"Where are you going?" Pappa asks me when he sees me putting on my shoes. "You just got here."

"Choir practice," I say. "I've missed the carol singing."

And so I escape. It's only when I'm outside do I remember that Emma will be there.

Emma and I became friends as six-year-olds and only seriously fell out once, twelve years later. She is the reason I haven't come home for Christmas two years running.

Our first meeting was at a parish picnic. I don't remember where they'd taken us—some big park by a lake. They paired us for the three-legged race. Note: six-year-olds do not possess the requisite coordination for the three-legged race; exposition for another day. One of the bigger boys laughed at us. It was that lout Aiden. Emma tripped him up while I walloped him across the face. He howled, and then his father whacked him for crying. It was all very hilarious back then. We talked about it for years.

Emma and I attended Mater Dei School together, and by some quirk of fate remained together in the same section from class one to class twelve. We had plans. We were always going to do everything together: we would become nurses, just like our mothers, work in the same hospital, and live next door to each other. Then I got through to medical college and she didn't—we'd both applied, of course—and I left. Vellore is two nights by train, followed by a bus journey.

"But you promised," Emma told me when I broke the news.

"I'm sorry."

"Be as sorry as you want. I'll never forgive you."

We walked away in opposite directions; neither was going to cry in front of the other. That was two years ago.

My heart is going like a fan on full speed when I walk into the cramped choir-practice room in our church, so fast that you can't tell where it stops or starts. I haven't been here in years, yet the stuffy warmth hugs me like an old friend. It's a relief to be in from the cold. A pile of sweaters, jackets, and mufflers lie piled on the bench along one wall. I discard my woollens there and turn towards the coffee and Santa-hat-shaped cookies someone must have brought. I start to calm down.

There's a low hubbub of voices in the room. No one has noticed me yet. I see many faces I recognise, including old friends from Sunday School and choir. I feel shy—an unforeseen circumstance—and suddenly my nerve is slipping out of my fingers. I want to snatch up my sweater and scarf and run out of there.

Then someone right in front of me turns around. I have to take a step back. The next half a second stretches out like the longest few minutes ever. This twelve-year-old boy in front of me looks so familiar. Then his eyes widen and his lips split in a smile. That's when I realise it's not a twelve-year-old boy; it's a twenty-year-old Emma.

My heart stops for a moment, and then the full-speed fan inside me is back in business. Emma looks just the same, yet there's something completely different about her. She's still tiny, of course, and she still favours her hair short, but this new pixie cut frames her delicate features so perfectly. There's nothing boyish about her, now that I look more carefully. It's the bulky sweater over her jeans that misled me. She feels preternaturally cold—she hates the winter.

"Kathy?" It comes out tentative. "Hi. Your mother said you'd be coming."

"Hi, Emma." We don't rush into each other's arms like nothing had happened two years ago. Instead, we watch each other warily. "How are you?"

"Good. You?"

"I'm good too."

She studies me for a good few seconds. I want to drink her in as well.

"I missed you," she says.

"Me too."

Then she opens her arms, and we are finally hugging. I feel like a broken part of me has been found. But I don't feel mended.

"I'm sorry for that stupid fight, about what I said."

"I'm sorry too. Stupid, childish fight."

"I want to be friends again. I have so much to tell you."

It's a silly conversation, me just repeating whatever she's saying. But I still say: "I have so much to tell you too." And so much I can't.

A jangle of guitar strings interrupts us. "Gather around, folks, let's begin." And the guitar belts out a jaunty "Jingle Bells" tune.

"Who's that?" I ask, nodding at the young man who's pulled up a chair and settled himself and his guitar into it.

Emma leans close to whisper in my ear as the group rallies around and the singing starts. "Brother Dominic, the new deacon," she tells me. She nods off to the side. "And Grumpy George is right there—remember him?"

I snigger. "Of course." The buzzkill of the whole Christmas choir experience.

"He can't stand Brother Dominic, no surprises. But the kids love him. Think he's so cool."

We segue into "Jingle Bells" like we never had a parallel conversation going. We click our fingers with the beat, like we used to, and look at each other and grin. By the time Brother Dominic leads us into "Go Tell It on the Mountain," it's like I've never been away at all.

We all wear masks. I read that somewhere. Such a simple statement, yet so deep, so true. We all wear masks because we are all hiding something. Something we are not brave enough to wear on our faces. We need our masks for self-preservation, for reassurance, for self-esteem, to keep ourselves sane and safe.

When I left home two-and-a-half years ago, I did not know I would return with a mask on. I wish that I could have my mask surgically attached to my face to spare me the effort of pretending to be someone else. And if that's not a miracle science can perform for me, perhaps it can build me a time machine to go back to being eighteen again, and innocent, when our dreams—mine and Emma's—of marrying handsome, fair-faced Anglo-Indian boys and having beautiful blended babies were real.

I walk back home after choir practice instead of taking the Metro. It's just one stop, so it's not a long walk, but it's not an easy walk. I need to feel that cold, smog-ridden winter air on my face, the grit in my eyes. I need the impatient honking of the buses, cars, and scooters to batter my ears. I need to smell the traffic fumes, deep-fried snacks, and Christmas with every breath. The anonymity of the big city is my cocoon. I feel as though I'm part of something when it swallows me, part of something big. I fit in. I need something to feel right in that way.

Can I ever tell Emma the real reason I had to leave? That getting into a college at the other end of the country and leaving was the thing that tore me apart and yet kept me together? Could I ever tell Emma about Damini?

My father is cracking eggs into a stainless-steel milk can when I reach home. The rich, spicy-fruity smell of rum-soaked dry fruits and candied peels fills the air. My cousin's wife is caramelising sugar. My mother runs around everyone, approving, rejecting, ticking off lists.

"Oh good, you're back. Help your father."

And seamlessly, I am part of the machinery. It's almost as if I've never been away.

Tomorrow is baking day. In the morning, we will rise early, gather all the cake things, and take them to the bakery, where we'll wait our turn at the ovens. My parents have been planning and prepping for this for months. I have missed being part of this tradition. It's just not the same in my ancestral home in Kerala where I spent the last two Christmases. Funny how you can feel so homesick in the middle of home, being part of something that was so entrenched in my growing-up years. I yearn for my childhood days suddenly, going from house to house distributing cake on Christmas Eve morning—mostly Hindu homes, some Sikh and Muslim ones, and just one other Christian household in the apartment complex—fending off offers of tea and snacks at every stop because we have so many houses to cover.

My grandmother, uncle, aunt, and little cousins arrive the next day. Ammachi hugs me and presses a two-thousand-rupee note into my hand. I protest; I'm not a little girl anymore.

But she'll have none of it. "I'm sure you have things to buy."

I'm secretly pleased she remembers this ritual of ours.

"Ammachi seems just fine to me," I tell my mother and aunt in the kitchen as we prepare to serve dinner.

"She is lucid most of the time on good days," my aunt says. She lives in Kerala and looks after my grandmother. She goes on to tell us how Ammachi walked out one day and got lost. A neighbour found her in the park behind the school, not a hundred metres from her house. But Ammachi didn't know where she was, and she was confused and distressed.

Mummy doesn't say a word as we heat and serve the food. I don't understand my mother's silence. She's always got on well with her sister-in-law.

Ammachi beams at me when I get up to clear the plates after dinner. "That was a lovely meal, Lucy. You're such a big girl now."

I stare at her, my arm still outstretched. Lucy is the name of her much younger sister who lives in Dubai.

"That's not Lucy, Mummy. That's Kathy, your granddaughter." My uncle's tone is firm, but there's still a gentleness in it. He says it automatically, like he's used to this.

"Kathy." Ammachi repeats the word as though it's an alien sound.

I want to run, but my feet won't move.

There is a sharp screech of wood on marble as my mother pushes back from the table. She snatches the plates from my hand, picks up Ammachi's, stacks it on hers and turns towards the kitchen. Her face is stony. Suddenly, I know why she's so quiet. I can't put it in words, but the knowledge drenches me like an ice-cold shower.

I am blinded by the tears that fill my eyes. I make for the bathroom. But there is no quiet corner in my house anymore. The bathroom door is ajar; the light is on. Splashes and murmurings come from inside. I push the door open. My young cousin Robbie is playing by the sink. He transfers water from a steel tumbler to a mug, back and forth, back and forth. Then he dips his hand into the mug and sprinkles water at the mirror, all the while muttering gibberish.

He freezes as he catches sight of me in the mirror.

"What are you doing?" I ask.

He blinks at me. "I'm playing Hindu-Hindu."

It takes me a moment to realise—he's mimicking Hindu priests. I start to laugh. Robbie stares at me for a few moments and then he begins laughing as well. I hug the little kid and laugh till there are tears rolling down my cheeks. I don't know if I'm laughing or crying.

Emma and I haven't exactly picked up where we left off, but that's a good thing. We left things awkward back then, and neither of us would want to be back there. Instead, it's like that blip never happened. Being friends with Emma again feels like a load has been lifted off me. Most of the time, when it's a relief to have someone to hang out with and talk to.

There are other times that being near her is the hardest thing in the world.

She calls me one evening a couple of days later. "Hey, you didn't come to choir practice today?"

"No. I'm home with my grandmother. My parents are out."

"Ammachi?" I can hear the excitement in Emma's voice. "She's here? You didn't tell me. Can I come and meet her?"

"Er…"

"Say yes, say yes."

Ammachi is watching the "Shashi Kapoor Super Hit Collection" on YouTube on my laptop. She grins as I sit next to her. "I love internet," she tells me. She leans forward, pauses the video, and then replays it. "See, I can stop and start whenever I want, and I can watch the same song a thousand times if I want."

I laugh. "Yes, the internet is amazing."

"Where are Robbie and Elsa? They would like this." She looks around.

My heart sinks. She has been having a good day. "They've gone to Agra, Ammachi. Remember?"

"Oh."

She doesn't talk again, but she nods to the music.

I get up to answer the door when the bell rings. My heart gives a little leap of joy as I catch sight of Emma through the spyhole. She comes bearing a box of rose cookies, which she must have stopped off at home for. I've always loved the rose cookies her mother makes at Christmas. I reach into the box for one, but she smacks my hand away with a mock frown. "These are for Ammachi."

My grandmother's eyes are swimming with tears. "Emma, how lovely to see you." She hugs her fondly. "Why don't you come around anymore?"

An embarrassed look crosses Emma's face.

I look at the floor guiltily as she replies.

"I'm here now, Ammachi. How are you?"

"I don't remember anything these days," Ammachi says sadly. "My brain is failing."

Emma shoots a panicked glance at me.

I shake my head. I hope she'll understand the *I'll explain later* that remains unsaid. "Tea?" I ask.

While the water boils, Ammachi and Emma chat away in Malayalam. It reminds me of my childhood Christmases, my grandmother coming down to Delhi, and she and Emma chattering away. They've always got on famously. I want to frame the picture for eternity—the two of them on the sofa, heads bent towards each other, giggling like schoolgirls.

As I arrange biscuits on a plate, I watch Emma. How did I survive two years without her? Now that she's back in my life, sitting in my home, it feels unbelievable that we were ever apart. That gesture with her hand, the impatient tapping foot, the quick smile. I have missed it so much. And that voice, low and soft—it could have been there at the end of a phone call.

A peel of laughter catches my attention. I have missed the joke. I'm awash with a deluge of gratitude towards Emma for insisting on coming over. I haven't seen my grandmother so animated since she got here. I go back to watching Emma through the kitchen door as the tea brews.

She rubs her head, an old, peculiar habit I used to tease her for. She has a twisted silver ring on her pinky. Her cropped hair stands on end. I smile. I want to reach over and pat it down. The little sideways fringe on her forehead is cute. Today she's wearing a red sweater with little yellow stars all over, and black jeans. The sweater hugs her body, not making her look like a preteen boy at all.

I tear my eyes away. My palms are sweaty.

"Kathy? Did you hear?" Ammachi's voice draws me back to reality.

"Sorry, what?" I call back.

"Emma is studying to be a nurse."

I turn towards them. "Yes, I know."

Ammachi leans towards Emma. "You know, Kathy also wanted to be a nurse. But now she's going to be a doctor."

Emma has that puzzled expression on her face again. She shifts away and stands up. "I'll help Kathy with the tea, Ammachi."

She comes into the kitchen and catches my arm just as I'm about to pour the tea into mugs. "Careful!"

"What's going on with her?" she whispers.

I purse my lips and put the pan down. Emma's hand is still on me. It sears through my fleece T-shirt, impeding my ability to think. I can't look at her; she's standing too close.

"She's been diagnosed with Alzheimer's."

Emma gives a gasp of dismay. Her hand flies to her mouth. "Shit!"

I stare down at the counter.

"Why didn't you tell me?" She turns me around and holds me by the shoulder, looking up at me—she's a good three or so inches shorter. "When did you know?"

"It's been less than a year."

She pulls me into a hug. "Are you okay?"

Her words are hot in my ear. I close my eyes, wrapping my arms around her. My family aren't the tactile kind. We rarely hug. Sometimes I forget how good it feels to be held.

I lean into her. Slowly, the awareness of how her body presses to mine seeps into me. Pulling away, I go back to the tea.

Emma doesn't stay long, but it feels like forever. I yearn to touch her again, but I don't of course. She squeezes my elbow as she leaves. I pull my arm back so her hand runs down my forearm till our fingers are interlocked. She looks at me.

"Choir tomorrow?" she says. Her voice is soft.

"Tomorrow," I reply. It feels like a promise, but maybe I imagine it.

Ammachi's eyes are gleaming when I go back inside to sit beside her. We've been eating rose cookies. I feel full—Mummy's going to be mad we spoilt our dinner, like we are five-year-olds.

"Are you happy, Kathy?" my grandmother asks me.

I smile at her. "Yes, Ammachi, I am."

Her gaze is penetrating. "You know," she says, very slowly, almost as though she's making up her mind what to say, "Shashi and I were also very happy. Nobody knew about us…"

My insides dip again. I want to scream. How can she be like this? Fine one moment, and then completely…*not* the next? I never know how to handle these moments. My uncle says to gently correct her, without making a big deal of it. But what are you supposed to say when your grandmother thinks her fantasies about a dead film star are real?

On the last day of rehearsals, Grumpy George is super grumpy because he thinks we've been goofing off too much during choir practice. We listen to him rant, in one ear, out the other. It's just a matter of letting him run dry. His meltdowns come around as regularly as raisins in Christmas cake, and all of us choir veterans are used to them. The younger ones look a bit upset, but Brother Dominic breezes in and cheers them up in no time.

Later, Emma and I buy cappuccinos from the Café Coffee Day down the road and take them into the park. The days are short, so it's already dark. Kids are laughing, running about, playing, screaming with laughter.

"Why do children sound like they're being tortured when they're actually happy?" Emma asks.

"Did we used to scream like this?"

"No way."

There are no empty benches, so we take a circuit of the walking track, sipping our coffees.

"It's not as cold as it used to be when we were kids, is it?" I observe.

"Global warming," Emma responds.

"Hmm."

We walk mostly in silence. Emma is a chatterbox and I'm not, but we've never needed too many words between us.

"What's it like in Vellore?" she asks out of the blue.

It takes me by surprise. "What?"

"You don't talk about it. What's it like?"

"I…er, it's hard work. I… We just… There's no time for much else apart from studies." That's not entirely true.

"But you have fun, right? You like it there?" A pause. "You must have friends."

There's a slight pause before *friends*.

"You don't talk about your college either. Or your friends."

Emma shrugs. "It's hard," she says, "to make friends after…" She's looking at me.

I am quite sure I forget to breathe. There's an expression on her face that I can't describe. I'm hot and cold at the same time. My skin is burning, yet I feel a sliver of ice running through my body.

"After?" I prompt.

"After what we had." She drops her gaze to the ground between us. We've stopped walking. Joggers and power walkers are detouring around us.

My head swims as I struggle to grasp her words. Lights swirl around me. Could it… Is it possible… Did we…? I don't know how those questions end.

Emma's hand is on my arm, gripping hard. I have to take a step or two to steady myself. My takeaway coffee mug is on the bricked path, the cover off and liquid pooling under it.

"Are you all right?" Emma's face is suffused with worry.

The walkers stare at us. A woman steps on my coffee mug.

I rub my hand over my face. "I'm fine, I just… I'm fine."

Emma drags me to her place, just down the road, through a tiny alley. She insists that I rest for a bit before I go home. I protest, but she insists even more. There's no one home except her fifteen-year-old brother. He's holed up in his room, studying for his board exams in March.

I plop down on Emma's bed and look around. Her room hasn't changed in two years. A single bed with its uneven mattress—"moulded to my body" she always said—and I even recognise the red-and-yellow block-print bed cover. A desk and chair are pushed up against the wall, on the other side of the wooden cupboard decorated with remnants of stickers from her younger days. The cane bookshelf is still in the same corner, with her textbooks, her modest collection of Mills & Boons carefully re-bound with Enid Blyton covers, and her actual Enid Blytons.

She sees me looking and grins. "Can you tell which are the real Blytons and which the MBs?"

"Of course. I haven't been away that long." I lie back on the bed, feet on the floor, staring at the ceiling. "It just seems long."

I stare at the fan. Its white blades are sparkling.

The bed dips. Emma mirrors my position.

I turn my head. Her face is inches away from mine.

"You didn't tell me about your new friends." She's so close that she only has to whisper. I can smell coffee on her breath.

I examine her face, her fine features, the rise of the bridge of her nose, the curve of her lips. The faint scar under her eye from a fall when we were ten. I know the place where her right cheek dimples when she smiles... I feel I know every scratch, every fold of skin of that face. A few years ago, I would have said I know everything that goes on inside her head too. We used to joke about an invisible wire that connected our brains.

But now...I don't know what to think. What will happen if I tell her what happened with Damini? Will she find me disgusting? What if I tell her about the real reason I *had* to leave? About how I had to go away and how it tormented me till I understood.

"There's nobody special," I say. I have to speak softly too.

She continues to look at me. "I feel like you've changed. There's something about you that's different."

I don't know how to respond to that. "Sometimes, do you feel like everything is out of control?" I ask instead.

"All the time."

I can see a sadness in her eyes.

I should clarify: there are certain things we don't talk about, we never have. Like her father's drinking.

The backs of our hands are touching. I push against her fingers and they slip into mine, entwining effortlessly. We are still staring at each other.

My heart feels like it's expanding. It's big enough to swallow me up. Swallow her. That invisible connection between us is palpable. We are coiled around each other, like threads in a yarn. The closeness I feel with Emma is almost as if she were an extension of me. And the fact that she's actually so close, her mouth just inches from mine.

I would barely have to move if I wanted to...

I pull back. I close my eyes and turn my head towards the ceiling. When I am able to look, Emma is sitting crosslegged near the head of her bed, her hands on her lap, her head down. As I sit up, she reaches for her phone. "I'll call you an Ola auto."

"It's fine, I'll take the Metro."

She shakes her head. "If you're taking the Metro, I'm coming with you."

"I'm fine, Emma, I was just…"

"Auto-rickshaw, then?"

I sigh. "Fine."

She doesn't look at me as we track the auto-rickshaw on the map, watching it come closer and closer, till I have to go.

All the ghosts of Emma's touches haunt me as I try to sleep that night. The hug in the kitchen, her hand on my arm, the linking of our hands. Blood is pumping through my body with a vengeance. I know it's not how it works, but I can imagine waves dashing against the walls of my arteries. My skin tingles, and the thick quilt is uncomfortable wherever it touches bare skin. I pull my arms out, but then I feel cold.

I turn and shift, trying to get more comfortable. Ammachi is tucked up right next to me. I start as I see her eyes wide open, staring at me.

"Shashi and I had so much fun together," she says. She speaks in a slight lisp because she's taken her dentures out.

God, I'm not in the mood for this. "Ammachi…"

She clucks her tongue impatiently, turning around to face me. "Nobody knew about us. We went everywhere together when we could, which was not very often, of course, because our fathers were very strict. But we found ways." She taps the side of her nose impishly. "Oh, yes, carol singing was so much fun. Loitering after Sunday School. Studying for exams together. Learning to cook…"

I can only stare, my mouth open. It's a little embarrassing in a way, that my sixty-nine-year-old grandmother has bizarre fantasies about a movie star, even imagining that they were childhood friends together. But it's also fascinating. She really thinks she spent her childhood with Shashi Kapoor? What are the memories that she's lost or is losing, and how and why are these blanks filling up with made-up things? Do we, with our "regular" brains, also do this? How much of our memories are real and how much wishful thinking? So much of the brain is still a mystery to scientists.

Ammachi is fingering the little gold crucifix around her neck. "Shashi gave me this," she says wistfully, "when I got married. We did not want to be parted, so I told my father I didn't want to get married." She laughs softly. "Of course, I would have happily married Shashi if it were possible. We even ran away together, Shashi and I. My uncle found us at the station and brought us home. My father slapped me. I was married very soon. But Shashi didn't give in. We met again, but I'll tell you that story later."

Just as suddenly as she'd started talking, she stops. Within seconds, she's snoring.

I feel weirdly disappointed. I want to know where she goes with the story. There are a thousand questions that I'll never have answers to. For instance, if Ammachi can construct an entire past with Shashi Kapoor in it, why could she just not have married him in her fantasy too? What makes her remember that marrying a Hindu man would have been a no-no—at least back in her village—but not other things?

We rendezvous at the church at seven-thirty in the evening for the first day of carol singing. A minibus is waiting, and Grumpy George is on a chair next to it, fanning himself with a magazine. An expression of extreme distaste covers his face as he berates a couple of seventeen-year-olds about something or other.

Nikhil leans in towards me and says, "Is he going to have a heart attack, do you think?"

The look on his face hints that that would be a favourable turn of events.

I nudge him with my elbow. "That's mean."

"You weren't here last year, you won't believe what he said…"

I don't care about what Grumpy George said last year. I look around, tuning Nikhil out. Where is Emma? Is she upset about yesterday?

But what is it about yesterday that she should be upset about? I don't know the answer. Just that there was something going on… My pulse quickens as I spot her. She's wearing a woollen beanie today. Her little fringe is poking out. She also has fingerless gloves. A smile leaks out when she spots me, and I feel like I'm walking on air. I smile back.

"Seriously, gloves?" I ask.

"What, it's cold," she shoots back.

"Hi, Emma." Nikhil looks a bit put out he didn't get to complete his story.

"Hello," Emma says.

Nikhil turns to me. "So, when are you going back, Kathy?"

"Er…what? On first January. Why?"

He takes out his phone. "I don't think I have your number."

"I… My number?"

Emma takes my elbow. "Oho, later. Let's go take our seats, Kathy."

We climb into the bus, leaving Nikhil looking bereft.

"I think he likes you," Emma hisses as we slip into the second-to-last row of seats.

"Is that why he's been hanging around us? Wait…what if he likes *you*?"

"No, no. He's had plenty of chances to hit on me. It's you." She narrows her eyes. "You, um, what do you think of him?"

I laugh. If only it were that easy. "He's not my type."

"What is your type, then?" Emma demands.

All right, I walked into that. I can't tell the truth—*You*. Yet she's looking at me with a determination that means she definitely wants a reply.

A stir of activity saves me from having to lie. The rest of the choir group pours into the minibus. Brother Dominic follows, lugging his guitar, and then Grumpy George lumbers inside too. A short, sharp exchange ensues between them about Nisha, the tambourine player, who hasn't turned up. Whatever Brother Dominic says calms Grumpy George down.

Then we're off. Our group is going to cover one part of the parish, starting from the outer edge, slowly working our way in closer over the next few days, until Christmas Eve.

The bus comes to a halt near a park by an apartment complex. Brother Dominic hands out Santa hats for us to wear when we get off. Then we trudge to the first house on our list. I love the looks of delight and surprise when they answer the door and see us. They're all expecting us, of course, but they don't know which locality we'll visit when. Sometimes, the kids spot us on the street and run ahead to tell their families.

For the next two hours, it's all about singing, eating Christmas cake and snacks, and drinking tea and coffee. I'm stuffed by the time we board the bus to return home.

"Don't be late tomorrow," Grumpy George tells each one of us as we get off.

I can't believe I didn't come home for Christmas for two years. Everyone gathers around the ginger wine and cake after Midnight Mass on Christmas Eve, asking me what happened, where I was, and how I could have been so busy that I didn't even come home.

"I went home to Kerala," I reply. Lying on Christmas Day—surely that counts as a major sin. Because Kerala isn't home, it hasn't been for me since I was five years old. I doubt even my parents think of it as home any more.

Robbie and Elsa, my cousins, run around with the other kids. Being legitimately allowed to stay up so late is part of the fun of Christmas. It reminds me of the time I was as young as them, when the midnight snacks, playing with friends so late, and going to bed at two was just another thing to look forward to at Christmas, just as much as the cakes and the feasts and the cousins.

Inside, people are still lining up to admire the crib and kiss Baby Jesus's feet. The wine, cake, and tea are disappearing fast. I wonder where Emma is.

The thought of leaving her in a week rips me apart. I don't know how I did it two years ago.

I shake my head, like that will make the thought go away. I can't think of things like that, not here, not in church. To take my mind off Emma, I try to see if I can spot my cousins among the kids.

"You looked cold."

I jump. And there she is, holding out a tiny paper cup of tea. I take it from her. "Thank you."

"And sad."

I force a smile. "You can't be sad on Christmas Day."

"Then why are you?"

I blow on the tea and sip. It's already cooling, and it tastes like sweetened hot water. "I'm a bit sad because I have to leave in a week."

Her face falls. She looks down at the ground. "But you won't disappear?"

"I won't, I promise."

"And you'll visit more often?"

"That too."

"Do you have internet at your hostel?"

"Yes."

"Good." She looks up at me and smiles.

Something breaks inside me.

Christmas Day is a mad rush. It begins with a breakfast of egg curry and appam. There have been very few Christmas mornings without Ammachi's special egg curry. After that, there isn't a moment to breathe. My mother has been getting things ready for Christmas lunch for days. The house is packed—my uncle's family is already here, plus my cousin who lives close by, and his wife, their kids. Twelve people in all to feed and entertain. The mutton cutlets, fish fries, sausages, and seekh kababs, served with onion salad, disappear as quickly as we bring them out. The main door of the house is open, and the kids play in the corridor. Some of the neighbours glance in to wish us Merry Christmas.

Of course, there's a lot of help, though it's mostly the women doing the cooking and serving. My father always gallantly announces that he will take care of the drinks—and my mother always rolls her eyes at that. When lunch is finally on the table, I am exhausted and I haven't even done much. There is fried rice, mutton curry, fish curry, raita, papad, salad, and pickle. And plenty of cake. There isn't enough place around our dining table to fit everybody, so it's a buffet.

I wonder if I'll have the time later in the evening to drop in at Emma's. Or if she'll come around to mine. I haven't even had the time to check my phone today.

Ammachi is having a good day. She's been completely lucid and helped with the cooking; she's been quite the life of the party. When we're clearing up, my mother and I catch a moment alone in the kitchen, and I tell her that.

"Yes, she's looking happy, isn't she?" Mummy tips a bowl of mutton bones into the dustbin. "Every time I look at her, I wonder if this is going to be the last time."

I glance at her. She seems pensive.

"But she doesn't seem so bad, does she?" I say. "She gets muddled sometimes, but otherwise, she's...fine." I glance at the door. Nobody seems to be around. "The story about her getting lost in the park—I... She doesn't seem so...you know?"

"It's just..."

My aunt comes in with a pile of dirty plates, putting an end to our conversation. I take the plates from her. "Mummy was looking for you, Kathy," she tells me. "She's gone inside to lie down for a bit."

"Go see what she wants," my mother says.

Ammachi is sitting on the bed, next to her is the antique wooden box with lacquerwork on the lid. She never goes anywhere without it. It's full of all sorts of trinkets. When I was a kid, she used to open it and show me things from inside it, and tell me stories. She never let me touch, though.

"Kathy, come and sit." She pats the bed.

I go obediently.

"I want to give you something before I forget and all the memories become a jumble."

I open my mouth to protest, but she shushes me. "I know I have dementia, I know I forget things and mix up people and places. Sometimes I don't know where I am."

I am silent.

She looks down at what she's holding, something small and thin, wrapped in yellowing tissue paper. "You told me that day when I asked that you were happy. Right?"

"Ye-es."

She turns her head up to me. "There are things that will make you happy, right?"

"Er, yes…" I'm not sure what she's asking me.

"Sometimes it isn't easy to have the courage to do what makes you happy."

I have no idea what she means. I'm starting to feel a bit uneasy.

"Shashi was very courageous, but I wasn't."

Reaching for her hand, I squeeze. "Ammachi…" I'm not sure what I'm going to say. "I was a great fan of Shashi Kapoor too. I was so sad when he died. But he wasn't your friend. Really, he wasn't."

She frowns, clearly puzzled. "What? What are you saying?" She grips my hand back. "We ran away, did I tell you? But we didn't get too far. I thought it was all over when I got married. But Shashi didn't give up. Here." She thrusts the tissue-wrapped package at me. "When I went to live in Kottayam with your grandfather, Shashi got a job in a school and came to live with…"

"Mummy, here's your medicine." My aunt bustles in with one of those long Monday-to-Sunday pill boxes and a glass of water. "You should rest now. You and Kathy can chat in the evening."

She smiles at me, and I smile back. I am grateful to her for coming in and interrupting Ammachi's fantasies, I suppose. I get up and go out into the balcony.

The package in my hand is haphazardly wrapped, like it was done in a hurry. I can feel something hard inside. I open it, and the gold chain with the cross that Ammachi wears slips into my hand. I stare at it. Why has she given it to me? She loves it. She never takes it off. Maybe I should ask Mummy if I can keep it or if I should return it. But won't Ammachi be upset if I return it?

There's something else in the package, something thin and papery. I pull it out—it is a black-and-white photograph. Of two girls—well, young women. They're dressed up in saris that I can tell are bright and colourful even though the photo doesn't show it, and dangly earrings and fancy necklaces. They have their arms linked, big grins on their faces, leaning against each other, shoulder to shoulder. I frown and peer at the faded, mottled print—is that Ammachi? I turn the photo around. Yes, it is. It says, "Rosa and Shashi. Christmas 1965". Then there's a heart. And below it, "Forever."

My mother is just ending a phone call as I burst into her room.

"What's wrong?" she asks, looking at my face.

I hand her the photograph. "Can you explain this to me?"

She peers at the photo. "That's your grandmother—and her friend. What was her name? Susie? She used to live with us when I was very small. I called her Susie Aunty. She was very fond of me. Why? Where did you get this photo?"

"Ammachi gave it to me. With this." I show her the chain and pendant. "Are you sure her name was Susie?"

"Yes, I think so…or something very like it. Why?"

"Could it have been Shashi?"

My mother's eyes light up. "Yes, Shashi. How do you know?"

I can't speak. I only stare at her.

My mother laughs as she studies the photo again. "Yes, of course, Shashi Aunty. How could I have forgotten? It was quite funny, because you know your grandmother's obsession with Shashi Kapoor—"

"T-they were friends?"

"Hmm? Yes, they were very good friends."

My head is reeling. What was it that Ammachi said the other day? *Nobody knew about us. But we were very happy.* Something like that. And another time, *I would have married Shashi if I could.* My legs feel like they can't hold me any more. I sit down next to my mother. "What happened to Shashi Aunty?"

Mummy shakes her head, frowning. "I can't quite remember. I think she went back to her village when her mother fell ill. But they kept in touch, your grandmother and she. I think she died when I was in my twenties. I don't know what happened. Why do you ask?"

I look at the chain in my hand. "I think this belonged to Shashi Aunty. Is it okay if I keep this, Mummy?"

"If Ammachi gave it you and she knew what she was doing, then yes, of course. Are you sure you're all right?"

I'm very far from all right. Could it be true? Ammachi and her friend Shashi? Or was it the Alzheimer's talking?

I go back out into the balcony and stare down at the narrow lane at the back of the house. Suppose it's all true, that Ammachi and her friend were, well, more than friends. Then why is she telling me this? How does she know about my feelings for Emma?

Oh my God! Is it that obvious? The thought sends me spiralling into panic. I gasp for air and grip the railing. I think I'm going to throw up. I run through my room, into the bathroom, and retch, but nothing comes up.

When I come out, Ammachi is lying in bed, her eyes closed. I think she's asleep, but her eyes snap open at the screech of the bathroom door.

"I won't tell," she says to me, and her eyelids droop shut.

I stand there for many minutes.

"At this time?" my father glances at the clock. "It's almost eight."

"I'll take an Ola auto," I say firmly. I try to sound like an adult, and not like the teenager Pappa still thinks I am. He's been struggling with the fact that it's not so easy to monitor my comings and goings. I can see he's a bit confused about it, about how much he should try. "I'll be back soon."

I escape before he can stop me. In fact, I walk all the way to Emma's house. My head has been buzzing since Ammachi's revelation that afternoon, and I need to clear it. I don't know what to think about her and Shashi, but one thing I'm pretty sure about—somehow, she knows *about* me...and how I feel about Emma.

As I ring the bell at her place, panic grips me. What am I doing here? I stare up at the star on their balcony landing, bobbing gently in the breeze. I have no idea what our church thinks about...you know. But if I had to guess, it would be nothing favourable. They probably think people like me are the worst kind of sinners.

"Oh, hello."

Emma is surprised to see me. I don't blame her. It was stupid of me. I should have called to see if she was free.

"Hi. Merry Christmas."

"Merry Christmas." She half frowns and then smiles. "This is a surprise. Come in."

"No, I... You must be busy. I think I'll come back later."

She grabs my arm and pulls me inside. "Don't be silly. Just come inside, will you? There's no one here. Jacob fell and twisted his ankle, and my parents have taken him to the hospital."

"Oh no. Is he okay?"

"Yeah, he's just a big crybaby. Never mind him. Why are you here?"

We sit on her bed again, side by side. I twist my hands in my lap.

"Kathy? Is something wrong?"

I shake my head, then I nod. Then, I laugh. "I...don't know. I found out something about my grandmother today."

"Is she okay?" I can hear the concern in her voice.

I nod. "It's about her childhood. Well, her younger days."

"Okay." Emma sounds curious now.

"Remember I was telling you how she's getting muddled and telling me stories about her youth with Shashi Kapoor?"

"Yeah."

"I misunderstood. They weren't fantasies."

"You mean she really knew him?"

"No, no. Of course not. Just that…" I twist faster and faster. I risk a quick glance at Emma. A frown pinches her brow.

"What?" she says again, impatient now.

"Shashi was her friend, a girl. I think…Emma, I think my grandmother had a…a relationship with her."

There is silence. I look up.

Emma is staring back at me. "Are you sure?"

Now I'm the one staring at her. I half expected Emma not to understand what I meant. But she does, immediately, without any judgement or shock.

"No, not a hundred per cent." I take the photograph out of my jacket pocket and show it to her, including the inscription at the back. "It's not incontrovertible proof. But I think they were, you know. She said that she would have married her if she could."

Emma studies the photograph and then hands it back to me. Her hand shakes ever so slightly.

"You're not shocked?" I say.

She shakes her head. She won't look at me. "Are you?" she asks, her voice soft.

"Well, she *is* my grandmother, so, yes, a bit."

"And what do you think about…the other thing?" At that, she catches my eye. Her look is keen, like the answer is important to her.

My heart races; my palms are sweaty. I feel so hot. I want to tear off my jacket. But I can't move. I'm locked in place by Emma's penetrating gaze.

"I think…" I pause, because it is only in this instant that I have actually allowed myself to think. "I think it takes a lot of courage to understand what you feel and to let yourself feel it."

I spent more than two years running away from how I felt. Ammachi was right: all I needed was a bit of courage. Remember what they say about fortune favouring the brave? It's true, isn't it? When I decided to come home and face my feelings—well, all right, it wasn't quite like that—but when I did, the universe conspired to help me unravel myself. Would I have ever found out about Ammachi and Shashi if I hadn't come back this year?

And that's not all. Here I am, with Emma just inches from me one more time. In my peripheral vision, I can see her chest rise and fall faster than it should. Her lips are slightly parted, and her eyes are bright black beads, studying me intently. As I look at her, her gaze drops, her eyelids droop. She's the one studying my mouth now. My lips feel dry. I lick them quickly.

There's an electrified knot of excitement deep inside me, spreading through my limbs. I inch forward, and Emma inches that much closer too. I close my eyes and gather all my courage inside me and let myself feel what I need to feel.

There's no one else in the house. The universe continues to conspire— we have all the time in the world.

So I take that leap of faith. Our lips meet, and my mask drops.

Love Just Is

BY JODY KLAIRE

Chapter 1

SNOW SWEPT OVER LUSH GREEN mountains still bearing scars of the coal industry beneath their thick pine forests. The white blanketed every row of terraced houses, some red brick or grey and some painted with garish colours, but all flashed, flickered, and sparkled like fairground rides under icing sugar. Christmas wreaths adorned monuments to lost loved ones: miners, children, families all buried for black gold in past centuries; seafarers, soldiers, and airmen. The cold stone and bronze glittered with snowflakes in the bitter moonlit night.

Through slush-filled lanes turned brown with the traffic, over hedges dusted white and fields painted in a snowy glow, lay a small village. Its rugged old cottages wore the same straw hats. All were gathered around one Tudor-esque pub and a grand old church with an illuminated cross on top.

Bryn Cariad. Its families were mainly retired people. Their children had escaped to the noise of the cities, but Christmas snow always brought them home before the roads were undrivable and the sleepy village settled in for the holidays.

Later than all the other children, Nia Jenkins chugged her ancient Land Rover up the ski-slope of a lane into town and willed the rattling excuse for machinery to make it. Living in the city of London, she always used the bus or taxis. Why splash out on a new 4x4 when she only ever used it once a year?

She flicked her window-wipers into "frantic" to clear the thickening white and gritted her teeth. "Don't forget to plan for the snow," Mam had said. "You don't want to be stuck out there."

Why hadn't Nia listened? She pulled her mouth to the side. When did she ever listen to her mam? If she had, she'd have married Robert Jones. She glanced out at the snowy fields his dad owned. No thanks.

"Come on," she muttered as the hunk of rattling metal stuttered. "Nearly there."

Slam.

She winced, braced, and her shoulder crunched into the door as someone clattered into her. Then she yelped as the 4x4 slid into Mr Jones' wall. A loud creak, groan, and a hissing noise filled the car. Great. Nice welcome home.

A woman in the craziest Christmas-bobble hat, which flashed on movement, ripped open the door to Nia's car. "I'm so sorry, I'm sorry, I'm so sorry..." The woman put her hands over her mouth. "I'm sorry."

Nia held up her shaking hands. "Yes. We've established you're sorry." She tested her shoulder. Still attached, if the pain was anything to go by. "Did you hit ice or just decide you didn't like my car?"

The woman bounced about on the balls of her feet. "I was making a house call. I didn't see you in the snow." She held out her hand.

Nia frowned. She looked too energetic for a GP. Then again, most doctors she saw were sat behind a desk with bored expressions and a prescription pad.

"Please, let me check you over?"

"I don't know, you might try finishing me off." Nia tested her neck. Oh, that was going to take a lot of painkillers. "You won't get partner if you bump off his daughter, y'know. Dad likes me...sometimes."

"*You're* his daughter?" The woman stared up at the sky, bobble hat flashing away. "Lovely."

Nia sighed, shunted over the seat, and grabbed her travel bag from the back. "Mr Jones might want to lynch you before Dad catches you though." The woman helped her out, and Nia tried out her wobbling legs. Bit of shock just to add to the mix. "So, do you have a name, or will that foil your ambush?"

"Sarah," the woman said, doctor's gaze on, scouring her like she might put her in a jar. "Sarah Kavanagh."

Ah, that was the Doctor Kavanagh Dad kept talking about. He kept saying that he'd not seen a doctor like her since Ieaun, Nia's brother, had been in the practice. "In that case, everyone will probably side with you." She thumbed to her crunched-up car and shivered. If it was cold in Swansea, it was always ten degrees lower up on the mountain.

"Let me give you a lift. I'll sort out your car. I can check you over then." Sarah led her over to a Land Rover Defender which didn't seem to have a scratch on it. "I should check you over now though." She shivered and hugged herself as if the huge, puffed-up coat didn't keep her warm enough. "Oh dear. I think *I'm* in shock."

"You're the worst attacker ever." Nia shook her head and got in the driver's side. "I know the lanes. I don't think you'll get to the surgery through this."

Sarah got in and managed, just, to do up her seatbelt. Wide-eyed, pale, and shaking. "I'll have to. I can't get home otherwise."

"Can you call?" Was the woman crazy? When the snow came down like this, the only thing to do was find a warm fire and a brandy. Medically approved or not, brandy always helped.

"No." Sarah shrugged. "Well, I could try, but I don't think the plant pot knows how to pick up the receiver."

"Then Dad will have you stay at ours." Great, that would make the already riveting conversation between Ieaun and Dad a three-way drone about medical drivel. "Just so you know though, Ieaun is currently single and you might somehow be married off to him."

That would be Mam's mission sorted until the snow let up. Yes, then they could stop trying to marry Nia off to Robert Jones and she could rehearse her lines. The show wasn't going to learn itself, was it?

"Oh dear. I don't think Ieaun is my type." Sarah frowned.

Her eyebrows weren't blonde, but they weren't dark in the interior light either. Mousey brown?

"You don't?" Ieaun was stout, jolly, and had a fascination with flower arranging. "Don't tell me you can resist romantic conversations about how long a petunia should be in a vase?"

Sarah blinked at her. "Why do I get the feeling you're teasing me?"

"I'm really not...on that." Nia smirked at Sarah and slid-drove them through the lane to her parents' cottage, right beside the church.

"Ah, so you do tease?" Sarah's cheeks had colour again.

"Intense medical professionals who need to lighten up, yeah." She pulled them off the lane and slid to a stop in the flowerbed. Oops. "If they ask me, I'm saying you parked." Nia jumped out—legs still wobbly—and retrieved her bag.

Sarah took her doctor's bag from the back—why? They had more medical equipment inside than the surgery—and nodded as if bracing herself. "I take full responsibility."

Nia rolled her eyes and shoved open the wide, thick wood door, ducked to avoid the mistletoe, stamped off her snow on the mat, and turned.

Sarah was still focused on the door. Her eyes were not quite brown, more cappuccino.

"Did you freeze?" She put her hands on her hips. "It's not *that* cold."

Sarah blinked a few times. "Steeling myself."

"Right. Well, I'm letting the heat out, *mun*." She pulled off her boots and wiggled her toes. Sarah was still standing like a statue. "Should I just shut the door and get Mam to bring you food?"

"I'm contemplating hiding in the car." Sarah shrugged and cooed at the bag. "I don't think I can take conversation."

"Why, you might like Ieaun. If you don't, tell them your fiancé is rich and a consultant or something." Nia tapped on the door. Was Sarah really comforting her medical equipment? Was that shock or insanity? "Unless you're hoping for hypothermia."

Sarah lifted her bag up, hugged it, then walked forwards, stopped, walked to the car, and then stopped and did the same again, twice.

"Did you concuss yourself?" What was with her?

"No. I'm always this dithery with family things." She glanced back at her car. "I don't like family things."

"You don't like dinner with two doctors, a vicar, and an actress?" She waved at the hallway, as it had always been: pale wood floor, coats hanging all along with shoes and boots below. "Just think, all we need is a butler and Colonel Mustard and we're Cluedo all by ourselves."

"Dr Kavanagh in the lane with a Land Rover," Sarah mumbled, then tittered and cooed to her bag again.

Hey, there could be humour in there. Who knew? "Yep, so pass go, collect some warmth, and if you stick a hotel on Park Street, I'm reporting you for assault." Nia offered her best smile. None of Dad's other GPs were this…shy? Crazy? Interesting? Most of them, she couldn't shut up.

Sarah hurried inside, and Nia shut the door before she bolted.

"Thanks."

"You're welcome." Nia took off her hat and coat and hung them on the hook, then held out her hand. "You can't seduce Ieaun in a puffer coat."

Sarah pulled it tighter around her.

"He's not *that* bad." If a girl liked long walks in the countryside taking pictures of flowers.

"Not my type." And Sarah was staring. Why was she staring?

Nia touched her hand to her head. "What?"

"Doctor Andi Mayflower," Sarah mumbled, then let out a long breath. "No wonder you're so good."

"If you start singing the theme tune to me, I will get violent." Yes, the long-running medical drama gave her a steady income and publicity, but people also thought she could perform brain surgery and give them a prescription.

"Sorry. I love the show." Sarah shrugged and took off her coat, still gripping her doctor's bag. "I've always loved the show." She stepped out of her boots. "Your dad never said that you were in the show."

"No. He wouldn't." Because only people from outside the village wouldn't know she was his daughter. "Let go of the bag, Sarah. No one is going to steal your stethoscope."

She stared down at it and smiled. "It's not my doctor's bag." She opened the top, and a tiny dog popped its head out. "Fredrick comes everywhere with me."

Okay, that was a relief: cooing to tiny pets was allowed. Nia grinned and fussed the miniature Doberman. "Now that will get you off the hook with Ieaun."

Sarah beamed down at Fredrick and kissed him on the head. "How so?"

"He doesn't like dogs. He has a cat." She led Sarah into the kitchen. All quiet. They must be in the church hall sharing a mulled wine with the rest of the village. She took a saucer from the cupboard and filled it with water.

"Saved by Fredrick." Sarah let the little guy—the size of a guinea pig—out, and he trotted to the bowl for a drink. "Guess I won't need romance after all."

"Exactly." Nia winked at her. "Who needs romance?"

Chapter 2

SARAH DUG INSIDE FREDRICK'S BAG and pulled out a pouch of food. She doubted he'd eat it. He wasn't a foodie, and the excitement of a new place to explore would distract him. They were both lone adventurers in a new land of rugby and sheep and very attractive actresses who were good natured considering Sarah'd ripped off the entire passenger wing of her car.

Nia seemed to love Frederick and had spent an hour attempting to play with him—she really should have told Nia that a tennis ball was half Fredrick's size and he'd hide, but Sarah wasn't really au fait with dogs. Trying to explain that he was her ex-girlfriend's who'd left when she opted for Bryn Cariad and not St. Thomas' in central London would be too much information. She hadn't even told Nia's dad she hadn't even wanted to be a GP. She'd wanted to be a urologist, but being a surgeon took steady hands and coordination. Clumsy did not go well with scalpels.

Nia was on her hands and knees with a cheeky grin, Nia Jenkins—a woman Sarah watched every week in scrubs—on the flagstone floor in a Christmas jumper, complete with musical jingle, wrestling with Fredrick who thought he was a Great Dane.

How did you make small talk with a puppy-wrestling actress?

"Must be hard trying to smuggle him in and out of the surgery," Nia said in her beautiful sing-song Welsh accent. Her character was a posh Oxford graduate with fitting upper-class speech, but the Welsh burr was oh-so much more…pleasant. "Doubt dogs are allowed."

"Guide dogs and assistance dogs are." Though she wasn't sure what Fredrick could guide or assist with. He could probably sleep in a shoe, not pull it off someone's foot.

"Well, he'd look cute in yellow." Fredrick sprinted at Nia, yapping away, and she rolled him onto his back with a swish of her elegant hand and tickled him until his leg twitched. "Not sure you qualify to be guided."

"Unless you count my driving?" Sarah leaned onto the table.

Nia lifted him up, placed him next to the saucer of water, and stroked him. She stood up and stretched out her back. "Good thing he was with you; he'd have been really upset in the house on his own."

Sarah nodded. "He comes with me everywhere."

"What made you buy a dog, as cute as he is?" Nia eyed her. Her blonde hair was shorter than it was on the show and more highlighted, but there were hints of red in it. Her green eyes were blue on the show, and her skin was much paler in person.

"I didn't buy him." And this was one awkward conversation she wanted to avoid. "I…er…acquired him?"

"Ah, break-up, then." Nia grinned, then took Fredrick to the back door and opened it.

"Are you stealing him?" She was too tired to give chase if that was the case. Surgery had started at eight, and it was—she checked her watch. Nine p.m. now.

"No, he needs the toilet." Nia raised her eyebrow, then smiled a cheeky smile. "Where would I go? You're in my parents' house."

Hmm. That took braincells Sarah'd battered in the collision. "You'll set Ieaun on me." She'd met Ieaun, twice. He was a gastroenterologist, a spectacular trauma surgeon, and a work-focused, networking doctor who didn't shut up about gardening. She'd never really been attracted to those qualities, and she had a pollen allergy. He'd called her a few times, and she'd completely forgotten to pick up. Funny, that.

"You pull that face whenever I mention him." Nia cheered at Fredrick, then fussed him. Why? Next, she hoisted him up in her hand and strolled over to the table, where she tucked him back into his bag. "Don't worry about it. Dad and Mam always try setting him up with registrars and new blood."

Sarah liked the Jenkins family, she did. Doctor Jenkins was a thorough doctor who knew all his patients. He wasn't always up-to-date, but he listened if she showed him the new BNF guidelines or latest research. Reverend Jenkins was boisterous, jolly, with a runner physique and more energy than anyone Sarah had met. She didn't want to disappoint them. She'd disappointed her own family enough. "How do I make them give up on the idea?"

"Well, they're not *twp*." Nia studied her, eyes flicking over her face in a familiar way, an intimate way, then she smiled. "You tell them you're gay."

Sarah blinked a few times. "*Twp*?"

"Stupid *yn Gymraeg*...er...in Welsh." Nia leaned on her fist, amusement in her sparkly green eyes. "Then they'll try setting you up with me."

Now that idea was far more welcome as was the Welsh. Sounded a lot smoother and sexier on Nia's tongue. Sarah cleared her throat. Possibly too welcome. "That would be awkward considering our violent history."

"Indeed." Nia held Sarah's gaze, her tone so soft. The door opened, Nia stroked her cheek with the warm pad of her thumb, and pulled away. "Look what rabble turned up on the doorstep."

Reverend Jenkins dashed through the door, then looked up, threw her hat onto the hook, and scurried across the kitchen. She yanked Nia to stand, squeezed her until Nia grunted, and pushed her back to fuss with her hair. "You lost weight again. You may be busy, but you're never too busy to eat."

Said Reverend Jenkins, who was so slight?

"What can I say? Single living means skipping meals." Nia kissed her on the head. They had the same smiley energy. "Practice what you preach."

Reverend Jenkins chuckled. "Are you coming to the service?" She checked her watch. "You have to come to the service." She glanced over, then grinned as her gaze met Sarah's. "Ooh, you will definitely have to come now. With two extra bums on pews, I'll have to break out the microphone, see?" She grinned. "I love using the microphone."

"Service?" Oh, that didn't sound like fun.

"Don't look so scared, *gul*. There's wine and Christmas trees and carols." Reverend Jenkins beamed at her. "And I can get the entire service done in under an hour." She nodded like that was highly impressive. "Then you get more wine. But it's mulled then... You like mulled wine?"

"Sarah is having the 'I don't think I'm welcome' moment," Nia said with a smile. "She's missed the whole fact that you're a *woman* in a dog collar."

Hmm. True. "I've never been."

Reverend Jenkins walked over and took Sarah's hands with soft warm ones. "Then think of it as discovering something fun. Do you think anything with me involved could be boring?"

"No?" Sarah liked her job. She could mimic fascination.

"Good. As you ploughed Nia's scrap heap into Mr Jones' wall and you're both stuck here, we'll have to show you a traditional Welsh Christmas. At least our way." Reverend Jenkins winked at her. "And the gentleman snoring in here"—she peered into the bag—"is welcome too."

"How?" Sarah frowned. "How did you know about the wall?"

Nia chuckled at her. "Small village, and Mr Jones has a loud voice." She pressed the nose on her snowman jumper, and it danced about and sang "Let It Snow." "Traditional just might surprise you."

Nia held her gaze, her eyes so full of fun and laughter.

"Welsh and traditional will knock your socks off."

Reverend Jenkins looked from Nia to Sarah and kinked her eyebrow, then grinned like she was up to something.

"Why not?" Sarah mumbled. A traditional Welsh Christmas? Should be…interesting.

Chapter 3

WITH FREDERICK AND SARAH IN tow, Nia closed the back door and headed across to the church at eleven thirty. The paths were gritted, but the grounds were blanketed in thick white. She held out her hand to Sarah, who looked like she was attempting to ice skate, and breathed in the crisp, cold air.

"Relax, will you? I've got you." Nia smiled at her as Sarah wobbled about.

"I'm nervous. I get clumsy when I'm nervous." Sarah fiddled with her Christmas-bobble hat.

"Good thing you aren't a surgeon, then." She flicked her eyebrow at Sarah and caught her elbow as she "ooh'd" and nearly took the church notice board out.

Sarah clung to her. "I have no idea how I'm supposed to act or what I'm supposed to do."

"That's why there's a booklet, *mun*." Nia took Fredrick off her—flying dogs were not Christmassy—and guided her through the group of neighbours at the door, hoping they were all far too short-sighted to notice them.

"Nia!" There was Mr Jones. Dai-cap, tweed jacket, smart trousers, and wellies.

"Dr Kavanagh!" And Mrs Jones. Reindeer headband on, pink everywhere, and loafers.

Nia met Sarah's eyes and smiled. Yep. Small talk. "*Noswaith dda*. Sorry about your wall."

"*Mae'n iawn*." Mr Jones wagged his finger. "Lucky it was only the wall. What were you doing driving in this weather?"

"Dad hasn't made the sleigh yet?" Nia held onto Sarah's elbow. How could she slip about standing still?

"I had a house call." Sarah said it like no one would know who she had visited. "But I can't really add any Welsh in, sorry..." She pulled her lip to the side and peered up at Nia. "I can count to three?"

"Well, counting is always useful in *meddyginiaeth*...medicine." Nia gave her a toothy grin. "Just remember that one and *diolch*...thanks...because I'm not sure if you can roll your Rs."

Sarah shook her head. "Ieaun found it hilarious making me say Llanelli." Which really sounded like Lan-elly when Sarah said it.

Nia tried not to chuckle. "A double L...you have to say a 'ch'...like a German 'ch' while saying 'luh' out the sides of your mouth. 'Llanelli.'"

Sarah stared at her in wonder. Easily pleased, then. "I'm not sure that should be physically possible."

"Welsh people make their own rules...Doctor." Nia chuckled. Oh, bless her. Sarah looked like she was going to practice pronouncing the town's name until she got it. Might take a while.

"John said the stuff you gave him is working great." Mr Jones tipped his Dai-cap to Sarah and looked Nia up and down.

He still wasn't happy she'd gone out with his daughter as a teenager and not his son. Ah well.

"Can't make the service, of course, but Betty is going to take him communion tomorrow."

Sarah pulled her mouth to the side. "I'm not sure alcohol will agree with the medication."

Nia bumped her hip, then steadied her as she slipped about again. "It's a mouthful unless Mam has to drive, then she tries to shovel it down you." She rubbed at her throat. The wine was strong, really strong even with water.

"Why?" Sarah peered up at her.

"Because otherwise she has to drink it all," Mrs Jones said with a chuckle. "Do you know how many eucharists she does?"

Sarah shook her head, blank look on her face.

"Service where she hands out the alcohol." Nia grinned and led Sarah into the church. "When Mam has a new curate... er...a registrar type...she always reminds them that, at some point, they'll get the amount in the cup wrong and get merry."

Sarah smiled, but her gaze was on the church as they headed through from the porch. Wooden pews shined up with red velvet covers. Tea lights on ledges all along with string lights casting a gentle glow over the stonework. The nativity scene laid out on real hay, stone steps up to the pulpit dressed with tinsel. One huge Christmas tree that filled the air with pine and smiling faces full of Christmas cheer.

She sat Sarah next to Robert Jones and winked at her. "Robert doesn't like flowers, and he can't say Llanelli either."

Sarah scowled back.

Nia chuckled and headed into the vestry. "Evening. *Yn iawn?*"

Dad, Ieaun, Mam, and the three other members of the choir turned and grinned.

"There you are. Quick, stick on your robes, *gul.*" Mam wrestled her into them and did up the back. "Remember that we really like those high notes. We love those high notes." She sighed and nodded to herself. "I really need help on the high notes."

Nia patted her on the back. "Maybe Sarah has a voice?"

"*Efallai,* maybe... Aye." Mam tapped her lip, and her eyes lit up. "In that case, you'll need to ask her out before she knows you too well." Cue cheeky wink.

Ieaun pursed his lips. "Ah, come on. Again?" He swatted her with the song book. "It's like Mary Griffiths all over again."

Nia averted her gaze. She'd gone out with her as a teenager too… Good memories. "Don't know what you mean."

Dad thwacked Ieaun with his song book. "Don't hit your sister, *bach*." He smirked at her. "She needs to keep Sarah wanting to stay in the practice."

"Glad I'm useful for some things." She kissed the three other ladies on the cheek. "You'd think I only came home to be married off, *mun*."

They nodded. "We could do with a wedding."

"It'd have to be a blessing at the moment." Mam pursed her lips and took a deep breath. "I'm working on that one."

The music started, and Nia closed her eyes for the prayer. She knew, full well, Mam meant it. Worth a smile just for that.

Chapter 4

SARAH CUDDLED FREDRICK WHO HAD wriggled out of his bag and decided he wanted to cuddle up on her lap.

Robert Jones grinned at Sarah and patted him on the head. He was very nice and didn't seem at all interested in dating. Although maybe that was the setting?

The music started, and Fredrick shifted as the choir, in long purple robes, strode out behind Dr Jenkins holding a gold cross. Sarah had only seen a church in an RE lesson, and it felt like watching a display or being at a museum. Then Nia appeared at the back in purple, one person behind her in white, and then Reverend Jenkins. Her white robe had an emerald tabard of some kind over it with a golden embraided cross.

Nia caught her eye and winked as they passed by to the altar.

Sarah cuddled up to Frederick and relaxed as hymns started. The rest of the congregation got up and down for every song, along with the choir. Up, down, up again, down again. It was more rigorous than aerobics, but the readings were happy and joy-filled, and then Reverend Jenkins walked up to the pulpit.

Sarah tensed, and Frederick wriggled in her arms.

"Sermon is a bit different this evening. Came to me while I was dancing in the vestry," Reverend Jenkins said, and beamed out at everyone. "Christmas wears a lot of different glasses."

Okay, not the opening Sarah was expecting, but Fredrick loved it if the tail wagging was anything to go by.

"And some people don't think they have glasses at all." Reverend Jenkins chuckled. "But the glass can be cold or warm, half empty, half full, but what's important is what the glass really means."

Sarah frowned. Glass was glass. It was see-through.

"The glass is love," Reverend Jenkins said, focusing on her. "And love doesn't have to be a shape, a size, a colour, or anything at all." She leaned on the pulpit. "Love just is."

Robert mumbled his agreement, as did the rest of the congregation. Wasn't expecting that.

"And, wherever you are, whoever you are, Christmas is meant to celebrate love. The birth of it, the promise of it, love and hope." Reverend Jenkins pushed back. "Depending what your glass looks like, that might mean you celebrate it at a time of year, as part of a festival, by celebrating freedom, equality, friendship, by going home to the person you share your life with, by caring for the people and creatures in your care." She tapped the pulpit. "I pray that you know love, however your glass appears, because in my heart love...pure, true love...sees no colour, no shape, no amount, no difference. Love is unfailing and everlasting. Love just is. Amen."

Sarah cuddled Frederick closer as another hymn was sung. The words seemed to hold her and warm her, and she met Nia's eyes once more.

Nia nodded to her as if she understood, as if somehow everyone in the church understood.

She looked around with Frederick wagging his tail, and a smile filled her. "Love just is," she whispered. She liked that. She really liked that.

Chapter 5

SNOW DRIFTED DOWN THICK AND cold, the wind making it dance and sway in the lights from the posts along the church path. Nia grinned as Sarah shuffled over to her with a peaceful smile on her face. Mam's sermons had a knack for doing that.

"And she didn't make you hide behind the pew once, huh?" Nia said with a chuckle. There was something about Sarah's intensity and—innocence?

Was that the right word? Naivety sounded like she knew nothing at all, and it was clear she was intelligent, not socially at ease, but more like a tourist discovering a new land.

"I feel…I needed that." Sarah slipped and slid along. "And I need snow grips."

Nia caught her elbow and rescued Fredrick before he flew through the air. "The pathway is gritted. Are you always this clumsy?"

"Outside work, yes." Sarah held on, then gripped tighter as Ieaun, Mam, and Dad wandered up behind them. "Merry Christmas." She tensed and met Nia's eyes. "That's okay to say, isn't it?"

"Why wouldn't it be?" Nia pulled her closer as she wobbled about until she was tucked under her arm and Sarah's arm slid around her waist. Hmm. Felt like they did it all the time. "You've had mulled wine in the hall, you are merry, and it is Christmas, right?"

Sarah poked her tongue out.

"Lovely to see you, *merch*," Dad said, beaming at Sarah. He was as thin and wiry as Mam but with grey hair, not blonde. "Glad that you have Nia taking care of you. It'll keep her from pining over Robert."

Nia rolled her eyes. "Aye, I'm the picture of lovelorn."

"I'd say you're the picture of smug, as always," Ieaun muttered, and poked her in the side. They were both in their thirties, but inside, they would always be bickering siblings.

"I have plenty of reason to be, *butt*." She poked him back. "I got the looks, and I have a miniature guard dog ready to eat you on command."

Ieaun looked at Sarah.

"Not me," Sarah said, and pursed her lips. "Fredrick."

Ieaun had a way with women. "Who is Fredrick?" He grinned. "Your boyfriend? I'm sure he is. What would you want with a wooden plank of an actress?"

Mam tutted. "She's a wonderful actress, *bach*, and they meant the dog." She spat on her hanky and wiped something off Ieaun's cheek.

"What dog?" Ieaun scowled and turned away as Mam linked her arm through his. "Don't tell me they're already shacked up together. No wonder she didn't return my calls, *mun*."

"Not yet," Dad said, giving Nia's elbow a quick squeeze on the way past. "But if they do, I'll get my golfing partner back."

Sarah's hand on her waist tightened.

"He means me. I'm mediocre with a club." Nia grinned down at Sarah, helping her along the path.

"It's not that. I've just never been…quite so…welcomed?" Sarah furrowed her brow, met Nia's eyes, then clattered into the gate and nearly dived into Mam's herb garden.

Nia righted her, and Sarah sighed. "I only drove into you. Yet they act like…well…we're…"

"A couple." Nia nodded and kissed her on the cheek. "That's probably because we're acting like it." Which was odd considering she'd never really been comfortable with her exes around her family. "You know, you tried to attack me, I took you home, we bonded over tiny puppies, visited a church, and you tried trampling Mam's basil. The traditional route, innit?"

Sarah kissed her on the lips. Lingered. Then threw her arms around Nia's shoulders and went for it.

Bit sudden. Warm lips. Ooh, really nice warm lips. Nia held Frederick's bag behind her back—too young for that kind of display—and pulled Sarah closer. Intense doctor: she could definitely work with that. Oh yeah.

Sarah pushed back, panting. "I…I'm sorry. I don't know… I have no idea what's come over me." She smiled a flustered smile. "I don't do that."

"You should. You're very good at it." Was she panting too? Her mist was puffing out like she was. Wow. That felt far too needed. When had she ever needed to kiss anyone?

"Definitely mutual." Sarah gazed up into her eyes. "But I'm going to sleep in my car."

Nia cocked her head.

Sarah pointed to the kitchen window. "They clapped."

Mam and Dad grinned back, and Dad held up a plate of mince pies.

Nia chuckled. "Dad's serious about keeping his GPs."

Sarah groaned and thunked into her chest, then groaned and pushed back. "How do I have a conversation with him now?"

"We have another Christmas tradition to go that will help." She pulled Sarah along with her; it was easier if she just skied behind.

"What's that?" Sarah mumbled as she clung on.

"Charades," Nia shot over her shoulder, then hoisted Sarah over the icy mat and inside. "Just try not to knock anyone out."

Chapter 6

SARAH WOKE UP WITH FREDERICK in her face yapping. She peeked open one eye and groaned. Charades had needed mulled wine and mince pies for confidence, and the mince pies had gone straight to her head. Yup, the pies, not the wine.

"Morning," Nia said, tapping on the door. "You look…rested?"

Sarah sat up and put her hand through her hair. Felt like she'd backcombed it. "Um…thanks?"

"We let you sleep in." Nia nodded to Frederick who bounced up and down. "But we've played in the snow, had breakfast, and now he really wants to open his presents."

Did dogs like presents?

"You've never owned a dog before, have you?" Nia leaned against the doorjamb in a Christmas jumper, jeans, and Christmas socks pulled up to her knee with bells and lights on them.

"No." She'd never seen socks like that before either. "I'm on call."

"Dad called in the registrar. You can't get down the lane on foot, let alone with your dodgy driving." Nia walked over to the window and drew back the curtains. "When it snows up here, it does it properly."

Sarah picked up Frederick and wandered to the window. One huge white blanket with some ridges where the high hedges must have been. "Ah."

"You're stuck with the in-laws for a while." Nia gave her a cheeky smile.

Oh no. Sarah had vague memories of telling Nia she'd fancied her on TV for a long time and maybe proposing? Oh no, had she really done that?

"I'm still not wearing scrubs to get married in though." Nia peered under her eyebrows and kissed her on the lips. Ooh wow. "And waving your arms around like you want to take off is not a good charade for *Chitty, chitty bang, bang.*"

"The car flies." Sarah lifted Frederick who yapped at Nia. Sarah hoped to hide the swirl, leap, and backflip for joy her stomach was doing. "See, Frederick got it."

Nia took Sarah's hand and led her to the bed, then pulled up a huge stocking. "You've got mail."

"But how?" Sarah took the stocking and sat on the bed. She hadn't had a stocking since she was a teenager, but somehow the feel of the wiry wool or cotton in multicoloured rings made her feel like a kid. Yes, she was an excited kid who might just have the biggest crush to the point she couldn't look at Nia without wanting to kiss her. How grown up.

"We don't buy things for each other." Nia sat beside her. "When we were kids, we had a big toy, a few little things. It's traditional for us to put time and effort in."

Sarah pulled out the presents, and Frederick dived at them ripping the paper apart, tail wagging.

"He likes unwrapping. Should have seen him go at Mam's stocking." Nia chuckled and patted Frederick on the head.

Sarah fished the present from the shredded paper and chortled—a bottle of paracetamol.

"I didn't really have enough time to make a lot, and Mam had to dig her way to church for the service." Nia laughed and leaned back on her elbows. "Powered by faith and coffee."

Sarah smiled and pulled out the second present. Frederick launched into action again. "I think I'll just buy him wrapping paper."

Nia nodded, eyes twinkling.

Underneath the remnants of paper was a wooden cross. She cocked her head and picked it up. Looked hand carved.

"Just to remind you what Mam said. If you keep it in your pocket, you'll always have a robust stress buster." She shrugged, waving her hand about like Sarah wouldn't like it.

"I love it." Sarah leaned in and kissed her on the lips—soft lips, warm. That was a present all by itself. "Don't ever be worried about sharing your heart with me."

Oh, that was deep. That was very deep. Was she still intoxicated?

Nia smiled up at her. "Who's worried now?" She tapped the stocking. "Apart from the orange at the bottom, and I've no idea why we have oranges, there's one more."

Sarah fished out the orange. "Vitamin C is always good in moderation." Then she pulled the third present out. Thin, small. Hmm.

Frederick set to work, tail wagging, and she pulled a laminated piece of paper from the rubble. A phone number?

"Seeming as you proposed, I thought it might be useful." Nia pulled Frederick onto her and cuddled him as he burrowed in. "Thought laminating it might puppy-proof it."

Sarah looked down at the phone number and hugged it. "You're being very reasonable considering I sounded like a dribbling idiot."

"I've never been proposed to mid-charade before." Nia laughed her soft, sweet laugh. "Mam was very moved."

"She just liked the fact I got a reference to glass in there." And she could now remember it in vivid detail. How had both parents and Ieaun cheered her? What was in the mince pies?

"It was very touching, even slurred." Nia cuddled Fredrick and gazed up at her. "Definitely worth a phone number."

"But is it yours or your solicitor's?" Sarah went to her clothes on the chair and tensed. Changing felt…intimate.

"That would be telling." Nia wrapped her arms around Sarah's waist. Warmth, much-needed comfort. When had she started needing that so much? "I have some warm joggers and suitable Christmas jumper for you, and some special equipment." Nia kissed her on the neck. Didn't that give Sarah goosepimples. "Grab your orange and I'll show you."

Sarah picked up Fredrick—who was making a bed of wrapping paper— her orange, and then stopped. "I'm sorry if I embarrassed you by being so… forward." She chewed on her lip. "Proposing, I mean."

"You didn't embarrass me." Nia turned at the door and smiled. "I said yes."

She strolled out, and Sarah stood cuddling Frederick. The recollection floated around her. Nia *had* said yes, and without hesitation? Her stomach clenched with some buzz of nervous excitement she'd never ever felt before. Nah, who proposed to someone they'd just met? Who accepted a proposal from someone they'd just met? Nah, it was just the wine, or jolly atmosphere, or shock, or concussion. Right?

Chapter 7

Nia checked her watch and shoved the rest of the food into the insulated bags. Ieaun was busy digging a tunnel down the driveway, and Dad was pulling out the sled from the garage.

"You're not all watching Christmas movies and stuffing yourselves?" Sarah asked as she slipped into the kitchen in waterproofs and a jacket. Must have wondered why Nia had left her those items of clothes.

"Nope, to be Welsh"—Nia turned and smiled—"maybe more so from Bryn Cariad, but no...no...I'd say Wales." She smiled as Sarah tucked her hair behind her ears.

Frederick poked his head up from the zip in her jacket. So cute.

"It's about caring. Our grandparents, our parents, they are treasured." She chewed on her lip. How to explain? "Celtic people...we're all born with...with this connection. When I see the grass outside, I feel connected to the ground it grows in, the land, our rugged land." She blew out a breath. "We call it *hiraeth*."

"Hir-I-th?" Sarah said, sounding more Jamaican than Welsh.

"Yeah, the connection to your homeland. That wherever you are or live, Wales always calls to you. We're not as loud as our cousins. The Irish bring cheer, merriment, and...Guinness." She stroked Frederick's head, tempted to tuck the loose strands of Sarah's hair from her face. Her own maternal grandfather was an Irishman from Cork. "The Scots, they bring that fiery passion, that steel...and whiskey." She grinned. Her maternal grandmother was a Scot. "The Welsh, we bring a deep-thinking soul, a calm, laidback welcome; and poetry, hymns, and daft rugby songs."

"And also whiskey, and ale." Sarah nodded with utter seriousness. "I've been drunk on it enough to know that much."

"How much?" Nia zipped up the bags and tried to hide her smile.

"Not in an alcoholic way." Sarah sighed and trudged over, studying the bags. "Your dad wanted me to experience Welsh life. We went to watch a rugby match against England." She narrowed her eyes. "You're not overly welcoming to people in English rugby tops."

Nia grinned. "Until the match is over." She winked and hoisted up the bags.

"So, deep-thinking soul." Sarah's lips twitched, and Frederick yapped. "Why are we hiding food?"

"Community." Nia headed out of the door.

Mam had her face screwed up, focus intense as she finished off her snow sheep complete with farmer and sheep dog.

"It's Christmas. Which means feeding elderly people with too much rich food and sugar."

Sarah wrestled on her wellies and hurried to catch up.

Frederick wriggled out of the bottom of her coat and charged at the snow-sheep dog. He leapt at it, yapping. Then he stopped. He looked down at the snow, yelped, and sprinted back to Sarah, shivering.

"He's the picture of bravery." Nia grinned at Sarah fussing over him and turned to Mam. "Got the lava bread and Bara Brith in here."

"Bara Brith is like a fruit loaf, isn't it?" Sarah cocked her head. "Lava bread?"

"A tasty seaweed thing," Nia mumbled. How to explain lava bread? "It's packed with active B12 and iron?"

"Although healthy—" Sarah tripped over something in the snow and threw Frederick.

Nia caught Fredrick before he hit the snow-farmer, and Mam caught Sarah before she took out the sheep.

"Best if you stay upright," Mam said with a chuckle. "Soggy knees are not much fun." She helped Sarah straighten up as Dad and Ieaun headed over. "We'll head through the village in a clockwise fashion," she said like a rugby coach. "Ieaun, you are on BP, pulse monitor, and checking medications."

"Mam, *ie,* Mam!" Ieaun saluted with his shovel.

"Wyn," she said, eyeing Dad. "You are on symptoms and blood sugar and making the tea."

"*Ie,* Ma'am!" Dad snapped to attention, whacking himself in the head with the string of his ski-gloves.

"Nia, you are in charge of small talk, food distribution, and sherry." Mam focused on her, a grin on her face.

"Mam, *ie* Mam!" She nodded to Sarah who was watching like she wasn't sure how serious they were being. Mam was as good in role as any professional actor.

"Sarah, *merch*," Mam said, full sergeant major hat on. "You are in charge of Frederick, checking any sores or skin complaints, and mince pies." She grinned. "You seemed to like the mince pies."

And there was the cheeky look at Nia.

Sarah snapped to her best salute, wobbling on her feet. "Um... Aye, aye, Reverend?"

They burst into laughter. Nia handed a food bag to Mam and pulled Sarah under her arm. She could get used to this, really used to it.

Chapter 8

BY SEVEN O'CLOCK, EVERY VILLAGER had been fed and watered and filled in the family on every tit-bit of family life over the year. They had been medicated and checked over, cuddled Frederick who was the hit of the holidays, and interrogated Sarah on her marital status which she'd been tempted to say was engaged to a gorgeous local. Crackers had been pulled... prizes lost beneath furniture or chewed by Frederick—she wasn't the best at crackers. Bad jokes were read out, trick questions solved, the Queen's speech watched...and all wearing paper hats. Exhausting.

Sarah clung to Nia's waist as the family skated their way back from the furthest farm towards the glow of the cross on the church. She sighed. Exhausted but feeling more merry than on the mince pies.

"That sounded contented." Reverend Jenkins beamed at her from the sled Dr Jenkins and Ieaun were pulling.

Too contented. It was starting to feel real. "I'm glad we sorted out Mrs Evans' sugar level."

Nia chuckled and looked down at her. "You're wistful over blood glucose?"

"Yes." It was easier than saying that it had been perfect. She'd dreamed of Christmases like it as a kid. Mum worked insanely long hours as a surgeon, Dad was a banker, Christmas was a meal out between business calls and beepers. "It takes skill to stabilise blood glucose."

Ieaun chuckled. "I'd say it was skill to remove a polyps from the colon myself, but I'll go with it."

Dr Jenkins "hah'd" and reached across and shoved Ieaun off his stride. "You see someone three times, cut them open, and leave us to do the hard work."

Nia rolled her eyes. "Here we go." She looked to Reverend Jenkins. "Next it'll be the argument on which antibiotic is the best." She narrowed her eyes at Sarah. "And, for the record, I don't care."

Reverend Jenkins let out a sigh. "I care but only if I have an infection. Right now, I just want a cuppa and to collapse on the sofa."

Ieaun pushed Dr Jenkins back. "When I cut someone open, you don't have to do anything else. I fix it." He flashed a dashing grin at Sarah. "And I look better in scrubs than her."

Sarah doubted it. Every week, she was glued to the TV screen and *Doctor Mayflower Investigates*. She didn't care about the crimes—in fact, she hated medical-based programs—but Nia Jenkins in scrubs. She sighed again.

Nia chuckled. "There's your answer."

Sarah cleared her throat and looked up. The entire Jenkins family was grinning at her. "I may like the TV show..."

They all nodded.

"I told you all that when I was drunk?" She cuddled Frederick who was asleep in her jacket.

They all nodded again.

"You quoted lines," Ieaun said with a shake of his head. "You know them better than she does."

"I did?" She really needed to lay off the mince pies.

"Yeah," Nia said, leading the way into the garden. "I'll have to get you to run through them with me."

Sarah stopped, skidded, and hit the snow farmer who was so frozen he didn't even budge. "You will?"

Ieaun rolled his eyes. "And you whinge about us talking medical stuff." He helped Reverend Jenkins off the sled. "Should hear her go on about acting."

Nia scooped up a fistful of snow and hurled it at him.

Thwack.

Right in his face.

Ieaun narrowed his eyes. "Oh, it's like that, is it?" He scooped up snow and hurled it back.

Thwack. It hit Nia in the face.

Sarah ducked behind Reverend Jenkins as Doctor Jenkins scooped up two fistfuls and hit both Nia and Ieaun with a clean shot.

Reverend Jenkins smiled and winked over her shoulder. "Hope you don't mind snow?"

"Another Christmas tradition," Nia shouted, diving at Ieaun and charging him into a pile of snow. "Pile on!"

Sarah scurried into the kitchen with Fredrick and peeked out the window. This tradition, with her clumsiness? No, it was best she sat this tradition out.

Chapter 9

THE EVENING HAD BEEN PERFECT. No matter how Nia looked at it: Board games, roaring fires, laughter, Sarah chomping mince pies, and chatting until early on Boxing Day.

Nia longed to stay, and longed for Sarah to stay, wrapped up in the Christmas bubble, but she had to get back to London. She'd not learned any of her lines, and there was the small matter of starring in a theatre production. Rehearsals started in January, and she really needed to know her lines by then. And, if she stayed in the bubble, she'd start to believe it could be real, that Sarah and her…that somehow they'd found love? Nah, that was… It was just crazy to think that.

Mam was in the kitchen as Nia headed downstairs. It was hard to leave normally, and she always hurried off before anyone could cuddle her and make her teary. She had to go. If she stayed… She glanced back up the stairs. Sarah was too easy to fall in love with.

"You know, love is a funny thing," Mam said, focus on the sandwiches she was making—they'd be eating turkey for days. "It tends to change the way you look at things."

"Rose tinted, you mean?" Nia leaned on the worktop beside her.

"No, it just shines light on the good things." Mam buttered the bread and shoved in some stuffing. "Brings out the good things in you."

"You sure? I thought love was supposed to be blind?" She stole a slice of turkey and chomped on it.

"No, lust is blind, love knows the faults. It just seeks to pull out the good bits." Mam put the turkey in the sandwich and closed it up. "It also tends to draw you to it."

"As in?" Wasn't like Mam to say a lot. She'd always let her make up her own mind.

"As in, it opens its arms and your heart responds." She met Nia's eyes. "Whether you try to ignore it or not."

Nia glanced back at the hallway. "I don't know her. Not really. We've talked, a lot. I know her history, but I don't even know why a doctor like her is here." She chewed on her lip.

"Does it matter?" Mam smiled at her. "Love makes you feel good and wraps you up. Walking away does the opposite. Trust your heart."

Nia took the sandwiches and sighed. "Dad is taking me to the station."

"Yes." Mam kissed her on the cheek. "The other thing about love is that it calls to you, but it's up to you if you listen."

Nia hugged her and picked up her bag. She hurried to the 4x4 before she turned around. She couldn't face leaving Sarah or Frederick. How was that?

"*Merch*," Dad said as she got in the car. He navigated them up the frozen lane, intensity in his eyes. "You're leaving even earlier than usual."

Nia nodded and stared out of the window. Her heart strained like she was tearing a plaster from it and burning it in the process. "Yeah. Work."

They passed her crunched-up car. Sarah: Clumsy, intelligent, quiet, intense, completely insane over a fictional TV show, and the sweetest, most empathic doctor she'd ever seen.

"I met your mother in a dance," Dad said, crawling past the car. "Knew I loved her the second I set eyes on her. I'd never dared talk to a girl before her." He smiled at Mr Jones' wall. "She ramraided my heart." He glanced her way. "Best thing I ever did was ask her to dance."

Nia blinked at him. He wasn't a man to talk about feelings. He didn't avoid them; it just wasn't the Welsh way. Things were done calmly, logically. It didn't sound a lot like logic.

"She turned me down, twice." He slowed down to a crawl. "I couldn't let her go…but she gave me a chance…" He sighed. "I took it… Are you going to?"

Nia stared at him. Sarah seemed to…to… She just… Sarah made her feel she could be who she wanted to be…who she was, who she truly was inside. Sarah: with no idea about dogs, who couldn't pronounce Llanelli even on mince pies, and was the worst person she'd ever seen at charades.

Sarah: who asked her to marry her, and she'd said yes. Her heart strained like it would shatter. She'd meant it when she said yes. She'd really *meant* it. "Stop."

He pulled over. "Go get her."

Nia shoved open the door and scrambled along the snowy roadway.

Mr Jones stuck his head out. "You forget something?"

She shook her head. "No." She scurried by the church, slid over the icy path, and scrambled into the garden.

Sarah was at the door with wellies on like she was about to give chase. "You were leaving?"

Nia nodded. She skidded into Sarah's Land Rover and grinned. "Felt like ripping my heart out."

"Mine too." Sarah clung to the doorframe and eyed the path.

"No. You stay there... One concussion is enough." She slid her way over. "I meant it...I mean...I meant it when I said yes. Always yes."

"I can see."

How did Sarah know what she meant? Did she? Could she?

"I meant it too... I can't explain why? It makes no sense... But I do, I really did mean it. I love you. I don't know... I just... I love you."

"*Dwi'n caru ti hefyd...* I love you too." Nia pulled Sarah into her arms and pointed up at the mistletoe.

"I know that tradition full well." Sarah yanked her in, and she sank into the kiss, her heart bubbling with the joy, her glass full of it, her soul full of it.

The snow fluttered down from the white puffy clouds, on the church, the straw roofed houses nestled around it; onto the car parked in Mr Jones' wall. The flakes swirled as if in triumph, whispered words danced upon it as if sending up a prayer of thanks, echoing the blissful new hope of two hearts called together. Love didn't need a reason or a tradition, and those words, simple words, captured Christmas in one snowy little village. Love just is.

Grand Market Bliss

BY FIONA ZEDDE

"Do you know what day it is?" A soft voice, threaded with a hint of excitement, pierces my half-sleep.

Do I know what day it is? Oh, yes.

Slowly, I open my eyes and blink, once. Twice. The sun flows into our bedroom past the new set of curtains Sinclair put up for Christmas. In shades of burgundy and warm gold, the drapes do nothing to shelter my sleep—because my beloved pulled them wide open to torture me awake. The afternoon light ribbons across the bed and floats dots of brightness through my half-closed lashes.

"It's Monday," I mutter, and turn my head, hiding my smile in the pillow that smells like us.

"Oh my god!" Fluttering fingers skate along my naked sides, then Sinclair's warm body tumbles down into the sheets with me. "It's Christmas Eve!"

I laugh-gasp at the full spill of her weight on top of me and give up any pretense of sleep. Delicious woman. My love. She is all long legs and spider arms, her loose hair rich with the scent of coconut oil and that creamy leave-in conditioner that makes her smell like something good to eat.

Her skinny fingers dig into my sides, and she laughs herself into a frenzy. After two years together, Sinclair damn well knows I'm not ticklish. But she's the ticklish one, so I give in to what she wants—a tickle fight that leaves her gasping for breath, cheeks warm and her house dress dragged above her hips for my questing fingers.

"Yes, it is Christmas Eve." I huff a low laugh and grin down at her. Then I try to kiss her. "With Grand Market and everything."

"Hunter!" She shrieks and turns away her head, hiding her lips from me. "Your mouth smells like something died in there!" But her thighs still fall open in welcome.

Underneath me, she is the miracle I never thought I deserved. Sharp fox teeth and eyes like the dark sky in summer, crinkling beautifully at the corners. The brown of her has been perfectly baked by the winter Jamaican sun, silken to the touch. Her thoroughly American voice is the music I hear in my dreams.

"Ugh! No! Morning breath!" She squirms and tries half-heartedly to get away.

After all this time, our morning sex is still something we both crave, but she hates to kiss me on the mouth. Most mornings when we're both so eager for it that we can barely talk, she allows me to do anything to her except kiss her lips. The top pair.

The sunlight pours over us, hot on my naked skin, in my long and loose dreadlocks moving in waves over my back. She's wriggling and beautiful and laughing and still trying to avoid my kisses.

"Hunter, stop!"

But she's laughing too hard to make it sound sincere. So I nip the corner of her jaw instead of tasting her lips like I want. The thin cotton of her dress rucks up under my hands, revealing acres of warm skin, flat belly, the bones of her hips that have become less noticeable since she's been here on the island with me.

"Why should I stop?" I ask, even though I've already ended my hunt for the treasure I want.

"Because people are outside!" She giggles, her head tipping back to offer me her throat and the tender line between her breasts. "Yes, remember?" But she's moving against me like she wants me to forget, her sun-warmed scent and soft skin temptation enough to stay in bed for another five minutes at least.

Okay, maybe ten.

It's Christmas Eve and Grand Market, the annual all-day celebration of the season with food, games, and music that takes over all of our little town. Although both sides of our families usually gather on Christmas Day for dinner, we decided this year to invite the family queers for lunch at our house then walk into town at sundown to celebrate Grand Market together. It was Sinclair's idea, and it makes sense. We have enough gays in the family to make it a decent turnout.

So, yes, we *both* decided on this. But damn, does it have to be so bloody early?

Sighing, I ask Sinclair the question in the soft shell of her ear.

"It's not early, love. It's nearly two in the afternoon." She laughs, joyful and sweet, draping her long thigh over my hip.

Delicate, swimming motions rub her against me. I shiver, oh-so close to giving her what she came in here for.

But we don't have time for any of that.

Vague sounds of laughter from the living room reach my ears. I lift my head and notice that yes, Sinclair closed the door when she came in. Maybe even locked it, too. Like I don't know what that means. But I give her hips a regretful squeeze and pull away.

Her thick twist-out fans dark and inky against our pillow as she blinks up at me in surprise and disappointment. "Already?" But there is a coyness to the edge of her smile.

My laughter tumbles out low and deep. "Weren't you the one telling me 'no' not two seconds ago?"

"But I don't mean 'no' right now." A familiar and addictive fragrance rises from between Sinclair's spread legs. Her bright teeth snag her own lower lip, and her lashes drop low over her eyes.

"Nope. You're not going to blame me for any foolishness of yours today." I jump out of bed and swat her thigh, then head toward the shower. "Don't make everybody think I'm in here molesting you and depriving them of your company."

By the time I get out of the shower and make my way into the living room, still twisting my waist-length locs into a high crown on top of my head, everybody we invited over has made themselves comfortable, laughing and talking all at once while the radio plays an old Dennis Brown tune.

Xavier, Sinclair's baby brother, isn't quite a baby anymore. A typical six-year-old, he's sitting on the floor at his mother's feet and playing with a set of toy trucks. Sinclair got him an iPad for his last birthday, but that didn't end his fascination with tangible games.

"It's about time you dragged your butt out here," my cousin Ebony calls out. She's dressed in a criminal mastermind's idea of Christmas best, thin jeans fresh from some European designer, complete with gold swirls stitched into the pockets, a white linen blouse showing off the black lace bra underneath, black combat boots. Her hair, long and straight, ripples like a dark river down to her waist. "I knew Sinclair wore you out last night, but Jeesam Peas!"

Ebony looks enough like me to be confusing from far away. Dark skin. Long hair. Just enough muscle not to seem weak. When my ex-girlfriend, Lydia, first caught sight of her, Lydia got on top of her faster than a rent-a-rasta on a sunbathing tourist.

"Hush up!" Lydia slaps Ebony's arm, jerking her head meaningfully toward Xavier.

"What?" Ebony didn't look the least bit sorry. "I didn't say anything he hasn't heard before."

Xavier drags his gaze away from the truck currently rolling across a bridge made up of hair combs and clothespins. "Are you wore out, Hunter?"

"Nope!" I squeeze the boy's shoulder and cut my eyes at my cousin. *Do better*, I tell her silently as I walk past and head toward the kitchen.

Of course, Ebony just rolls her eyes and keeps on doing whatever the hell she wants. I tell you, this cousin of mine has the perfect job for her big ego and careless ways.

In the kitchen, I find Sinclair bent down in front of the oven. She's baking, and the smell of Christmas cake flavors the air, rummy and sweet, but it's the perfect curve of her butt under the thin dress that tempts me.

The oven bangs shut, and she backs away from it, carrying the steaming cake between two potholders. I want to touch, but I also don't want to give either of us third-degree burns. The little metal stand rattles when she puts the cake down on it to cool. Before she turns, I put myself in her path.

"Oh!" We collide, and she grabs me with the potholders still on her hands. "I could've burned you with that cake, Hunter!" Her eyes are wide with concern.

I pull her into me to kiss the sides of her mouth.

"But you didn't. Come here and kiss me properly." She tries to stay mad, but a light stroke of my fingers along her ribs has her curling into me, laughing. I playfully nip her earlobe. "My breath is nice and fresh, and you can smell me anywhere you like."

Her soft breath brushes my throat. "Why are you always so dirty?" But it's a part of me she loves. Dirty in bed, in the kitchen, anywhere I can get her alone. Her potholder-clad hands drape around my neck, and the softness of her body slopes into mine like a plant seeking the sun.

"For you, American girl, anytime. Anywhere," I murmur before claiming her lips.

She tastes so good. Of warm desire and home and all the things I'd been yearning for before she came into my life. Our lips press close, mine slick and cherry-flavored from the lip balm I wear, hers soft and welcoming, naturally made to fit mine. Lips to lips we stand, breaths slow and easy, our eyes open and smiling into each other.

"I love you," she breathes.

The tip of her tongue teases my mouth open and gifts me with the flavor of sweet cakes and mint tea. I take everything she has to give, our tongues sliding together, reconnecting in that dance we've come to perfect over the years. I can't help it; I groan and pull her closer, sucking on her tongue and wishing that every single person in our living room would just disappear so I can make love to my woman in peace.

"Didn't you two just leave the bed? Give it a rest already." My cousin Tima's voice comes out of nowhere a second before her laughter blows away the haze of desire clouding my judgment.

Reluctantly, I pull away from Sinclair.

"Don't you have someplace else to be?" I ask Tima just as Sinclair steps delicately away from me, licking her lips, her pretty eyes ducking away. She can't hide her smile, though, and the promise of "later" that it shows.

"This is where I need to be, cuz." She waggles her empty cup at me. "Your guests need refills." Tima looks runway ready with her perfectly arched eyebrows, deep purple lipstick, and sexy black dress. Nothing like the street-weary cop she is.

I suck my teeth. "We don't have any guests here, man. Only family. Get what you want."

"That's what I'm doing." She tosses her mane of straightened hair, the asymmetrical bob immediately falling back into place under her sharp cheekbones. "I didn't plan on making my way through a porn shoot just to get something to drink!"

"Don't even start—"

"Here you go, Tima." Sinclair appears with the pot of hot chocolate. "Unless you want tea this time."

"Now, this is how you play a good host." Tima throws me a look and holds out her cup. "Chocolate is perfect, oh beautiful woman to whom there is no equal."

Now she's just doing too much. "In case you didn't realize what you walked in on, this woman here is mine." It's stupid. I know it. But that doesn't stop the low growl from my throat at my pretty cousin. Sure, I'm playing with her (a little), but she really is out of order. Tima is arguably the most beautiful woman in the family. Plus, she's noble as hell, a good cop working in a system that usually only rewards the ones looking out only for themselves. Women always find that sexy for some reason.

Sinclair backs away with the hot chocolate, an arch to her eyebrow. "Quit playing, Hunter." She lightly elbows me in the side. "Let me go out there to see who else needs anything."

But I tug her into my arms again before she can get too far. As always, her slender body falls into me beautifully, and it's all I can do not to kiss her again. "Let me do it," I whisper against her cool forehead. She's probably been on her feet all morning while I was sleeping in, snoring in bed like a dude knocked out after one orgasm. At least I was able to convince her to take the day off from work, coaxing her out of the office and away from her hectic freelance schedule. "I know I interrupted you earlier." I take the pot from her unresisting hand and head out to the living room.

"Be nice to them," she calls out to me before the swinging kitchen door settles closed between us.

"You two are so sickening, it's sweet." Tima follows me out of the kitchen, but I ignore her. "Acting like you're married or something."

Across the room, a look stutters across Nikki's face. It's too fast for me to read, but she bends down to say something to her son who only looks up at her like he has no idea what she's talking about.

"Finally!" Another cousin, Cliff, shouts when he sees me, or more to the point, sees the pot with the hot chocolate. "I'm dying of thirst out here."

"How come with all these grown-ups in one room not one of you can pick up a pot to bring it out here?" I ask.

"That's what you're here for, darling dear." Cliff lifts his empty cup high, pale gold eyes sparkling with humor. "Now, be a dear and fill up Papa's cup."

I throw him a disgusted look.

No matter how many times we get together, I'm a little overwhelmed by how *good* it feels to have our families with us. Sinclair's and mine. Together in one house, laughing and sharing stories. I want this to last for as long as we're alive.

God, this Christmas season is turning me into mush.

When Sinclair finally comes out of the kitchen, she presses a kiss to my jaw. Then, leaving me with the scent of browned sugar and mint tea, she floats over to sit on the arm of Nikki's chair. Although it shouldn't be possible, it seems like she didn't leave her young stepmother's side for the rest of the afternoon.

We lock the door behind us at 6:30 p.m. sharp. Xavier hops up and down, impatient with us to get going so he can join the kids a few houses down and rack up the gifts and free sweets from the shopkeepers on the square.

"Go." Nikki, her face pinched and a little tired, waves a hand to her son. He takes off like a bullet toward the small group of six or so kids flooding from the neighboring houses and heading toward the main square.

"Hunter!" A voice arcs over the fence, then a bright brown face pops up. "Hey." Our neighbor, Ruby, newly relocated from Toronto, waves a brightly wrapped package.

Beside me, Sinclair makes a startled noise, then dashes back into the house.

Ebony jerks her chin in Ruby's direction. "Damn, I'd love to hit that," she murmurs loudly enough for just about everyone to hear. She's an ass.

Ruby is older than any of us, a softly padded and sexy fifty-something with straightened, gray-streaked hair down to her shoulders. Since she moved here, all the neighborhood men have dropped gifts on her doorstep, trying to get her into bed. But she's yet to take any of them up on their offers, which is a good thing since most of these guys are married, and to vicious women at that.

The last thing we need is another knifing incident in the neighborhood.

"Hey, Miss Ruby." With a wave toward the others, I let them know it's cool to walk ahead. Sinclair and I will catch up.

"For the last time, *Hunter*." She stresses my name with a dimple-deepening smile. "I'm just Ruby around these parts." Elegant hands rest on top of the fence. "This is the part of Grand Market I missed the most when I was in Toronto. Exchanging gifts with neighbors is such a good way to show how much you appreciate them."

Since moving here, she's been eager to make friends and establish herself as part of the community. In the beginning, I tried to warn her off. With some trigger happy, bible-thumpers around, she was bound to find it a little harder to make friends if she readily accepted and socialized with the neighborhood dykes. But she didn't bat a single eyelash at me and my woman. So far, everybody in the neighborhood is still talking to her.

The front door of our house clicks shut behind me, and Sinclair clatters down our steps. The package she waves at Ruby is wrapped in burgundy and gold. Appropriately festive.

"I'm glad we caught you," Sinclair says with a smile. "We've had this all week."

She flies across the grass toward me and Ruby while her pretty new dress, in blues and greens like the sea, swirls around her legs. The dress is backless, beginning low on her spine and leaving inches of her beautiful skin bare. My favorite part. Out of sight, her hand pats my butt in the dark slacks. She and Ruby exchange packages and smiles over the high fence.

"Thank you, dear." Ruby holds onto the package like it's something precious.

"It's just a little something," Sinclair says. "But I hope you can put it to good use."

Ruby sniffs the package, and the dimples wink in her cheeks. "I'm sure I will," she says. "I hope you'll take kindly to my gift, too."

Sinclair tucks Ruby's package under her arm. "Whatever it is, thank you. We appreciate you thinking of us and being such a kind neighbor and friend." There's more behind the words than just those few syllables, and Ruby seems to know exactly what Sinclair means.

"Thank you both. I won the neighbor lottery when I ended up with you two next door."

The woman who used to live next to us sold her piece of property and moved to America someplace. She was nice enough but remained distant. That was better than being a murderous, homophobic asshole, though, so I was okay with it.

"We both got lucky," I tell Ruby.

"True." She smiles again. "Anyway, enough blah blah blah from me. Enjoy Grand Market."

"You're not going down?" Sinclair's voice rises with the question.

"Later on. I have some company coming over. After they leave, I'll make my move down there."

Company? Good for her.

"Well, enjoy yourself, Miss…uh, Ruby. We'll see you later on."

"Yes, dear. I'm sure you will." With a wave and another smile, she drops down behind the fence and disappears.

"That's nice for her." Sinclair leans into my side once we're away from the fence and trekking down the paved road toward the town. "*Company* is always nice to have." Her look is pure naughty speculation.

As usual, we're on the same page. "It sure is. Warm cockles are nice this time of year."

We burst out laughing like kids.

The streetlight overhead glows softly over us, illuminating the dense green of the landscape. Banana trees bare of fruit, tall mango trees with their wide branches heaving under the persistent caresses of the night breeze. The warm air brushes my face and, for a moment, it feels strange—this hot Christmas.

Despite being born in Jamaica and raised here until I was a teenager, years of cold English Christmases have left me feeling a slight disconnect from the warm weather, light-strung coconut trees, and Santa-print bikinis here.

Sinclair slips her hand into mine. "Miss Ruby deserves a little something good. It would be a shame for her to come here as a single woman and have to keep her snatch dry because of the poor pickings in the area."

"Poor pickings?" I'm not even touching the "dry snatch" comment.

"From the men, hell yes. If she decided to switch teams she'd have better luck even though I already got the sweetest one from the bunch." Sinclair's eyes crinkle under the streetlights.

"Why do I suddenly feel like a ripe banana?"

"Because you're delicious?" She teases me with a light pinch on my butt. Unable to resist, my lips seek her own.

"You two are really getting on my nerves with all this lovey-dovey stuff," Ebony mutters from far too close.

Without meaning to, we'd walked fast enough to catch up with her and the rest. Xavier and his friends are so far ahead all we can hear is their laughter.

"Yes, man. Give it a rest. Two years is enough time to lord it over the rest of us about how happy you are," Tima chimes in, but she laughs as she says it.

Ebony pulls out a chew stick, her eyes devouring Lydia.

She and Lydia weren't able to make it work when they got together. No big surprise there. Ebony has a thin streak of cruelty in her, just like Lydia. During their six-month collision, they cut each other to pieces, often in front of anybody unfortunate enough to be nearby. My cousin needs somebody kind to make her see that the world isn't full of predators. Lydia could use a firm hand on her backside, and maybe a closeted woman with thick skin.

"I can't take much more...!" A little way ahead of us, Nikki's voice rises briefly. Then the rest fades away in a sound like a sob.

"Oh no." After a quick squeeze of my hand, Sinclair rushes toward her stepmother in a swirl of skirts. Worry throbs faintly in my belly, but I only watch her go. Whatever it is Nikki's going through, I hope it'll okay in the end. I don't deal with any of the gossip running all over the place like poison ivy, but still, I have a vague idea of what's happening with her.

"What's going on?" Ebony asks, looking at Nikki.

"Something that's none of my business." I shrug and keep walking.

"Cousin, you are just too nonchalant. All of this *should* concern you. Poor Sinclair looks worried enough to fall over." She peers into the darkness toward where Sinclair disappeared to comfort her young stepmother.

"If it's my business, Sinclair will tell me. For now, it's about her and her family. I like to keep my fork in my own plate."

The noise Ebony makes is far from attractive. "Ah, the high and mighty English queen."

My lips curl in instinctive irritation, but I keep my mouth otherwise shut. My cousin has a lot of opinions about me, some of them based on nothing but her own bias. But today is not the day to confront them.

"Easy, man," I finally say, and she lets it go, too.

Nikki and Sinclair are far in front of us now, walking quickly, their arms linked. Their words are lost to the breeze scattering different scents at us. Jerk pork and other meats. Roasting corn. Freshly baked bread. A spurt of hunger races across my tongue and makes it wet.

"Smells like a little bit of heaven around there." Ebony gave up meat a few months ago but talks about jerk pork like it's her latest girlfriend—often and with obvious lust.

I wonder if she'll give in and eat meat tonight.

It's true that Grand Market is huge for the kids. They get to stay out as late as they want. Dance in places their parents normally scold them to stay away from. Eat candy from strangers.

But it's big for adults, too.

Grand Market is a time to eat food we've otherwise denied ourselves, to receive special blessings, and say words that are forbidden the rest of the year.

With a hand in my pocket, I rub my thumb over the gift I have for Sinclair.

Up ahead, my woman is everything beautiful to me. Her hips sway under the moonlight, stoking the ever-present flame of my desire for her. From the tilt of her face toward Nikki, I can tell she's saying something kind but firm. Her blue dress looks almost gray in the light now.

"What's going on with Nikki?" Lydia drifts back to me and Ebony, away from Tima who's laughing with Clifton now. Tima looks carefree and careless. But I know my cousin. She's keeping an eye on Lydia. And waiting for…something. I don't want to be around for explosion that will happen between these three.

"Not sure." I answer Lydia's question with a shrug that's becoming my default reaction of the night. "You should ask her."

"Not everyone's as straightforward as you, Hunter," my ex tells me.

"Amen," Ebony mutters.

Oh, Christ. These two…

We walk through the cordoned off parking area at the top of the sudden and wide hill and then the town square appears. Bright and glittery, the whole place is strung with Christmas lights of every conceivable color. Music bursts from the band on center stage; some guy I don't know sings a reggae classic while other members of the band sweat and play their instruments under the warm winter sky. The music is loud. Perfect for dancing.

Excitement obvious in our hurried steps, we all flow down the hill and into the square. The kids have gone ahead, and Nikki looks after them with a sort of longing on her face. At her side, Sinclair turns. Her eyes meet mine. Then she says something to Nikki and comes back to me.

The hem of her dress brushes my slacks. Her arm curls around mine. "She's sad," Sinclair says.

Lydia and Ebony watch Nikki who seems like she's disappearing into the darkness. One after the other, they move up ahead until it's only me, Sinclair, and Ebony. Apparently sensing the turmoil in their midst, Clifton and Tima abandon their conversation and crowd Nikki, spinning her into an awkward three-person dance that somehow puts a smile on Nikki's face.

"That looks like fun," Ebony says a moment before she's with them, too, trying to lure Lydia into a dirty bump and grind while the band plays PG-13 oldies. She only half-succeeds, hands on Lydia's waist while Lydia tries to turn away, ambivalence in every line of her body.

Games.

"Your cousin is a mess," Sinclair says with a soft laugh. But dark clouds float in her eyes, hiding their usual brilliance.

"Nothing to do with me." I curve a hand around the back of her neck and drop a quick kiss on her forehead. "Tell me, what's wrong?"

Sinclair has been cautious with Nikki all day. At the house, it was easy to overlook, the two of them tucked away on the sofa and talking quietly in the midst of everyone else's chaos. But now, their melancholy is obvious and impossible to mistake for anything other than what it is. I did lie to Ebony before. I do care, especially since this affects Sinclair's happiness. But I won't pry unless I'm invited.

With a trembling sigh, Sinclair tucks her face into my throat. "Nikki and Daddy are breaking up." Her voice trembles, filled to the brim with unhappiness.

"Okay." It's what I expected.

Sinclair's father had been a serial cheater back in the day. He had a wife—Sinclair's mother—but that didn't stop him from getting caught with pretty young things all over the district. Everyone ignored his wandering dick. Everyone including Sinclair's mother who'd been sowing wild oats of her own, only with women instead of men.

Cheaters usually don't stop their little games, no matter the quality of the ass they have at home.

Sinclair's gaze flies up to meet mine. "You don't seem surprised."

"I'm not." Did that sound dismissive? I might need to work on that. Something else for later. "Is it just a rough patch or will she leave him?"

Her lips droop with a worried frown. "I don't know. Nikki's really hurt. She feels really distant from him right now, and it's hard since there's nobody at fault. They're just...I don't know...growing apart or something."

"Really?"

"Oh! Now *that* surprises you." Her dark eyes gleam with a hint of anger, or some other emotion on her father's behalf. "Why is that?"

"Beasts don't stop being beasts, you know."

"You shouldn't damn my father for something that happened years ago."

The back of her neck feels tense under the steady stroke of my thumb. "It's hard to put something completely in the past when it stares at you every day." Sinclair and her sister, Lydia, have different mothers but were both born while Sinclair's parents were still together.

My fingers slide up into her hair to stroke her scalp. Blunt nails sink into Sinclair's skin and she whimpers softly, drawing in a sudden breath. But she doesn't lean into me like I know she wants to. She's still a little angry with me. I can feel it in the deepening tension of her neck, the way she refuses to yield to the physical comfort her body craves from mine.

"Difficulties crop up for every couple," I finally say, the most diplomacy I can spare for her father and his history of bullshit. Cheaters get no sympathy from me.

She sighs. "Hunter..."

"Yes, my love?"

A faint sound of distress leaks from her lips, but she doesn't say anything else about her family. Which doesn't mean she's not thinking about them and the looming elephant of divorce. I give her neck one last squeeze.

"Come on, gorgeous. Let's get at least one dance in before Grand Market is over."

"You're not slick," she mutters, but allows me to lead her away from her melancholy and into the thick of the celebration.

Along the edges of the square, the kids dash from vendor to vendor, their faces getting sticky from the free cakes and candy. The dancehall at the end of the street is packed tonight. Its doors regularly open and close as people head inside for more than the PG-13 dancing and music going on in the square. Of course, some kids will sneak in, but that's part of Grand Market, the rare freedom allowed to the children and everyone else.

In the middle of the crowd, I pull Sinclair close. "You feel good," I murmur in the coconut-scented haven of her hair.

The cloudy thickness brushes against my face. Just like it had last night when we kissed and whispered into each other's mouths and I strained between her legs, my thigh flexing against the heated mound of her while her gasps of pleasure overwhelmed our bedroom. Just like that. If she would have me, I wanted her like that for the rest of our lives.

My fingers dance down her bare back and settle on her waist.

"Bliss Sinclair."

"Hmm?" She moves against me, dreamy and soft. "Yes, Hunter Willoughby?"

The crowd around us isn't very big. Just the usual size for Grand Market, full of our neighbors and their families and with enough room to breathe and move our elbows without jabbing anyone. Mouth just above her ear, I ask her the question that has been burning in me for months. "Will you marry me?"

Sinclair jerks against me in surprise, her rhythm and dreaminess gone. She stops dancing. "What?"

Not quite the response I was expecting. But maybe she didn't hear me. I repeat the question and tighten my hand on her hip, fingers digging into her skin to let her know how serious I am. My other hand reaches for the ring in my pocket. "Will you share your life with me? Here in Jamaica? For as long as we're on this earth together?"

Her eyes are big and shocked under the moonlight, streetlight, and stars. "I... Oh, Hunter."

The answer is so very far from what I expect that my knees suddenly feel like they've turned to water. I let go of the ring and hold on to Sinclair with both hands. She's trembling so hard, it feels like we're vibrating against each other. I swallow thickly, wondering and afraid.

"Whatever your answer is, I can take it." But the words feel like a lie once they leave my mouth.

We've been together for nearly two and a half years. In most of that time, we've been happy. Moving, I thought, toward forever. Have I been wrong all this time?

Our friends, Radha and Madeline, have been a couple for ten plus years. They've lived here on the island as wives, even changed their last names to match. Just a few months ago, they returned to England, where they are both citizens, to get legally married and now seem more solid together than ever. That's what I want for me and Sinclair.

And that's apparently what I'll never get.

"Am I a fool?" I ask her.

"No!" She clutches my hand, but nothing else comes out of her mouth.

People keep moving around us, dancing and singing along to the Christmas song the band plays. My chest feels cracked in two. The lump in my throat is impossible to swallow. I wet my dry lips and force myself to say what I need to.

"It's okay, Sinclair. Whatever your answer is." The fault line that feels strangely like heartbreak cracks open a little wider in my chest. All my foundations begin to shake.

But maybe I *am* the fool Ebony always says I am for giving Sinclair an out like this. But I'd rather Sinclair be happy being whatever or *wherever* she wants in the world than unhappy shackled at my side. One thing I always admired about Sinclair is that once she knows what she wants, she sails toward it without looking back.

It seems that she doesn't want me like that, though.

"No!" Little pains explode in my bare arms. Sinclair's sharp nails sinking into me. "That's not what I mean. I just…I just can't right now."

Past her shoulder, I see Nikki and Lydia and the others moving in the crowd, their faces alight with cautious happiness, or maybe just caution. Nikki is still sad.

"Tell me," I demand, willing my voice to remain steady. "Tell me what you want."

"I don't... It's not that simple."

"No? I want to spend my life with you. I asked if you want to do the same. What's simpler than that?"

My cousin is right. Sometimes I can be too direct. But why does the world want me to be less honest, less than I am? If people were more upfront about everything—their feelings, their fears, their fuck-nos—then we'd all be better off. Being less straightforward comes with more confusion. I don't want that. I want the truth.

"There are other things to consider," Sinclair says with a hint of desperation in her voice. "Other—" She abruptly stops and half-turns away from me. "The last thing I want to do is hurt you." She bites so hard into her lower lip that it looks ready to bleed. Her thick halo of hair waves in the breeze as she shakes her head. "Shit. I can't...I can't do this right now." Another curse and she is rushing away, pushing through the crowd to escape our conversation.

"Sinclair!" I frantically call her back to me.

But the dancing crowd surges, dozens of hands flying up in the air when the song from the stage suddenly changes to one the entire world knows. People start singing loudly, dancing like mad things and pushing me farther from Sinclair. The herd of wild horses masquerading as my heart gallops out of control.

Sinclair's splash of ocean blue-gray quickly disappears.

"Hey, cousin of mine. What's going on?" Ebony appears out of the crowd.

Her presence right now feels like a mockery. The ring in my pocket burns against my hip, a bad idea, a betrayal of myself.

"Nothing's up," I tell her, and dive into the crowd. I don't have enough in me to deal with her right now.

Grand Market festivities swirl around me. The laughter of children. Winking lights. Music from the stage weaving through the air. I imagine the intimate whispers of nearby lovers and cringe. Although I don't know exactly where I'm going, my footsteps are swift and sure. The rock in my throat grows bigger with each breath, each step. I fist my hand around the rejected ring in my pocket.

How did I get this all so wrong?

At the edge of the square and higher up the hill where various vehicles are parked, self-styled "bad men" stand around their tricked-out cars and motorcycles playing dominoes on folding tables. They are loud and aggressive with each other, but friendly, too. From there, the whole of the square spreads out below me, a little valley of happiness and sparkling lights.

"Hey," one of the men calls out as I pass. "Isn't that the dyke from up the road?"

"Leave her alone, man!" comes an answer. "She's all right."

"Since when?"

There's more, but I tune them all out and keep walking.

Is this the reason she doesn't want to tie her life to mine—the threat of being harassed and more just for living proudly as we are? Being in Jamaica and being visibly gay is sometimes hard, but I've gotten used to it. Maybe Sinclair never did.

"Fuck..."

Footsteps thud swiftly behind me, and I turn around in time to see Ebony approaching through the gauntlet of men, a chew stick perched at the corner of her mouth. "You didn't answer me, cousin. What's the trouble in paradise?"

Really? Can't this woman take a hint?

"I don't want to talk to you, Ebony," I say, just to make it a little clearer.

"Really? I couldn't tell." She falls into step beside me, her stride fast and heavy in her military-issue boots. "Why are you running away? You love all this Christmas stupidness."

Love. What an assumption to make.

"I just need some air." Hands in the otherwise empty pockets of my slacks, I walk faster. The pavement slaps against the bottoms of my yellow Converse sneakers. As we walk, the tall trees surrounding the long rectangle of a green space and the parking lot rustle in the wind. It's a lonely sound.

"There's plenty of air right here, Hunter. You go any further and you'll end up floating all alone in the sky." She grabs my wrist, forcing me to stop. In the breeze, her hair ripples around like an obsidian scarf, long strands brushing against her cheeks, shoulders, and waist. It's the only soft thing about her.

"I'm not looking to score anything illegal if that's what you're talking about."

"One illegal career and now everybody thinks I'm trying to sell them coke." She does a credible impression of an innocent woman, but her eyes are all bright mischief. "So, no my dear cousin. I'm just trying to have a conversation with you. No drugs involved."

"I *don't* want to have a conversation with you."

"What's with everyone tonight? Lydia looks like somebody stole her favorite piece of candy, Nikki's soon-to-be-divorce is making us all sad, and Sinclair's pretty face is a wreck because of you."

A wreck? "What are you talking about?" She seemed fine enough when she walked away from me. Or at least nearly so.

"If Lydia is into it, I think I can work that angle and get some of her sweet Christmas candy tonight—" She moved the chew stick around in her mouth, looking playful.

"No. That's not what I'm talking about and you know it." Ebony plays too damn much.

"It's always about you, isn't it? Always so selfish. It's not enough that you got the sexier sister—"

My body feels too tight, too raw to entertain any of her foolishness. "Don't fuck with me tonight, Ebony."

She rolls her eyes, looking more like my little cousin who refused to eat her vegetables than the criminal mastermind who runs half the valuable secrets and high-end hookers in queer Kingston.

"Wouldn't dream of it," she says with a smirk. But those words don't mean a damn thing. "So, are you guys breaking up or what? You know I've had my eye on that twin fantasy you and I talked about back when we were kids."

First of all, it was a fantasy she talked *at* me about. And second of all—

"You really want me to kick your ass, don't you?"

"You, kick somebody's ass? More like talk them to death, *professor*." There go her eyes again, around in a complete and infuriating circle. "Or maybe you'll just send them a computer virus."

Even though I know she brags about her cousin "the uni professor," Ebony makes fun of my job to my face whenever it's convenient. Like now.

"This is not the time, Ebony."

"It's the perfect time." She pauses, moving the chew stick to the other side of her mouth. The breeze shifts and ripples her hair toward me. "I know you bought a ring."

Everything in me freezes and stops dead. How, when I didn't tell anyone? Then I remember just who Ebony is. My locs slither over my shoulders and back as I shake my head. "It doesn't matter anyway. Sinclair doesn't want it."

"But she wants *you*, though," Ebony says with a certainty I don't have right now.

"Does she?"

"You're the only person who has any doubts." She steps away to lean back on one of the trees ringing the parking lot. Despite the music coming from down below, I hear the harsh scrape of the bark against her thin blouse. "So what happened, you just didn't get the answer you expected?"

Expected? No, not exactly.

"She seemed…scared or something when I asked her." Christ, the expression on her face. Nausea rolls in the pit of my stomach.

Ebony makes a sound of exasperation. "Look over there." Her chin jerks down toward the celebration going on without us.

"What am I supposed to be looking at?" I don't notice anything but people having a good time. Nothing unusual.

Then I see them. Nikki and her husband, Victor. Sinclair's father. They're arguing.

Standing at the edge of the festivities and wearing dark colors when everyone else wears some color of the rainbow, Nikki and her husband are easy to spot. With her arms crossed tightly over her chest, Nikki's mouth moves quickly. Her head snaps back and forth to bring home whatever point she's trying to make. Victor's face is a thundercloud, and his hands slash through the air. Even from so far away, it's obvious they're shouting at each other.

Nearby, their son, Xavier, throws worried glances over his shoulder but doesn't come closer.

"You can't blame her for hesitating to jump into legal union with this particular marriage exploding right in front of her face," Ebony says. "She loves you. You love her. Enough real problems exist in the world without you making up something to push Sinclair away." Her eyebrow ticks up.

"Anyway, if you're going to let that lovely creature go off into the wild on her own over a bit of nothing, you don't deserve to have her. Let the rest of us get the chance to fulfill a lifelong dream." She pulls the chew stick out of her mouth with a downright dirty look, licking the end with her obscenely long tongue.

"I'm going to murder you in your sleep," I mutter.

"Come on, Hunter." She cuts me off before I can lay out any more empty threats. "This is your dream woman. She's out, she's Jamaican. Sure, she's a little bit on the skinny side, but she's willing to try anything your perverted little mind comes up with. Don't make a hasty decision you'll regret later."

"Who's perverted?"

I almost jump out of my skin when Sinclair appears out of nowhere. She repeats the question, looking between me and Ebony.

Of course, my cousin says something without much more prompting. "You already know who." She gives Sinclair a filthy look I'm sure she thinks is sexy.

Sinclair loosens a pale imitation of her usual smile. "You're the most perverted thing on two legs, Ebony. I won't let you convince me of anything different."

Pride throbs in Ebony's quick burst of laughter. "Too right, my dear."

Then after a silence that gets a little awkward, my cousin pulls out her phone. "I'm going to…ah…" She waves her phone at us and backs away toward the madness of the square.

"Sure." I give Ebony a grateful nod despite everything. "See you over there."

She nods back. After a meaningful look at Sinclair, then at the family drama taking place in that corner of Grand Market, she turns and walks away.

Sinclair clears her throat. "So, it's Christmas Eve and everything. Come enjoy it with me, nuh?"

My breath catches at her simple plea. She's radiant under the sky. A brilliant neutron star that lives in my heart, no matter what any legal document says we are or aren't to each other. I sigh and release the fear I'd been holding onto. My emotions from before seem like a temporary madness.

I pull Sinclair to me and smile when the hesitant look on her face disappears. "Yes. Let's go do that," I murmur into the scented cloud of her hair. "What do you want to try first? I hear Miss Esther has some nice gizzadas tonight."

"Whatever you want," she says, biting the smiling corner of her lip.

With our hands joined, we head back toward the square, skirting the group of domino players in the parking lot. The night is brilliant, and it's Grand Market. I asked my love a question, and she gave me her honest answer. But she's still my love. I was stupid to forget that.

I swim up to the surface of sleep with the awareness of a slight weight on top of me. The weight is sweet and soft. Bare skin, the low sound of a moan, hands in my thick and heavy hair.

"Good morning," a beloved voice whispers a moment before teeth sink into the side of my neck. My consciousness may be only semi-aware, but my body knows perfectly well where it is and what it wants. I caress Sinclair's waist with both hands, my fingers wandering down to squeeze the lean curves of her butt.

"Hey." I grip handfuls of her soft flesh and she laughs into my throat, a huff of warm breath. "You're up and in a very…excited mood," I murmur.

Beautifully naked, she's moving on top of me in a subtle and slow wave. She tongues the side of my neck. "With you, I'm always excited." Soft bites and licks tease my throat, and I wake up just enough. My thighs fall open to receive whatever she's in the mood to give me.

Grand Market ended with us sitting on the front steps of our house, watching the hints of pink spread across the sky although we were both too tired to do anything more than hold hands and lean into each other in pleasant exhaustion. It's a miracle we made it to the bed.

We love each other. That's it.

Like Ebony reminded me, what Sinclair and I have is wonderful. Just about perfect. We've squabbled about food and where to put the laundry basket and if we should have a TV in the bedroom, but those are all minor things. Barely a blip on the radar of our lives as a couple. The only real issue that came up was when I opened my big mouth and asked Sinclair to marry me. I created a problem where there was none.

That was and is my fault.

"Why are you so beautiful?" Sinclair asks softly, rising from her feast on my throat to look down at me. Her brown eyes are luminous in the morning sunlight with no trace of the clouds that were there last night.

"Because you think so?" I open my thighs even more, and she slips between them. The movement of her furred sex against mine drags a moan out of me.

"Ah." A smile curves up the corners of her mouth, and her tantalizing waves continue between my legs, pressing into me, dripping desire from me.

Then she leans down and offers me kisses. Softly on the corners of my lips, and my eyes can only flutter shut to savor the sensation, kisses like butterfly wings, her hands in my hair, her sensual movements stirring up more of my desire.

Merry *fucking* Christmas.

Her tongue traces the seam of my lips, moist and delicate, and it's only surprise that makes me surrender to her kiss, opening my mouth for her. Immediately, she takes what she wants, licking deep into my mouth with a shocking morning hunger. My hips buck, and a moan splits me in two, vibrates my chest. The surprise drags a gasp from me, but I'm too much of an opportunist not to instantly pounce on what she's given me. The sweet and hot Christmas gift of her mouth in the morning, the taste and scent natural, her fingers roaming up my sides and over my breasts to tease.

Her taste is incredible. So perfect. And the sexiest thing I've had on my tongue in what feels like days. She's giving me this—her breath, her taste, her surrender. Her love.

This is what I want. Forever. It doesn't matter whether or not some piece of paper gives us permission. Christmas is about valuing and loving the family we have. I don't need a ring or a judge to make what we have any more real.

"Baby…" I groan into her mouth. "Sinclair."

She lifts her head like she doesn't know exactly what she's doing to me. "Yes…?"

Her eyes are swimming with love. How could I have doubted her, doubted what we share?

"I'm sorry about yesterday," I tell her softly. "I take it all back. I didn't mean to make you sad." Her wild hair crinkles under my palms rough-soft. "I don't want you to marry me, okay?"

Sunlight dances in her eyes. "But what if I *want* to marry you?"

"What?" Everything stops. The birds. My heart. The throbbing pulse of desire between my legs. "What are you saying?"

Her fingers tug once on my hair and then she pulls back, palms flat against my ribs. "I love you," she says.

"I know—"

"Let me finish."

Fine. "Okay."

"I love you. I love us. Yesterday, I was scared that we would end up like Daddy and Nikki or any of those other couples who just couldn't make it work. The thought of losing you to something like this—indifference or apathy or whatever—instead of something real and unavoidable like…I don't know…death, squeezed my insides so hard I thought I was having a heart attack. Especially when you asked me to marry you."

"I'm sorry," I interrupt, unable to stay quiet for another second. "I won't ask—"

A hand clamps over my mouth. "And then I realized we're not everybody else."

"Huh?" Under her hand, my question comes out muffled and a little idiotic.

"You and I are simply you and I. Not Nikki and Papa. Not Ebony and Lydia. Not my parents. We are making our own lives here and we're creating our own love together. So, since you want to get married, we'll get married."

"Umm umm umm," I mutter from under her hand.

"What?" Then she looks down at her hand over my mouth and blushes. "Oh, sorry. What did you say?"

"I said it's okay. Marriage and rings and all that aren't for us."

Her gaze narrows, then slowly the lines of confusion clear from her forehead. "Oh, you threw the ring away, didn't you?"

More than a little embarrassed about doing exactly that, I can't meet her eyes. Instead, I slide a hand down to stroke her wetness. A stuttered gasp tumbles out of her.

"Oh, Hunter…"

The words fall from her, a mix of passion and exasperation. But she should be used to me by now. With a quick motion, I flip her over, dropping her onto her back and pinning her hands by her sides.

"Who cares about engagement rings and weddings when I have the most perfect woman in my bed and in my life."

She gasped out a laugh and pulls me closer with a leg hooked over my hip. "You sweet, sweet woman."

For her, yes, I'll be sweet. Grinning wide, I nibble her throat, the dip of her collarbone, slowly heading lower. The scent of her rises to invite me closer. My love moans my name.

"Now, open up," I growl with my lips ghosting over her quivering belly. "I have your Christmas present right here."

Orphans' Christmas

BY CHEYENNE BLUE

"You've no excuse this year." Megsie, perched on the kitchen counter, swinging her legs and shovelling cereal straight from the box into her mouth.

"For what?" I turned the box so I could see the label. "Why are you eating this junk?"

"Nothing else to eat." Megsie shrugged. "I'm crazy hungry. Don't change the subject. You've no excuse not to come to Orphans' Christmas this year."

"I have every reason. Just as I did last year."

"Last year you were working. Although I still haven't figured that out. Why does a physiotherapist have to work on Christmas Day? Do you have emergency squats or something?"

"It's a hospital. They have emergencies." I took the cereal box from her.

"Urgent back massage." She giggled.

"You must have a sugar high if you find that funny." I put the box in the cupboard. "I skipped lunch today and I'm starving. Wanna go eat?"

"Sure." Megsie jumped down from the counter. "How about Sinbad's?"

"Sounds good." I grabbed my phone and stuffed a credit card in the back pocket of my jeans. "I'm ready."

"I don't know how you do that," she complained. "You haven't combed your hair, no make-up, of course, and you don't carry *stuff* with you." She picked up her bag. If it was weighed at an airport, it'd be over the carry-on limit. She rummaged through it. "Lemme check I've got my phone, purse, toothbrush, lipstick, and then I'm ready."

"Got your leg irons and a spare alternator for the car in there?" I teased.

Megsie marched down the hall, leaving me to follow. "Maybe. And you still haven't answered my question about Christmas."

The neighbourhood where Megsie and I lived was one of those shabby-chic areas of inner-city Melbourne. It was an eclectic mix of Victorian terrace houses, some almost bowed in the middle under the weight of the wrought-iron lace work, others shabby to the point of dilapidation. Old industrial warehouses, now turned into luxury apartments, butted up to architecturally designed houses. Our house was one of the dilapidated ones: freezing in winter, boiling in summer, due to the lack of heat and air conditioning. But it was cheap, and both of us wanted to live in the inner city, rather than in some soulless suburb with a two-hour commute.

Once we were settled in Sinbad's, a plate of kofta and two cold beers between us, Megsie returned to her attack.

"Christmas." She studied me over the table. "What's the excuse this year?"

I picked a piece of lamb from the platter. "I really don't do Christmas. It's not my thing."

"You think it's mine? I'm a born-again atheist. I wouldn't suggest religion and carols to you."

"I'm just not comfortable in big groups of strangers."

"Hannah, *honestly*." She scooped hummus onto a piece of flatbread and regarded me fondly. At least I hoped it was fondly. The exasperation in her voice said I was trying her patience. "Yes, there will be lots of people there. No, most of them will not be like you—that is, most of them won't be introverted Irish lesbians, but you gotta broaden your horizons. Meet people."

"Straight people."

"So? You don't have a problem with me."

I was silent. My excuses were falling like drunks at closing time.

"You can sit alone and eat yourself into a coma. It doesn't matter. Orphans' Christmas is exactly what you want it to be. No one will force you into the cricket match if you don't want to. You can come with me and Will. It's just a community gathering. In our local park. With beer." She lifted her bottle. "*Sláinte*, as you Irish say."

"*Sláinte*," I replied automatically.

"So, you'll come?"

I ate a carrot stick while I thought. Megsie made it sound appealing. It would be good to meet people who didn't work at the hospital. But I'd made a promise to Mam, and if she had to return to Ireland, then there was no way I could go to Orphans' Christmas. In fact, I wasn't even sure I could keep living with Megsie, and that was why I hadn't mentioned it to her yet. Megsie was the best housemate I'd ever had. There for me if I wanted to chat, but silent if I curled up with a book. Her boyfriend, Will, was a sweetie too, a cuddly giant of a bloke, the strong and silent type. I liked Will.

"I'll think about it," I said. "I need to check on a few things first."

Megsie was used to my evasiveness, and this time she didn't push me. "No worries." She drained her beer and divided the last kofta on the plate into two. "Are you on early shift tomorrow?"

I shook my head.

"Fancy a beer at the Corner on the way home?"

"Sure." There was a barmaid at the Corner who I liked. *Really* liked. I could sit and chat with Megsie and try not to stare at the barmaid and wonder if she was a lesbian. And if she was, what, if anything, I would do about it.

"She doesn't work Thursdays," Megsie said.

"Who doesn't?"

I can't have been very convincing, as she said, "The barmaid you always pretend not to watch. I've never seen her except on the weekend." She stood and yanked me to my feet. "But that's okay. I'll go with you Saturday arvo, same as always, so you can get your fix."

"I have to go, love. I booked the flight for next week." The worry in Mam's voice came clearly over the phone. "I don't like leaving you here alone."

"I have work and my friends."

"But it's so far."

"It's only one day on a plane." I pushed down the nugget of anxiety that bubbled in my throat. I'd never been more than a couple of hours from my Mam in my life. Not a normal thing for a twenty-seven-year-old, I knew, but then Mam and I were close, and we'd only got closer after Da died one week after we arrived in Australia. He was the one with the Australian dream. He wasn't supposed to die and leave us alone in a strange country. "You go. Granny Guilfoyle needs you."

Mam was silent.

"Go," I said more firmly. "I'll be okay. And when you come back… after…we can have a late Christmas dinner, just the three of us." *After.* After Granny Guilfoyle had finally let go of the world and gone… Gone where? I didn't know.

Sometimes I thought it ironic that Mam and I always celebrated Christmas, even though neither of us were religious anymore. Australia had done that to us. Just one of the ways we had changed.

"—and I think it's best. She's agreed. I don't see how it would work otherwise."

With a start, I realised I had no idea what she was talking about.

"Um," I said, my tone non-committal. Hopefully, she would keep talking and I could catch up with the conversation.

"I had a look at it. There's bingo. And it might only be for a short time."

My incomprehension vanished in the sound of a sharp intake of breath. It was her mother dying in Ireland. Her own mam. Sure, there were her five brothers and sisters over there already, but it was her *mother*.

I clenched the mobile in my hand. I couldn't even begin to imagine how I'd feel if it were Mam who was coming to the end of her life. Even working as I did in one of Melbourne's biggest hospitals, death wasn't too immediate. Not for me as a physio.

"—so does that suit you, Hannah?" Mam asked.

I realised I'd again missed what she said.

"Gramma agrees that it's daft to mess up your work. She's happy to go to Sunny Court while I'm in Ireland. It's near enough that you'll be able to visit easily. Even after work, when you're on an early shift."

I was silent as I tried to work out what she was talking about.

"Hannah?" she prompted. "Have you heard something about Sunny Court? Is it not a good aged-care home?"

Aged care. I swallowed. Gramma would hate being in a home. And I would hate her being there. Gramma—my da's mother—was all we had left of Da. She lived with Mam, who was her carer.

"I can stay with Gramma at your house," I said. "That would be better."

"You can't, sweetie. You'll never get the time off work, not at Christmas. I've talked with Gramma. She's happy to go to Sunny Court. It's only until I'm home again."

Mam had said "home". Normally, "home" was Ireland, and the swathes of bog land and purple hills of County Offaly. Where her family was, where our roots were—hers, mine. And Da's too, until he couldn't wait to come to Australia for a warm climate and all the construction work he could hope for. Well-paid work with a contract, not a slap on the palm and a promise, which was all he'd got in Ireland since the Global Financial Crisis.

"I can stay at your place," I said again.

"No, Hannah. It's settled. I don't want to disrupt your life more than necessary."

"Gramma isn't a disruption. You know that."

Her sigh drifted down the line, as ethereal as bog cotton nodding in a spring breeze. "I know, sweetie. You're a grand girl to even say it. But it's arranged. Just make sure you see Gramma as often as you can. And if I'm not back by Christmas, don't leave her alone then."

"I won't," I said.

At work the next day, I related the conversation to my friend. Kim's family was from Vietnam, although she'd been born in Australia. But she understood the whole immigrant thing.

"Does that mean you'll be spending Christmas at Sunny Court?" She snagged her lunch from one of the microwaves in the break room.

It smelled delicious, and my mouth watered. She had lemongrass chicken and vermicelli, and she dumped on a handful of fresh herbs from her parents' backyard. My own crumbly sandwich looked pathetic in contrast. I bit into it, trying to summon enthusiasm for stale bread, cheese, and ham.

"I was going to ask if you wanted to spend Christmas with my family, seeing as your mum will be overseas."

"You don't celebrate Christmas."

"No, but we always make it a big family time. We gather at my parents' house, and they cook a pig on a spit. You're invited, if you're not spending all day at the oldies' home."

That would have been fun, but I shook my head. "That's sweet of you, but I can't leave Gramma alone."

"You could bring her." Kim made the offer hesitantly, and I didn't blame her. Gramma was eighty-six and still feisty, but she was frail and spent much of her day in a wheelchair. Kim's parents' house, with its twisty narrow paths and steps, would be too difficult.

"I don't think it would work. But thank you. My housemate wants me to go to Orphans' Christmas in the park. I'll have to turn that down too."

Kim grabbed chopsticks from the drawer. "Okay. But if you change your mind, the offer's still open."

I stole a piece of chicken from her plate. "Thanks. Now, tell me how you're going on your Meet Cute crusade."

Kim sighed. "Not good. I went to the restaurant four nights in the last week. She was there on three of them. I've been trying to flirt, but I can't tell if it's working, or if she's just being friendly. I don't even know if she's a lesbian. I've got a freezer full of Indian curry, and I don't even like it that much. But that's the only way I know of trying to find out if she's interested."

My mouth watered, and I put down my stale sandwich. "I'll eat the curry if you don't want it."

"Okay." She sighed. "It's her parents' restaurant, and they're there in the kitchen. Sometimes I think I'm the only out Asian lesbian in Melbourne."

"Not true. I know of at least one more. There was a girl I dated a couple of times last year. She was from Thailand. Her parents were fine about it, she said."

"Well, I never meet any." Kim bit her lip. "And my gaydar is now so faulty, I can't tell if she's straight or in the closet. I'll probably end up in Sunny Court when I'm eighty, all alone, wondering if the cute grey-haired darling in the chair next to me likes women."

I laughed and squeezed Kim's hand. "No chance."

I saw Mam off at the airport two days later, her bags laden with gifts for her huge family. We hugged at the departure gate.

"Look after yourself, Hannah. And look out for Gramma too. You're all she has now."

"I will." I clutched Mam tighter, unwilling to let go. The absence of her was already closing around me. "Email me. Skype. Call. Let me know how Granny Guilfoyle is doing."

Mam nodded, dashed at her eyes with the back of her hand, and with a last squeeze of my fingers, she turned and headed for the security line.

I hung around, waiting until she'd cleared security, and with a final wave, she was out of sight. I turned abruptly. I'd taken the day off to take Mam to the airport, and the rest of the afternoon yawned empty. My fingers closed on Mam's car keys in my pocket. I'd drive over and see how Gramma was doing at Sunny Court.

The nursing home was in a leafy suburb on the south side of the Yarra River. It was a cluster of buildings with small brick courtyards in between. Gramma had a room in Bellbird—each cluster was called after an Australian bird, all very pleasant names like kookaburra or lyrebird. I wondered if the booby had a group of rooms named after it, and that thought kept me grinning as I rounded a corner too fast and went smack into a woman and toddler coming the other direction.

Our shoulders banged, and I stood on her foot. Her bag fell to the floor. The child howled—I think I'd knocked him as well.

"Sorry, sorry. I'm a total eejit. I wasn't looking where I was going." I smiled apologetically. "Are you okay?"

"No damage." The woman rubbed her shoulder. She crouched to gather the child to her. "Hey now, Ryan. You're okay, buddy. Just a fright, eh?"

Ryan nodded, his tears already drying as he leant into his mother.

I crouched too. "Sorry, Ryan. Are you okay?"

He stared at me, eyes wide, but didn't say anything.

His mother rose, and I followed suit. "No harm done," she said, and smiled.

Oooh. Butterflies jumped in my stomach at that smile. It was soft, not practiced, just the sort of shy smile one stranger gives another, but it crinkled the corners of her eyes—brown eyes, I saw, as warm as her smile—and brought her face to life. She wore the blue tunic and pants of a nursing assistant.

I bent and picked up her bag and handed it to her. "Sorry, again. I was in too much of a hurry to see my Gramma."

Ryan tugged at her pants. "Mama. Icey-cream."

"We're going now, sweetie," she said. And then to me, "Enjoy the visit with your gran."

I wondered if she looked after Gramma. I continued on my way, and after a couple of wrong turns, I found Bellbird. Gramma was dozing in her wheelchair on the terrace. Her eyes sprang open as I approached. "Hannah, my darling girl. Aren't you a picture!" Her soft Irish lilt warmed my heart, as it always did.

I bent to kiss her soft cheek. "You're a picture yourself." I sat on a bench near her. "How are they treating you here?"

"Just grand." Her eyes twinkled with life. "I've the most comfortable room and my own bathroom. The food's very good. And there's all sorts of activities. It's like a holiday camp."

"Bingo?"

"Pole dancing." She chortled at my startled expression. "Hannah, you are such a prude."

"You know me too well. Do you want to show me your room?"

"That can wait. Have you got time to come to the shops? There's a couple of things I need."

"You should have told me. I could have picked them up on the way here."

"It's not those sort of things," Gramma said. "And there's a minibus twice a week anyway. No, I need to go today. It will be easier if you come too, help get my chariot up the kerb." She slapped the side of her wheelchair affectionately.

"Sure. If that's what you want."

"I do. And I'm ready." Her handbag was propped between her feet, and she wore a broad-brimmed sunhat.

"Do we have to tell anyone we're going?" I looked around for a nurse. Maybe the smiling, dark-haired woman of earlier.

"Already done all that." Gramma flapped a hand. "Let's go."

I walked beside her as her motorized chair buzzed down the wide corridors to the entranceway. Once in the street, I paused. "Which way?"

"Left." Gramma turned in that direction and we trundled along.

"Did Áine get away all right?" Gramma asked.

"Without a hitch. She's probably in the sky by now."

"Any more news on how Fiona is doing?"

I hesitated. Gramma was in fine health most of the time, but I wasn't sure if I should tell her that Granny Guilfoyle—who was three years younger— was now in a hospice and the curtains were slowly closing. Would that be tactless of me? But Gramma knew why Mam had gone over to Ireland.

Gramma halted her chair. "Hannah, you darling girl, you can tell me. We're all going to die one day—even you—and not talking about it doesn't make it further away."

I pressed my palms to my cheeks, stretching my eyes in the hope the wetness would go away. I looked at Gramma, her exuberant grey curls that age couldn't tame, and her kind expression. Gramma was a pragmatist. And she made sense. I was the one not facing up to the way it was. "Mam said it would be a few days. Maybe a week. No more." I couldn't stop the tears then.

I hadn't cried when Mam told me last night. Now, in the middle of the street in suburban Melbourne, with people hurrying past, I was about to fall apart.

"Fiona's ready to go." Gramma reached up and pressed my elbow, until I lowered my hand to clasp hers. "She told me, last week when Áine and I spoke to her on that Skypey-thing. She's not scared; she's ready. It's us who are sad."

I took a deep breath. Another. "I know." The stone in my chest lifted a little. I emerged from the grey mist in my head, back to the sunshiny afternoon and noise and bustle of Melbourne. "But I'll miss her."

Gramma squeezed tighter. "We all will." She waited, my hand in hers, until I gave a short nod. I was okay. We could go on. Without a word, we restarted our journey down the road.

I expected Gramma to want lollies or an iced cake—she had a notoriously sweet tooth—but she wheeled on past the baker and the supermarket and turned into a side street.

I paced beside her, wondering where she was going. There were a couple of smaller shops, and a pub, one of the old-fashioned art-deco ones that was probably once painted cream or white but was now a rather lurid purple.

Gramma passed by the shops and stopped the chair at the bottom of the ramp to the pub. "I think you'll have to give me a push."

I shot her a glance. Gramma liked the occasional whiskey, but she wasn't a big drinker. I didn't say anything, just gave her chair an extra push to help the rather feeble motor propel it up the ramp.

Inside was just what you'd expect: a dimly lit bar, with a long counter and a row of tradesmen drinking beer after knocking off for the day.

"What would you like?" I asked.

Gamma didn't glance my way. "Nothing to drink." She wheeled through the bar to the corner where the TAB was. It was like any betting shop: a bank of TVs showing the racing, the trots, and the greyhounds. Gramma retrieved her bag and fumbled in it until she found her wallet and a folded piece of paper.

Then she went up to the counter. She was there for a long time and handed over what seemed like quite a thick wad of notes, and she received a dozen or so betting slips in return. Gramma was betting? Betting big time, it looked like. Chalk that up as well; I'd never seen her do more than slip a dollar into a poker machine.

She returned to where I stood. "I'm done."

I followed as she trundled back to the street. It was the middle of the afternoon and scorching hot. Melbourne was in the middle of the first heatwave of summer and temperatures hovered in the high thirties. The heat hit me like a wall after the air-conditioned pub. I flapped a hand in front of my face. "Where else do you want to go, Gramma?"

"That's it. We can go back to Sunny Court now."

"Want a cold drink or an ice-cream?"

"That would be grand. There's a little place on the main street. I've been there with a couple of the ladies from the home."

I waited until we were settled at a table by the broad window where we could see the street, dishes of ice-cream in front of us. "So, what's with the gambling, Gramma?"

That evening, Megsie and I sat on our veranda with a cold beer. Melbourne was sweltering, and our house felt like a pizza oven. At least outside there was the barest hint of a breeze. I lifted my hair off the back of my neck. The movement of air felt good against my damp skin.

"Gramma's been at Sunny Court for two days, and she's already got herself into a betting ring." I took a deep swig of beer, enjoying how it slid down my throat. I pressed the cold bottle to my forehead. "It's a syndicate, all women, all residents of Sunny Court. Apparently, one of the women has a system for betting on the dogs. Gramma was quite cagey about it—she's been sworn to silence as to how it works. I took her to the TAB."

"Haven't they heard of online betting?" Megsie asked.

"Their average age is eighty-four. They're not that up on things like that."

She nodded. "Did they win?"

"They *always* win. I'm going back tomorrow with Gramma to pick up the winnings."

We waved at our neighbour walking her dog. Then Megsie said, "Did you decide about Christmas yet? It's next week, in case you're deliberately blanking it out. I got the food list for Orphans' Christmas this morning. I've put my name on the bottom, along with what I'm bringing, and now I send it to the next person on the list."

I was silent, twisting the stubby of beer in my hands. The more I heard about Orphans' Christmas, the better it sounded. If I couldn't be with Mam, then a cheery, multicultural, secular community event sounded just the thing. I probably wouldn't join in with much, but I could eat great food, sit in the shade, watch, and enjoy. I might not meet my own "cute", as Kim liked to call it, but that wasn't what it was about. I was tempted. "I can't," I said at last. "I can't leave Gramma on her own. Much as she seems to love Sunny Court, I can't not spend the day with her. I imagine there'll be some sort of gathering that I can join."

"Bring her along." Megsie drained her beer and wiped her mouth with the back of her hand. "There's all ages coming. Babes-in-arms to oldies. I think Gramma would be right at home. She's probably more social than you."

I thought of the betting syndicate she'd talked her way into. "She's definitely more social than me."

Megsie stood. "You think about it while I get another beer. Want one?"

I nodded, and she disappeared into the house, letting the screen door bang behind her. Megsie was right about one thing: Gramma was the social sort. That was how she'd taken to Sunny Court like the old duck she was. She'd probably love a big eclectic gathering in the park. As long as it wasn't too hot. Even now, at nine at night, sweat trickled down between my breasts.

Megsie returned with the beers and handed one to me.

"I'll ask her," I said. "If she says no, that's the end of it, okay?"

She nodded. "Fair enough."

"I'll ask her tomorrow on our jaunt to the betting shop. Will that be enough time to get our names on the list if necessary?"

"Yup. Just let me know by the evening."

I was on early shift the next day, so it was mid-afternoon before I arrived at Sunny Court. I knew the way this time, but I still walked fast, and as I rounded the corner where I'd collided with the nurse and her kid, I thought again about those warm brown eyes. Lesbian or straight? I sighed; my gaydar was as faulty as Kim's if I couldn't tell. I'd always been able to pick a lesbian at ten paces. Now, not so much. But that was as much about changing times. I was too young to remember the days when your choices as an Irish lesbian were to stay in the closet or be out and proud with big army boots and a shaved head. No need for gaydar in those days.

Gramma wasn't in sight when I entered Bellbird lounge, so I looked around, wondering where her room was. She hadn't shown me last time. I spied a nursing assistant in a blue uniform in one corner, so I went across. She straightened from adjusting pillows behind someone's back and smiled. It was the woman I'd nearly mown down the last time, she of the warm brown eyes who'd been in my thoughts only a minute ago.

"Hello again," she said. "Can I help you?"

"I'm looking for my gramma," I said. "Eithne O'Reilly."

She had a lovely smile, and I got the full force of it. "I'll show you."

She led me along a corridor and paused at an open door. "Eithne?" she called. "Your granddaughter's here."

Gramma was ready, all dressed up for the trip down the road. I smiled my thanks at brown-eyes and tried not to watch her back view as she returned to the lounge.

Gramma and I left on the short trip to the pub. She returned from the counter chortling. "Nearly three hundred dollars!" she said. "Split five ways, that's sixty bucks each. Here," she handed me a twenty. "That's for ice cream."

"What's happening for Christmas?" I asked her as we headed back. "Is there a meal at Sunny Court I can join in with or something?"

"If you want." She pushed the stick so that the wheelchair motored a bit faster. "Haven't you anything better to do?"

"I'd like to spend the day with you. As we always do."

She stopped then. Maybe I sounded forlorn, or maybe she thought I wasn't being entirely truthful, as she said, "Hannah-girl, you do not *have* to spend Christmas with me. I'm making friends here, and there'll be all sorts of grand and festive events. If you want to come, there's a family-and-friends' dinner on Christmas Eve. Why don't you come to that?"

"Nothing on Christmas Day?"

"I'm not sure," Gramma said vaguely.

"Megsie's trying to persuade me along to Orphans' Christmas. It's a community thing for people without family at Christmas. Or with families, and they like to come anyway. We all bring a plate to share, and chip in for a marquee and ice and the like. She said you might like to come."

"One of the nurses is going to something like that," she said. "It sounds like good craic. I'd like that—unless I'm going to be in the way."

"You're *never* in the way, Gramma. I'd rather be with you. If you're sure you'd like it? I'd take you back here whenever you've had enough."

She nodded. "You're a good girl, Hannah. I know it's hard for you this year, without Áine."

"I have you."

We were back at Sunny Court. Gramma led the way down to the lounge. "We're in time for afternoon tea."

Indeed, one of the nurses was handing around cups of tea. Not the brown-eyed nurse. There were plates of small cakes and plain biscuits. Gramma took me over to four bright-faced ladies sitting in a corner and handed one of them the envelope with the winnings.

She nodded, as if it were not unexpected, and tucked it into her bag.

We sat and drank tea, and I ate too many biscuits, simply because one or the other ladies would press another on me. Eventually, bloated from too much sugar, I left. If I hurried, the rush-hour traffic wouldn't be too terrible.

I walked fast and rounded a corner straight into someone. Our shoulders glanced off each other, and the folded sheets she carried fell to the floor. I stopped.

"I'm sorry, I was rushing. Are—" I was looking into the amused gaze of the brown-eyed nurse from before.

"You again," she said. "We must stop meeting like this." Her eyes crinkled as she spoke the corny line.

I smiled back. "We're making a habit of it."

She bent to pick up the sheets, smoothing the ruffled cotton with a palm. "Did you have a good visit with Eithne?" she asked.

I nodded. "Yes. We went down the street for ice-cream."

"That's not all you did down there, I'll wager." Her grin told me she knew exactly what else we'd done.

I didn't want to give away Gramma's secrets, so I said, "Ryan not with you today?"

"My friend drops him here sometimes for the last part of my shift. Ryan loves it; the residents spoil him rotten. I think it's a good thing too, for him and for them. He doesn't have grandparents of his own; and many people here don't have grandkids—or if they do, they seldom visit." She peeped at me sideways. "Eithne loves him."

"Yes, she often tells me not to forget to have children."

"Do you want them?"

I shrugged. "I'm not cut out for single parenthood."

She opened her mouth, as if to say something, and then closed it again. Maybe she thought the conversation had dived too deep into the personal for two strangers. I wondered if Ryan's father was in the picture. Maybe I could get Gramma to find out. A little reconnaissance mission was right up her alley.

Another nurse popped her head out of a room. "D'you have those sheets, Luce?"

"Right here," Luce replied, and then to me, "Excuse me."

For the second time that afternoon, I watched her rear-view hurrying away, her figure neat and compact in the unflattering uniform.

"So, what should I put you down for?" Megsie turned the tablet so I could see the list of things people were bringing. It was a long, long list, and I had no idea what many of the items were.

"What's that?" I pointed to one. "Ants climbing a tree. It doesn't sound good."

"Oh, but it is. It's a Sichuan noodle dish, very delicious. You'll love it."

"Do most people bring something from their own tradition?"

"Some. Not all. It's a good idea though. You can have too much of chops and potato salad. Can you do something Irish?"

"Irish Christmas is turkey and veggies. Christmas pud. Very stodgy and dull compared to ants climbing a tree."

"What about that potato thing you made once? Sort of smashed-up spuds with cabbage and bacon? I bet that would go down well."

"Colcannon? Would that do as Gramma's contribution too?"

"Yup. There's no gatekeeper going to turn you away."

I fanned myself with the tablet. "I hope it cools down before next week, or I'll just lie in the shade of a tree and go to sleep. And Gramma would melt. She's not used to this heat."

Megsie snatched the tablet back. "So, colcannon it is, then." She typed fast with two fingers. "Done."

And then it was still so hot that Megsie and I went out to the front veranda and ate hummus and carrot sticks and drank all the cold beer we had in the fridge.

I woke in the night with a start. For a second, I couldn't think what the loud and shrill noise was. My head was groggy from too much beer, the fog of sleep still on top of me. The noise continued, and in another second, I realised it was my phone, with its ringtone of crashing saucepans. I snatched it off the bedside table, heart pounding. Phone calls in the middle of the night were seldom good. I looked at the screen. It was Mam.

"Hello." My hand shook as I clutched the phone. I sat up in bed and groped for the bedside light.

"She's gone, Hannah." Mam's voice was thick, flat and weary, as if she'd been awake for days.

Tears started instantly; they welled up and overflowed down my cheeks. Granny Guilfoyle. My granny. The person who'd given me my first teddy bear—still sitting on a shelf in my room—who'd minded me after school while my parents worked and I was too young to be left. She'd made me thick doorstep sandwiches of batch bread for my school lunches. We'd sung along to the radio together, and she'd taught me how to play tin whistle. I'd pinched apples from her orchard and harassed her hens, and she'd told me off soundly for both.

She was gone.

"Oh, Mam." My voice cracked, and I couldn't say any more.

"She slipped away peacefully. We were all here, all her children. It was a good way to go."

"I wish I was there with you."

"I wish you were too, sweetie." She paused. "The wake's on Friday. Just before Christmas."

"How are you doing?"

"I don't know. I knew this was coming, of course, but when it actually happens… Well, that's when you realise you're never as prepared as you think you are."

Tears ran down my cheeks in silent streams, and I couldn't answer.

"Hannah, will you tell Gramma?"

"Yes."

"Thank you. I don't want to call her in the middle of the night. I'm sorry I had to wake you."

"I love you, Mam."

"Love you too, Hannah."

It was after nine when I walked into Bellbird lounge. I hadn't seen it so quiet before—maybe the residents were late risers or still at breakfast. I went to Gramma's room, but it was empty. I sat on the edge of her bed to wait.

There was a picture on the wall: Gramma, Mam, me, and Da. It was taken on our second day in Australia. We were on St Kilda pier, eating fish and chips and drinking wine out of plastic glasses. Our hair was blowing everywhere, and there was a seagull in one corner of the picture. We were laughing. I remembered that time, when we were still high on our new country and what we could be here. About a second after the photo was taken, that seagull had swooped down and made off with Gramma's fish. Da had laughed and given Gramma half of his.

Da. Granny Guilfoyle. Both gone. I sniffed, trying to hold back the tears, at least until I saw Gramma, but it was no use, and I curled up on Gramma's narrow bed, face to the wall, and bawled.

A weight depressed the bed behind me, and a gentle hand rested on my shoulder.

"Hannah, are you all right?"

I recognised Luce's voice, but explaining was too hard, and I wasn't ready for my grief to be public. I curled tighter and choked back my sobs.

"Hannah," Luce said again, and then she was gone. Her footsteps crossed the floor, then there was the sound of the door closing. Luce returned, and the bed sagged again as she sat. But this time she lay down behind me, fitted her body loosely to mine and draped an arm over my waist. "Cry," she said. "Let it all out. You'll have to tell Eithne soon; she'll be back from breakfast. But cry now. It's okay."

Her arm was light on my waist, and her body only barely touched mine—near enough to be comforting, enough distance that she wasn't intruding. There was space for me to move away if I wanted. But I didn't want. I pressed my face to Gramma's pillow, smelling her warm scent— lilacs, the light perfume she always wore—and cried harder.

A tiny part of me wondered how Luce knew, but I figured Gramma had talked about Granny Guilfoyle. But I didn't really care. My tears dried, and my shoulders stopped heaving. I dragged a deep breath. Luce moved away and sat up on the bed.

I rolled over and swung my feet to the floor. We sat, side-by-side, facing the door.

"Thank you. I'm sorry you had to do that."

"Don't worry." Luce found my hand and gave a gentle squeeze. "All part of the service."

I gave her a watery smile.

Her eyes searched my face, as if checking I was okay. She stood. "Eithne will be back any moment."

I nodded and stood too. The quilt was crumpled, and Gramma's pillow was bunched in a soggy hillock.

"I'll bring a fresh pillow case." Luce slipped out leaving the door ajar.

I used Gramma's washbasin to splash water on my cheeks. That brought the puffiness down, but my eyes were still red. Nothing I could do about that. I went back to her bedroom to await her return.

Christmas came. Megsie and I spent Christmas Eve cooking: boiling potatoes, chopping cabbage, frying bacon, and threading chicken on skewers. Megsie made a huge pan of satay sauce, which was mostly peanut butter but tasted amazing.

The emails from the Orphans' Christmas organisers came thick and fast. They asked for volunteers to erect the marquee in the park, to set up tables and chairs, and to wrap presents for the children. I'd said I'd be there to help at seven, so I had time before going to fetch Gramma.

It was early when I arrived in the park but loads of people were there already. A tall bloke in a Santa hat seemed to be handing out tasks. I hovered nervously on the edge until he noticed and sent me to join the gang of people erecting the marquee. In no time, I was heaving on a rope as the canvas rose precariously into the air and swayed on its poles while people rushed around securing it.

Someone handed me a bacon-and-egg roll, and I stood taking in the scene. The organised chaos, the shouts and laughter, the smell of bacon wafting in the air. Megsie and Will arrived, and then someone shouted that they had mimosas. Megsie was first in line and returned with two glasses of bubbles and orange juice.

"Is there any better way to start the day?" She knocked her plastic glass against mine. "*Sláinte.*"

It was mid-morning before I got away. I found Gramma in the lounge with a mimosa of her own. From her bright eyes, it wasn't the first of the morning.

"Hannah, my darling."

I bent and kissed her cheek, hugging her around her skinny shoulders.

She was wearing a scarlet T-shirt with "Tell Santa I've been bad this year" printed on the front. Someone had twined tinsel around the armrests of her wheelchair.

I handed her my present. It was a family tradition to wrap presents in anything at all—so long as it wasn't wrapping paper. My present was wrapped in banana leaves and tied with a blue band, the sort used for Pilates stretches.

Gramma's arthritic hands had a bit of difficulty pulling the band off, but I knew better than to try and help. Finally, she succeeded and opened the banana leaves to find an internet radio.

"You'll be able to get your programs from Ireland this way," I said. "*Radio na Gaeltachta* and the like."

"It's perfect. You couldn't have thought of anything better. Those annoying morning hosts on the radio here give me the irrits." She handed me an envelope. In keeping with our tradition, the recycled envelope used to contain Gramma's meal choices for the week.

I slit the top open carefully and pulled out a folded piece of paper. "'To my dearest Hannah'," I read. "'All winnings from Eithne O'Reilly's share of the Sunny Court betting syndicate from this day forward will be payable to Hannah O'Reilly'." I looked up. "But Gramma, it was sixty dollars the other day."

She nodded. "And nearly two hundred this week. What am I going to spend the money on, Hannah? I have everything I need. You'll get it all when I'm dead and buried; you might as well have something now."

"It's too much." My hand shook as I studied the paper. "What if you need the money for something? Medicine. Something important."

"I have enough for my needs. But I promise, if ever I need money for something important, I'll come to you. Will that do?" Birdlike, she cocked her head on one side and studied me. "It's polite to say thank you."

"Thank you." I squatted in front of her chair and took her frail hands in mine. "I'll use it wisely and well. I won't squander it."

"Squander away, Hannah. Wine, women, and song. I can think of worse uses."

The park was bursting with people when we arrived back, and there wasn't a parking spot for blocks. I unloaded Gramma at the entrance and called Megsie to take charge of her until I could dump the car and return. It was nearly twenty minutes later before I made it back. I pushed my way through chattering groups of people, dodged a group of kids, and skirted the cricket match where a bloke with a wobbling beer gut and a shaved head plastered with zinc cream was bowling to a tiny woman in a long skirt and a hijab. There was a cheer as she thwacked the ball past the boundary line for a six. I passed the long tables laden with food. In keeping with the sharing nature of the day, everyone's food went on the tables. I looked for my colcannon—Megsie had promised to heat it up and bring it—but there was so much food I hadn't a hope of seeing it.

I found Megsie and Will in the marquee, tucking into a mix of food. A bottle of bubbles sat beside them. I flopped on the grass and took a long drink from Megsie's glass. "I thought I'd never get here." I stole a chicken wing from her plate. "I had no idea there'd be so many people."

"Over a hundred, according to the email this morning." Will leant over and kissed my cheek. "Happy Santa Day."

"Where's Gramma?" I peered around the marquee but couldn't see her.

"She got whisked away to play Frisbee," Will said.

"*Frisbee?*" My mouth fell open.

"I think that's happening on the Carrington Terrace side of the park," Megsie said.

"*Frisbee?*" I said again.

"There's a couple of people in wheelchairs, some little kids, and of course a dog on each team. She was here maybe five minutes when she was recruited. She's having a ball."

"I'll go and find her." I clambered to my feet and dusted off the grass seeds. "Will you be here when I get back?"

"Sure," Megsie said. Will just nodded through a mouthful of food.

It took me a few minutes to find Gramma. Sure enough, she was in her chair, about to catch the Frisbee floating towards her. She caught it and flung it back at the other side, where a blue heeler stopped barking long enough to make a massive leap, caught the Frisbee in its mouth, then ran around, evading all attempts to catch it. Gramma laughed as the dog romped from person to person, its jaws still clamped firmly around its prize.

I went over to her. "How's things? Enjoying yourself?"

"I'm having a grand time."

"Ettie!" A shrill child's voice sounded above the general hubbub, and a small boy-shaped whirlwind came dashing through people's legs to hurl himself at Gramma's chair. He grasped her by her legs and hugged tight.

"How's my favourite boy?" Gramma ruffled his tight curls.

The boy looked familiar. Head on one side, I considered him. It was Ryan. I scanned the crowd. If Ryan was here, Luce wouldn't be far behind. My heart jumped in my chest. Then she was there, taking Ryan by the hand, separating him from Gramma.

"Be gentle," she cautioned him. "Ettie needs your most gentle, special love." Her eyes met mine over Gramma's head. "Hello again, Hannah."

"Hi, Luce." It was hard for me to meet her eyes, awkward to remember how it had been the last time we'd met; how she'd been there for me as I cried. The warmth of her slight body near mine.

Her hand reached towards me, hovered for a moment.

My fingers twitched. I wanted to take it, but I wasn't sure what she meant by the gesture. Would it be comfort, or an informal handshake clasp? Or would it be a lingering like-to-know-you-better touch? What if I made it more than she meant? Fear of rejection kept my hand by my side.

After a moment, she withdrew her hand, and her attention switched. She bent to kiss Gramma's cheek. "I didn't realise this was where you were coming today, Eithne."

"Hannah lives a couple of streets away." Gramma's bright eyes moved from Luce to me and back again. "She lives in the worst house on the best street."

Luce grinned. "Heating?"

I shook my head.

"Off-street parking? Air conditioning?"

I shook my head again.

"1950s kitchen and bathroom?"

I nodded.

She grinned. "Sounds like my place. I'm in Burnett Street."

"Yarra Street." My voice croaked, the words sticking in my throat. It shouldn't be hard to talk with her. She was a nurse; she probably comforted people all the time.

"D'you ever go to the Phoenix Tavern? That's my favourite haunt around here."

"Sometimes." I made a mental note to drag Megsie there the next time we wanted a beer. The cute barmaid at the Corner couldn't compete with Luce's smile.

Ryan sat on the step of Gramma's chair, and she moved her feet to one side to make room for him. "Shall you and I go and find something to eat?" Gramma asked him.

His little head bobbed up and down. "Yeah!"

Gramma flicked a questioning glance at Luce.

She nodded in response. "Be good, Ryan. Look after Ettie."

With Ryan standing on the step of Gramma's wheelchair, leaning against her legs, the two of them wheeled in the direction of the food. That left me with Luce. When I looked back at her, she was closer, enough that I could see the dark flecks in her warm brown eyes.

"Eithne's lovely with him," she said. "Many of the residents are, but Ryan's independent. He has his favourites, and his Ettie is right at the top of the list."

"Has he found her lolly jar?"

She grinned. "I hope not, but possibly. That could be the reason for his crazy energy lately."

A teenager chasing a football knocked into me, pushing me closer to Luce.

"Sorry," I muttered, and would have stepped back, but she put a hand on my forearm.

"Are you okay, Hannah?" Her words were soft, wrapped in caring and concern.

"Yes. Thank you. I'm sorry for crying all over you the other day. I hope you didn't get into trouble for being late for something."

"That doesn't matter. You can cry on me anytime if you need it." Her hand was still on my forearm. She glanced at it and rather stiffly removed it.

I missed the slight weight, the warmth.

"It's always harder when you lose someone at Christmas. I know you don't celebrate in a religious sense, but it's a family time. You have Eithne with you… I hope you don't mind, but she did tell me about your parents."

"That's okay." I swallowed. "Do you have family here?" Maybe she was here at Orphans' Christmas with her handsome husband, who was somewhere drinking beer with one hand and jiggling a fat baby with the other.

"No. It's just me and Ryan now. My partner left us just after he was born."

I waited. If she wanted me to know more, she would doubtless tell me.

"Ryan was planned. We both wanted to parent, but when it came to it, when there was this noisy, smelly, demanding little person in the house, Angie couldn't take it. She left." Luce shrugged. "I think she's over in Perth now."

Her ex was a woman. Well, that changed things. Or did it?

I looked over at the food tables trying to see Eithne and Ryan. I thought I caught a glimpse of Eithne's chair.

Luce must have caught my glance. "I know I'm only a nurse—"

"There's no such thing as *only* a nurse."

Her mouth quirked upwards in a most fascinating way. "Thank you for that. It's hammered home to me sometimes by people demanding to speak to the doctor for the most trivial of things. They tell me I'm *only* a nurse, so I couldn't possibly understand." The tone of her voice showed her amusement. "What I meant to say was that while I'm only a paid carer, rather than a real friend, to most of the residents, most of them love seeing Ryan. He has five or six surrogate grandparents in Sunny Court."

"Including my Gramma?"

"Including Eithne. I hope you don't mind sharing."

"I'm happy to share with Ryan. I just hope he's happy to share with me."

Too late, I realised how my comment could be interpreted. A slight pink stained Luce's cheeks. Great. Now she thought I was putting the heavy word on her. "Sorry, I think that came out wrong. I was talking about grannies. Not—"

Luce put her hand on my forearm once more. "Don't beat yourself up over it. I knew what you meant. Although, for what it's worth, I would like to get to know you better, Hannah. Eithne talks about you a lot."

"There you are!" Megsie rushed up, glass of bubbles in one hand, a samosa in the other. "Come and eat now, because you'll be roped into the cricket match soon."

"Have you eaten?" I asked Luce.

She shook her head. "No, and I better go and find Ryan. He's hard enough to chase down on two feet. Eithne in her wheelchair wouldn't have a chance."

"You're Ryan's mum?" Megsie said. "He's fine. He's stuffing his face with cake."

We walked across the park. Before we reached the food, where we would be with Gramma, Ryan, Will, and a cricket match that wouldn't wait, I hung back and stopped. "Luce?"

She halted and tucked a strand of dark hair behind her ear. There was a half-smile on her face.

"Would you like to have coffee sometime? You and me? If you prefer, Ryan and Gramma can come too, but I was hoping it would be you and me."

Her half-smile bloomed to a wide one that crinkled her eyes. "I'd like that very much." She reached for my hand and squeezed my fingers. A moment of hesitation, then she pressed a kiss to my cheek. Her lips were soft and didn't linger. I wanted them to. "You know where to find me," she said.

I wanted to press my fingers to where her lips had touched. I wanted to let the strand of her hair float free again. I wanted to know if it was as silky-smooth as it looked. I did none of those. One small step.

I smiled at her. "I'll find you."

And The Bells Are Ringing Out

BY LOLA KEELEY

THERE ARE ANY NUMBER OF things about this charming London pub that Eden doesn't care for on a daily basis. Whether she's complaining about the cleaners cutting corners, or having to train the bar staff how not to shatter glasses every time they get distracted, most days of the year, this is a place of work.

Funny what a bit of tinsel and closing the doors can do for the place. As manager, Eden has taken the executive decision to gather the various waifs and strays that comprise her staff, with a couple of their lonelier regulars, and have Christmas Day together, before the bar reopens in the evening for punters looking to escape their families.

Klaus, their resident chef, initially refused, but Eden was waiting with her secret weapon: creative freedom. No sticking to the menus and ingredient lists approved by the brewery, their overarching lords and masters. No, this Christmas is about having it however they want, and each invited guest is to bring something that means Christmas to them. For Eden, that meant excavating her crockpot from the depths of a cupboard and throwing together chicken yassa overnight. She can pick the smell of the lime-soaked onion out of the air even now, and it's going to be the first thing on her plate despite the rest of the feast on offer.

The two long tables pulled together are already brimming with cakes bought from supermarkets, and even a few homemade attempts at dishes that Eden isn't sure she can identify. Tupperware of every size and shape is filled with colours ranging from the richest browns to slightly alarming greens. Potatoes and rice flecked with herbs and oils and different vegetables fill mismatched bowls. There's even a homemade sponge cake that looks like an attempt at a *Bake Off* entry, albeit with structural issues that aren't often seen outside of Pisa.

She misses her mother at times like these most of all. She misses the few years she can remember in Senegal, when celebrations like Christmas and Eid were a welcoming, mixed party to shower the cousins and neighbours with food and drink, regardless of their particular beliefs. Teranga, the sense of hospitality, of sharing, of there always being room around the table for one more—that's what she remembers.

Eden wipes away an unexpected tear and finishes setting the chairs around the table.

That's what she's tried to arrange today—a secular gathering that's more about not being alone than about anyone being born in a manger. Working Christmas also means she can justify taking off for New Year, and getting out of London is priority one. This corner of Fulham is rich and leafy, almost untouched by the urban sprawl in places, but lately the city has become claustrophobic in a way that Eden doesn't recognise.

Klaus sticks his head out of the kitchen door, instead of sending a helper for once. "Dinner in ten!" he calls out in that booming voice of his. From their various corners, or propping up the bar with comped drinks, everyone startles and heads towards the table.

"Come on," Eden urges them, spreading her arms wide to welcome every last person, just as her mother used to do. "Grab a chair! I want to see clear plates when you're all done."

The staff nod out of habit, used to following her orders. The regulars follow their example, and Eden takes the seat at the head of the table for herself. Klaus can have the other end, ready to carve the traditional goose and show off. It's not something Eden has ever tried, but like everything else on offer, she's game for at least a taste.

It's fun to watch as everyone else picks up platters and bowls, investigating the food or explaining their contributions. It brings a particular smile to her face that Mikey, ex-boxer and bouncer, is so proud of his trifle. Apparently his nanna's recipe. Then there's eighty-year-old Florence, who lives in one of the little cottages at the end of the road by herself, who promises that her turkey curry is hot enough to "melt their faces". Eden is going to need to try at least a spoonful of that.

She glances to the seat at her left, unused to not having an automatic person to fill it, even now. Christmas is a hell of a time to be recently broken up. After pouring herself a rich glass of red, she calls the table to order just by raising it.

"Thank you all for coming," she begins. "And for sharing this day and this food with each other." There's a lump in her throat, like she might really cry this time, but Eden chases it off quickly.

"Cheers!" The cry goes up, and she's relieved to join in. Maybe she's not in such a hurry for a new adventure, not while Fulham still feels a little bit like home.

Six days later, she's stepping off a train in the Scottish capital. Eden has friends here, old friends and good ones, and it's been all the excuse she needs to book a very overpriced train for New Year's Eve tonight and a few days after that.

She pulls the collar of her leather jacket up against the cold. She'd be better with a parka, one of those massive ski coats that doubles as both a quilt and an igloo, but she's not a total martyr to fashion. Under her fashionably distressed sweater, there's a thermal layer, leaving only her extremities vulnerable to the insistent damp sting of an Edinburgh winter. She's glad she went for box braids, protection from the cold moisture in the air that does her natural hair no favours.

The train station is packed like the end of days, and it might as well be since there are no trains for two days after this. Hard not to be suspicious of a country that celebrates the turn of the year so thoroughly that they need forty-eight hours to recover. Once upon a time, Eden might have called these carousing Scots her kind of people. Now she finds the very idea exhausting.

Catching her breath once she's spit out onto Princes Street, Eden finds herself seduced for a moment by the postcard quality of it all, looking in both directions at sparkling lights against a rapidly darkening sky. The

Balmoral hotel looms behind her, ostentatious flags flapping in the brisk breeze that's getting up.

Stacks of metal barriers line either side of the street, ready for the men and women in fluorescent jackets to spring into action. This is party central, ground zero for revellers who'll drink too much tonight and not feel the cold, waking up in a new year with bruises and aches they don't entirely remember earning. Well, she'll be having absolutely nothing to do with that.

Her destination isn't far, and she's visited often enough to walk there with only a cursory glance at the app on her phone to make sure she doesn't set off in entirely the wrong direction. Eden rarely does, being the lucky owner of an almost flawless inner compass. Maybe it comes from moving around so often, but usually within an hour of landing somewhere new, she gets her bearings as quickly as any local. Geography makes sense in a way that few other things do.

Especially relationships.

Running a pub isn't much in the way of glamour; in fact, it's bloody hard work and a lot of smiling at people she'd sooner were drinking somewhere else. Trouble is, she's good at it. So good, in fact, that the brewery she works for, out of nowhere, suggested she go and run their newest acquisition: a tourist-trap pub in the old and spooky end of Edinburgh. Not that she can wrap her head around whether to agree or not just yet.

When she's in the mood, she'll joke that her pub-running skills come from having a father who spent more time propping up the bar than being at home with his only child. It only got worse once her mum passed, leaving him more sorrows to drown. The real reason, though, is somewhere between fending off loneliness by being surrounded by people and needing a physical enough job to wear herself out. Sleep doesn't come easy to her, and the late hours to cash up and lock up have always suited her.

Which makes her a disaster as a girlfriend. At least with the nine-to-five power-lesbian types, the ones that just so happen to be her kryptonite. It's charming at first, how they like to come into the bar and hang out for that steady stream of free drinks, monopolising her attention and pissing off the regulars. Then there are the evenings they want to go elsewhere, whether it's their mother's for dinner or the opera, and Eden has to explain that she can't just take every work night off. It rarely goes well.

Still, this trip is going to be her sorbet, her palate cleanser. Usually she would have ignored a good friend's Facebook invite to a Hogmanay party, especially one four hours away by train. Once she'd Googled what the hell Hogmanay was—other than a particularly creative take on spelling mahogany—the prospect of a friendly gathering to toast the midnight "Bells" with whisky, good company, and song sounded absolutely perfect.

She's always surprised by how small and distant Edinburgh Castle looks, even lit up in its festive glory. The fireworks will launch here in a few hours, not that Eden is planning to be sober enough to see them. It looms a bit closer as she crosses the bridge with its wide-angle view over the glass roof of the train station.

Eden finds herself cutting across the Royal Mile. Cobbles test the grip on her biker boots, well-loved and worn-in though they are.

Ticking off the landmarks as she goes keeps Eden on the right path until she hits university terrain. There's a subtle shift in the type of shops, the style of cafes, and it means it's not far now. Samuel is one of her oldest friends, raised on the same estate in Peckham.

Showing up at Samuel's, she's greeted by his wife, Hamako. The flat is huge, but warm and bright in a way that makes Eden think of a more welcoming art gallery. Hamako is shorter, barely up to Eden's shoulder, but her hugs are rib-cracking in their intensity. Samuel shows up with a dishtowel tossed over his shoulder, faded T-shirt sporting the crest of his beloved Chelsea, spattered with whatever he's been cooking.

"My prodigal sister returns," he says, tugging on her braids like the big brother she's always sort of wished he would be. "And you didn't show up empty-handed for once."

She hands him the overpriced bottle of Scotch and smacks him on the arm. "Are we starting on shots this soon, or are we going to pretend to have self-control?"

"Ah, none for me," he says, with a furtive look at his wife. "Someone made me promise to stay off the booze for as long as she has to."

"You're hosting New Year, in Scotland, sober?" Eden can feel the realization creeping up on her, like an ice cream headache, only at the back of her skull. "Wait, has to? You're pregnant?" She asks Hamako, whose beaming smile is answer enough. That sets off another round of hugs.

"So save your drink for now," Samuel says, reaching for a jug in the centre of the kitchen table. The deep red liquid splashes against the side, the scent of hibiscus tickling Eden's nose as the ice rattles. "And have some bissap with me. They don't serve this in your old-man pub, do they?"

"No, but I can buy it in bottles from the shop by my flat. I should have brought you some."

"We have some stores here now. The little things, right? I remember my dad bringing me this sobolo back every summer. It was better than Christmas, finding each little bottle hidden in his luggage." Eden smiles when he uses the Ghanaian word for it this time. It was sweet of him to defer to her in the first place.

"So, baby makes three? Your parents must be thrilled."

"Like you wouldn't believe," Hamako says. Before they can get into particulars, the doorbell is ringing again.

"Now as for you," Samuel says as Eden finishes her drink. Her father would have added more ginger to his, and probably a large splash of rum. "…There's someone I want you to meet tonight."

"No fix ups," she warns him. "Single and ready to mingle, yeah. But no more than interesting conversation and maybe a good old-fashioned singsong. I don't need complications if I do move here."

"That would be wild, if you ended up living down the street or something."

"Don't think it means free babysitting, before you get your hopes up."

The next couple of hours blur into a mêlée of introductions, a few familiar faces that Eden just about scrambles up the names for, and some delicious food that banishes lingering memories of train snacks seemingly made of cardboard. Eden has to separate herself from the sushi platters before it gets embarrassing, but every other arriving guest has brought something else to tempt her. She almost draws the line at haggis, but when it's presented on an oatcake, Eden is too polite to turn it down. Like lightly spiced mince in the end, perfectly fine as long as she doesn't think about it for too long. As Scottish delicacies go, Eden is definitely a bigger fan of their bottled stuff.

"Are you and the Bruichladdich exclusive, or can anyone have a drink?"

The accent wraps around the soft 'ch's like only a native can, and Eden turns around to find a tall redhead waving an empty glass gently in one hand.

"It's more of a trial basis, since I got separated from the Lagavulin. You a Scotch drinker by choice, or does it just come naturally up here?"

As opening lines go, Eden could do better. She's definitely trying not to stare. That red hair is eye catching, there's no denying it. It's that brassy Hollywood red, too, not the traditional Celtic ginger. Pale skin with that is a given, but when your family are from Senegal, most people are pale by comparison. Next to Eden's skinny jeans, with their strategically placed rips, her company has opted for the classic little black dress.

"Well, they start us on milk, but it's right onto Famous Grouse after that." Eden unscrews the cap, gesturing for the glass to be brought closer. "It's not Scotch in this company though. Just whisky. You're a friend of Samuel's?"

"We go way back. What about you, bride or groom's side?"

She takes a long sip from the glass, and Eden instinctively offers the bottle for a refill.

"Oh, I wasn't at the wedding."

"No, I would have remembered you," Eden points out, as though it's obvious. "And I didn't get your name yet."

"No, I don't suppose you did." She finishes her drink, and Eden thinks she might actually walk off without telling. That would be a record, in a new low sort of way. "Simone. Nice to meet you."

Simone actually offers her hand, formal as you like. It's all Eden can do not to bow when she shakes it.

"Pleasure."

And oh, Simone actually blushes. Like her inner compass, Eden's gaydar has rarely let her down. Even three drinks in when it's more hope than science. "Oh, and I'm Hanako's friend. Well, I'm also their vet, but we had some friends in common."

"Eden!" Samuel is grabbing at her elbow, and the last thing she wants is an interruption. Except she did say no more women, especially not here in the city where her new life could begin. Through gritted teeth, she tells herself that Samuel is actually doing her a favour.

"What, man? I'm playing nice, I promise."

"What? Oh, Simone's good people, it's not about that." She loves him for how his sharp London vowels still come through on the 'a' sounds. "Listen, we're gonna announce to the party when everyone's here, but I wanted to ask you first. You up for godmother? There'll be a bit of church, and I know that's not your scene no more, but you know."

"Godmother?" Eden's stomach does a funny flip. She's not that friend, never has been. Nobody asks her to be bridesmaid, to come stand witness. That's always been fine, or so she told herself. But the fact of being asked has turned that upside down. Suddenly, she can't think of many things she wants more.

"One condition," she says.

"What's that?" Samuel narrows his eyes, and they're the calm in the middle of the party's growing storm. Even with huge rooms, it's starting to feel crowded.

"You let me show the child a decent football team, and they can decide for themselves."

He laughs, pulling Eden into an easy hug. His stained shirt has been swapped for a button-down in light blue, and Hamako bustles into the kitchen with some empty plates, drafting them both into action whether Eden is hosting or not.

"Who did you want me to meet?" she asks when they're loading up new plates with fancy snacks. "Before, you said there was someone."

"You already met her," Samuel answers with a grin. "That girl I pulled you away from, 'Mako says she bats for your side. Don't say I'm not good to you, girl."

"We were talking about whisky. Don't write our wedding invitations just yet."

"Still, not bad for a white girl, eh?"

"You just have good taste, Sam," Hamako reminds him, urging them out of the kitchen and back into the throng. "Don't you mess my girl Simone around now, Eden. I know you're a heartbreaker when it suits you."

Eden nods in acknowledgment, carrying trays that seem destined to spill everywhere. But she makes the rounds with the food, a fair chunk of which she helps herself to in order to soak up the early drinking. The whole time she keeps an eye out for that red hair. Nothing, not even on the stairs, which is the official backup location for the people who didn't manage to colonise the kitchen.

Still, it's a good party. Samuel and Hamako have a lot of friends, a ready-made network that seems ready and willing to draw in anyone it encounters. It might be easier here—no spending an hour on the Tube every time Eden wants to see her friends. She can see herself playing Frisbee on the Meadows with those nice guys who work with Samuel at the university, or getting brunch with Hamako and her Pilates buddies, maybe. It all seems within touching distance, if she just makes the decision to go for it.

Every new person she talks to, from the nonbinary geophysicist who's trying to explain magnetic fields with cans of cider, to the butch sculptor who works out of Hamako's art studios, seems like an invitation to stay here, to give it a shot. Still Eden can't convince herself, because it's all too good to be true. The only time she's felt those nagging doubts slip away so far was when... Well, that doesn't mean anything.

Because she. Is. Not. Looking.

Not for Simone, who seems to have vanished from whichever room Eden walks into. She takes to staking out the table full of drinks eventually, keeping an eye on the Bruichladdich in case it has a magnetic effect on redheads. The evening wears on, and although she's pleasantly buzzed, Eden feels adrift in this place full of relative strangers. She's good at belonging, sometimes, but only ever for a little while.

There's no point seeking out anyone to say good-bye. Not her style. Instead, she unearths her jacket from the bedroom, the one non-party zone, and slips out the front door to tackle the stone steps of the old tenement building, one foot in front of the other.

"Oh!" A familiar voice echoes in the space. The only other sounds comes from competing sets of muffled music and voices, more than one party going on behind closed doors. "You're leaving?"

"I have a room booked," Eden starts to explain. "I should have checked in before I got here, really."

Simone comes past her, her lightly spiced perfume wrapped up in the chill she brings from outside. Her black dress and most of those appealing legs are covered by the kind of puffy coat Eden was craving earlier. Locals always dress better for the weather.

"But you will come back?"

Eden shrugs. With a glance at Simone's green eyes, she's starting to feel that pull again, that creeping certainty that there's something here for her. It would be beyond stupid to upend her life over a woman. Again.

"Might do."

"Well, why don't I come with you? I'm guessing you don't know the city that well? Then we can come back together. And you can help me ward off my ex, who isn't really taking the hint after nearly a year apart."

"Are they giving you trouble?" A pronoun hedge, because if Eden's going to make a fool of herself, she's at least going to bark up the right tree.

"Nah, he's just a bit pathetic about it still." It's damning in that brisk accent, and Eden almost feels sorry for the guy. Only she's feeling sorrier for herself if that dating-men thing turns out to be exclusive. Then again, why would Samuel be so insistent they meet? "He just can't accept that I'm also attracted to women…"

Simone tugs at the sleeve of her coat, adorably self-conscious. "Of course it's all about his ego and not what might actually make me happy."

The fact that Eden manages merely a dignified nod is the best feat of self-control she's ever managed. Inside, she's turning a cartwheel, starting a wave, and ready for a full-on Meg Ryan-style chorus of "yes, yes, yes!"

So much for not being interested in anyone new.

They walk downstairs in tandem, Simone's heels clicking in time with the jangling of the buckles on Eden's boots. When they open the heavy door downstairs, the drizzling rain has finally stopped, and they step out into a cool, crisp Edinburgh night. The turn of the year is less than an hour away, and Eden finds herself wishing time could slow down just a little. Just to see if this might be something.

"Do you smoke?" She blurts out the question that's been on her mind since Simone caught her on the stairs.

"What? No, no." Simone shakes her head in apparent disgust, and Eden's glad in that moment that she gave up ten years ago. "You don't…?"

"No, I just wondered if that's why you popped out."

"Ah, no. Duty calls, I'm afraid."

"Vets work on New Year's Eve?" Eden is surprised, and Simone isn't exactly dressed for vaccinating hamsters.

"Just a favour for one of my regulars. She lives over there." Simone points to the lower buildings across the street. "You know how the old dears are with their wee dogs. Nothing to worry about, but I wanted to look in on the pup and put her mind at rest. Of course, you have to stay for tea and a biscuit, or it's a great personal insult."

"That's kind of you. Most people when they're off the clock, they just switch off. I know I do."

"What is it you switch off from? I didn't ask, before." Simone shoves one hand in her pocket and then hesitates for a moment before linking the other arm with Eden's own. They draw together at that, fending off the cold a little.

"Nothing exciting," Eden says. "I run a pub, actually. In London."

"Just here for the festivities, then?" It might be fervent imagining, but Eden could swear she hears disappointment.

"In theory. I've got a job offer for a bar here in town though. It would be a big upheaval, but there's nothing keeping me down South, not really."

"London's hard to give up," Simone replies, with a sideways glance. "I trained in Glasgow, where I'm from, and moved down there after uni. Three years, I lasted. Properly chewed me up and spat me out, running home to my mammy."

"Really?" Eden raises an eyebrow in surprise.

"Not really." Simone stifles a laugh. "I liked it fine; I just got offered a place here with a practice I could buy into, become a partner. And where does any Glaswegian go to start fresh? Edinburgh, of course. Still, I suppose I've put down my roots."

"Roots, yeah." Eden bites her lower lip. "I keep meaning to get some of those. Closest I've come is keeping the same flat for six years. Anyway, this is me."

The modest hotel is a chain now; another family guest house bought out and turned into an identikit set of rooms with sterile-looking beds and vending machines in the hall. The charge for tonight is more like a five-star suite, but Eden's days of crashing on friend's couches are long behind her, and her lower back especially.

"Well, let's get you checked in. You can come and go as you please then." Simone has that jolly-hockey-sticks head-girl quality about her, all can-do attitude and apple cheeks. It was irritating in the girls she boarded with at school, but switched up into a Scottish accent and combined with killer legs, Eden has to concede that she's charmed.

Charmed enough that she isn't even too surprised when the hotel has lost her booking. She knows the look from the clerk in an instant. No special measures or little favours are going to be produced tonight. He's seen the colour of her skin and the woman on her arm, and he's not inclined to do much beyond an insincere apology and a cursory glance at the email she printed out.

"Well, this is awkward." Eden sighs as she gets a promise of a full refund and a number to call when the world blinks back to life properly on the second of January.

"I dunno, you're pretty cute for a temporarily homeless urchin," Simone tells her.

Standing on the steps of the hotel that's screwed her over, Eden doesn't see the first kiss coming. She likes to think she adjusts with a certain level of smooth, returning the sweet pressure with her own lips.

"Was that okay?" Simone asks when she pulls back, the brief seconds of her mouth against Eden's nowhere near long enough.

"Yeah," is the only eloquent response. "Now we should get back to the party and make sure nobody's spilling drinks on the couch. Since I'm going to have to sleep there and all."

"Sure, good plan." Simone starts down the steps, this time holding out her hand for Eden to take. "Or, hear me out... I also have a flat."

"You do?" Eden feels that little thrill go up her spine. There's no harm in a one-night stand, surely? Very welcome to the neighbourhood. Or at least welcome to the new year, if they take their time about it. "I suppose you would have to live somewhere, yeah."

"Mmm, just a few streets from here." Simone gestures to the west. "And I don't mean to brag, but there's a killer view of the castle. You know, if you wanted fireworks?"

"Hard not to be convinced by a girl promising you fireworks." This time, Eden initiates the kiss, and she makes damn sure it's not a quick one. Simone's lips part, granting her access, and they're lost in the kiss when a car speeds past, horn beeping and vague shouts of encouragement being yelled drunkenly from the windows. Eden spares a brief thought to hope at least the driver is sober.

"Mmm," is Simone's informed response. They're still holding hands, which seems oddly sweet. With a gentle tug, she's leading the way again, and they walk at that giddy pace between even steps and skipping. Every few yards, they stumble or stop, taking turns to try out another kiss. Each time a little deeper, a little more adventurous. It's hard to get a real hold of Simone in her slippery coat, but Eden gives it a good try regardless, hands starting to wander of their own volition.

"I suppose you'll think all Edinburgh girls are easy now," Simone says as they push open the front door of her building, so similar to Samuel and Hamako's. "Does that make you more inclined to move here, at least?"

"It doesn't hurt, admittedly."

They have to make it all the way to the top floor, and even though she considers herself fit, Eden feels the rake of the stairs in her calves from halfway up. These buildings are not for the fainthearted. Their improvised waltz of a few jumbled steps before stopping to kiss each other again makes for slow progress, and one accidental bump against a random neighbour's door gets them an elderly woman peeking out with the chain still on the door, tutting at their behaviour. It only serves to make them laugh, taking the last flight of stairs at a quicker, slightly more breathless pace.

It seems like a perfectly nice apartment, from the little Eden sees between the front door and whichever room they stumble into. Living room, she concludes, once their jackets are off and Simone pulls her down onto a ridiculously comfortable couch. Shoes are kicked in one direction, Eden's boots in entirely another.

"You can have the tour later," Simone promises, as both of their phones start to beep with a flurry of texts. The inevitable 'trying to beat the network crash' from friends and family who just can't wait. Eden moves in to kiss Simone again, letting her hands roam over that little black dress now it's on display again, but Simone stays sitting up, pressing a finger over Eden's lips. She kisses that instead, pouting just a little.

"Watch," Simone says, turning towards the huge windows that take up most of one wall. The curtains are pulled back, and the panoramic view of the city is so stunning that Eden finds herself standing to take it in better.

"Holy—"

"Makes all those stairs worth it," Simone says, standing beside Eden and wrapping an arm around her waist, managing to touch bare skin beneath her jumper and base layer. "And you know, less time in the gym."

There's a party somewhere nearby, faded sounds floating through the one small window that's partially open. Gunpowder in the air, mingling with the old-fashioned smell of coal fires. Then the first *bong* of Big Ben sounds, suffocated by walls and windows, but distinctive all the same. Four hundred miles away, a sound she never listens out for at home, but hearing it through some stranger's television, it sounds like Eden's own heartbeat.

That's why the first of the fireworks catch her off guard. The castle is lit up for the occasion anyway, just like she saw it from the bridge earlier. Vibrant blue and purple and white streaks pepper the impossibly dark sky, smoke starting to billow like clouds.

She turns to Simone, watching the new colours play out across her face. Genuinely lost in an innocent kind of wonder at the display, she squeezes absently at Eden's hip. They can pause, for a few minutes. Watch something wonderful, a sight that only really comes round like this once a year. No harm in letting go of the past year's mistakes, letting the new year wash over them both.

When the rate of explosions and screaming rockets finally begins to slow, Eden holds her breath. She doesn't have to wait long, because once Simone is freed from her reverie, they're on the move again. That dress turns out to have a bloody stubborn zip, but Eden is persistent enough to have it falling to the floor before they hit the bedroom. She's less graceful at yanking her tops up over her head, letting her braids rattle against her back as they fall back into place.

"Your hair is gorgeous," Simone says as she occupies herself unbuttoning Eden's jeans. "I just thought I'd mention that." Then she's brushing some errant braids back over Eden's shoulder and kissing the bare skin that's exposed in their place.

Happy New Year, indeed.

Morning is a brief flicker of daylight, a dash to the bathroom and water drunk straight from the tap, before crawling back under luxurious navy-blue sheets and passing out until well after lunch. When Eden opens her eyes again, tentatively feeling out the extent of her hangover, she's pleased to find that other than raging thirst and the need to stretch some tight muscles, she's feeling something close to utterly fine.

"Afternoon, sleepyhead," Simone says from the doorway. She's wearing one of those silky robes, a deep blue to almost match the bedding, and it lands pleasantly mid-thigh, only the loosest of knots holding the damn thing closed. She comes bearing mugs of something steaming, and that's all the encouragement Eden needs to get herself upright against the cloudlike pillows.

"I might have been up earlier," Eden says, accepting the coffee. No instant muck, something rich and strong. "But someone insisted on wearing me out."

"Well, start the year as you mean to go on, and all that?" Simone sits on Eden's side of the bed, casting a hungry glance over her still-naked form. They sip at their coffee in companionable silence. "Speaking of which, I have an odd request."

Eden tilts her head. This is not a woman who's shy about asking for what she wants. Not in bed, anyway.

"I don't know what your plans are; you might have somewhere to be. But if you are leaving now, or soon, can you hold on for a second at the door?"

"I can go if you want me to?"

"No, I don't want that. I was going to ask if you wanted to go for some kind of late lunch, actually. But if you weren't coming back here, I'd just need a tiny favour before you go."

"Well, ask me anyway and maybe that will answer when I do it."

"It's silly, but once you leave, if you could knock on the door, and then step back in again when I open it?"

Eden swallows her coffee too fast. "Wait, what now?"

Simone groans, flopping back on the bed and still cradling her mug over her lap. "It's absolutely daft. I can't believe I'm asking. It's just we got in right before midnight, right? And there's this whole thing. I haven't thought about it in years, I'm not usually home to worry about it... What I'm asking is will you be my first foot?"

"First foot is, what? The first person to step across the threshold?"

"Exactly."

"I guess so? It's not a big thing to ask, really. Of course I can. I'd do it now, but I might scare your neighbours." Eden has a change of clothes—two, in fact, stashed in her backpack. She could get dressed right now and look willing, but she's curious as to why Simone is blushing about some old wives' superstition.

"It's not a big deal. In fact, I don't think it's supposed to count if you're in the house and go out, just to come back in. Only my granny always said the person who's your first foot, your qualtagh, sets your luck for the rest of the year."

"I'm not sure I'd be good luck." Eden squirms a little under the responsibility, preferring to concentrate on where Simone's dressing gown has fallen open.

"Are you kidding? You're the best luck I've had in a year."

That's enough to make Eden set her coffee aside. So much for not getting into anything. She's giddy already, and it's only getting worse with every awkward smile that Simone gives her.

"Well, I'd hate to disappoint your granny." She leans in for a coffee-tinged kiss, before wriggling off the bed and taking custody of the bathroom. A long shower will be in order, but for now Eden reaches for the T-shirt and faded shorts that she brought to sleep in. Quite unnecessarily, as it turns out.

Without another word, she pads along the hall barefoot, opening the front door and stepping out with a hiss onto the freezing stone floor. There's the briefest panic as the door closes itself behind her, that she's just locked herself out from her wallet, her phone, her sensible clothing, all to make a pretty girl smile some more. Luckily—there's that word again—Simone doesn't keep Eden waiting when she turns around and knocks.

"First foot?" she says, in her best serious voice. "I'm supposed to bring your luck, Doctor."

"Oh, 'doctor' now, is it?" Simone teases, opening the door wide. "I don't really get the title from my patients. Well, the parrots sometimes."

It's delightful to be back in the warm, back in Simone's arms. It isn't supposed to be this easy, not this soon, but Eden can see this for what it is now: her luck changing. The sign she didn't realise she was waiting for, telling her whether to stick or twist. With an open return and a few days off still to spend as she pleases, there's no reason not to set up that final interview and nail down a job in Edinburgh. A pub's a pub, after all. It isn't even that far from Simone's flat, not that anything is in a city this compact.

"I was going to offer you first dibs on the shower," Simone says, resting her head against Eden's shoulder as though it was meant to fit there, as though the slightest curve in her collarbone has just been waiting for its complementary person. "But if we shower together, we can go for something fried and unhealthy much sooner."

"Hard to argue with that logic," Eden answers, but she's already caught up in plans for that shower that should last until the water runs cold. She lets Simone go long enough to go and get the water running, taking in a proper view of the flat in weak daylight. Tasteful art on the walls, fresh flowers on the table instead of just discarded keys and mail, though that's in evidence too.

Wandering back into the bedroom, Eden pauses by the window, open just a crack. From the street outside she hears laughter, people shouting "Happy New Year" across the quiet road with its parked cars. Maybe they're friends and neighbours, or maybe just friendly strangers still inebriated from the night before.

Well, if this is the level of hospitality around these parts, then Eden thinks Edinburgh could make for the perfect home city after all.

"Are you coming?" Simone calls from the bathroom. The steam is already drifting out into the hall as Eden approaches.

"Yes!" Eden replies. "Yes, I am."

Paula Gets a Pony Ranch

BY PATRICIA PENN

December 22nd

WELL, HOME, SWEET HOME. IT wouldn't be Germany if it didn't start
with a clogged autobahn. Or maybe some gods out there just wanted to
make extra sure that I had the worst Christmas in a while. Pick one.

Alas, I'm writing this in a quaint little guest room under a sixteenth-
century roof, filled to the brim with mismatching antiques, smelling both
of nostalgia and promise. This is, of course, a misleading impression.
Somewhere else in the house, a twenty-four-year-old called Timo is
receiving the worst parental lecture since he bullied kids in kindergarten,
because he made the grave mistake of antagonizing the woman who holds
his family's future in her hands. Somewhere outside, the butch version of
Audrey Hepburn is mucking the stables. If the roof window wasn't covered
in snow, I could open it and listen for the whinnies of twenty-three beautiful
horses, all of them mine.

Yeah. That last one still freaks me the hell out.

So I was late. I was late because the world sucks, and what's with all
the construction on the A3 anyway? Only satnav saved me in the end,
leading me faithfully to my destination at the ass-end of the Lower Taunus
Mountains. And those non-existing gods snickered, I swear I heard them,
because when I drove down to the Rosenbrock Valley, which holds the
Rosenbrock Ranch, the sun was going down—fervent and majestic,
throwing crimson shadows all across the meadows. An electric fence runs

along the street, all the way down to the ranch building, and the grazing herd perked up curiously at the engine sound. Pitch-black steeds threw up their curly-maned heads, like I'd stepped into a Disney movie.

Unfortunately, that would make me the villain, but heck. Call me Ursula, gimme my eels.

That's sure in accordance with the Staplers' view on me. Tight-knit, hardworking, traditional family, predestined to be the heroes of stories. When I arrived, they spilled out of various annexes to expect me in the yard, four people overall—I knew from the crappy website that the Stapler family was made of a couple and their two sons. Frozen dirt crunched under my heels when I left the car, though miraculously I didn't end up with soaked McQueens. That was pretty much the only good news today.

It was Ulf Stapler who took the lead. He's been in charge of this place for thirty years and he looks the part: beanstalk of a man, haggard from the top down, probably by nature rather than the professional dread he'd recently been suffering. Firm handshake. Broad local accent—the kind of countryside Hessian that sounds like he's decided there's no need for those pesky last syllables that might as well be dropped.

"Good to meet you, Dr. Keller," he greeted me with a shameless lie. "Sorry for your loss, and all. She was a great lady, your aunt."

That why she let this place rot? was what I didn't reply.

Instead, I tried my hand at a lie of my own. "I'm so sorry I have to disrupt your holiday like this." I'm really not. "I only have a small window to make a decision, unfortunately, or I'll have to pay taxes no matter whether I end up liquidating the business or not."

"Better than sitting on our asses underneath the Christmas tree and waitin' for the other shoe to drop," Ulf Stapler drawled, like he almost meant it.

Carola Stapler shouldered in then, virtually stepping into my sight line, like a particularly petite and out-of-breath quarterback. "We are so, so excited to have you here." She was a harried but slender forty-something, with an unruly blonde ponytail and a false smile that looked both manic and exhausting.

This isn't big business. I'm used to Japanese associates sneaking into empty offices to liberate the company secrets, to pseudo-proposal calls for jobs already promised to somebody's cousin. I'm trying to tell myself these people will not know to play that kind of gamble.

But—I dunno—something about Carola Stapler's forced enthusiasm sets me on edge.

The two remaining young men were the sons of the family. If I'd had to pick, I'd have supposed that son number two, name of Yannik, would screw up first, because he was barely eighteen and still lived at home and helped with the farm, as Carola babbled at me when we shook hands. He just glared at me, though, and muttered something under his breath that might have been a greeting, or possibly a Klingon declaration of battle intent.

Son number one, Timo—who I was proudly informed studied to be a vet in Budapest, and only visited for Christmas—gave me a corresponding look that said in a very pleasant way that he'd already decided where to hide my dead body.

"No time like Christmas to ruin people's lives, huh, Dr. Keller?"

Carola gurgled, coughed, and shot Timo a glance that promised slaughter.

So. Here it was. Out in the open. Right off the bat. Awkward.

I imagine there was a much more diplomatic reply available, but then I don't make seventy grand a year because I'm such a terribly likable person.

"No time like Christmas to decide whether I should, anyway," I replied in my gentlest voice.

After that, it took a very short time for everybody to decide that that was enough discomfort to take for the time being; we'd reconvene in the morning. Yannik was entrusted with fetching my suitcase, which resulted in another Klingon grunt. Carola pushed an admittedly delicious spread of bread rolls and some plum schnapps on me, then deposited me in the guest room. She probably breathed a sigh of relief the moment the door fell shut behind her.

Is this why you gave the ranch to me instead of your real daughters, Auntie Elsie? Because you know I won't mess around?

Susie doesn't have the nerves for a stare-down with an adolescent wannabe alpha male. Christina would melt, and try and make everyone happy, but lose everybody's money. Me, though, you knew I'd have the guts to shut this place down.

You always said I had no heart.

December 23rd

Usually I would have spent today at the Frankfurt office. I can see the Römer from up there, through the glass wall, seventeen floors below. The Christmas fair closed business for the year yesterday, so tiny, ant-like workers would have been busy packing up all across the plaza. People mentally prepare themselves for gifts and spritz biscuits on the 23rd, which means no phone calls, so I could be immersing myself in the year-end accounts closing right this minute. The Staplers, on the other hand, would have probably been busy wrapping those gifts. Instead, they had to give me the grand tour.

First, they pacified me with a really great breakfast. I'm not beyond admitting that it worked, too, considering those cooked eggs had still rested under the resident hens an hour prior and the local sausages make angels sing. Plus, Christmas cookies—they've got those *Bethmännchen*, that Frankfurt Christmas pastry made of marzipan and rosewater. Still, never mind that everybody referred to their operating resources as "our ponies," or Carola's continuing fake smiles as she assured me of how much "the local refugee children" profited from healing riding lessons. It was still a sales event, a pitch. Naturally, the Staplers wanted to keep their home and jobs.

So, Auntie. Facts. For whatever tea leaves you'd smoked, you bought this place almost exactly a decade ago, in the summer of 2008. Forgot all about it in no time, I'm sure, when you were distracted by the next shiny thing that crossed your path—some community arts project for the homeless, or some scantily clad belly dance instructor. But it was not before throwing a generous amount of cash at the place without any thought on what should be done with it.

The only reason the ranch had been on the market in the first place was the fact that it was marinating in the red, after all, so you probably figured that'd cure all ailments, Keynes style. Thing is, while Ulf Stapler undoubtedly knew how to handle a horse, he made for a crap custodian.

With no proper business plan or anything resembling a strategy in evidence, the money might as well have been fed to the resident dogs. The proud breeding days of the Rosenbrock Friesians ended with the loss of the prized stallion to a broken femur. Apparently, his name had been

Agamemnon, and he used to bless the ladies with Olympic competitors by the dozen.

You, dear Auntie, had unfortunately already lost interest in your project when he moved on to the Elysian Fields. You'd stopped answering the Staplers' calls. Since they knew a hard business evaluation would probably result in a shutdown, they didn't try so hard anyway. They proceeded to run their shabby little riding school, and supplemented the aging purebreds with cheap teaching horses. Sucks to work around an incompetent boss.

That's not how the Staplers tried to sell it.

Friesians are currently having their big break in dressage, I was informed. I looked it up, and it's even true. Lots of new business opportunities looming on the horizon, if only the breeding got going again.

A part of the grazing land had been repurposed to grow hay, an example of the Staplers' stellar grasp on cost efficiency—whatever dictionary had supplied them with that term. Allegedly, all that ails these poor, misunderstood businesspeople is the need for a lot more money, and they'll proceed to both make a profit and a better world. If they think I'll risk my reputation by signing a loan application on that logic, they're sorely mistaking me for, well…you.

"And then, of course, there's Olga," Ulf said as we were standing at the fence and admiring the majestic black beasts—probably an attempt to appeal to my romantic side.

I caught a glimpse of Carola shaking her head at him in alarm, though when I turned, she was the picture of gravity.

"Who's Olga?" I asked.

"Our horse trainer," Ulf said. He hesitated, side-eying his wife, then apparently decided that it was too late to abort. "Olga. Olga Nikiforow. We're lucky to have her. She teaches, too, at the international level. She brings in plenty of business."

Carola changed gears, now that the conversation was happening. "Sometimes professional riders come in for a week or two, stay at the inn over in Limbach, just so they can work with her," she supplied.

"Last year we had Karla Messner over," Ulf said. When I had no particular reaction to that name, he added helpfully, "She won silver at Olympic equestrian in 2012. Needed help to work out some kinks with a new pony of hers."

I waited.

"She ain't here, though, Olga," he added in a very determined voice. "She went home for Christmas. To see family. Won't be back for days. Weeks."

"She's from Bucharest," Carola finished brightly, as if Romanian immigrants come with a particular equestrian qualification of which I'm unaware.

They left me alone for a bit then, and yeah, when they were gone, I leaned on the gate and let myself enjoy the horses. They *are* beautiful, is the thing. They're astonishing. The Friesians have gleaming black coats, all the more pronounced by the contrast of the surrounding patches of snow. They almost seem to reflect light, and you can see firm muscles playing underneath.

They have these feathery strands of hair on the back of their legs, like dainty little accessories. And you can see how curious and intelligent they are. They remind me of the riding lessons I took as a child. I thought horses were magical then. I thought there was no better place to be but in a saddle. I remember my mother standing at the sidelines during lessons and looking on with so much pride, just days before the accident.

A short one—a mare, I think, a yearling going by her slenderness—broke from the herd when she noticed my attention, showing herself off with a cheerful set of bucks. Then she trotted over and stuck her nose out at me.

"Didn't think to bring you any treats," I muttered, presenting my palms to her so that she could investigate. "I'm sorry."

As I petted her head, she leaned closer, neck relaxing, eyes half shut, blissed out.

I'd loved horses, once.

I'd like to think that's the real reason you gave me the farm, Auntie.

Not sure if you even knew that, though.

Ah well. At least their filing system is sufficiently…

Scratch that. To hell with sarcasm! Their filing system is amazing. I love their filing system. I want to heart it and squeeze it and carry it around in my pocket.

I've written so many articles and corporate blog posts on what makes competent business management, I've honestly lost count. So it's a really good feeling to step into a back office that could serve as a best-practice illustration in one of them.

Despite her abysmal acting skills, it turns out Carola and I are practically soulmates of record keeping.

Who knew that tiny woman with the dirty jeans and straw on her sweater had it in her?

"Organization is the key to a successful business," she said eagerly. "I try to solve all possible problems before they arise."

"I've often said that myself!" I said.

I mean, I've published a book on it and all.

We spent a good half hour talking tech, on what software she uses and how she manages the budgeting requirements. Or maybe I talked and she listened with rapture, but good enough.

The thing is just this. I mean, Carola is responsible for everything to do with the back office: the finances, the taxes, the organization, everything. And the whole thing is spotless. Literally spotless—there's no smear of dust, no sign of wear in that entire office. How can she have such a firm grasp on the business side of things but at the same time run this enterprise into the ground like that? Where's the flaw? What's the secret?

Eh, I'm gonna know soon enough. I've got seventy-two empty hours of Christmas cheer in front of me. Enough time to read through the financial records back to when the main building was built during the times of Karl the Great. I'll figure it out.

December 24th

Ah, screw it.

Thanks to you, Auntie, I can't hide from the holidays this year. I've got to intrude on a mysteriously intact family that's bound to deserve something better. And I get to feel bitter. Want to venture a guess as to why feeling like an intruder in another family poses such a trigger for me, huh? Of course not; you're dead. And the fact that I felt like a parasite at your dinner table because I never was flighty and happy enough to fit in always went over your head anyway.

I remember my first Christmas with you, uncomfortably perched on the couch, while you and Susie and Chrissie invented a new holiday tradition of dancing a conga line around the tree. Remember the last Christmas with Mom and Dad, too, how Mom went "Shush, Santa is coming and bringing the presents" although she knew I'd figured out long since that Santa was Dad. Their joy was in playing pretend, not in lying.

I spent the day getting started on the finances, working the books. Then, when it got dark, I made the mistake of deciding to go and stretch my legs.

Sure, I'm quite aware of the date, but all that domesticity is still foreign enough to me that I startled a little when I found the farmstead covered in Christmas lights. They illuminated the entire yard in dim red shadows. The scene, strangely, didn't remind me of the ominously lit endgame scene of a first-person shooter, as it rightfully should have. It just looked a little bit romantic and warm.

Burying my hands in the pockets of my coat, I came to a halt when I looked through the window to the Staplers' illuminated living room like frigging Oliver Twist. They had a huge Christmas tree, decorated entirely in homemade-looking straw stars, plus thin strands of silver tinsel. Maybe the exchange of presents had already commenced, or it would follow after the meal, because the family was currently gathered at the table. Unlike Mom and Dad, who'd never done any special food for Christmas Eve, or Auntie, who'd take us out to restaurants, they seemed to make a big deal out of it. Something out of the oven, it looked like—maybe some kind of braised meat.

I could see Yannik's face, and he was not muttering in Klingon; he seemed to be laughing so hard at something his brother had said that it gave him a hiccup, making him look impossible young. Ulf entered the room carrying a tray, and Carola got up to help him set down the food. She bumped her shoulder against his. The smile she threw him was neither manic nor forced; it just was.

What was it, Auntie, huh?

You didn't even tell me you were sick. I only heard about it when the notary called about opening your will. I asked both Christina and Susie why they'd never let me know, and from the way I could practically hear them shuffle their feet through the phone, I assume they acted under your orders.

Goddammit.

I suppose I shouldn't even be surprised. You might have claimed to love me, but you never acted the part. And hell, I could respect that. You'd tell me I'd been the one who didn't make an effort to stay part of the family once you'd fulfilled your legal requirements and paid my college fees. You'd be right, too. I'd always stayed the orphan charity case, never transformed into a real daughter, and that's both on you and me, maybe even more on me, since accountability has never been your strongest suit. You'd have done better inheriting a niece who'd accompany you to yoga retreats and make plans to climb the Kilimanjaro.

But still, why give me anything, then? Why spend a year dying slowly and never saying good-bye, and then give me a *horse ranch?*

A horse ranch.

Fifteen Friesians, eight other breeds, five employees, zero income.

Maybe it's just that seeing my name and the words "pony farm" in the same sentence cracked you up.

That makes as much sense as anything.

I'll try and use the silent, holy night to read through the next batch of tax records.

I did not read through the next batch of tax records.

It was too depressing to sit in my little room under the roof when I didn't even have a bottle of red, or a delivery service open on Christmas Eve—not this far out. So I went out again, wrapped in coat and scarf, with a vague plan to maybe hop in the car and take a trip to Wiesbaden or Frankfurt. I'd find an open bar there, drink something Christmas-y with cinnamon and sugar and appropriate amounts of alcohol. Hell, there'd be a church concert somewhere; they're short enough on real believers to let the atheists attend, too.

Surely the Staplers were still up given the time and the fact that the Christmas lights were still on. I avoided looking at the illuminated windows, though, which was how I noticed somebody had turned on the light in the stables. I could make out a whinny, and what sounded like hooves banging against wood. Since the herd lives outdoors all year round and the handful of boxes are supposedly only put to use on special occasions, that got my curiosity piqued enough for a detour. I mean, that was one of my assets whinnying in there.

The gate creaked ominously when I pushed it open, and I was hit by the dry scent of hay and a sharp note of saddle oil. An aisle led past a handful of comfortable but empty boxes on each side. The first two on the left held cleaning supplies, and the last contained a horse that was snorting frantically, marching around in circles. A woman was leaning on the chest-high wooden door, chin propped on her hands, looking in. One of the stable hands. I'd seen her around, although we hadn't been introduced. And yeah—she was hot, all right? There was no way not to notice her—Hepburn in *Robin and Marian* through and through, slender features and all, except for even shorter dark hair and, oh, the tattoos. She wore a short black shirt with work jeans; her arms were covered in dragons and skulls all the way down to the back of her hands. No hope to ever again be hired for a desk job. But boy, that ass. Nobody has a right to have an ass like that. She was Audrey Hepburn, if she'd starred in James Dean movies. *Rebel Without A Cause*, butch style.

She looked up when I came in, though turned toward the horse again when I stepped up to her for a glance of my own. She never took her elbows off the gate.

"What's wrong with her?" I asked when I laid eyes on another girl I'd seen around before —a stocky mare with a dark grey mane, pacing, emanating the occasional sound of discomfort.

Hepburn gave me an appraising glance. Maybe I haven't gotten laid in too long, but it was intense enough and she stood close enough to make me shudder. Especially since a woman can't ping on a gaydar any louder.

"She's having a baby," she said, calmly.

I gave her an alarmed look.

She chuckled.

"Not now," she said. While she spoke with the fluency of somebody who'd grown up in these parts, she retained a soft, faint accent, something Eastern European. "At least I doubt it. She got restless, so I brought her in, and she's sweating a bit, but I think it's false labor. She hasn't really been waxing, so it'll probably be another week or two. We don't know when exactly she conceived. It's hard to tell."

"Uh, wouldn't it be better for her to stay with her buddies?"

She shook her head, eyes on the mare that had retreated into the back of the box skittishly when I showed up, although now was back to pacing, swishing her tail and kicking her hooves. "You'd think so, but they didn't really hit it off. We only got her in September, see. Our other German Riding Pony, Zsa Zsa, got early-onset arthrosis. Didn't know Heidi was preggers then—got to have been a grazing accident at her old stable that nobody knew of. So she keeps getting fatter and we're thinking, what the fuck, but really we're busy trying to figure out how to get her to be friends with the others. She's the only white. Horses don't like it when someone looks funny. It didn't go over well."

Something told me that that explanation constituted a particularly long speech for this woman, who looked like she told people to go fuck themselves on the regular. She smelled faintly of cigars and as though she'd spilled beer on her shirt not too long ago.

She turned and held out her hand. It was accompanied by another gaze up and down my body, this one definitely very appreciative.

"Nicky," she said. "I help out here sometimes."

"Paula." I shook her hand as my own gaze trailed down her chest, past more tattoos peeking out of her neckline, which a voice in my head insisted was nowhere near low enough.

She caught my eyes with hers. A slow smile curled around the corner of her mouth. She'd seen.

Not that I'd tried to be subtle.

"I know," she drawled, with an obvious awareness of what was happening, and leaned against the door to focus all her attention on me.

Very, very brown eyes.

Suddenly, it was quite easy to shove aside my Christmas woes.

"Why aren't you asking me yet if I'll shut down this place?" I asked, because it wasn't possible that she didn't know what I was here to do. Also, I'm a provocative kind of gal, and she made me bristle, in quite the welcome, heated, challenging way.

The corner of her mouth twitched again.

"Thought about it," she granted. "Suddenly got distracted, though."

"By what, for example?" Now I was smirking, folding my arms in front of my chest.

"By what's hidden underneath that coat."

Oh, this was not a woman who fucked around when she found something she desired.

Being so clearly and so openly *wanted* has always done things to me—for completely Freudian reasons, I'm sure. Though thanks but no thanks, Auntie; I refuse to discuss you and sex in one breath.

Nicky's voice had become pleasantly husky. I really expected her to just go for it when she rose to step past me. She paused, close enough for me to feel her breath on the side of my neck. Still I tensed, though, appreciating the game for what it was—daring her, even though this was a stable with a whimpering mare, not the lesbian brothel in Cologne I'll maintain I've never visited, and nobody can prove anything different.

Then Nicky raised her head, distracted by something behind me, and a moment later I heard it myself—heavy boots on the yard, the creek of the gate.

"Yannik? That you?" Ulf Stapler.

Nicky gave me a last, heated glance. "Just me! I brought Heidi in!" She neatly stepped aside and made her way to the door. "Doubt she'll be foaling tonight, though. Shame. No baby Jesus for us this year."

A moment later, she was gone, slipping out to talk to her boss, and I looked past her with a lot of feelings, half of them really, really welcome, but the others somewhat confused.

Why wouldn't she want to be seen with me by her boss? Sure, these people thought my PhD was in heinousness, but clearly the staff were all also under orders to play nice.

And in the five minutes I'd known Nicky the stable hand, I hadn't gotten a sense that this woman cared all that much for what other people thought.

Eventually, I heard the voices of her and Stapler getting quieter, as they walked away, even though it would have made much more sense for her to let the man come and check on his horse. She had to be leading him away from me on purpose.

Weird.

So instead I gave Heidi a last look, told her, "Good luck with that. I hope he was worth all the pain," and made my way back to my room.

Probably not gonna get any more work done before bedtime.

December 25th

There's something wrong with the financial records.

It's Christmas Day, my dead aunt left a decrepit horse ranch under my tree, and there's something wrong with its records.

For one terrible, terrible moment I honestly considered whether your real reason for buying this place was money laundering, Auntie. Not sure for what, but I wouldn't put it past you to have supported some radically left political party on the sly, protected some leftover RAF officer from the sixties. Or, this being you, maybe one of your husbands or lovers had secretly been a mafia boss.

That would require discretion, organization, and patience, though, so probably not.

So either the Staplers created some kind of tax chaos, which also wouldn't surprise me terribly, despite my love affair with their filing system—and despite the fact that such a thing shouldn't be *possible* with that filing system, that's its whole *point*. Or somebody fiddled with expenses on purpose. Or nobody had fiddled with expenses on purpose, just with their records.

And because that's the way my luck runs, when Carola Stapler enticed me with another breakfast this morning filled with coconut macaroons and Santa-shaped butter cookies, she informed me that the family would visit the grandparents over Christmas and return on the 27th. The stable hands would take care of the horses. I'd told her I was fine with it. There were lists for emergency contacts pinned to the wall in the office, she said, then handed me the keys to the office.

Shame that this is happening between Christmas and New Year's, when all the companies close shop. So inquiries to my associates at the credit bureaus will have to wait.

December 26th

It's quiet here without the Stapler family.

Way too quiet.

Sure, it's not like I'm in charge of anything in their absence. The stable hands are still around, and have been taking horses to the ring for ground exercises and work on the lunge line all day.

The groaning fridge has leftover Christmas goose, stuffed with a super-traditional filling of apples and macaroons, plus red cabbage and potato dumplings and some porridge thing to do with cinnamon. There's no one typical Christmas dish in this country to my knowledge, but I swear nobody told the Staplers.

I saw Nicky from a distance, once or twice. But from the way her face closed off, and she retreated and was seen speeding off toward the woods on one of the blacks shortly thereafter, I'll say she's avoiding me.

I talked to this woman for all of five minutes. Why is she acting so weird, and never mind that—what's with the tax records and Carola's furtive looks, and how could these be connected?

Instead of finding out, I'm wallowing.

If I'm evil Ursula, that makes Nicky Arielle, except probably less naïve and way more forward, so how should her reaction surprise me? She probably was just horny last night, or feeling provocative, then came back to her senses. She's gotta be aware that I could fire her, even if I should decide to keep the ranch running.

But hell. It's the second Christmas holiday today. A woman who could have jumped straight out of a filthy dream avoids me so hard she literally saddles a horse and gallops off, and my aunt, who raised me, has been dead for three weeks.

She's been dead for three weeks.

Fuck.

Stable hand Annika bravely dared to walked up to evil me to let me know that she's the last one to leave for the day, but that everything is taken care of, with Heidi in the box but calm enough, and the master keys in the tack room et cetera, et cetera. So it's just me now.

I walk across the grounds. I hear no dogs—the Staplers took them along—and if a fire broke out, all that would save the place would be me. All of a sudden, it weighs down on me in a scary way, the fact that this place belongs to me.

This is my place. I'm responsible for this.

Those whinnies belong to horses that I own, fifteen Friesians, eight others.

Five employees, zero income.

God.

I did it. I called Christina.

Aside from the recent contact regarding the will, and during the funeral that I almost didn't attend, I haven't called my almost-sister in years. She's got a whole family of her own keeping her busy now—kids, hubby, picket fence.

"Why did she leave me the ranch?" I said when she answered, rather than introducing myself.

"And a merry Christmas to you, too," Chrissie replied.

"Why the ranch, Chrissie?" I was standing outside the house, wrapped up in my coat, phone clenched between my fingers. It was freezing. The air promised snow. Far away in the distance, I could make out the herd, grazing uphill. "And why me?"

"Geez, I don't know, Paula, maybe because Mom loved you and she wanted you to have something nice for yourself?"

"The place is a ruin. It'll take months to liquidate. Five people will lose their jobs and three will lose their home. The last word I'd use to describe the situation is *nice*."

"Oh come on, they've been around for decades, it can't be that bad." Whatever kind of logic that was supposed to be, I could picture her rolling her eyes. Cheerful denial is strong in this one, as it is in the rest of that branch in the family tree. "Plus, if anybody can save a business, it's you. Who else should she have given the ranch, huh? She loved this place, you know. That caretaker sent her pictures of the horses every year, and she kept all of them. I looked at the scrapbooks when we started cleaning out. She used to tell everybody of her little thoroughbred farm."

"Friesians are carthorses," I said automatically.

"See how qualified you are?" she replied with no trace of irony whatsoever.

I didn't deign to answer that.

Chrissie sighed.

"You wanted money? Shares?" she said. "You'd be bored with money and shares. You'd just have thrown it back at the notary with some smartass comment about how cash can't buy you absolution." A pause. "Now tell me why you really called."

"Why didn't she tell me she's dying, Chrissie?"

Chrissie has always read me better than I read myself—I hadn't even known that I wanted to ask that. The words just appeared, in a thin voice that didn't quite sound like mine. It reminded me of when I'd still expected Chrissie to magically take on the traits of a big sister.

I found myself staring at the faraway herd, trying to discern which of the black dots might be the mare who'd come to say hi the other day. I remembered Heidi the German Riding Pony, who couldn't join in because she hadn't been accepted by the herd and might have gotten hurt.

Chrissie hesitated.

"She didn't want you to know." Then she fell silent.

I'm not much of a crier. I did so much crying when Mom and Dad died, I've just been sick and tired of it ever since. Still, now my eyes burnt.

I'd have understood if she just didn't want to include me, as much as that would have hurt —it would have been consistent. But why cut me out, then leave me something anyway? And such a *useless* thing at that? Or was it really just because she expected me to clean up her mess?

Why give me anything?

I wasn't aware that I had said some of that aloud until Chrissie replied.

"Paula," she said, sounding very careful now, almost reserved, the way she never sounded with little sis Susie. "Paula, you despise weakness."

"You think I'd blame her for being *sick*? She was in her seventies, for God's—"

"Well, none of us have ever been all that good at figuring out what you need—"

"I needed her to say *good-bye*!" I snapped. "I needed her to *want* to see me one last time!"

What's so hard to figure out about that?

But screw it, a part of me knew from the start that this conversation wouldn't lead anywhere—or only to places that would hurt. I was angry, then, so angry, so when Chrissie tried to start pontificating and pacifying in that way she had, I just told her that it couldn't be changed anymore anyway—because it can't—because now Auntie is gone, and hung up.

I really was crying at that point, and I would have liked to hit something.

That's where being alone came in handy, at least. Nobody to stare at me like I'd lost it.

Soon-to-be twenty-four horses, five employees. It might have meant cutesy framed pictures and bragging rights to my aunt, but to me it was twenty-nine live beings to take care of, twenty-four horses who might go to the butcher if I couldn't find homes for them, five incomes cut off, the livelihood of an entire happy family destroyed.

Also, local refugee kids, apparently, losing access to the integrative riding lessons.

Thanks, Auntie Elsie. I'm sure your intentions were angelic.

December 27th

Well. Things turned to hell in a handbasket with surprising speed in the last twenty-four hours, and even more surprisingly, I'm A-okay with that. Now I am, at least. It might have something to do with the fact that I'm writing this in my nostalgic little guest room, heat turned up, on a bed that still smells of company.

Really good company.

Let's rewind.

So. Last evening, it started snowing.

At first, I didn't even take notice of it much. I was too busy staring at a decade of account information, spread out all around me on the yet virginal bed, trying to reconcile the total chaos among the actual hard cashflow information with the beautiful if bullshit official records. That's where the Staplers' decision to leave me alone with the back office keys bit them in the ass.

I'm not a country kid. Never have been. I grew up and have lived and worked in cities—Cologne, Vienna, Luxembourg City. All that snow means to me is the occasional seasonal logistics problem in wholesaling.

So when the roof window got covered with more and more of the stuff, all I did was turn on more light absentmindedly.

It was fairly late in the evening when I left the house again for one of my now habitual walks. I broke into abject terror when I realized I'd have to stomp through at least thirty centimeters of snow to do so—ridiculous amounts of it, everywhere I looked. The only reason I could still open the front door was the little awning that covered the stairs.

My eyes searched for the herd. I found them huddled up against each other tightly under a set of trees. The only escape route from the valley—the road—had been swallowed, nothing left but the upper half of the fence that ran along it.

Thing is, I was the only human around.

Did this constitute an emergency? Did I have to do something?

Did these people have a snowplow or something I could use? I didn't see how a shovel would be helping me any, and the law says the inhabitants of houses have to clear the sidewalks in winter. Except I have no idea what constitutes a sidewalk outside of city limits. And what about horse rugs—I know such things exist for winter—where would I find those? And was I supposed to cover twenty-three horses in them, and how was I even supposed to reach them, if so?

I reminded myself that I'm a problem solver. I forced myself to work the problem. So I made an executive decision that the road was not my responsibility, and it had no sidewalk, and surely the Staplers had listened to the weather forecast, so they would have let me know if there was anything that needed doing in this scenario.

Meanwhile, I trudged to the chicken house to make sure its inhabitants hadn't been suffocated by snowbanks, but it appeared well-fortified. I Googled "snow" and "electric fences" on my phone and learned I was probably cool there, too. I figured I'd leave checking on Heidi for last because I didn't see how the snow could possibly be affecting her in the stables.

After I managed to push the gate open and slink in, I'm pretty sure I said aloud, "You have *got* to be kidding me."

Not that anybody but Heidi was present, and she was way too busy with herself to care.

Now, my childhood riding classes didn't exactly equip me with any veterinarian knowledge, and neither does my business acumen, but it wasn't exactly hard to make deductions here.

As I stared at Heidi in her box, for a good five minutes, she lay down, just to get up again, and go down again. When she was up, she paced. Her neck and flanks looked damp, covered in sweat, and she frequently twirled her head around to look at her sides and swished her tail. Most worrisomely, she kicked at her belly. That just couldn't be good.

I had not considered this question before, but who in the hell left for two days when one of their mares was in foal?

Somebody who's organized for someone else to look in on her, that's who.

But whichever stable hand had drawn check-up duty certainly had no way of reaching us now.

Crap.

Why me?

Never mind.

Again. I tried to remind myself that I solve problems. They pay me the big bucks for that. Granted, usually it involves moving money while intimidating people, but heck, I can improvise.

Not like I had a choice.

So off I went to snow-stalk to the back office, where Carola had promised I'd find emergency contacts. I did, too, thanks to her fantastic and intuitive organization, and then I stared at the names on the list for a while.

There were the four Staplers, including Timo although he studied abroad, but right now they could all be considered as MIA.

There were three vets listed for some reason. However, there were no pointers as to who would be helpful right now. Or who had snow chains.

I scanned the list of employees, looking for Nicky.

Annika Vögele. Olga Nikiforow. Theresa Podolski.

No Nicky.

It clicked, then. Though I didn't really have time to get blinded by the sudden flash of that light bulb.

I made my way back to the stables as I dialed.

"Yeah?" came Nicky's voice, fortunately wide awake, and filling me in equal parts with relief and a tingling sensation of an entirely different nature, despite the situation.

"This is Paula, the, uh, evil heir," I said. "Heidi is about to foal. What do I do?"

"Oh," Nicky said. "All right." Infuriatingly, the news seemed to leave her quite calm. Something rustled in the background, as if she got up, or left the room. "What are her contractions like?"

"How in the world am I supposed to know that?"

"... Right." I imagine she smirked, or something equally unhelpful, displaying an infuriating lack of empathy for my predicament. "Uh. Usually, she should make do by herself. 'Course, we don't know the dad, though. I mean, if he was much taller than her..." She must have heard me taking an abrupt breath, because she paused, probably smirked *again*, since my panic was so *amusing*. At least she refrained from finishing that thought. "We don't usually call in the vet unless something goes wrong, so she should be fine. Now, I'll try to find a way to come, but I only have my bike..." Of *course* she only had a *motorcycle*. "... But I'll figure something out. You stay put."

"But what do I *do*?" This far out in the hills, it'd probably take *hours* until she was here. And anyway—what was she going to do, borrow a Husky and harness it to a sled?

"If she lies down too close to the wall, make sure there's enough room for the li'l one when it comes out. If she starts foaling standing up, you're gonna have to catch the foal so it doesn't hurt itself falling down, all right?"

Oh, yeah. Right. Sure.

If that's all.

Nicky kept me on the line for a while longer, quizzing me on Heidi's behavior and, to my dismay, agreed that it definitely looked like she was going into labor for real. Then she said, ominously, "Gotta shut up now, or someone will hear me."

What on earth did that mean?

Nicky didn't explain and abruptly hung up.

Cue the two most nerve-wracking hours of my entire life. Easily.

Living through it again might give me the heart attack I narrowly escaped when it was happening for real, so I'll keep it short. Suffice to say, I approximated cardiac fibrillation every time Heidi lay down—because she might get started now—and then again when she got back up—because she might do it standing and force me to *assist*.

Judging by the amount of white in her eyes and the sweat covering her trembling torso, she wasn't having the greatest day of her life herself.

When finally the gate rumbled and Nicky appeared, she looked to me like a particularly laid-back angel bearing salvation. Getting out of her jacket and throwing it across the door of an unused box on the way in, I would have been willing to kiss her from sheer relief, not that I would have needed much of an incentive to do that in absentia of Heidi.

It's much more marvelous a thing, watching a baby pony coming into this world, when there aren't any responsibilities involved.

When it was clear Heidi didn't plan on getting up another time, Nicky joined her in the box, approaching carefully, producing soothing sounds. I watched her cleaning the membrane thingy of the foal's nose so that it could breathe—while it wasn't entirely out yet, which was a bit weird—and study other things that came out after that with an expert expression. Then, covered quite thoroughly in goo, she joined me outside to watch the little thing lifting its head and trying to open its eyes, and finally getting up on very thin, very trembling legs. It is pitch black and has impossibly large ears. Heidi looked pleased.

"Damn, I'm tired." Nicky stretched her neck by rolling her head so that bones cracked audibly. Morning sun was illuminating the stables from what a look out the window told me was a now clear and unbelievably blue sky.

"Maybe a shower, first," I recommended, with a nod at her ruined sweater and jeans.

She smirked at me then, and it was as if she consciously chose to let all tension seep out of her body, transforming back into the irredeemable flirt from Christmas Eve.

Needless to say, I approved.

"Yeah?" she said, communicating quite clearly how she'd chosen to interpret that suggestion. "Lead the way, then."

Somehow, that woman has a way of making me want to laugh.

Apparently, the adrenaline of the night had been enough for her to shelve her plans of avoiding me and go back to what she made very clear she actually wanted.

Auntie, I've spent way too much time addressing you directly in the past couple of days to go into detail about the rest of the morning.

All I'm going to say is that Nicky kisses like neither Audrey Hepburn nor James Dean presumably would have. She kisses like Nicky, or like what I've seen of her so far, unhurried and sensual and like all that existed in her world right then was me.

We lay in bed with each other for a long while after, partly because we both were way too tired to move by now—sprawled out, the both of us, taking up as much space as we wanted and staring at the ceiling and letting our exhausted minds wander.

"So," I said when I remembered, when my brain had finished rebooting. "Olga Nikiforow. Nicky."

There had been really good orgasms just then, and it didn't seem like such a big deal in light of those. Certainly not enough to bitch. I felt mellow and gracious.

"Ah," I heard her say after a moment, when she caught up, slightly embarrassed. "Right. That. Sorry about that."

"Why would the Staplers try to hide you?"

It took a while until I got an answer. "Uh," she said, eventually. "They thought, uh, I wouldn't leave the right impression, 'cause you're such a professional and all. What with the tattoos. And the bike. And the flirting? I sort of can't shut that off. And, uh, my problem-solving techniques."

"Your problem-solving techniques?"

"Ah, I might have borrowed a snow blower to get here? From my neighbor? He works for the winter-service people. I left him a note, though," she hurried to add, like an afterthought. "I don't think he'd press charges."

I snorted a laugh.

"I keep doing that." She sounded almost apologetic. She turned her head to look at me without bothering to move the rest of her body. "I love this place. It's a great place. Ulf and Carola…they work so hard. They put up with me, although I am the way I am, I get focused on one thing and forget the, uh, big picture."

"Like focusing on how to reach the pregnant mare and her overwhelmed midwife?"

"Like sleeping with the boss type although it could cost all of us our careers." While it seemed like she was attempting to joke, the guilt in her voice still won out.

It came to me then, and I groaned.

"You looked me up on the Internet." It suddenly seemed obvious. I'm not the only person with the power to Google. My thoughts on back-office organization are a matter of public record. I've opened my mouth about reputation management, on quality of service, and on marketing. Some of my projects have made it on the news, and I'm active on both LinkedIn and XING. "You read my articles, and my book. Carola tried to make it look like she works with my system."

Nicky kept gazing at me. "Did it work?"

Despite myself, I giggled. "Yes," I admitted. "Yes, it did. They'd have done better looking for my dating profile on *Lesarion* and sic you on me directly, though."

Nicky started chuckling at that, too, and for a moment we just lay there, laughing into the pillows companionably, too tired to much contemplate the relative stupidity of that entire situation.

Not as cunning as big business, my ass. I've underestimated everything. These people are fighting for their lives. So they've lied. And falsified. And made it look like their ranch is anything but totally, dismally fucked.

Not that you *can* make much of a profit if you have no business or investment plan, no strategy, no way to systematically draw in new customers.

There are way too many people out there mucking around with their own businesses but no idea what they're doing.

I noticed then, after our laughter had long died and made way for this lazy kind of exhaustion again, that Nicky had returned to looking at me, once again observing my face, waiting.

"What?" I asked.

"So you've decided to do it? Shut the ranch down, sell it all in parts?"

I returned to staring at the ceiling a little bit longer, mulling it over. "Nah," I eventually said.

January 2nd

Today, I got to use my favorite sentence in the world. Turns out it's even more of a pleasure to say when it's in regard to my very own project, rather than a client's.

"Here's how it'll work."

I don't screw around once I make up my mind. I make a call, I commit, and then I keep at it until shit is done—not that businesses are ever done. They run on and on and on and become a huge, impossible-to-sideline part of your life. In this case, the calls I made were mostly to my accountant and my lawyers, who know there's enough money in this kind of thing for them to gladly spend time on it on January 1st.

Ulf and Carola Stapler were sitting in front of me at their kitchen table then, equally serious expressions on their face. Timo and Yannik loomed in the background, both looking suspicious, but also somewhat amendable for the first time since I met them.

"We're going to apply for that credit," I said. "There's no way around that. It's illusory to try and raise the revenue without a considerable investment and a lot of change. We're going to renovate, and we'll separate out guest rooms.

"You'll be in charge of the hotel part of business," I addressed Carola. "Ultimately, we will hire a manager, if we launch successfully. For now, I expect you to take a management class."

She nodded at me, multiple times.

"We'll need a new website, a Facebook account, possibly Pinterest or Snapchat. Run a number of ad campaigns. I'll hire a marketing consultant who'll walk you through those. You will do everything according to the business plan," I said, hopefully looking very stern.

Ulf nodded soberly. He knew as well as the rest of us what was at stake.

"You'll run every investment by me," I warned. "Your power-of-attorney days are a thing of the past."

They both nodded.

"We will expand the riding school and partner with the local schools to offer special courses, and if—*if*—we see signs of amortizing according to the predictions three years from now, we'll start looking into that new stud."

They looked hopeful at that.

"We could look into working with the refugee center," Carola proposed with a shy eagerness that I was still getting used to. "Maybe we could get aid money from the community for that."

"There's no money in refugee kids," I said categorically.

The following silence was very loud.

I raised my head from my notes to see Carola just looking at me in an intense way.

"I'll look into it," I grumbled without looking at either one of them.

These people.

They better spend the next couple of years pouring the exact same amount of dedication and passion into running an actually successful company as they did when they tried to fool me by fiddling with the books and hiding the employee with the criminal leanings.

Fortunately, they seem perfectly happy to agree to any and all terms, and even relieved to hand the parts they suck at over to the professionals. Not that they'd been at liberty of doing much with a boss who refused to acknowledge their existence.

I *do* like being needed.

I like it a lot.

You know what, Auntie? That's the first explanation for why you might have given me this place that I'd be willing to accept.

Sure, I grumbled a lot all through the past couple of days, but let's face it—that's just how I roll.

You weren't right for these people. You weren't ever right for me, either, and I sure was never right for you. The Staplers, though, and the Rosenbrock Ranch? I like the idea of building something from the ground, something that relies on me, I really do.

I might make them name Heidi's foal after you, Auntie, that ridiculous little thing with its donkey ears and dubious descent, the kind of animal that everybody will always call "peculiar" and "unique" for lack of anything else positive to say. You don't get to complain; you gave me a pony ranch.

You know what they say—don't look a gift horse in the mouth, eh?

Yeah, that's a terrible joke.

Will finish later, as much as there might be left to do before we'll start getting anywhere with this endeavor. Still need to take a shower and decide on something to wear, for now. Nicky said she'd pick me up in twenty. No idea if she's the punctual type.

Four Chanukahs and a Bat Mitzvah

BY CINDY RIZZO

A Bat Mitzvah – I'm 13

THIS PARTY WAS REALLY FUN until Amelia Perlman kissed me in a hidden corner of the large function room of my synagogue's social hall. Did I mention that it was a kiss on the lips? And did I forget to mention that I kissed her back?

Maybe it was because I'd let down my guard after getting through the Saturday-morning bat mitzvah service I'd been dreading for months.

The party—complete with a large buffet, a chocolate fondue fountain, and a DJ—started hours after I had tortured my extended family and friends with two horrendous Torah and Haftarah readings. They'd all had to sit and listen to my horrible voice as I tried to remember which of the Hebrew words were important enough to be chanted at a high pitch for an extra beat and which I could zoom through. And after all that, I still had to read my essay on the ten plagues to everyone and hope that they would magically tune it out.

Luckily, my parents had agreed to the basketball theme I wanted for the party, which was a good thing since basketball is kind of my life. They also let me wear pants instead of a dress. I would have died without having any pockets. Even if I had nothing to put in them, I'd need to do something with my hands.

That's where they were—my hands, that is. They were jammed in my pockets when Amelia leaned close and whispered, "Erica, you did great this morning." Then she laid it on me.

Soft and fruity, tasting and smelling of raspberry lip gloss. I breathed it in and relaxed my own lips against hers after the first few seconds of shock and surprise wore off. I tightened my hands into two rigid fists, the pads of my fingers pressing hard against my palms.

Suddenly the force of what was happening hit me like that time a kid from Monroe Middle School threw a basketball right at my head. Amelia and I were kissing! And if we kept kissing, we'd actually be making out. I just couldn't. Not now, not here. So I pulled back, nearly jumping away from Amelia, and mumbled something about needing to be around for more pictures (which was a lie). And I ran away, back toward my table, only slowing when I heard my name and felt a hand on my shoulder.

"There you are, Erica."

I turned to face my mother.

"You almost missed the Hora."

Amelia and her family left right after the party. They had an early morning flight back to San Francisco, so we never had a minute to ourselves to talk about the kiss.

You see, Amelia's mom, Sharon, is best friends with my Aunt Barbara, who also lives in California. Since we're the same age, my parents, my aunt, and Amelia's parents have been putting us together ever since we were little. Every time my family went to visit my aunt, there were always dinners and outings with Amelia and her two moms.

I thought Amelia was pretty nice, even though we didn't seem to have a lot in common. She likes books and learning about history. I like basketball and computers. When I visited, she always asked me to help her figure stuff out about her software and the internet. I taught her Boolean logic search commands and sent her links to websites she might like. She told me I would love reading graphic novels. So I went to the Strand Bookstore and bought a few. She was right. I was hooked.

Between visits we'd email occasionally. So it wasn't a total surprise when she emailed me after the bat mitzvah.

"E," she wrote (we always called each other by the first letter of our names). "I hope you're okay with what happened. Please let me know. A."

The truth was, I didn't want to dwell on it. It's not like I had a problem with gay people. Barbara was my favorite aunt, and she's gay. I looked up to her because she'd made a killing in the business world and was now investing in new companies and teaching at Stanford. My mom is an elementary school teacher and my dad is an accountant. By comparison, Aunt Barbara is up in the stratosphere.

I decided to send Amelia a quick reply. Short and to the point.

"Hey A. No worries. It's cool. Thanks for coming and thank your parents for the gift, though I'm sure I'll soon be tied to my desk and forced to write thank you notes. E."

The First Chanukah – I'm 15

It was one of those weird years when Chanukah overlaps with Christmas. That's the problem when you have a holiday that doesn't stay still on the calendar. I remember once when I was little, Chanukah came during the long Thanksgiving weekend. That was really crazy.

When I asked my mom why the Jewish calendar was so funky like that, she told me it wouldn't seem funky if I lived in Israel.

"But I don't and it does," I told her, knowing that I was sounding a bit like a whiny two-year-old, even to myself.

"Well," she asked, "have you ever noticed how Easter jumps around various Sundays in March and April, sometimes overlapping with Passover?"

She had me there. This wasn't just some weird Jewish thing. Maybe instead it's all a grand scheme to get Jews and Christians (and people of other religions, I don't know) to have to pay more attention to the fact that our holidays are coming. But then why is Christmas always on December 25th? I guess there are some things I'll never understand.

Anyway, the reason I bring all of this up is because that year Amelia and her family were coming for our annual Chanukah party. They wanted to see

New York City during the Christmas season. You know, the store windows and the tree at Rockefeller Center and all that. Nobody I know who lives here steps foot in that area until after New Year's because it's so crowded it takes forever to walk one block. But tourists don't seem to care.

They were only staying a few days and then flying down to Florida to go on some kind of gay family cruise that sounded totally cool.

Oh right, the gay thing. Well, it was two years since that night at my bat mitzvah party when Amelia kissed me. Since then, I'd managed to figure out just why I kissed her back and why that sent me into such a state.

Big surprise, I finally realized that I'm gay. This basketball-playing computer nerd walking around in sweats, with my short brown hair tucked under a knit beanie, is a total stereotype. Hey, it's not like I wasn't this way before I came out. I've always dressed like this and kept my hair short. Maybe that's why Amelia thought it would be safe to kiss me.

We'd been emailing a bit more that year and started to text and chat on WhatsApp a bit. Someone took a really great picture of me leaping up to make a crucial game-tying point when we played Brooklyn Tech, and I sent that to Amelia.

"Awesome! You're amazing!" was the reply I got back. She continued to tell me about graphic novels I might like, and when I snuck the "I'm gay" line into a very long sentence in an email, she texted me with a "yay" response that had about a million exclamation points and emojis. Pretty funny.

So right away she had me reading stories about girls who like other girls. Sweet stuff about coming out and scary stuff about Christian conversion camps. Also, there was one about vampires that was kinda fun. And she texted her cute school picture. She'd grown out her wavy, light-brown hair past her shoulders, and the braces she'd complained to me about had come off, so she was smiling with her mouth open a bit. Her hazel eyes sparkled in the picture. She had the kind of eye color that seemed to change depending on the light. Sometimes her eyes looked green and other times I'd notice a greyish-brown color.

They arrived on December 22nd after settling into their hotel and walking around to see the store windows at Macy's and along Fifth Avenue. Amelia ran right over to me and gave me a tight hug and one of those meaningful looks, her eyes fixed on my face, a half-smile on her lips. I stood rigid with her arms around me, holding my breath and swallowing a gulp.

"Hi, E," she whispered, and gave me a quick kiss on the tip of my nose.

I quickly got a hold of myself and said hi back followed by a big grin so she'd know I was glad to see her. I wondered if I should kiss her, like really kiss her. But I thought maybe it was too soon to start with that only seconds after she walked into my house.

Instead, we injected ourselves into the crowd of family and friends that had gathered for my parents' annual Chanukah party. Every few minutes, my mom had another thing she needed me to do.

"Erica, find the large slotted serving spoons."

"Erica, bring the folding chairs in from the den."

"Erica, watch the latkes so they don't burn and transfer them onto the paper towels when they're brown on each side." (Like I didn't know to do that after spending fifteen years in this family.)

The house had taken on that amazing Chanukah smell of grated potatoes and onions frying in oil, a smell that would stick to the walls and linger for days. With the oven on all day, the stovetop burners going, and the windows closed, the house was too hot for winter clothes. I had pulled my sweater over my head and was walking around in a UConn basketball T-shirt with my lightweight sweatpants. My mother pleaded with me to "dress up a bit for company," but I refused, telling her it was too hot and I wanted to be comfortable.

Amelia happily accompanied me on all of my chores, watching the frying pan while I looked for the spoons and carrying her share of folding chairs. When we finally got a break, we sat on the couch together, the sides of our legs touching, and brought each other up to date on school and basketball and friends.

Then it was time to light the candles. This was no small thing. My parents always told our guests to bring their own menorahs (or menorot, as I was taught in Hebrew school) so we could light them all at once. Positioned along the sidebar cabinet in our dining room, each with five candles spanning a spectrum of colors—including the rainbow ones I had bought—a member of each family held a long wooden kitchen match and lit the shamash, the middle candle, of their menorah. Amelia and I stood together watching as both of our younger brothers, guided by a mother, slowly lit each of the four candles that marked the fourth night of our eight-night holiday. A few voices began to chant the first of the two nightly blessings in Hebrew, thanking God for just about everything, but especially for commanding us to light the Chanukah candles. Then I heard my mother's voice rising above the din.

"I know it's traditional to only say this on the first night, but since this is the night we are all together, and our good friends are visiting us from San Francisco, I thought it would be fitting to chant the *Shehecheyanu.*"

And so we did, and once again we thanked God, but this time it was for bringing us to this day and to this occasion. Amelia and I smiled at each other in a silent understanding that we couldn't agree more.

Then I coated my latkes with sour cream while Amelia poured applesauce on hers. This, of course, led to a debate about which was better, and a minor food fight that left each of us with one another's preferred topping all over our faces. After that we stuffed ourselves on those little jelly-filled munchkins from Dunkin' Donuts that my mother had bought in a panic after she realized she didn't have time to make her own *sufganiyot.* Finally, full to the point of not being able to move very much, Amelia and I escaped to my room and shut the door.

I cued up a playlist of music we both liked, and we sat down on my bed. Now was the time to be brave, to shoot for the three-pointer from outside the box just before the buzzer sounded. I took Amelia's hand in mine, and she laced our fingers together.

"I'm so happy to see you, E," she said, her voice soft. "I think about you..." She trailed off.

I kept my eyes on her, focusing on her lips as I leaned over and kissed her. She scooted closer to me and threw her arms around my neck. Our soft, sweet kisses became more intense, and our hands explored each other's shoulders, arms, and backs, both of us remaining fully clothed. I brushed over Amelia's breasts lightly with the palms of my hands, and she let out a soft moan. I felt her hot breath on my ear followed by the warning, "Parents on the other side of that door."

I nodded my reply still holding her and whispered, "Right. Too bad."

The Second Chanukah – I'm 16

It was all over the internet, and it even made the *New York Times.* *"California Teen, 16, Rescues Kindergarten Class on Field Trip."*

The teen in the headline was Amelia. She was doing some kind of community service project working at a nearby school where my mom said that most of the kids got free lunches (code words for "they were very poor"). The real story that we got from my Aunt Barbara was a bit different from what we read in the newspaper and on the net.

The class had gone on a field trip to a children's museum in the city on the same day that a crazy ex-employee snuck in through a side entrance with an automatic rifle that had the capacity to end a lot of lives in a very short time. Amelia was shepherding a group of six little kids. They had just entered a cave exhibit and were exploring the interior when she heard a series of loud blasts, like firecrackers followed by screams. She'd been through these drills in her high school and knew immediately what was happening. But now she had a group of five-year-olds in her care. What would she do if the shooter came after them?

A few minutes later, she got her answer. She had the kids sitting on the floor of the cave against a side wall, their hands in their laps and heads down. They crowded around behind her as she tried to shield them. Every few seconds, she had to twist her body to quiet their cries and outbursts. Then the light from the cave entrance about ten feet away was blocked by a tall figure holding something that he was swinging from right to left and back again.

"I know you're all in there laughing at me," a voice strained with anger and pain called out.

Just then, she heard a strange noise, not the explosions of fire, but a series of clicks and the high-pitched screech of metal on metal. "Oh shit. Don't fuckin' jam on me now," the angry voice muttered.

Amelia put her finger to her lips, urging the kids to remain quiet. Then she made a downward motion with her opened hands, telling them to stay put, while she stood as quietly as she could.

She looked around for something to grab onto and noticed fixtures on the wall shaped like wooden torches. They gave off only a glimmer of light to preserve the dimness of a cave, but prevented the exhibit from being completely plunged into darkness. Amelia reached for one, and to her surprise, realized that they weren't fastened to the wall, but were instead held in place by the kind of brackets that enabled you to lift them up and hold them.

She looked at the shooter who was bent over his gun, trying to fix the jam. Lifting the light from its bracket, she happened to feel the outline of a small flip switch and shut off the flickering light. She inched her way along the side of the cave, taking advantage of the fact that the shooter's back was to her as he focused on his gun. His posture was lowered as he worked, so she had a good chance of hitting the back of his head with the light torch.

She swung it with all her might. A groan escaped from him, and she feared that she'd only fueled his anger. But then he dropped to his knees and fell forward, the gun clattering onto the floor. She used the torch to move it away from him and screamed for help.

Amelia hadn't killed the guy, but she'd knocked him unconscious long enough for the police to arrive and get everyone safely out of the museum.

None of the kids in the cave were physically harmed, but before he'd reached the cave, the gunman had managed to kill two museum employees, a parent chaperone accompanying her child's class, and two children. Amelia's actions had prevented him from adding to the body count.

I tried to contact her by email, chat, text, and finally phone, and all I got back was one text that simply said, "I'm fine E." My mom and Aunt Barbara said to give her time. She'd been through an ordeal.

Then her parents called and asked if one of them could come with Amelia to New York for Chanukah. They wanted to get her out of the glare of the spotlight and into an environment where she wouldn't be stopped on the street or hugged in the hallways at school. My mom thought it was a great idea, and I breathed a sigh of relief that I'd finally get to see her.

Even before all this took place, I'd never gotten a clear fix on what we were to one another. Were we girlfriends or friends with a mild case of benefits? I had hoped for the first but was worried that Amelia wanted the second. The truth is that I was too chicken to ask her outright. But maybe when we were together, we could talk and figure it out.

As soon as I laid eyes on her, I knew this was not going to be an easy visit, and I doubted we'd ever get to that talk about us. Dressed in skinny black jeans with a black hoodie, her wavy hair tied back, Amelia sat hunched over looking down at her lap.

I sat down next to her and wrapped my hand around her arm. "A, how are you?" I kept my voice quiet, trying to muster as much concern as I could.

She shrugged in response and didn't look at me, her head still bowed.

"Do you want to talk about it?"

She shook her head vigorously. "No!" she said almost as if I'd asked her if she wanted to jump out a window or eat worms or something.

I decided to keep trying, so I put my arm around her as gently as I could. She jerked her shoulders from side to side and stood up, finally looking at me, her face twisted in anger.

"I don't want to be touched or coddled or helped, Erica. I just want to be left alone by everyone, including you. I didn't even want to come here, but my parents made me!"

I pulled back, stunned by her anger. What had I done? I was three thousand miles away when all this happened, and all I'd done since then was try to make contact with her. What was going on with her?

"Amelia." It was clear that she was no longer interested in our little nicknames for one another, so I went back to using full names. "I know this has all been hard…"

"You know nothing, Erica. Nothing."

I stood, feeling uncomfortable being shouted down to. At least I could gain some confidence by asserting my height since I was a head taller than her. All of my hopes about the two of us. All of the dreams I'd had of making something of what we'd started last year. I had to give it one more try.

I reached my hand out to her, but kept it a few inches from her arm, hoping she'd close the distance. "How about we get out of here together? We could see a movie or go into the city and walk around. I know a bookstore you might like."

She nodded slowly, her hands buried in the pockets of her hoodie, clearly not interested in the hand I still held out like hope itself.

"I do want to get out of here," she said almost in a whisper. I started to smile thinking I'd finally come up with the right solution, but then, as she turned away from me, she blurted out, with that same anger in her voice from before, "But alone, not with you."

I stood there in shock for a few seconds until the sound of our front door slamming jolted me awake like an alarm clock.

The remainder of the three-day visit wasn't much better. Amelia was either out of the house or sulking somewhere inside still dressed in her funeral outfit. Nothing my parents or her mom did—not the sweet overtures or the pleading or even the threats—helped at all. She wouldn't participate in the Chanukah rituals or eat the potato pancakes I brought her smothered in applesauce, just the way she liked them.

It was like she was a different person. And if I heard the words "Give her time" once more, I felt like I was going to scream and run out of the house myself.

None of this was fair. Not to Amelia, to our families, or to me. It was a major relief when she finally left to go back to California. The Amelia who'd kissed me and who I'd finally had the courage to kiss back was gone forever. I'd just have to live my life here in Brooklyn without her.

The Third Chanukah – I'm 17

This time it was me who didn't want to go. My parents were insisting we fly to San Francisco to spend the holiday with Aunt Barbara so that I could also tour Stanford University, which had been recruiting me for a basketball scholarship. But I had my heart set on the University of Connecticut, which was also recruiting me.

My mother thought I was crazy. "Stanford versus UConn, Erica? There's no comparison, especially if you're studying computer science. You'll have a million opportunities out there in Silicon Valley when you graduate. And you promised me that basketball would end when college did. Are you planning on going back on that promise?"

I wasn't keeping score, but this was likely the twentieth time we'd had this conversation where my mother listed all the reasons why I shouldn't go pro and try out for a WNBA team. While I had a minor interest in wondering what new heights I might be able to achieve, I actually agreed that I'd be much better off sticking with computers. I loved watching the women pros, but it wasn't an easy life touring around the country and playing on European teams off-season. That whole running-around-the-world thing isn't really for me. I like being rooted somewhere. So I told her that college ball was it.

But I wanted that college to be UConn and only reluctantly agreed to check out other schools. UConn had been my dream since I'd first played on a youth team when I was nine. They were always in the final four, regularly coming out on top. I wanted to learn from their amazing coaches and to play with teammates who were as serious about the game as I was. I didn't really care if I saw Stanford or not.

The truth was I had no interest in going all the way to California. I wanted to spend Chanukah and Christmas break at home playing basketball and hanging out with my friends, especially Sofia, who I'd just started to call my girlfriend. She was new to my school and to New York. Her family had arrived from Estonia, a country I knew nothing about, except that it was where Skype was headquartered. She was really pretty with long dark hair and velvety soft, dark brown eyes, and was only a few inches shorter than me. For the second time in my life, I was smitten, but at least this time, the object of my affection lived close by and didn't hide herself under a black hoodie.

As I toured around Palo Alto, I had to admit, Stanford had one beautiful campus, and you couldn't beat sixty-degree weather in December.

My mother looked up from her iPhone and gave me a knowing smile. "I just checked and it's fifteen degrees in Connecticut with snow expected."

I shrugged back at her, not wanting to give her the satisfaction of the response she was expecting. "So?" was all I said.

The high point of the trip really was seeing my Aunt Barbara and her girlfriend Ellen, who was a genuine San Francisco police officer. She was totally cool and even took me to a park to play a little "round ball," as she called it. She was a good sport, especially since she could never beat me when we played one-on-one.

Barbara had let me know ahead of time that Amelia and her family would be joining us for a night of Chanukah.

"That's fine, really," I told her. "Amelia and I are not really in touch anymore so it's no big deal."

"That doesn't surprise me," Aunt Barbara said. "It's still pretty rough going with her. She's hanging out with people her mom calls hoodlums, and Ellen has had to pick her up in the Mission drunk off her ass and bring her home in a squad car. Plus, she's got a girlfriend whose goes by the name Spike."

I shook my head. "Spike, huh? Does she have a big point on the top of her head?"

Aunt Barbara chuckled. "I don't think so, but she's not in school and hustles through life in not very honest ways. Even though Amelia's been grounded and forbidden from seeing her, she just ignores every limit placed on her. So Sharon and Paulie have decided to accept this Spike and invite her to dinner and other family events. You'll be meeting her at my house for Chanukah."

I rolled my eyes. "I can't really say that it'll be nice to see Amelia again."

When she walked into Barbara's condo and saw me, Amelia seemed to freeze for a few seconds, her eyes fixed on me. I saw her head dip and rise slightly as she looked me up and down. I thought she'd known ahead of time that I'd be there, but maybe not.

"Hello, Erica," she said in a voice that lacked warmth but wasn't ice cold.

I smiled a little and nodded back to her.

"Who's that?" The voice was loud and a bit gruff.

It didn't take a genius to figure out that this was the famous Spike, or maybe infamous would be a better word. She was a little shorter than Amelia (much shorter than me, I might add), and her black hair was, well, spiked. Her round face was very pale and framed by the outline of the hood portion of her black hoodie. A black leather jacket was layered on top. Her shoulders and chest were wide. With her body type and forward leaning stance, plus the hair and clothes, she was definitely pulling off a tough-girl look.

Amelia responded that I was "Barbara's niece," as if we'd never known one another. I wasn't sure whether to be totally pissed at being so dissed by her or amused by the threatening looks I was getting from Spike. I'd been working out a lot over the last year in order to up my game and attract the college recruiters. I figured with all the strength and aerobic training I'd had, I could take Spike if she started anything with me.

I looked back at Amelia and purposely rolled my eyes, letting her know that none of this impressed me. I noticed then that she wasn't wearing her black hoodie. She was wearing skinny jeans, ripped at the knees, and a button-down forest-green shirt that brought out the green in her eyes. She looked amazing, much more like the old Amelia of two years ago. I forced myself to look away.

After that awkward introduction, I tried to keep my distance from them.

I couldn't help but notice the very warm reception I received from Amelia's moms. There were hugs and compliments about how nice I looked (Paulie called me a "powerhouse") and many questions about school, basketball, and the college search. At one point I caught Amelia looking over at me while I was talking to her parents. She tried to keep her face neutral, but I noticed that she didn't just look and turn away. She watched us for a good couple of minutes.

Once the candles were lit and the food brought out, I saw Amelia putting on her jacket. Spike hadn't taken hers off, and believe me, Aunt Barbara's condo was steamy. Spike caught me looking, and with that same menacing forward stance, she walked over to me.

"Hey, Green Giant," she said, still not at all friendly. "Wanna ditch with us?"

I looked over at Amelia whose mouth was open in surprise, her head shaking a silent "no."

There was no way I was gonna lose face with Spike by rejecting what I was pretty sure was a challenge. I'd come up against tougher girls on the basketball court and never backed down from them.

I shrugged back at her. "Sure," I said, trying my best to sound bored.

As we walked along the streets leading away from my aunt's building, Spike asked me where I was from. I had a feeling that my answer, "Brooklyn," might have earned me a little street cred, though it was likely because she had no idea about how gentrified my neighborhood of Park Slope had become. Amelia knew, but surprisingly, she didn't let on. In fact, she was pretty quiet after we left Barbara's place.

"So where are we going?" I finally asked.

"You'll see, Brooklyn," Spike replied.

I huffed out a chuckle and shook my head. I guess Brooklyn was a better nickname than Green Giant.

We seemed to be in a neighborhood with a lot of homeless people looking for a bit of change, just like you'd see in New York. One guy was laying on the ground in a heap, his face and hands filthy.

Spike stopped right in front of him. "Hey, Georgie, want a little job?"

The guy looked up. "Oh, it's you," he said in a voice that seemed to lack enthusiasm and contained maybe a bit of fear.

Spike pulled something out of her pocket and then held her hand out to Amelia, who gave her money.

Spike bent over to where Georgie was sitting and held the cash out to him. "Here's ten," she said. "Get a big one."

With great effort and no help, he lifted himself up off the sidewalk and took the money. I watched as he headed into a store a few doors away from where we were standing. I looked at Amelia, but she wouldn't meet my eyes. Something told me to just stay silent and wait to see what was going on.

A couple of minutes later, Georgie, in his torn T-shirt and ragged navy-blue sweatshirt came toward us holding a paper bag. Spike took it from him, and when she held her hand out, he dropped some money into it. She looked in the bag and then stared at the cash in her hand.

"You know it's not a good idea to hold out on me, Georgie. Remember last time?"

Georgie stood swinging his arms back and forth, swaying a little. A minute later, he reached in his pants and held one dollar out to Spike, who grabbed it and shoved it in her pocket with such force, it was as if she was afraid it would disappear.

She opened the bag and it looked like she was gonna pull out whatever was in there, but she only let about an inch of what looked like a beer can become visible. She popped the top and took a long swig. "Ahhh, that's better. Okay, Georgie, you know what to do."

I couldn't believe what happened next. Georgie cupped his hands together, and Spike poured beer into them. Immediately some of it dripped onto the ground, but enough remained for Georgie to lift his hands to his mouth and drink.

I stared at Spike, no longer able to contain myself. "You made him drink from his filthy hands?"

Spike looked at me and did that thing where she leaned forward. "What? You want me to drink from the same can he did? No way."

My stomach lurched with nausea as I thought about poor Georgie having to drink beer laced with the filth from his hands. I clenched my own hands into fists and shoved them deep into my pockets to avoid the temptation to haul off and punch Spike in her big mouth. The only thing that kept me from bailing on them was the fact that I had no idea where I was. Well, that and my concern for Amelia, who I wasn't sure deserved it.

We continued walking, I have no idea where, and I watched as Spike handed the paper bag to Amelia, who lifted the can to her mouth and drank. Then she passed it to me.

There was no way I was going to drink beer. First of all, I was in training and it was forbidden. Second, walking the streets of a city I didn't know with someone like Spike meant I had to keep my wits about me. I lifted the bag to my mouth and used my tongue to block the liquid. This made it look like I was drinking so I wouldn't have to deal with any hassles from Spike.

The sun was setting, and we would soon be in the dark on unfamiliar streets. Since I didn't trust Spike, and Amelia seemed to just be going along, I wasn't particularly comfortable with this whole thing. Then I heard the familiar thump, thump of a basketball repeatedly hitting pavement. Up ahead was an outdoor court, lit up for nighttime play, not something you'd see in New York, but a real possibility in the warmer weather of California. I stared in the direction of the high chain-link fence and stopped at the opening, watching a group of guys play a game of three-on-three, shirts versus skins.

"C'mon, Brooklyn." Spike pulled on my arm.

"You want to play, don't you?" Amelia's voice was soft in contrast, almost pleasant. I'd forgotten that she was capable of speaking to me without that harsh tone I'd come to expect.

I pulled my arm from Spike's grip and walked onto the court area.

"What the..." was all I heard from behind me.

Cupping my hands around my mouth for volume, I shouted, "Someone wanna take a time out?" Nothing happened, so I repeated myself.

This time one of the guys closest to me raised an arm and yelled to the others, "Whoa, whoa, hold on for a sec." The game stopped and all of them turned toward me. They were a mix of brown and black chests and faces, shining with sweat.

"You serious?" asked the guy who had stopped the game.

"Yeah, I haven't played in a few days and I'm antsy to get back to it."

"You're antsy, huh?" said the tallest one in the group. "What makes you think you can play with us?"

A quiet voice behind me said, "Erica, maybe we should just go."

Amelia.

I ignored her.

I stood tall, showing them all five feet eleven-and-a-half inches of me; my feet firmly on the ground, my hands on my hips. "Oh, I can play with you. The question is whether you'll let me. Who's ready for a little break?"

"All right," said the tall one, "let's see what you got, girl." He twisted his body toward his friends. "Go easy on her, boys." Then he tossed me the ball.

"Don't bother," I told them.

They thought I'd be bent out of shape by the fact that the guy who'd given me his spot was playing with the skins. But I simply rolled up the sleeves of my T-shirt, pulled it out of my jeans, and tied it under my breasts. This way I was showing skin too.

There were catcalls and whistles, but I ignored them, choosing instead to pay attention to the rush of energy I was feeling in anticipation of that first run toward the basket and the inevitable jump. I picked up the ball and approached the two other skins, holding out my fist. They bumped it and we began.

They didn't have much of a passing game, so I focused on shooting. After my first two baskets, I could tell that they'd stopped easing up on me. The play was more aggressive and more to my liking. When I scored a three-pointer, I got two atta-girl backslaps from my teammates, just like at home. I intercepted the ball from the other team a few times and sent it along to another skin who scored. I was in the zone.

At one point, as I was running after another player, I turned side court and saw Spike bent over the benches where the guys had put their jackets and shirts. Amelia stood in front of her looking nervous. Shit, I realized in a split second, she was stealing their stuff.

The guy who'd given me his place in the game noticed me looking over and in that same instant saw what I saw.

He jumped up and down, yelling, "Stop the game! Stop the game! They're stealing our stuff."

In a flash, six sets of feet ran for the benches toward Spike.

"Fuck it!" one of them called out. "This whole thing was a set up."

I had no idea how Spike was going to get away from them, but while they moved in on her, I lifted Amelia up under her arms and started to run. I knew she'd never be able to keep up if she ran beside me and the adrenaline rush brought on by intense fear made her feel light as a feather.

We ran like that for a block and turned the corner. I wasn't sure if we'd been noticed, but I wasn't sticking around to find out. We crossed a street and I spotted a store on the corner. It was like the bodegas we had at home, with fruit and vegetables out front. I slowed down and felt my heart pumping furiously in my chest, my breathing labored. I looked back in the direction of the basketball court listening for the sound of running feet hitting pavement. The street was quiet and empty.

"Erica!" Amelia's voice was strained and pleading.

Before she had a chance to say more, I relaxed my hold on her and led her by the hand inside the store. We stood together in back hiding behind a display of bread and cakes. I pulled her close to me so we couldn't be seen.

When my breathing slowed enough for me to speak, I glared at Amelia.

"What the fuck were you thinking, stealing their stuff? We could have been killed."

Her body trembled against mine, her breath ragged and eyes wet.

She looked down and a sob escaped. "Spike said to guard her." She was crying. "She said it would be okay."

I wanted to answer, "And you believed her?" but Amelia's tears had extinguished my anger, and all I felt like doing was pulling her closer.

We stood like that for a while, and during that time I decided that it would be a good idea to at least do something to help Spike. She wasn't my favorite person, but that didn't mean she deserved to be beaten to a pulp. I called 911 and had Amelia give the cops the location of the basketball court. I hoped they'd come quickly.

Amelia continued to quietly cry, pressed against me. I tried to calm her by rubbing the back of her neck and combing my fingers through her soft hair like I had that first night in my room when we'd kissed. After a little more of this, I thought we were finally safe and that no one was coming after us. I whispered into Amelia's ear, "I think it'll be okay to go now."

She started shaking again. "What if they come? What if they have a gun?"

Then I realized that she was thinking about the shooting at the children's museum. I abandoned the plan to leave and continued to hold her, resuming what I hoped were soothing touches. I didn't know if this would be welcomed, but I lightly kissed the side of her head and whispered. "It's okay, Amelia. You're safe. I'm here with you."

She leaned into me. "Oh, E," she said through her sobs, "I've been such an asshole to you, and I'm so sorry." She looked at the floor.

"It's okay," I said in my most reassuring voice.

"No, no it's not." I felt her raise her body up so she could look at me. Her nose was red, and her face was streaked with tears. "You deserve so much better. You... You..." She breathed out and reached up with both hands to cup my face. "There's no one like you," she whispered.

The Fourth Chanukah – I'm 18, Finally

By the next Chanukah, I knew I'd be heading to UConn at the end of the summer. In the fall, I'd been invited to spend a weekend in the dorm where a lot of the team lived and then encouraged to apply early. My acceptance had arrived right before Thanksgiving along with a full basketball scholarship. There'd be no need to apply anywhere else. I was set.

I was pretty happy with college in the bag and my last season of high school basketball about to begin, even though I no longer had a girlfriend. Sofia's dad had been called to Washington, DC, to work in Estonia's embassy. She'd told me it was a big honor. She'd also told me it didn't make sense for us to continue being together since we'd be living in different cities and soon after that we'd be in college.

It was kind of a bummer since I really liked her a lot and, well, she was my first, you know…experience with sex. But I knew it was better to make a clean break than to sit around and watch this thing we had fade away.

Besides, Amelia and I were talking again. She'd broken up with Spike, saying all the stuff you say when you break up with someone, like "What was I thinking?" and "She was a disaster." I tried my best not to enthusiastically agree, but it wasn't easy.

She'd also been accepted early decision and would be going to Fowler College in western Massachusetts.

"*That's a great school.*" I texted. "*I'm glad they realized how smart you are.*"

"*Please E. I'm a legacy. My mom went there.*"

"*Still…*"

"*So we're coming for Chanukah because I was invited to spend a weekend at Fowler.*"

"*I know.*"

I followed that up with some smiley faces and a thumbs-up sticker.

I was excited at the prospect of seeing Amelia again, but also nervous and a bit confused. What did I want from her? What did she want from me? Was there a chance we could have something?

As I've gotten older, some things my family does every year have become boring. Like, for example, the annual summer trip to Montauk, which used to be so much fun, has felt like a big drag the past few years. Once I've gone to the beach and the pool, ridden a bike to the lighthouse, and looked at all the stores, there's nothing more for me there. No friends, no basketball, and only my computer to keep me company.

But the yearly Chanukah party has never gotten old. It's still something I look forward to, even after the year that Amelia and her black hoodie ruined it for me. I still strip to a T-shirt and sweats and follow all of my mother's orders without complaint. I still breathe in the smell of potatoes and onions frying in oil and look forward to the sight of lit candles set into a dozen menorahs brightening our dining room when my father has turned out the lights.

I haven't looked at the Jewish calendar for next year, but at least I'll be close enough to home to try to get back for this party, even if Chanukah doesn't overlap with my winter break. I wouldn't want to miss it. And while I'm probably getting ahead of myself, it would also be possible for Amelia to come as well.

When she walked into my house this time, we both stood and smiled at one another. Her hair was loose, the waves reaching right below her shoulders. She looked healthy, in like a glowing way. Her eyes were bright and her stance was comfortable and open.

I walked over to her and put my hands on her shoulders. "Hi, A."

"Hi, E," she whispered.

I took her coat and backpack, and she followed me to my room.

She took the backpack from me and zipped it open. "I brought you something."

She handed me three paperback books, each with a picture of a female basketball player on the cover. "They're books about lesbian basketball players."

I stared at the covers and turned one over to read the back. "Wow, these are awesome."

I leaned over and decided I would go for it. I kissed her, softly at first, and then I felt her respond with a much more intense kiss, her tongue stroking my bottom lip. I opened my mouth, and our tongues met and began to explore one another. I heard Amelia's soft moan, and I pulled her closer.

After a few minutes, she broke the kiss, and we both sat there catching our breath. She laid her head on my shoulder, and I held her there. The vision of us standing in that bodega behind the bread display came into my head. I ran my fingers through her hair, knowing that holding her here in my room where it was warm and safe was so much better than our scary adventure last year.

I didn't know if she wanted to take this further, but I knew I did. Despite her rejection of me two years ago, and despite the other relationships we'd both had since, my heart had always been with Amelia.

I kissed her cheek and spoke quietly into her ear. "I was wondering. Our neighbor is away for a few days, and I'm taking care of her cats and watering the plants. We could be alone there. No parents."

"Erica Mandel," she said, and giggled. "Are you propositioning me?"

I thought she was teasing but I was a little nervous that maybe she wasn't. "Well…uh, I mean, we don't have to. I just thought…"

She pulled back so she was facing me and smiled, then gave me a sweet little kiss. "I was just making sure that you were really propositioning me before I said yes," she said, and threw her arms around my neck in a tight hug.

I grabbed onto her, and we both shook with laughter, mine more from relief.

"How soon can we leave to go to your neighbor's? Can we tell everyone that her cats must be starving?"

I moved out of our hug and took Amelia's hands in mine. "We should get through the candle lighting first so nobody gives us a hard time."

Amelia got up and walked around my room, looking at my books and the pictures on my walls. I put on some music.

"So, uh, Fowler, huh? You excited?"

She turned to me. "Extremely."

"You know it has a reputation as a lesbian school. I guess you'll have your pick of girls there."

There was some truth to that statement, but I'd said it to test her. Despite all our kissing and the promise of more later, I still wasn't sure who we were to one another.

Amelia just shrugged in response. "What about you, E? Don't you think every gay girl at UConn is going to find the new sexy basketball player irresistible?"

Wow, she called me sexy. I couldn't hide a wide grin until I realized that she might be taking it as a sign that I was hoping she was right.

I went to her and pulled her to me. "There's only one girl I want to be irresistible to, and she's right here."

"Well, E, I'm glad to hear that because I may not be as much of a computer whiz as you, but I do know how to use Google Maps. Did you know that Fowler and UConn are only an hour away from each other?"

I kissed her. "Mmm, my girl is so smart."

"Yes she is." Amelia nipped at my earlobe with her teeth.

I was sure she could hear my heart pounding. I grasped her arms so I could remain standing. When I regained some control, I kissed her along her jawline. Her breathing accelerated.

"So, A," I said, my voice low and as sexy as I could make it, "did you know that because of my scholarship I'll have enough money to buy a car next year?"

She moaned in response, just as we were both shocked out of our private little world by the loud knocking on my bedroom door, followed by my father's booming voice.

"Erica! Amelia! Candles! Now!"

It was the moment when all the candles were lit that always made me smile. Tonight was the seventh night, so it was quite a little bonfire lighting up our dining room. Amelia and I stood close, our fingers laced together. I didn't care who saw. In fact, I hoped they all did.

Once again, my mom made her little speech about the fact that we should say the *Shehecheyanu* in honor of our gathering. And so we recited it in Hebrew, followed by the English, thanking God for giving us life, for sustaining us, and for enabling us to reach this season.

I put my arm around Amelia, and in my head, I repeated that last prayer of gratitude. *Thank you, for letting us reach this season.*

The Night Before Christmas—a Cumbrian Tale

BY ANDREA BRAMHALL

SAMANTHA KING CLIMBED OUT OF the car and followed her husband up the steps of the tiny chapel overlooking Buttermere village and lake, careful not to slip on the ice reflecting the moonlight. Not that the light lasted long. It was quickly buried beneath the mass of pregnant clouds clamouring to fill the sky.

She checked her watch. Ten forty-eight p.m. Only twelve minutes to make nice to the in-laws before the start of the Christmas Eve midnight service. Just one of the many family traditions she'd suffered through during the fifteen years of her marriage. It wasn't the chapel or the sweet carol service she objected to. It was being forced to make nice to Tim's parents while every year, his and his family's traditions took precedence over her own.

One more dried-out, overstuffed Turkey dinner, with more food than any sane person should try to stuff down their throats. Christmas cake served with cheese. Cheese. For pity's sake. *We're from Yorkshire*, Tim tells her, *we've to uphold our Yorkshire traditions even if we are in the Lake District now*. So, every time she tried to buy brandy sauce or that lovely new Bailey's cream concoction she saw at the supermarket, a twisted scowl carved itself upon his face, and his traditions speech started all over again. *Christmas cake is served with a lump of hard cheese.*

She adjusted the headband touting reindeer antlers she was wearing and supressed the smile that tugged at her lips when she thought about her promise to herself. This would be the last year she'd be forced into this event. The last time she'd be obliged to sit down with Tim and his parents and sing "Once in Royal David's City" and "Good King Wenceslas."

Sam leant forward to receive the one-armed hug and kiss, that didn't touch her cheek, from her mother-in-law, received a grunt of acknowledgment from Tim's father, and took her seat on the hard wooden pew. She felt a moment's regret that she wouldn't be here next year as she looked around at the small sea of merry Santa hats and antler headpieces. The little chapel was a quaint throwback to bygone days that flooded her with warm feelings of nostalgia.

Sam shook off the thoughts and turned the pages in the program. The words of every song were firmly imprinted in her mind. She didn't need to read them; she just needed the distraction.

Merry fucking Christmas, Sam. She scoffed at herself and covered it with a cough as eyes turned to stare at her. If only her naivety—no, her gullibility—were as easy to conceal.

Tim held out an unlit candle to her. The faint smell of smoke thickened the air as wicks were lit from each other.

Tim frowned. "What's up with you?" he whispered gruffly. "You've got a face on you like a slapped arse." He held his lit candle to hers. "At least try to pretend you're having a good time. My mum and dad'll think we're arguing again if you keep this up."

She hitched an eyebrow and straightened her back a little as she pulled away from him. The tiny flame of her candle dying as she moved too quickly for it to hold the meagre beginnings of heat it had started to gather. *Says it all, doesn't it?* She stared at the blackened wick as it cooled swiftly and hung over at the tip, like it was hanging its head in shame. It was Christmas Eve, she was surrounded by people, most of whom she knew, many she had treated in her GP surgery, she was stood next to her husband…and she had never, ever, felt so alone.

Sam rose when Tim nudged her with his elbow as the vicar led them all in the first song of the service. Fairy lights twinkled on the Christmas tree, giving Sam something to focus on, something to get lost in. As she whispered the gentle words of "Silent Night," she imagined each coloured bulb was a wish she could grant herself when she walked out of the church. Each dancing pulse of electricity lit the growing need in her. The need to stretch further than she'd been able to, to reach higher than she'd been encouraged to believe she could, and to feel the freedom she'd been denied too long.

When the service ended, the usual tradition was to go back to Tim's parent's house, for a nightcap. Sam had no intention of that happening tonight.

She leant over to whisper into Tim's ear, "Tell them whatever you want, but I'm not going back to your parents' tonight."

"It's tradition, Sam," he whispered back hoarsely. "We always—"

She cut him off and said quietly, "If you want to go with them, give me the keys and I'll drive myself home." She held out her hand, not expecting him to hand over the keys to his precious Audi, but it made her point. He scowled and shook his head.

When the service finished, Sam didn't wait for him to speak; she didn't even say good-bye. She walked straight out of the chapel and made her way to the car in the dark and rain. She didn't care that she got wet waiting for Tim to make the rounds, and excuses for her absence. She didn't care that she was cold and her teeth were chattering.

The orange lights of the car beeped and the internal light came on, startling Sam and she pulled open the door. Sliding into the passenger seat, she wrapped her arms around herself, chaffing at them for warmth. The cold was finally making itself known.

Tim's face was red, blotchy, and angry. "I told them all you were coming down with one of your migraines and you needed your medication. That we'd see Mum and Dad tomorrow for lunch. Don't make a liar of me when they ask you tomorrow."

Sam clipped her seatbelt into place but didn't say anything.

"What the fuck is wrong with you?" he demanded as he started up the engine and jerked the heater up to full blast. "Why'd you just run out like that?" His blond hair showed in stark contrast to the blood red of the rest of his face, and his blue eyes were hooded with temper.

She'd thought him handsome once. The slightly flabby jowls and the stomach hanging over the top of his pants detracted from that, but he was still a good-looking bloke for his age. At almost fifty, she wondered if he was ready for what lay ahead of him.

Pressing her head back against the head rest, still rubbing at her arms, she said, "I didn't run out. I walked out."

He grunted. "Why?" He turned to face her. "It's not like you to be rude. What's up? Time of the month?"

"Fuck off, Tim."

He snorted derisively. "Sounds about right."

He pulled off the grass verge, his wheels sliding a little on the soft ground. There had been so much rain lately that everywhere was saturated. Lakes, rivers, and streams were swollen, and everyone was on flood alert. Another downpour was not a welcome event.

Sam sighed heavily. Suddenly, tomorrow seemed just too far away. She didn't want to continue the charade anymore. She was done. "Tim, we need to talk."

"Isn't that what I've been asking you to do since we got in the car?"

"Lucy Booker came into the surgery this morning."

Tim's knuckles turned white as his grip tightened on the steering wheel. "I didn't know she was your patient."

"She isn't. It was an emergency appointment, and I was free."

Tim stared silently out into the night, hands guiding the car, the muscles in his jaw bunching and releasing under skin that had gone pale.

"She's twenty-two, Tim."

"What does her age have to do with me?" he asked through gritted teeth.

"You'll be fifty in February."

"I'm still not seeing your point. What does she have to do with me?"

Sam hadn't expected him to make it an easy conversation, but she had professional ethics to consider. If he was going to make it a dirty fight, she at least needed to protect herself. "I can't discuss anything medical with you, as you know. But I can tell you that she confessed to being in a relationship with you."

The engine revved harder as Tim's anger made his foot rest heavier on the accelerator. The narrow road up the Newlands Pass wound tightly around the crags and crevices of the fell, clinging like a black ribbon to the side of the rock- and grass-covered mountains. Sharp turns, blind bends, and the pitch-black night made Sam nervous.

"She's lying," he spat out.

Original. "I don't think she is."

"You believe some jumped-up little tart over your husband?"

"She has a way to prove it, Tim." She looked at him and swallowed down her nerves as the car got faster and faster. Carrying on this conversation in the car didn't seem like a good idea. She should have waited until they'd gotten home, but it was too late now.

He growled and slammed his fists on the steering wheel, accelerating more.

"Tim, slow down. The road's too wet to be doing sixty."

"I'm not doing sixty."

"Fine. The road's too wet to be doing fifty-nine miles an hour." She gripped the handle over the passenger door with her left hand and her seat with her right. "This road isn't safe to be doing this speed on a dry day, never mind a wet night."

"Am I the one who's driving?"

"Yes, but…"

"If you want to drive, just say so."

"Fine. Pull over."

He grunted but didn't pull over.

"I'll drive. You're driving like a lunatic, and you're going to get us both killed if you're not—"

Sam screamed as Tim yanked on the wheel and the car lost contact with the road.

Chloe Dexter stuffed the last bite from her stash of her mum's world— okay, Lake District—famous only-ever-made-for-Christmas mince pie into her mouth and caught her buzzing mobile phone before it rattled itself off the dashboard where she'd only just tossed it. She finished clicking her seatbelt into place and straightened the Santa hat on her head—good for customer relations apparently equalled good for donations to keep the team well-funded, well equipped, and well trained—before she glanced at the screen. A slew of messages from the Cockermouth Mountain Rescue team's base station filled her in on developments across the area. It wasn't good.

0021: ALL TEAMS ALERT. FLOOD WARNINGS ACROSS COUNTY. GOLD COMMAND ADVISE THIRLMERE RESERVOIR IN DANGER OF BREACH. ALPHA PLAN TO COMMENCE AT 0130 HRS. ALL TEAM MEMBERS ADVISE OF STATUS AND AVAIBLBILITY.

0022: SWIFT WATER RESCUE TEAMS PLEASE REPORT TO BASE STATIONS ASAP.

0022: WHINLATTER PASS CLOSED.

0023: HONISTER PASS CLOSED.

0023: CRUMMOCK WATER BURST BANKS. ROAD IMPASSIBLE DUE TO FLOODING.

"Fan-fucking-tastic. And a Merry Christmas to you too," Chloe muttered under her breath, and thanked her lucky stars that her rescue gear was already stowed in her car and that she'd been expecting something like this to happen. Sod's law, it would be tonight when the shit hit the fan.

Five years on the Cockermouth Mountain Rescue team had taught her a thing or two, and her remote location on a farm at the bottom of the Buttermere Valley was both a blessing and a curse. Tonight, it was going to cause her all manner of problems. Lakes and mountains to the south blocked her way out; passes to the east and west were now closed. There were two routes North: Whinlater Pass—already closed—and Newlands Pass.

Given the heavy falling rain, the overfull rivers, and already swollen lakes across the area, the implementation of Alpha plan was going to cause terrible flooding through Keswick and Cockermouth. Quite simply, to preserve the water source for hundreds of the thousands of people, they were going to open the reservoir flood gates. Sacrificing hundreds of homes and businesses across the two towns and in between.

"On Christmas Eve too." Chloe sighed heavily and grabbed her radio.

Keying the mic, she said, "Charlie base, this is Charlie Chloe, come in, over."

The silence of the car was only disturbed by the pounding of rain on the roof as she waited for Cockermouth base to respond to her call.

"Charlie Chloe, this is Charlie base, go ahead, over."

"Charlie base, be advised that I am en route but having to come over Newlands Pass as the only route left out of the valley, putting me closer to Keswick than Cockermouth. I know their SWRT leader is still out after dislocating his knee. I have my gear in the car, and Keswick will be first and worst hit when Alpha plan goes ahead. Please advise them that I will head their way. Over."

"Charlie Chloe, received and understood, will advise Keswick team to expect you. Please be aware we are receiving advisories that the river at Braithwaite is under threat. Drive careful, drive safe, but drive fast if you're going to make it out of that valley. It won't be long before nothing is going in or out of there. Over."

"Shit," Chloe said to herself before she keyed the mic one last time. "Understood, Charlie base. Safe and fast. I'll let you know when I get there before I turn over to Keswick radio frequency. Over and out."

She let go of her radio mic, checked her mirror as she turned on the engine to the old Range Rover she drove, and pulled out of the farm yard. Glad she had a snorkel fitted on the huge vehicle, because she was damn sure she was going to need it.

Chloe kept her radio on and listened to the chatter across the frequency as she powered her vehicle across the dark tarmac, sending wash after wash of spray up from her wheels. The windscreen wipers slid across the glass as fast as they could, but visibility was still conservatively shit. She slowed as she approached the right-hand turn that would take her past the church and up onto the Newlands Pass.

Chloe eased up on the clutch and started to climb, grateful that whatever Christmas tourists were about were safely ensconced in their cosy hotels, apartments, or better yet…the pub, and weren't out to slow her down. The Newlands Pass was the easiest of the three passes out of the valley, probably why it was usually one of the last to close, but that didn't mean it was an easy drive. There were numerous sharp bends, steep drop offs, blind dips, and the amount of water running down and across the tarmac made it slick; the danger of aquaplaning was very, very real. And drivers unused to the roads and conditions…were another hazard entirely.

A quick glance at the clock on the dashboard told her it was almost half past midnight and they had only an hour to clear the overflow zone in Keswick before people would be caught in their homes and in their beds, when the river burst its banks and started to fill the streets, overwhelm the sewers, and flood people's houses with the foul gunk they flushed away. Not a Christmas present anyone wanted…nor deserved. No matter how naughty you'd been.

Shifting down a gear as the road got steeper, she crested the top of the pass and slammed on her brakes as a man stumbled into the road, one hand held up to block the lights from her car and the other pressed against his Santa-hat-clad head. Red blood seeped between his fingers and ran down his cheeks in thin rivulets. His clothes and hands were caked in mud.

"Jesus," Chloe shouted as her training kicked in and she pulled on the handbrake. Without a second thought, she threw open the door and rounded the vehicle until she was in front of the man. She gripped his elbow and turned him towards her headlights so she could see him more clearly. "Sir, can you hear me?"

His eyes looked glazed, his skin was pale, and his mouth opened and closed without forming words.

"Sir, can you tell me your name?" Chloe tried again.

No change. It was like he didn't even see her.

She shook his arm as she spoke to him this time, hoping for a response. "Sir, what's your name?"

His gaze suddenly seemed to focus on her, and his lips formed meaningful shapes. "T-t-t-tim," he mumbled.

"Nice to meet you, Tim. I'm Chloe. I'm with the Mountain Rescue Service. Will you let me take a look at your head?"

He nodded, and Chloe led him to the back of the Range Rover. She dropped the tail flap and managed to get him sitting on it. The split tail offered them a roof of sorts as she pulled out a head torch and some first-aid supplies, but it did little to protect them from the rain that was almost coming at them sideways.

"Can you tell me what happened, Tim?" Chloe snapped on a pair of latex gloves and wrapped a silver space blanket around his shoulders. She pulled his hand away from his head, whipped off the Santa hat, and tilted his chin down so she could see the relatively small gash at his temple.

"Car…" He pointed into the darkness where the road dropped off by the side of Robinson fell.

"Car crash?" she asked, trying to clarify what had happened as she cleaned blood off his face with alcohol wipes.

"Y-y-yes." His teeth were chattering with the cold.

She needed to get him in the car and warmed up, but she wanted to make sure he had no other injuries first. "Does anything else hurt?"

"N-no, just my head."

"Okay, that's good. I'll get this cleaned up and then we'll try and get you warmed up. What were you doing out tonight?"

"Ch-church." He pointed back down the road towards Buttermere.

"Ah, the midnight service?"

"Yes. We were on the way home after…"

"We?"

He nodded as she applied a couple of steri-strips to the small cut.

"There was someone in the car with you?"

"My wife."

"Is she still in the car?"

He nodded again.

Chloe turned to look in the direction he'd pointed. She knew the mountain, the area, and the waterfall that cascaded down the side. It was a long drop to the bottom, and the waterfall was a raging torrent with the heavy rainfall. She shuddered at the thought of going over the edge. At the thought of being anywhere near the icy water that was gushing down the side of the mountain.

"Can you show me where?"

Tim pointed again in vaguely the same direction.

Chloe tugged on his arm, pulling him to his feet. "Come on, Tim. I need you to show me exactly where your car went off the road."

He stumbled, and she caught him under his arm. He was significantly taller than her, but she managed to assist him across the layby that was a popular parking area for tourists to take pictures of the waterfall and the view down to the valley below. When he pointed down the side of the cliff, she gasped as she saw the car perched precariously, wedged against the rocks under the waterfall, with the front end of the vehicle looking like it was half buried into the mud and grass on the other side of what was essentially a small ravine. Below the middle of the car was empty air, and a drop of probably another hundred feet.

The back end of the Audi A4 saloon was pointed lower than the front end by about thirty or forty degrees, and the way it was wedged, Chloe knew she wouldn't be able to open the passenger-side door. It looked like it had spun in the air before getting lodged. The window might be a possibility though.

"Tim, were you driving?" she asked, noting that the windscreen on the driver's side had a hole in it.

Tim nodded.

"You managed to climb out?"

"Yes, she needs help."

"Your wife?"

"Yes. She's stuck in there. I couldn't get her out."

Chloe assessed the side of the slope down to the vehicle and managed to supress a whistle. It wasn't vertical, but it wasn't far off. Tim had had to climb up and out of there. Little wonder his hands and knees looked caked in mud.

"Was she conscious?"

Tim shook his head.

Shit. Her next question needed to be asked, but she was well aware that it could send Tim off emotionally. Chloe took a deep breath and asked calmly, "Was she alive? Did you feel for a pulse of check her breathing?"

Tim nodded. "She was moaning a little bit, but she was pretty out of it. Didn't seem to understand when I told her I was going to try and find help."

Moaning. That was a good sign. "What time was that? Do you know?"

"No. We'd just left the church after the service when I-I…when I lost control of the car."

"It's a wet night, Tim. Accidents happen. Now, I need to get down there to get a look at your wife. What's her name?"

"Sam. Samantha. King."

"Okay, but first things first, we need to get you somewhere you can get a bit warmer and drier, and I need to let my team know where I am and see if we can get some more help up here."

Tim shook his head. "Just help Sam."

Chloe put a hand on his arm. "I will, Tim. But I'm pretty sure I'm going to need some help to do that for her safety as well as mine. And if you don't get warm, you're going to be no help to your wife when I do get her out of there."

"I'm not going anywhere while she's stuck—"

"I want you in the Range Rover, with the heater on full blast. I've got a set of overalls in the back, some blankets, and a thermos of coffee. There's a sleeping bag in my kit too. I want you to get out of those wet clothes, get a warm drink, and warm up in the car. You'll be right here when she needs you."

He nodded. "Thanks."

"Don't mention it." She hurried back to the car, keying her mic as she walked. "Charlie base, this is Charlie Chloe, come in, over," she said, her mouth close to the handset as she dug through the boot to free the items she needed.

"Charlie Chloe, this is Charlie base, reading you loud and clear, over."

Chloe smiled as she recognised her mother's voice over the crackly connection. Rita Dexter had been a member of Cockermouth Mountain Rescue Team for twenty years.

Keeping the radio protocols in place, Chloe depressed the button and started to speak to her mother. "Charlie base, I'm at the top of Newlands Pass and encountered the victim of a car accident in the middle of the road. The car has gone off the cliff and is wedged into the fell side and rocks between the road and Robinson almost directly under the waterfall. There's a woman still trapped in the car. I could use some help up here. Over."

Chloe waited a moment as she lifted a couple of overall sets, making sure she found the spare that used to be her dad's and was considerably larger than her own. She suspected it would still be a little small for Tim. But it was dry and considerably warmer than what he was wearing now.

"Charlie Chloe, the river at Braithwaite burst its bank. The road is flooded and impassable, even with our snorkelled vehicles. We can't get anyone out there to you. Over."

Well, fuck a duck, isn't that just a wonderful turn up for the books. She slapped the handset to her forehead while she thought about what she needed to do to try and rescue the woman, and what might be needed after that. She had a winch on the Range Rover; she could use that as her safety line and to pull the woman up after she got her out of the car. It was going to be getting her out of the car that was going to be the problem. Chloe cast a glance at the gear she had in her car. Dry suit, first-aid pack, O2, Entonox, and she even had the morphine kit locked away in the safe.

"Charlie Chloe, this is Charlie base, do you read me, over?"

"Charlie base, I'm here. Just assessing my very limited options. Over."

"Charlie Chloe, switch to channel four and fix your line open. I'm going to stay on this one with you. Do you copy? Over."

"Charlie base, I copy. Switching to channel four on an open line. Over and out."

Chloe quickly adjusted the frequency on her radio set and keyed the mic line constantly open.

"Chloe, baby, are you there?"

"I'm here, Mum."

"Good. What's your plan?"

Chloe tossed the overalls at Tim and dumped blankets and a sleeping bag on the back seat of the car. She turned her back as he quickly began to strip out of his wet clothes.

"I'm going to use the winch on the Rover to get down to the car and assess the patient and situation as it is there. I'm going to get into my dry suit first though. The waterfall is practically hitting the roof of the car and looks like it's pouring in through the broken windshield."

"Good plan. Do you have any assistance up there, honey?"

Chloe knew what she really was asking was asking how useful the victim she already had with her was going to be. She looked him over critically. He seemed to be doing better now that she was talking to him and he had things to do. She wasn't confident that would last when she had to leave him alone.

"The woman's husband is here with me." She pulled out the bag that contained her water gear and started to gear up. "I'll show him how to operate the winch from the Rover and leave the radio on in the car. He'll be able to communicate with us both on that. He's cold and wet, but we're working to change that now, and I'm hoping a cup of my world-famous coffee will help with the rest."

Chloe knew her mother would be able to read between the lines. She attached her climbing harness over her dry suit and tugged at the first-aid kit, added the morphine, and attached extra web straps to the pack that she kept around for emergencies. She secured the two cylinders to either side of the heavy bag, slid in an ice axe—just in case—and hefted it to test the weight. Damn, that shit was heavy. She was immensely glad she was going to be relying on the winch to secure her weight, up and down, because the pack was going to make her unbalanced and ungainly.

"Tim, can you come here a second?"

Tim rounded the back of the car; the dark green overalls barely reached his ankles and didn't cover his wrists, and he had the silver foil space blanket wrapped over his head and shoulders as a makeshift poncho. The sight of him would be funny in other circumstances. Instead of laughing, Chloe pointed to each of the packs in the car, explaining what they were.

"I won't be taking the winch off my harness. I've got a spare in my kit. If I can get it on your wife, and attach her to the line, I will. But that may not be possible. If it isn't, I have other options. Not as injury friendly, but they will save her life. You okay with that?"

He nodded. "Save her. We can deal with whatever happens from there. I just… It's my fault. Just don't let her die."

"Right, jump in." She climbed in the driver's side and crawled the Range Rover as close to the edge where the car was as she could possibly get, explaining the operations of the radio and winch as she did. "Okay, let's go see if I can give you the best Christmas present ever."

Tim looked crestfallen, but he nodded.

When they were in position, pack tightly strapped to her back and the winch secured to her harness, Chloe told him to start lowering the winch. Slowly. Very slowly. It took him a few seconds to get to grips with the speed function but not long at all. By the time she was halfway to the car, she had turned on the head torch attached to her helmet and was looking over her shoulder as much as she could to gauge the distance left to the vehicle. Wind and rain whipped her face, and her heels slid on the muddy ground and slippery rocks, but this was what Chloe lived for. The chance to help someone when few others could.

"Chloe?" Rita's voice crackled from the handset she'd clipped to the shoulder of her suit.

"Yeah, Mum?"

"How're you doing?"

"Almost at the car."

"Can you see a safe approach?"

"Define safe?" she said with a chuckle.

"Chloe Annabelle Dexter, don't piss me off."

"Sounds like you already are."

"Chloe." Her mother's voice was little more than a growl.

"Fine, fine. I'm going to approach the passenger side first. It's close to the rocks, so I'm hoping I'll find some purchase without having to add my weight to the vehicle. I don't know how securely wedged it is, and don't want to risk making it fall if I don't have to." She crept a little towards the passenger side and shone her light into the windscreen. Chloe could see the woman now. She wasn't moving.

There were perches on the rocks for Chloe to put her feet, but precarious was an understatement. Still, it was better than nothing. Wind cut through the gorge, whipping frozen pellets of rain into her face and stealing the breath from her before she could suck it into her lungs. Rocks, sharp as blades, sliced through the wet and tender skin of her hands, but she ignored every painful sensation as she secured herself as best she could to try and help the injured woman. She'd been right; there was no way she could get the door open, and with the woman unconscious, the only way she'd be able to access her here would be to break the window. Not ideal with an unconscious and uncovered patient.

She knocked on the window. "Sam? Samantha King, can you hear me?" She knocked again. "My name's Chloe Dexter, I'm from the Mountain Rescue team at Cockermouth. I need you to wake up, Sam."

Nothing.

"Mum, I can't get any access to the patient from the passenger side, she's unconscious and unresponsive. I'm going to have to try another option."

"And that would be?"

"I'm open to suggestions. Right now, the only thing I can think of is try to pull off the already broken windscreen or climb into the car on the driver's side through the broken windscreen."

"Not the driver's door?"

"That's hanging over about a hundred feet of empty air, and jostling against the car is as likely to dislodge it from its perch as climbing on the bonnet and getting access that way."

"How did the husband get out?"

"I climbed out through the smashed window and across the bonnet of the car," Tim said over the radio.

"You a big guy, Tim?" Rita asked.

"About six foot two, and a bit heavier than my wife, the GP, tells me I should be."

"Then that car should be safe enough for you, Chlo."

At five foot three and slim to the side of skinny, Chloe was inclined to agree. She still didn't like how risky it was. Not to her. She had on a harness and was attached to a car that weighed two and a half tons without all the additional gear she had on hers. No, Chloe was worried that dislodging the car would without doubt mean it plummeting further and killing her patient. The weight of the water accumulating in the back of the car was not going to be insignificant. And there was nothing Chloe could do about that. But sitting there doing nothing wasn't going to help her patient either.

The wind shifted, and suddenly, Chloe became very aware of just how cold the spray of water from the torrent tumbling over the side of the mountain actually was. It was icy. It felt like needles prickling at her skin. Knowing that Samantha King had been exposed to that frigid temperature for well over half an hour now made up Chloe's mind for her. Hypothermia was a killer.

"Okay, I'm going to step onto the bonnet and make my way inside the car."

"Take it steady, and keep double check your safety line, kiddo."

"Yes, Mum," Chloe responded into her mic.

She slipped her kit bag off her shoulders and laid it as gently as she could onto the red metal, then worked her way around the bonnet.

Chloe took a deep breath and steadied herself. With one last tug on the harness and carabiner about her waist, she stepped onto the precariously perched vehicle. The raw sound of metal grating against rock assaulted her ears over the howling wind and pouring rain. She held still, breath caught in her throat as she waited for the car to plummet to the bottom of the ravine.

It didn't.

Swallowing hard, she took another step, her full weight now balancing on the slick bonnet.

One step.

Two.

Her footing gave way.

"Shit," she squawked as she slid the last foot to the windscreen. She managed to brace her hands on the roof of the car before she slammed into the shattered glass.

"Chlo? What happened?"

Chloe caught her breath and answered, "Just slid on the wet metal. I'm fine." She crouched down and peered into the car. There was a lot of water inside the vehicle. A lot. And more was added every second as the frigid waterfall continued to fill up the enclosed space. She was going to have to deal with that before too long, but first things first. Was she still alive? Was she still breathing? Was she trapped or just unconscious?

Come on, it's Christmas, Universe. Don't let me have to deal with a DB on Christmas.

After stepping through the hole in the windscreen, she crouched onto the driver's seat and put her hands on Samantha's shoulders. Shaking her, she asked, "Sam, are you awake? Can you hear me?"

Nothing.

She shook again. "Sam, come on, open your eyes for me."

Sam's head rolled to one side, and Chloe could make out a thin line of blood running down her face from her temple. Potential head injury. Potential spinal injury. Unresponsive to sound or stimuli. Chloe pinched at Sam's upper arm and got a groan from her patient.

Chloe smiled. "Well, alrighty then. Patient responding to a good old-fashioned pinch on the arm. She's alive and breathing of her own accord." She put her hand under the woman's collar. Her own hands were cold, but Sam felt like ice beneath her touch. "But she's damn cold."

"Chloe, I don't need to remind you that I can't—"

"I know, Mum. The valley's cut off and the air ambulance can't fly at night." She reached behind her and retrieved the cervical collar from the first-aid-kit bag before she slid it gently behind Sam's neck. "I'm on my own in getting her warmed up once I get her out of here."

"I'm sorry, kiddo."

"Not your fault." She pulled a space blanket out of the kit bag and covered it over Sam's body. "I need to get the rest of the windscreen out of the way. It's the only way I'm going to be able to see what's going on and get her out of the car."

"Whatever you need to do, kiddo. I trust your judgement."

"I'm seeing indications of a head injury. I've got a collar on, but I can't ascertain if there's any spinal injury. Mum…"

"Understood. She has to live before anything else can be a worry."

Chloe didn't need to spell out her concerns that getting Sam out of the car and back up the cliff could exacerbate any potential injury she might have. Or cause another one. But if Chloe left her where she was, she would die. Soon. That had to be her priority.

She grasped the ice axe and used the sharp edge to score along the rubber seal as far around the window as she could reach, then, getting her back under the glass, she pushed up with her thighs and pushed her right arm out. The rubber seal gave way under the pressure, and the window popped out without shattering over Sam. Within seconds, the glass pane was careening to the bottom of the cliff and lost from sight. Now able to get much closer to Sam, Chloe could see that one leg was caught on some protruding metal coming into the foot well from the engine. Reaching down, she felt up and down Sam's calf.

"Okay, the glass is clear, and I can see what she's caught on. I'm pretty sure it's only caught on fabric, but the angle is awkward. I'm going to drop the seat back and see if that gives me enough room to free her leg."

"Chlo, Mike suggests getting a rope around her and tie her onto your harness in case the movement jostles the car."

Chloe smiled; she'd already grabbed the spare length of rope that was in the pack and was passing it under Sam's arms and around her back before tying a bowline knot about her chest, then repeating the process under each thigh. "Already on it, Mum."

She gave the rope enough slack to accommodate the chair sliding back, but no more. Offering a silent prayer to whoever might be listening, she grasped the metal bar at the front of the seat and gritted her teeth. She pushed until it released the lock with a grating pop and the chair shifted, Sam's legs immediately sliding free of their entrapment. She groaned, but otherwise didn't stir.

"Got her legs free, and she's secure to me." Chloe gathered the items she'd taken out of her pack, stuffed them inside, and with great difficulty slid it back on her back. She didn't know what she might need when she got Samantha back to her house to warm her up. She couldn't afford to leave her kit behind if it was at all possible.

"Do you think you can get her out of there now?" Rita asked.

"Not on my own. Tim, you there?"

"I'm here."

"How're you doing, mate?"

"I'm okay. I can feel my hands again."

"I'm very glad to hear that, because I'm going to need you to use them and very, very slowly lift me and Samantha out of here on that winch. You up to it?"

"Whatever you need."

"Okay, give me one sec here." She reached into the footwell and one by one lifted Sam's legs so that her feet were on the bonnet of the car, then wrapped the space blanket around the back of her shoulders and head. Given the awkward way they were harnessed together, this was going to be the best Chloe could do to protect Sam's legs and feet from getting stuck on the way out and her head and shoulders from being bashed into the car at the same time.

"Right, Tim. Are you ready?"

"I'm good."

"On three, then, very, very slowly ease back on the winch."

"Got it."

"One." She tightened her grip on the space blanket. "Two." She tugged the blanket forward a little, easing Sam into the sling it made. "Three."

The tugging at her waist began to lift them both, millimetre by tiny millimetre, out of the clutches of the cold and wet carcass of the car. As the ropes tugged Sam forward, her feet slid and her head and body swung out of the car far easier than Chloe had imagined it would.

"Mum, Tim, we're both clear of the vehicle now." Chloe slowly walked herself step by step up the cliff, travelling backwards so she could see Sam every step of the way.

Sam's feet scrapped and dragged against the mud and rocks, making her body spin and twist on the end of the rope. Chloe used the blanket to steady her as much as she could, but there was little that could be done to stop it from happening.

She glanced over her shoulder, waiting for the top to arrive with every step. Her first step over the edge of the cliff and back on to level ground caused her to stumble, and she went to one knee with a soft grunt. Grabbing the ends of the blanket in her right hand, she used her left to guide Sam's body with the harness so that she turned her to get her bottom onto the grass verge and then lay her down.

"Okay, Tim. Stop." The mechanical whirring stopped; she hadn't even realised she could hear until it was gone. Chloe dropped her backpack and began to untie the knots that had secured Sam to her body. After ten seconds, she looked up and saw Tim. "Give me a hand getting her into the car."

He hooked his arms under her legs as Chloe hefted her under the armpits, keeping her neck and head as still as possible. Chloe led Sam's body on to the back seat. She used the space blanket to cover her, then grabbed the sleeping bag and wrapped that over her loosely too.

"Mum, she's in the car and I'm going to head back to the farm." She crawled out of the opposite door, grabbed her bag from the ground, and slung it into the boot, slamming it closed once she had. "Get in," she ordered Tim. He climbed into the passenger seat, staring over his shoulder at Sam all the way.

Chloe kept the Rover in second gear all the way down the pass, and still the 4x4 slid on the wet and greasy road as she crawled back to the warmth of home.

"Chloe, do you have any saline at your place? Any way to get a warmed bag into her?" Rita asked over the radio.

"I've got a cannula and tubing in the first-aid pack, but I've only got the two bags of saline in here. No more."

"That's better than nothing. I've got Dan here with me." Dan Winters was one of the GPs who advised and trained the rest of the team in the advanced first-aid techniques and treatments they were able to use. "He says heat it up in a microwave for a minute and a half. It's not ideal, but better than the alternative."

"Right."

"Remember, warm her up slowly, core first, then extremities, or you'll cause cardiac arrest."

"I remember."

"I'm on with the air ambulance, there's one going to head to you at first light from Preston. Unless…"

"Yeah, unless…"

Unless she didn't make it.

They were silent as they continued down the valley, Chloe driving as fast as she dared. She wished she was in the back with Sam, monitoring her condition. It would help her make the best plan for her treatment, but it couldn't be helped. Tim was in no fit state to drive, and she knew the roads. She'd get them there faster. He wasn't even thinking clearly. He was in shock, Chloe could see that, but at least he was responding to instruction. Warmth, fluids, maybe some food, and rest were the best medications for Tim. Sam, on the other hand… She still didn't really know.

Chloe pulled into the farm yard and almost skidded to a stop in the mud. Cutting the engine, she said, "Tim, you grab her legs again, I'll get her torso, and we get her on the sofa."

He followed her instructions to the letter, carrying Sam, then running back to the car to fetch her bag from the boot while Chloe started to cut the wet fabric from Samantha's body.

"Tim, can you run upstairs? Second door on the left. Spare bedroom. Bring the duvet down, would you?"

He nodded and left her to her work. By the time he had returned, she'd stripped Sam naked and covered her with the space blanket while she dug the saline out of her kit bag and set it in the microwave.

Tim removed the foil blanket and wrapped the soft duvet around his wife, then reached for her hand.

"Jesus, you're so cold," he said, and began chaffing at her skin.

"Don't do that. We need to warm her core before her extremities. The heart and brain need the warm blood more than her fingers and toes do right now." She swabbed the crease of Sam's arm with an alcohol wipe after securing a strap to her bicep. Damn, her veins were all shutting down; finding a place to insert the cannula was not easy. It took her at least a minute to locate the vein and slide the needle in.

The microwave pinged, and Chloe retrieved the bag and secured it to the wall lamp that hung over the sofa before she attached the line and let it run wide open into Sam's bloodstream. "Tim, you need to get out of those clothes again. The suit's wet now too. Upstairs third door on the left is the bathroom. There are clean towels in the cupboard. I'll find you something to put on after you've had a shower."

"Don't you need to get warm too?"

"I will. When I've got Sam sorted. You go now."

"You don't need me here to help?"

"You've done everything you can for the time being. I need to do a few things, and then it's pretty much up to Sam."

"Then it'll all be fine."

Chloe offered him what she hoped was a reassuring smile. "I sure hope so, Tim."

He ducked his head once more and disappeared. His footsteps were heavy on the stairs.

Chloe busied herself, setting the thermostat in the room and stoking the fire. Next, she went to the mud room and climbed out of her dry suit, shed her shoes and wet clothes, and slipped on a pair of ratty old sweat pants and a hoody.

"Okay, let's see if I can see any causes for concern, Sam." She slipped quietly back into the front room and carried out a top-to-toe survey of her patient, noting the bruises that were forming over Sam's shoulder and ribs. Seatbelt injuries, judging by the pattern. "You're gonna match the Christmas stockings I've got hung up," she mumbled to herself, and chuckled. The massive red-and-white-striped stockings had been a firm family tradition since Chloe was a child. In fact, her mum had a framed photo of said stocking with Chloe bundled inside it. "And I'm gonna burn that just as soon as I can get my hands on it." She grinned gleefully at the thought and went back to her task.

Sam's knee looked swollen, and there was a two-inch gash on it. Possibly from the rock, or it could have been from the metal in the car. Chloe didn't know, but she cleaned it up and applied steri-strips to keep it closed before she moved on. It was the head wound that she was concerned about. She used her pen light to check Sam's pupils. They were even and reactive—a good sign. The best she could hope for right now.

She went to the kitchen and put the kettle on to boil. Two cups of tea, with sugar, later; she was waiting for Tim to re-emerge. She'd put a pair of her dad's old pyjama's outside the bathroom door for him—best she could come up with on short notice—and brought down some more duvets and blankets.

Sam's pulse was getting stronger and more regular, her breathing was returning to a normal rate, and Chloe was quietly optimistic that she was going to be okay. At least on the hypothermia front. She still hadn't woken up, and she was still only responding to painful stimuli, but she was getting there.

When Tim came into the room, looking warm and pink from the hot water, she excused herself. She showered and changed before phoning the base station with an update. Then she warmed the second bag of saline, ready to hang it for Sam, and finished making tea for herself and Tim, choosing the "Bah Humbug" mug for herself and one with a dancing elf on for Tim. She appreciated the irony of the visual.

"Will she be okay?" Tim asked, when he took the mug of tea.

Chloe nodded, put her own mug down, and started to change the bags over. "I think so." She checked Sam's pupils again—no change. "She's warming up nicely, and her vital signs are getting stronger. We've done all we can to give her the best chance right now, Tim. I'm sorry, but I can't do any more."

He smiled weakly. "I know. You've been amazing. I'm… I was… I was useless."

"No, you weren't. You got out of there, and you got help. I needed equipment to get Sam out of the situation, and I needed you to help me. Without those things, I would have been even more useless."

"I doubt that."

Chloe chuckled sadly. "It's true." She sat down and sipped from her mug, letting out an appreciative hum of the builder's style tea—hot, strong, sweet, and barely an introduction to the milk. "Nothing beats a nice brew. So, what was I saying? oh yeah. You did everything you could, and together we got her here. Sometimes that's all you can do."

"It was my fault."

Chloe frowned. "What was your fault?"

"I was driving too fast."

"Ah," Chloe murmured, understanding dawning. "It's easily done. It's easy to misjudge the condition of the road. No lights make it hard to see the slick patches. It was an accident. You can't blame yourself."

"She kept telling me to slow down."

"Well, how long have you been married, Tim?"

"Fifteen years. Why?"

She shook her head pitifully. "And you still haven't learnt the cardinal rule."

"What's that?"

"The wife is always right."

He chuckled. "Yeah. I must be slow on the uptake."

"You always have been." The voice from the couch was hoarse and little more than a whisper, but it was one of the nicest sounds Chloe could ever remember hearing.

"Welcome back." Chloe knelt beside the sofa close to Sam's head. "Silly question, but…how're you feeling?"

"Did you get the registration number of the truck that ran over me?"

"That good, huh?"

"Only when I open my eyes." She closed them again. "Or breathe."

"Well, I'm certainly not going to advocate for you stopping breathing, but feel free to keep your eyes closed while you tell me what hurts. Specifically."

Sam was quiet a moment. "My head and my knee mostly."

"Okay." Chloe reached for her hands. "Squeeze my fingers." Sam did so, and Chloe uncovered her feet. "Can you wiggle your toes for me?"

"Yeah."

Chloe watched as Sam's toes danced, considerably less grey than they had been earlier. "Fabulous. I need to check your pupils, but then I'd recommend sleep for a little while."

"Got anything for this headache?"

Chloe sighed. "I suspect a concussion," she said, checking the reaction of Sam's pupils again. "Which means until you've been checked out by a doctor, I'm not going to give you anything. You're not in screaming amounts of pain, and I'd rather not mess with your brains if I don't have to."

"Spoilsport," Sam mumbled weakly, and closed her eyes again. "What happened?"

"You were in an accident."

"Hospital?"

"I'm afraid not. The roads are flooded, so I've brought you both to my farm until the cavalry arrives."

"Hope you bought a big turkey, then."

"Why's that?"

"It's Christmas. I'm looking forward to the full works."

Chloe chuckled, enamoured by her patient's sense of humour even though she'd only just come around and gone through a traumatic event. "Is that right?"

"Yeah."

"And what part of you need to be checked out by a doctor before I can give you anything did you miss?"

"I am a doctor."

Chloe glanced at Tim.

He nodded and offered a weak shrug.

"Is that so, Doctor King? Well, I do believe there are limitations in treating oneself. Makes your palms go hairy or something like that."

Sam chuckled. "I believe that's masturbation."

Chloe shrugged. "Same thing."

Tim laughed loudly.

"Funny," Sam said. "And you can be quiet too. I remember who was driving."

Tim sobered. "I'm sorry, babe. I should've listened to you. You just made me so mad. You wouldn't listen to me."

"And I'm not going to. I meant what I said. It's over, Tim."

"It doesn't have to be. We can work things out, Sam. We've got fifteen years of marriage behind us. We can make it work. I want us to make it work."

"And what about Lucy Booker? What about the baby she's carrying? Your baby."

Chloe wished she could fade into the background. Instead, she sat totally still, hoping that if she didn't move, they wouldn't see her. Hey, it had worked for the kids in *Jurassic Park* when the T-Rex was chasing them. And yup, she could totally see why Tim thought it was all his fault. She could even agree with him…in the privacy of her own head, of course. Not out loud.

She glanced down at Samantha King. Light-brown, shoulder-length hair curled into little wisps about her face as it dried; the strong, bold planes of her face were beautiful and spoke of a strength of character. She estimated her to be in her mid-forties, but Sam's face was free of lines, but for the few that whispered away from her eyes. Full pink lips, with a deep cupid's bow, curled up at the corners even in repose. Lips that were made for smiling, laughing. And the eyes Chloe had seen when she'd examined Sam were such a pale blue they were almost translucent. Ice blue. Startling and twinkling like diamonds in the reflection of the light. She was beautiful, funny, clearly intelligent if she was a doctor, and they'd been married for fifteen years. A woman like Sam would be Chloe's perfect woman. In an ideal world… where she was in Tim's place and not…never mind. She wouldn't want to be him; the man was clearly an idiot.

He was overweight, slightly balding, gotta be hitting fifty—and he was cheating on her, with Lucy Booker, and had got her pregnant! Chloe knew Lucy from the pub. Everyone did. She was twenty-two and had been looking for a man to trap since she was fifteen.

Jesus. Poor Sam. That's one hell of a Christmas gift.

"You know?" Tim whispered.

"Yeah, I know."

"It was just once, Sam. It was a mistake, I swear—"

Sam's laugh was a bitter sound that made her wince. "You said that before. I believed you then." She turned her head and opened her eyes to look at him. "I don't anymore."

Chloe could see the pain in her eyes, but also strength and resolve. *Good for you, Sam.*

"Merry Christmas, babe." Sam whispered the words so harshly it sounded like a curse. "I want a divorce."

It's in the Pudding

BY EMMA WEIMANN

THE SCENT OF ROASTED GOOSE and red cabbage hung in the too warm air. Bing Cosby sang White Christmas and almost managed to drown out the clattering of cutlery on plates.

Ida carefully opened the top button on her pants and exhaled. She was stuffed. But being stuffed didn't mean that she wouldn't be able to eat just a tiny bit more. Ignoring the noise around her, she peered past the blinking miniature Santa Claus standing next to the bowl of cabbage. Two caramelized potatoes were left in the bowl. It would be a pity to let them go to waste. She slowly slid her plate a few inches toward the potatoes.

"Aunt Ida?"

Damn. Ida turned toward her niece and couldn't help but grin. Was there anything cuter than a frowning four years old? "Yes, Christina?"

Christina rubbed her nose. "Why did you open your pants?"

Heat shot through Ida's face. "What?"

"Yes, Ida. Why?" Her brother Tobias smirked at her from across the table and put the two potatoes on his plate.

Ida suppressed the urge to throw the blinking miniature Santa Clause at him. Sometimes, having to be on your best behavior because children were present really sucked. "You know," she said to Christina, "your grandmother is such a good cook that I couldn't resist and ate too much."

"Oh." Christina blinked. "But then you have no more space for dessert in your belly."

Tobias burst out laughing. "How sad."

"Tobias, stop teasing your sister." Ida's mother took the serving spoon out of the potato bowl. "And if I were you, I wouldn't eat too much dessert anyhow. Your shirt is getting a little tight." With the spoon, she pointed at the shirt that stretched over his belly. "You wouldn't think you're both over forty." She took one of the empty bowls and stood. "Everyone who helps clear the table gets to open one present right after dessert."

Christina and both of her brothers grabbed their empty plates and sprinted to the kitchen.

Tobias put one potato into his mouth, took a pile of plates, and followed his children.

"Kids." Ida shook her head.

"Well, three of the four suspects are children." Maria, Tobias's wife, stacked two empty bowls but made no move to get up. "As an only child, I find the dynamics between grown-up siblings fascinating."

"I still think he got mixed up with another child at birth and isn't really my brother." Ida lifted her wineglass.

Maria laughed. "That's what he keeps saying about you."

Groaning, Ida's father got up from his chair. "I'll be right back. I'm going to lend your mother a hand." He took a bowl and two plates before he disappeared into the kitchen.

Only the blinking Santa figurine and a few sad-looking pine branches remained on the table.

Ida took a sip of red wine and put the glass back down. "Just to update the statistics. Three of the five suspects are children." She pulled down her pants' zipper a little farther and sighed relieved. *That is much better.*

"No matter how many times I have spent Christmas with your family, it's fun every time." Maria winked at Ida. "And as a psychologist, I find it highly interesting."

Ida snorted. "Interesting? Is that the politically correct way of saying profoundly disastrous?"

Maria waved her away. "Oh, come on. You're like the Simpsons. A bit dysfunctional, but you stick together when it really counts."

Ida reached for her napkin, crumpled it up, and threw it at Maria. "I'm not dysfunctional."

Maria threw the napkin back. "Not on your own. But as soon as you and your brother get together, you both start behaving like children."

"Not true." Ida crossed her arms over her chest.

"Come on, let's go smoke a cigarette."

"I gave up smoking."

"Good for you. But you can still keep me company on the balcony. Or do you also want to go earn a second helping of almond pudding?"

Ida leaned back in her chair. "Yeah, sure. And then live off water and not much more for the next few days." She peeled out of her chair, pulled up the zipper, and buttoned her pants. "Sometimes I wish mom wasn't such a good cook."

Maria lifted her eyebrows and smirked.

"Okay, let's go freeze our asses off."

Ida squeezed past the Christmas tree, which—like every year—looked as if a decoration machine had exploded in front of it. The tree disappeared beneath a ton of Lametta, brightly colored balls, candy sticks, stars, ribbons, and garlands. The floor beneath the tree was covered in wrapped gifts.

In the hallway, Ida took her jacket from the coatrack and put it on. Surprised, she watched Maria put on her coat and wrap her woolen scarf around her neck twice. Normally, Maria was tough when it came to cold temperatures. She had won the snowball fight last New Year's Eve in a thin sweater. Something was not right here.

"Let's go." Maria opened the balcony door and disappeared into the darkness.

Ida followed and closed the door behind her. Snow creaked under their boots. The cold winter air took her breath away for a moment. She pulled up the zipper of her coat. "Wow, Maria. My uterus is getting frostbite."

"Mine doesn't have time for that. It's busy with other things." Maria grinned.

Ida grimaced as if she had taken a bite of lemon. "Please! That's definitely too much information. Really. That's my little brother you're talking about."

"It's not what you're thinking." Maria caressed her belly. The smile on her face was strangely enraptured. "Well, maybe it is. But what I wanted to say is that someone is living in here."

Ida's heart started beating faster. "You're pregnant?"

"Yes. Four months." Maria was grinning from one ear to the other. "You'll be an aunt again."

Ida whistled. "Wow. Congratulations." *Hold on a second.* She put her hands on her hips. "And you're still smoking? Are you out of your mind?"

"You're worse than a mother hen. I don't smoke. I just wanted a few minutes of peace and quiet and a little time with my favorite sister-in-law."

Ida shoved her hands in her coat pockets and stared at the floor. "You only got one sister- in-law."

"Yes, and isn't it great that I really, really like her?" Maria stepped up to the railing and looked in the direction of the snow-covered trees at the edge of the property. "It's still snowing lightly."

"Incredible, isn't it?" Ida took up a position next to Maria and wrapped one arm around her shoulders. "How long has it been since we last had snow on Christmas?"

Maria leaned against Ida. "It's been a few years. But last year we had a white surprise on New Year's Eve."

"Yes, and the snowball fight to end all snowball fights." Ida traced her lower lip with her tongue. Sometimes, the small scar she had sustained in last year's family snowball fight still smarted.

"Hey, we could wish for snow. And if you or I find the almond in the pudding, we'll have snow tomorrow."

"I wish I was a child and could believe that wishes would come true." Ida exhaled. "If they did, I would have one that is more important than snow."

"What would you wish for?"

"I can't tell you. Otherwise, the wish won't come true."

"I tell you what I wish for, and you tell me what you wish for." Maria's eyes glittered.

Ida wiped snow off the railing with one hand. "All right. Since wishes don't come true anyway… tell me, what do you wish for?"

"That your brother won't make a fuss when I tell him he should get a vasectomy."

Ida made choking noises. "I'm going to throw up."

"That's probably what he'll do when I ask him." Maria grinned broadly. "And what do you wish for?"

"Other than for you to stop telling me things I don't want to know?" Maria nodded.

For a moment, Ida stared off into the distance. A snowflake floated from the sky and landed on her hand. Wet and cold. And beautiful. She glanced at Maria before she stared straight ahead again. Her wish seemed silly. "Someone in my life. I'm wishing for a relationship next year. I'm tired of being alone."

Maria leaned her head against Ida's shoulder. "How long has it been?"

"Almost three years."

"A long time."

"I got a Christmas card from Stefanie last week. From Aspen." The words left a bitter taste in Ida's mouth.

"Stupid fool."

Ida laughed. "Yes, stupid fool. But a happy, rich fool who enjoys tormenting me once a year." Ida's stomach clenched as she remembered the day Stefanie had suddenly disappeared without an explanation, only to reappear two months later with furniture packers who took half of the furniture, including some things that didn't even belong to her.

"Maybe she'll break her leg skiing."

"Maybe."

"And there's only a twelve-bed room left in the hospital."

Ida grinned. Nice thought.

"And the nurse ..." Maria giggled. "She weighs four hundred pounds, comes from Russia, and doesn't like Germans."

Ida could easily imagine her ex's pained expression when the nurse was torturing her. What a nice thought. "Yes, if there's any justice left on earth ..."

For a few moments, both were silent.

"Do you think you're ready for a new relationship?"

Ida shrugged. "I don't know. Sometimes I think I am, and sometimes I think that I never want a relationship again. Truth is, that I'm lonely." Saying those words out loud hurt. "But sometimes I wonder if being single isn't the lesser evil to opening up again and inviting someone into my life, who will stab another knife into my back. I'm not sure I'll be able to recover from that."

"You know what?" Maria's face lit up.

"Mmmmhhh?"

"I'll also wish that you'll soon find someone worthy of being in a a relationship with you. That'll increase the chances of your wish coming true."

Ida shuffled her feet through the snow. "And the vasectomy?"

"I'll just tell Tobias that him getting a vasectomy is what I want for my birthday."

"Great idea. We can all club together and get you a gift certificate for a vasectomy."

Maria laughed. "Yes. And please tie a ribbon around it. Around the gift certificate. Not around little Tobias."

"Maria! Stop it, or I'll wash out your mouth with snow."

The balcony door creaked open behind them.

Ida turned around.

"There you are." Tobias stuck his head through the doorframe. "Dessert is served. Come on."

Ida covered her face with her hands and shook her head. "Damn. How will I ever get the image of the ribbon out of my mind?"

Maria started laughing.

Tobias furrowed his brow. "Did I say something funny?" He wiped his mouth. "Is there something stuck to my face?"

Ida joined in Maria's laughter until tears trailed down her cheeks. Hoping to rein herself in, she turned her back toward Tobias.

"What's the matter with you two?"

Maria cleared her throat. "Nothing. We just had a discussion about gift certificates."

Ida turned and looked at Tobias. "Special gift certificates."

Maria began to laugh again.

"Women." Shaking his head, Tobias closed the balcony door behind him.

"Ouch."

Maria was still giggling. "Perfect timing."

"Indeed. Come on. If we don't hurry, they'll start without us."

Maria sighed. "I bet Tobias will put on more weight than I do during my pregnancy."

"Then you can diet together afterwards. Isn't that great?"

Maria shoved Ida. "No, that's not great at all."

A little later, the family was gathered around the table. Not only the children were staring at the bowl that held the Christmas pudding, as if they could force their will on it.

"All right." Ida's mother took a big spoon and looked at her grandchildren. "As every year, there's an almond hidden in the pudding. The person who finds it gets to make a wish. An old Danish tradition says that the wish will come true next year."

The children nodded enthusiastically. Even Ida gave up on projecting a poker face. This was her year to go first. And she would find that damn almond. And her brother would be jealous. She allowed a smile to spread across her face.

Her mother continued, "And each year, someone else gets the first helping. This year, it's Ida's turn. Then comes Christina. And Christina gets to choose who'll be next. Only Tobias will be last because he had his turn last year."

Linus, the oldest of Tobias's children, groaned. "But I wanted to be first."

"It'll be your turn next year. I promise." Ida's mother caressed his light brown hair.

Ida's mouth watered. Almond pudding was her favorite dessert since she had first tried it as a child. And her mother's pudding was the best. She had tried to make the pudding using her mother's recipe, but it just hadn't been the same. Maybe its magic only worked on Christmas. Maybe it needed the right mix of sentimental feelings and sugar that adds the right amount of spice.

"Here you go, darling." Her mother handed her the spoon.

"Thanks." Ida pulled the bowl toward her. *Come on, little almond. Where are you hiding this year?* She tried to discover any uneven patches in the pudding. *Where do I put the spoon?* She had just one try. Then it was Christina's turn. If she found it, that would be okay too. Christina deserved to have her wish come true—even though Maria would not be happy if, in addition to a new baby, a new puppy would be moving in.

"Hurry up, Ida. We all want to take our turns sometime today." Tobias held his spoon in his fist.

The expression reminded her of a bad-tempered pug.

Maria looked at him through narrowed eyes. "Last year, it took you five minutes to decide where to put the spoon."

"Hey, whose side are you on?"

"On hers." Maria pointed at Ida.

"Me too." Ida's mother folded her hands on the table. "And now be quiet. Everyone else will take their turns before you anyway."

Ida grinned at Tobias and wiggled her brows. Having strong women in the family was great.

"Hurry up," Ida's father mumbled.

All right. She would do something that would cause a storm of indignation. With a quick move, she drilled her spoon into the middle of the pudding and heaved a big portion of it onto her plate.

"Not from the middle, child. Now the pudding looks awful," her mother said.

"Mom, Aunt Ida is destroying the pudding." Linus's eyes nearly fell out of his head.

Ida forced herself not to look in Tobias's direction. She didn't want to see the expression on his face. With relish, she put the first spoonful of pudding into her mouth—and encountered a hard object. I can't believe it. She traced the object with her tongue. Wow. "I got it!"

A relationship. I want to be in a happy, life-long relationship next year. She bit down on the almond. Gosh, this is hard. She bit down again.

Something crunched like a crumbling pile of stones in her mouth.

Ida closed her eyes. *Oh, shit.* Her stomach roiled. She spat the almond onto her hand. The skin was still attached. And a few strange pieces. And a bigger piece of something. The filling of her tooth. "Oh. Shit."

"Ida!" Her mother sat up straight.

Ida felt the tooth with her tongue. "The fillin' 's gone." She felt along the tooth again. "An' a piece of the tooth."

"Oh no." Maria looked at her with big eyes.

"Aunt Ida." Christina tugged on Ida's shirt. "Aunt Ida, does it hurt a lot?"

Ida laid the almonds with the filling splinters onto her plate. She'd lost her appetite anyway. "No. I think that's the tooth with the root canal. It doesn't hurt. But the tooth is damaged."

"And that now of all times, when no dentist is available." Ida's mother rubbed her face. "Horst, check in the newspaper to see if there's a dentist on call for emergencies."

Ida's father obediently stood and hurried into the kitchen.

"Nonsense." Ida shook her head. "It doesn't hurt. It can wait."

"No, you can't." Her mother furrowed her brow. "It might not hurt now. But who knows when pain will set in. It'll be even more difficult to find a dentist in the middle of the night. Maybe he'll be tired and drunk by then. You better take care of it now."

Maria put her hand on Ida's shoulder. "Let's go to the bathroom to check it out." She glanced at Tobias.

He nodded and turned toward the children. "Okay. Who wants dessert?"

Christina shoved her plate away. "I don't want damaged teeth."

The brothers looked at each other and slid their plates over to their father.

"I'll take Christina's portion and mine," Linus said.

Stefan nodded and pushed his plate more toward his father.

Christmas dinner sat heavily in Ida's stomach. Going to the dentist. On Christmas Eve. That wish thing worked really well, she thought bitterly. The only wish she had now consisted of three words, 'Please don't drill.'

"Come on." Maria shoved back her chair and stood.

The bathroom was as clean and tidy as the whole apartment. The sink gleamed like a diamond. The flashlight lay on the windows sill, as it always did.

Maria picked it up. "Open wide."

"Where did you get that commanding tone?" Ida opened her mouth and bent a little.

"I'm a wife and mother of three. How do you think I survive on a daily basis?" Maria directed the flashlight's beam into Ida's mouth. "Oh. The tooth is a goner. There's really just a ruin left."

Ida closed her mouth and squeezed her eyes shut. Her temples pounded. *Damn. Damn. Damn.*

"Hey, you okay?"

Ida nodded. She opened her eyes. "I don't want to go to the dentist."

"Aww, poor you." Maria laid her hand on Ida's arm.

"It doesn't hurt. I will manage somehow."

"Ida. That's nonsense. You can't wait until after New Year's Day. Who knows what else will break off in the meantime."

Ida sat down on the edge of the bathtub. This was a nightmare. Who wanted to visit a dentist—on Christmas?

A knock on the door interrupted them. Her mother stuck her head into the room. "A Dr. Stahl in Niedbach is on call during the holidays, and the receptionist said you can come right over."

Niedbach. That's twenty minutes by car. That wasn't too bad. Maybe Maria was right. It wouldn't be fun if the pain set in tonight. She could do that. Act like a grownup. "Do you know Dr. Stahl?"

Her mother shook her head. "No. But that's a good sign. If he were a bungler, we would have heard."

Ida took a deep breath. "All right. I'll go."

"I'm coming with you." Maria put the flashlight back on the window sill.

"Nonsense."

"I'm coming with you. And that's that."

Ida rolled her eyes but was thankful that she didn't need to go alone. If she wanted anyone to come with her, it was Maria. "Okay. You can be really bossy."

Maria's only reaction was a sugar sweat sweet grin.

When they entered the hall, the family had gathered around the coatrack. All gazes were fixed on Ida.

Maria is right. We might be dysfunctional, but we stick together when it really matters.

"If you're lucky, you'll be back in time for Little Lord Fauntleroy." Ida's father handed her the jacket. "Drive carefully."

"Do you want me to drive?" Tobias directed a questioning gaze at his wife, who shook her head.

"I'll drive her."

"It's snowing."

Maria chuckled. "I don't need to remember you who in the family had an accident this year."

"The other guy didn't stop," grumbled Tobias. "It wasn't my mistake."

"Aunt Ida?" Christina said.

"Yes?"

"Please make sure that all will be well quickly."

Linus put his hand in Ida's. "Please."

She crouched down and looked into Linus's light brown eyes. The color reminded her of the almond that had caused this disaster. "I'll do my best. I promise."

Maria, who was fully dressed by now and wearing a red woolen cap on her head, caressed her son's hair. "Are you afraid that you won't get to open your presents tonight?"

All three children nodded vehemently.

"Aren't they cute?"

Ida put on her jacket and rolled her eyes. "Just adorable."

The streets of Niedbach were deserted. A cat that carefully waded through the snow was the only creature outdoors. Everyone else was probably opening presents, sitting in their warm living rooms, having fun. For the hundredth time, Ida trailed her tongue over the ruin that had once been her tooth. She sighed quietly. This wasn't how she had imagined this night to go.

"I think we'll be there soon." Maria shifted gears. "Ah, there, house number three. That's it. And there are parking spaces directly in front of the dentist's office. Great service." Skillfully, Maria pulled into one of parking spaces.

Ida opened the passenger door. A gust of icy air yanked her from her sleepiness.

Snowflakes inaudibly floated down onto her head. "Cold, cold, cold." She pulled up her jacket's zipper.

"Oh, yeah. Let's go in before we freeze." Maria pulled her red cap over her ears and burst out laughing.

"What?" Ida looked left and right but didn't see anything that might have caused Maria's merriment.

"You know the stickers on cars saying 'class of 2011,' right?"

Ida nodded.

"Well," Maria pointed at a bright red SUV parking next to her car, "someone has a sticker with 'divorce 2011' on their car."

"You're kidding?" Ida stepped next to Maria. And there it was. The windshield of the SUV displayed in proud letters "divorce 2011." Ida grinned. "Either someone has a weird sense of humor, or they really had something to celebrate."

"Or both."

They trotted through the new powdery snow to the entrance. The front door was decorated with stenciled pictures of reindeer, stars, and bats.

"Bats? Are those really bats?" Maria traced her fingers over one of the pictures. "How bizarre. It fits with the divorce sticker on the car."

Ida's stomach clenched. She hoped that it wasn't the dentist with a penchant for macabre things. She loved black humor but she really didn't need someone who worked close at nerve-endings to be a fan of black comedy.

"Oh." Maria pointed at the practice sign. "Dr. Stahl is a woman. Your mother said it was a guy."

"I guess it's because even today people automatically assume that a doctor is male."

"Only too true." Maria rang the doorbell and only seconds later the buzzer hummed.

Now it was really too late to run away, which she wouldn't have done anyhow. She didn't want to appear as a coward and a bad example for her nephews and niece. But sometimes, being grown-up really sucked.

Ida braced herself and climbed the steps to the first floor.

The typical dentist office scent hit her as soon as she entered. Even blindfolded, she would have known where she was. What was that smell anyhow? Surely, she couldn't be the only one whose flight reflex was triggered by it.

The smell however was soon forgotten.

A blonde woman with a short-sleeved T-shirt, a nose piercing, and a set of reindeer antlers on her head sat behind the receptionist's desk. Blinking strings of light hung on the walls, almost making Ida want to put on sunglasses. Someone had draped an eye patch over the left eye of the inflatable Santa in one corner.

No way was she staying. She wouldn't leave her tooth in the hands of insane people. Ida stepped back and collided with something soft.

Maria groaned. "Watch it. That's my foot."

"Good evening. How can I help you?" The blonde smiled and rested her muscular, tattooed arms on the desk.

Oh shit. They're probably not even using numbing shots. She felt queasy. "I.. I called. Or rather my father called, I think. A filling and a part of a tooth broke off. Because of an almond. But it's not too bad. So, if you're too busy ..."

The blonde wrinkled her nose. "Ouch. No, no. We do have time. Can I have your insurance card, please?"

Ida swallowed.

Maria took off her cap and her coat and hung it on the coat rack. "I'll take a look at what's new with the royal families worldwide." She sat on one of few chairs and opened the newest issue of Gala.

Traitor. With trembling hands, Ida slid her insurance card across the desk.

A minute later, Ms. Tattoo handed her the card and two pieces of paper. "Okay. Please fill this out. Then we can get started."

Ida took a pen from a box and sat down next to Maria.

Totally immersed in the magazine, her sister-in-law didn't even look up.

Ida peeked at an article. The Spanish royal house and its marital crises. Photos of Princess Letizia of Spain always made Ida want to order a double-cheese pizza. Once really couldn't get much thinner. This wasn't what a happy person looked like.

Filling out the questionnaire didn't take long. She was healthy, except for her knees that weren't the same anymore after too many years of field hockey. "Done." Ida got up and handed Ms. Tattoo the completed questionnaire.

"Great. Please follow me. I'll show you to the treatment room."

Ida turned around. "See you later, Maria."

"What?" Maria looked up. "Ah. You can do this, Ida." She pointed at the article. "I'd love to do a family constellation with them." She returned her attention to the magazine.

With drooping shoulders, Ida followed Ms. Tattoo, who was the exact opposite of the Spanish princess. Athletic, muscular ... Ida's gaze wandered down the body in front of her. And a really nice ass.

"Here we are." Ms. Tattoo held open the door for her.

Ida wasn't sure what she'd expected, but definitely not this. Instead of a sterile, white room or a torture chamber, she entered a room decorated in light pastel shades. A painting covered the wall across from the treatment chair, showing a forest clearing that was suffused with light. Looking at this beautiful painting was much better than staring at silly photo wallpaper or an empty wall. It probably wouldn't make the treatment less painful, but it was nice anyway.

"Please take a seat."

Ida sat on the treatment chair. Her gaze wandered to the tray with the tiny drill bits that she didn't want anywhere near or in her mouth. Hot and cold shivers raced through her body—and they didn't have anything to do with the temperature in the treatment room. *I want to go home.*

Ms. Tattoo put a dental napkin with dancing reindeer around Ida's neck. "Dr. Stahl will be with you in a minute."

Ida nodded. She looked at the window. The blinds were closed. *Are there bars in front of the window?* If not, maybe she could climb out and escape. Since they were on the first floor, it shouldn't be a problem. But Maria was sitting in the waiting area, and she couldn't leave without her. *Damn. I'm trapped.*

Steps approached.

Ida clutched the armrests of the chair. Her heart started racing.

"Thanks, Yvonne," a deep female voice said.

So Ms. Tattoo's name was Yvonne. The name didn't match her appearance. An Yvonne was someone delicate with long blond hair and blue eyes. Without tattoos.

Someone entered and sat on a stool next to Ida. "Good evening. I hear you lost a fight with an almond?"

Ida swallowed and looked at the dentist. Her breath caught. That couldn't be. "Theresa?"

Dr. Stahl lifted one eyebrow. "Ida? Ida Maurer? Is this you?"

I can't believe it. "Hi. Hello. Gosh, what a coincidence." Theresa. Her first big love. The girl who had helped her discover that she didn't want pubescent, pimply boys in her life but beautiful soft women. And the girl, who broke her heart when she left for university and never contacted Ida again.

Theresa laid a hand on Ida's arm. "How long has it been?"

"No idea." Ida shrugged. "Ten years, give or take." Theresa still held those soft, brown eyes and the long, elegant fingers that had driven Ida crazy as a teenager. And the cute smile that had turned Ida's knees to jelly at the class reunion eight years ago. But Theresa had been in a relationship back then. She had brought her girlfriend, a rich lawyer, to the class reunion.

"Ah, yes, the class reunion, right?" Theresa put on light blue latex gloves.

That night hadn't been any fun. Twenty more or less straight classmates, who were all super successful and happily married. Plus one lesbian classmate who brought her partner. And broke Ida's heart for the second time. Later that night, when Ida was slightly tipsy a totally drunk Uta had tried to talk her into demonstrating the Sapphic lifestyle on Uta's surgically enhanced body. A night, she was not proud of. Ida shook herself. "Yes. 2004 in the Roaring Deer. Nice evening." Not.

Silence settled between them for a moment.

"And now we meet again. Thanks to an almond."

"It's nuts, isn't it?" Both laughed about the bad joke.

"When did you get back? I thought you were living somewhere in the Ruhr area?" What Ida didn't want to ask and what she really, really wanted to know was "and are you still together with the bitch lawyer?"

Theresa nodded. "In Cologne, so it's not really the Ruhr area. But I came back here a few months ago. I needed some space from my old life and my memories." She pressed a pedal with her foot.

The chair on which Ida sat slowly rotated back.

"Did you break up?" The moment the words had left her mouth, Ida wanted to slap herself. Dignity was what she should have wished for earlier this evening.

Theresa tilted her head and gazed at her through narrowed eyes. "Why?"

Heat shot through Ida's face. *Shit.*

Theresa grinned. "Good to know that some things never change. You're still blushing whenever you're slightly embarrassed."

Ida covered her face with the reindeer napkin and shook her head. So much for a good first impression after so many years. *Please kill me now.* "I'm sorry. I shouldn't have asked. It's none of my business."

"We got married two years ago. You remember Andrea?"

The lawyer? Ida nodded.

"Well, we got divorced last year. The only thing I kept is the name. I was too lazy to go through all the paperwork for the name change again."

Oh. Thankful that the napkin covered up her stupid grin and at the same time horrified that this message caused more happy emotions to run through her than it should, Ida said, "I'm sorry."

"No need to be sorry. I'm just sorry that it took me so long to realize that it was better to leave."

A knock on the door interrupted them.

Out of the corner of her eye Ida saw a happily grinning Yvonne stuck her head in. The set of reindeer antlers on her head bounced up and down. "The next patient will be here in half an hour—minus one incisor. Seems opening Christmas presents with teeth didn't go so well."

"Thanks. We should be done here by then." Theresa turned toward Ida. "You said in the questionnaire that the tooth had a root canal."

"Yes. Five or six years ago. My dentist said the tooth wouldn't make it for very long and recommended a crown. But up until now, it's been fine."

A smile darted across Theresa's face. "You don't like going to the dentist, do you?"

"No." *Oh damn.* Quickly, she added, "But I have nothing against dentists. Really."

"That's good to know." Theresa pulled the tray with the torture instruments closer. "Then let's take a look."

Ida leaned her head back and opened her mouth. A thousand thoughts raced through her mind. Theresa was single. Very likely. She was no longer married in any case. *As soon as I make the wish not to be alone anymore, I meet Theresa.* Was that just coincidence? It had to be and surely didn't mean anything. Nope.

Pain shot through her teeth. She flinched. "Ouch."

"I'm sorry. The gums are irritated. But I don't think you'll need a shot. The troublemaker really seems to be the tooth with the root canal. But if you'd feel more secure, I could give you a light numbing shot."

Ida didn't even have to think twice about it. "Thanks. My name is Ida, I'm a sissy, and I want a shot."

"No problem." Theresa laughed. "More power to those who know what they need."

While Theresa prepared the injection, Ida—as a believer in the head-in-the-sand method— averted her gaze. What she didn't see didn't exist and wouldn't cause her pain.

"Okay, open your mouth. You'll just feel a bit of a prick."

Ouch! Little prick. Sure. Her hands clutched the armrests. As much as she hated shots, they were the lesser evil.

"It's over already. Within a few minutes you won't feel a thing. The shot doesn't last very long, so you'll be able to eat Christmas cookies later."

Ida ran her tongue along the tooth.

"Do you still live in Frankfurt?"

"No. Do you live here?"

"No." Theresa chuckled. "I didn't want to live where I work. Gossip is a big thing in small towns like this and faster than you know, everyone talks about what you bought in the supermarket."

"So, you moved somewhere where you can buy chocolate or something equally unhealthy for teeth without the whole town chatting about it?"

"Exactly." Theresa glanced at her watch. "Is the numbing medication working?"

Ida swallowed. "You're really looking forward to getting your hands on me, don't you?"

Smiling, Theresa nodded. "Totally my plan, yes."

Was she flirting? *Am I flirting?* Looking at Theresa still made Ida's heart beat a bit faster, as it had when they met for the first time. Theresa's dark hair was streaked with a few gray strands. Laugh lines around her eyes revealed that she wasn't sixteen years old anymore. But she was still as attractive as ever. No, that wasn't right. She was more attractive.

A little embarrassed, Ida felt the gums surrounding the broken-off tooth with her tongue. It was weird but totally reassuring that she couldn't feel the touch. "Yes, it's working."

"Okay, then let's drill. Please open your mouth wide." Theresa hooked the awful suction device that sounded like a dying vacuum cleaner into Ida's mouth.

Shit. Ida clutched the armrests so tightly that her knuckles turned white. Her muscles were stretched to breaking point. Even though she knew it couldn't hurt, fear triumphed over logic. The sounds of the drill weren't helping. They sounded as if Theresa was crushing a rock in Ida's mouth. She felt the vibrations going straight to her brain.

"Okay." Theresa put away the torture instrument. "I drilled a gap into the old filling so that the provisional crown will stay in place. But after the holidays you should make an appointment with your dentist. This won't last forever."

Ida nodded. Maybe she could make her follow-up with Theresa. It would only be logical. After all, Theresa was already familiar with the tooth. And then I could see her again without coming up with a stupid excuse.

"Isn't it strange to meet again under these circumstances?" Theresa stood and prepared something behind Ida's back. A minute later, she returned to the stool.

Why did dentists always ask questions when their patients couldn't answer? Ida nodded slightly, trying not to move her head too much to avoid having the suction device wander around in her mouth.

"I actually thought a few times about calling you ever since I moved back."

Really? Ida swallowed the wrong way and coughed.

"Everything all right?" Theresa bent down and directed a concerned gaze at Ida.

"Shpit. Shwallow'd."

A deep furrow formed between Theresa's brows. "Are you okay?"

Ida nodded.

"Let's continue. We'll be done in a few minutes."

Already? Ida watched Theresa pick up a tool with a weird substance.

"This is a composite filling."

A biting smell spread through the room. Ida wrinkled her nose.

Theresa laughed. "I know. It doesn't smell so nice. But it's really the best solution, and the smell is only temporary."

Theresa grasped a tool that looked like a broken-off electric toothbrush. "Okay, let's harden the filling. It'll take a minute. Please keep your mouth wide open."

A short while later, Theresa said, "All done." She took a piece of foil from the tray. "I want you to bite down on this so that I can see if everything fits."

"Okay." Ida obediently opened her mouth and bit down on the foil while she was pondering asking Theresa out. For a coffee. Just to talk a little. To indulge in old memories. She was equality excited and terrified of the idea to spend time with her.

Theresa took the foil. "Okay. I'll have to retouch one small area."

Ida opened her mouth without waiting for further instruction. *She wanted to call me.* At least that's what she said.

"All done." Theresa took off the latex gloves.

Ida loosened her grip on the armrests. A grin spread over her face. *I'm a hero.*

"You look like a child who just got the Christmas present she wished for."

"That's what I feel like. A small step for mankind, a huge victory for me."

"You can rinse your mouth if you want."

"Thanks." Ida reached for the cup adorned with dancing Santas and took a big sip.

"Almonds in the pudding. What's the tradition again? If you find the almond, you've got a wish, right?"

Ida spat the water into the little sink and stared at the whirl that formed. She didn't dare look at Theresa. "Yes, that's right."

"Did you have time to make a wish before the almond attacked your tooth?"

"Yes, I did." She put the empty cup down and looked at Theresa.

Theresa lifted her brows. "Was it an interesting wish?"

Ida would rather have another root canal procedure than talking about her wish. With Theresa. "Yes. But I'm not allowed to speak about the wish before it comes true."

"Theresa?" Yvonne entered. "Sorry to interrupt, but the patient with the broken-off incisor is here. And the next patient is on his way over too. He lost the filling in one of his molars." Yvonne pointed at her right cheek.

"Oh, boy." Theresa got rid of her latex gloves and rubbed her eyes. "It's going to be a long Christmas Eve."

The ringing of the phone echoed through the dentist's office.

Ida wrinkled her nose. "I guess you won't get bored today."

"No. That's for sure." Theresa turned toward Yvonne. "I'm almost done here. Just a few more minutes."

"Okay." Yvonne put her hands in her pants pockets. "No problem. I'll answer the phone."

"Thanks." Theresa smiled at Yvonne.

Was there something going on between those two? Ida swallowed hard. As far as she knew, Yvonne wasn't really Theresa's type. Back then, Theresa had always preferred more feminine women. The bitch lawyer had been rather feminine as well. Ida cleared her throat. "It's tough to have to spend Christmas Eve working."

Theresa shrugged. "I'm new to the area, so it was my turn to be on call for most of the holidays. Yvonne didn't hesitate. She said that it didn't matter to her whether she opened her presents today or tomorrow and that her mother's roast beef tasted even better after sitting for a day. Her boyfriend is going to be back from visiting his family tomorrow. And to tell you the truth," Theresa winked at Ida, "I prefer working to spending time with my nagging mother."

"Some things never change, eh?" She remembered Theresa's mother Maria well. She had tested everyone's patience twenty-five years ago and her attitude of being little Ms. High and Mighty probably hadn't gotten better with old age. Plus, she had been the driving force behind Theresa moving away for university. Ida stood and stretched. Satisfaction coursed through her when she caught Theresa looking at her breasts. "Thanks. This has been one of the most pleasant dental appointments I ever had."

A hint of red spread over Theresa's cheeks as she looked up and into Ida's eyes. "I'm glad to hear that." She got up from the stool. "Please don't wait until the provisional crown collapses. Make an appointment."

"Will do. Would it be okay to come back for that tooth?"

"Yes. Absolutely." Theresa's smile lit the room. "I'll escort you to the door."

Ask her out, idiot. Ida followed Theresa, unable to say the words. As much as she wanted to, truth was that she was scared. What if Theresa didn't want more than a meeting between old friends? And even worse— what if she wanted more? The Theresa of today wasn't the old Theresa, whom she had been in love with as a teenager. Ida ran her tongue over the temporary crown. It was smooth even though it didn't feel like a real tooth.

Maybe she would ask Theresa out after the next appointment. Yes, that was a good idea.

A middle-aged man and woman sat on the chairs next to Maria in the waiting area. The man was red-faced and held an ice pack to his right eye. The woman sat with her hands folded on her lap and stared at the floor. They were not only not talking with each other, their silence was louder than any words could ever be. *I guess more than just the tooth bit the dust.*

Theresa looked at Maria and cleared her throat. "Oh, you've got someone waiting for you."

"Yes. That's my sister-in-law. She accompanied me for moral support."

"Ah."

Was that relief on Theresa's face?

Theresa laid a hand on Ida's arm. "It was really nice to see you even if it wasn't under the best of circumstances."

"Yes, it was nice. I mean, seeing you again." Ida trailed her hand through her hair. Why couldn't she be as eloquent and cool as the women in lesbian romance novels often where?

"Have a nice Christmas Eve, and please say hi to your parents for me." Theresa gave her a short nod before she turned to the couple. "Good evening. I'll be with you in a minute." With a smile on her face, she turned and walked back toward the treatment room.

Too late. Damn.

"And?" Maria held out Ida's jacket.

"Everything's fine. For now. And it barely hurt."

"Good. But what I meant is, who is this good-looking dentist? Did your Christmas wish just come true?"

Ida took her jacket from Maria. "Oh, please. Yes, we know each other. But that's all. Come on, let's go home, so the kids won't have to wait for so long. I want to continue being their favorite aunt, not the one who spoiled Christmas for them."

Maria patted Ida's shoulder. "Don't worry. We've got savings accounts for the kids that will help them pay for their therapies later."

Ida burst out laughing. "You're really crazy sometimes."

With a dismissive wave of her hand, Maria turned and opened the door.

Ida stared at her. "You're joking, right?"

"Sure."

Ida closed the office door behind her and climbed down the steps. "You can't—"

"Ida, wait!" Theresa's voice echoed through the staircase.

Her heart pounding, Ida turned around.

Theresa stood on the top landing, holding a piece of paper. A nervous smile trembled on her lips.

For a moment, time seemed to stand still.

Theresa lowered her gaze and slowly went down the stairs. She rubbed her neck with one hand. "Maybe it sounds a little weird, and maybe it's totally inappropriate, but ..." She paused in front of Ida, took a deep breath, and said in a rush, "Would you have coffee with me tomorrow?"

Ida blinked. *Wow. She's definitely braver than me.* "Yes. Sure. I'd love to." She shoved her hands in her jacket pockets. "But is there something open around here over the holidays?"

Theresa's eyes shone. "My kitchen is open. I'm not on call tomorrow."

"Oh." Ida forced back a Cheshire cat smile. "Great. Sure. When?" She sighed inwardly. Since when wasn't she no longer able to speak in full sentences?

Grinning broadly, Theresa held out a piece of paper. "Here's my cell phone number and my address. Why don't you call me tomorrow around eleven? Then we can set up a time."

"I'll do that." Ida took the piece of paper and glanced at it. Her phone number and address.

Maria cleared her voice behind Ida.

"See you tomorrow, Theresa. We have to go now, or I'll get in trouble with my niece and nephew's. They're waiting to open their gifts."

"Oh. Sure." Theresa gnawed on her bottom lip. "Then, um, drive safely. I'll see you tomorrow."

"Yeah." Ida nodded enthusiastically. "See you tomorrow." She turned, looked at Maria, and held up both thumbs in a way that Theresa couldn't see it. I've got a date. I've got a date.

"And Ida?"

Ida turned back toward Theresa.

"Yes?"

"No more pudding for you tonight." She winked.

About the Authors

ANDREA BRAMHALL

Andrea Bramhall wrote her first novel at the age of six and three-quarters. It was seven pages long and held together with a pink ribbon. Her Gran still has it in the attic. Since then she has progressed a little bit and now has a number of published works held together with glue, not ribbons, an Alice B. Lavender certificate, a Lambda Literary award, and a Golden Crown award cluttering up her book shelves.

She studied music and all things arty at Manchester Metropolitan University, graduating in 2002 with a BA in contemporary arts. She is certain it will prove useful someday…maybe.

When she isn't busy running a campsite in the Lake District, Bramhall can be found hunched over her laptop scribbling down the stories that won't let her sleep. She can also be found reading, walking the dogs up mountains while taking a few thousand photos, scuba diving while taking a few thousand photos, swimming, kayaking, playing the saxophone, or cycling.

CHEYENNE BLUE

Cheyenne Blue is the author of the "Girl Meets Girl" series, four standalone stories with interconnecting characters. *Never-Tied Nora*, *Not-So-Straight Sue*, *Fenced-In Felix*, and *Almost-Married Moni* are also available from Ylva Publishing. Her short fiction has been included in over ninety erotic anthologies since 2000, including *Best Lesbian Erotica*; *Best Women's Erotica*; *All You Can Eat: A Buffet of Lesbian Romance & Erotica*; *Sweat*; *Bossy*; and *Wild Girls, Wild Nights*. She is the editor of *Forbidden Fruit: stories of unwise lesbian desire*, a 2015 finalist for both the Lambda Literary Award and Golden Crown Literary Award, and of *First: Sensual Lesbian Stories of New Beginnings*.

Her collected lesbian short fiction is published as *Blue Woman Stories*, volumes 1-3, with more to come. Under her own name she has written travel books and articles and edited anthologies of local writing in Ireland. She has lived in the U.K., Ireland, the United States, and Switzerland, but now writes, runs, makes bread and cheese, and drinks wine by the beach in Queensland, Australia.

LOLA KEELEY

Lola Keeley is a writer and coder. After moving to London to pursue her love of theatre, she later wound up living every five-year-old's dream of being a train driver on the London Underground. She has since emerged, blinking into the sunlight, to find herself writing books. She now lives in Edinburgh, Scotland, with her wife and three cats.

JODY KLAIRE

Jody has been everything from a serving police officer to working in kitchens before finding her home in writing. She can often be found chuckling to herself at her own jokes; being pounced by her golden retriever, Fergus; eating cake or chocolate or preferably both, and sometimes, when Fergus hasn't run off with her keyboard, she writes stuff.

SHERYN MUNIR

Sheryn Munir is a big fan of romances. After reading countless lesbian romance novels based in Western countries, she wanted to read a lesfic based in India. She didn't know how long she'd have to wait for that wish to come true, so she decided to have a crack at writing one herself. *Falling into Place*, is the result of that endeavour. Sheryn was born in Lucknow and grew up in Delhi, India. Though she started writing from the age of seven, she was only recently inspired to write an entire book in a genre close to her heart that is about her own people. She has studied journalism and freelances as a writer, editor, and web developer. While she likes visiting new places, the journeys are a tad unpleasant. She has a weakness for chocolates, Indian street foods, and British television dramas. She lives in Delhi with three laptops and an e-reader.

PATRICIA PENN

When Patricia was a teen, her school's job qualification test said that she should be a surgeon since she has a big ego, and she doesn't like other people. Later, she read a theory about how all authors secretly are social outcasts anyway, and decided that the pen suited her even better than the scalpel. She currently also sells her soul to a day job in marketing in Frankfurt, Germany. She lives with her dog in a small town near Frankfurt, and has given long-distance relationships a new meaning with her girlfriend, who lives in Massachusetts.

CINDY RIZZO

Cindy Rizzo lives in New York City with her wife, Jennifer, and their two cats. She has worked in philanthropy for many years and has a long history of involvement in the LGBT community. Cindy is the author of *Exception to the Rule*, a lesbian romance and winner of the GCLS Debut Fiction award. Her second book, *Love Is Enough*, was released in September 2014. Earlier writing includes essays in the anthologies, *Lesbians Raising Sons* and *Homefronts: Controversies in Non-Traditional Parenting*. She was the co-editor of a fiction anthology, *All the Ways Home*, published in 1995 (New Victoria) in which her story "Herring Cove" was included. Cindy serves on the boards of *Congregation Beit Simchat Torah*, and *SAGE (Services & Advocacy for GLBT Elders)*. She and her wife have two grown sons, a wonderful daughter-in-law, and a baby granddaughter.

ALEX K. THORNE

Alex K. Thorne graduated from university in Cape Town, South Africa with a healthy love of the classics and a degree in English Literature.

She assumed that this entitled her to a future of pretentious garden parties, while drinking fancy tea and debating which Brontë sister was the wackiest (Emily, obvs).

Instead, she spent the next few years, teaching across the globe, from Serbia to South Korea, where she spent her days writing fanfiction and developing a kimchi addiction.

When she's not picking away at her latest writing project, she's immersing herself in geek culture, taking too many pictures of the cats and dreaming about where next to travel.

EMMA WEIMANN

Emma Weimann knew at an early age that she wanted to make a living as a writer. She knew exactly how and where she wanted to write the books that would pay for her house at the beach and the desk with a view of the ocean.

Even though she has had those dreams for over thirty years now, neither the house nor the desk exist. Not yet. But she's making a living producing books, not just as a writer but also as a publisher, establishing Ylva Verlag and its international pendant, Ylva Publishing, in 2011 and 2012.

She also is the author of *Heart's Surrender*, a 2015 Golden Crown Literary Award Winner for lesbian erotica.

LEE WINTER

Lee Winter is an award-winning veteran newspaper journalist who has lived in almost every Australian state, covering courts, crime, news, features and humour writing. Now a full-time author and part-time editor, Lee is also a 2015 and 2016 Lambda Literary Award finalist and has won two Golden Crown Literary Awards. She lives in Western Australia with her long-time girlfriend, where she spends much time ruminating on her garden, US politics, and shiny, new gadgets.

FIONA ZEDDE

Jamaican-born Fiona Zedde currently lives and writes in Atlanta, Georgia. She is the author of several novellas and novels of lesbian love and desire, including the Lambda Literary Award finalists, *Bliss* and *Every Dark Desire*. Her novel, *Dangerous Pleasures*, was winner of the About.com Readers' Choice Award for Best Lesbian Novel or Memoir of 2012.

Her short fiction has appeared in various anthologies including the Cleis Press Best Lesbian Erotica series, *Wicked: Sexy Tales of Legendary Lovers*, *Iridescence: Sensuous Shades of Lesbian Erotica*, and *Fist of the Spider Woman*.

Other Books from Ylva Publishing

www.ylva-publishing.com

ROCK AND A HARD PLACE

Andrea Bramhall

ISBN: 978-3-95533-902-9
Length: 289 pages (100,000 words)

Jayden Harris is an expert climber filled with demons after surviving an avalanche. When she and marketing executive Rhian Phillips are forced to work together for a reality show, she expected it to be hard. They both expected things to get rocky—they are facing snow, ice, and a daunting mountain range, after all. But neither of them ever expected the hardest thing would be resisting each other.

THE BRUTAL TRUTH

Lee Winter

ISBN: 978-3-95533-898-5
Length: 339 pages (108,000 words)

Aussie crime reporter Maddie Grey is out of her depth in New York and secretly drawn to her twice-married, powerful media mogul boss, Elena Bartell, who eats failing newspapers for breakfast. As work takes them to Australia, Maddie is goaded into a brief bet—that they will say only the truth to each other. It backfires catastrophically.

A lesbian romance about the lies we tell ourselves.

CHASING STARS

(The Superheroine Collection)
Alex K. Thorne

ISBN: 978-3-95533-992-0
Length: 205 pages (70,000 words)

For superhero Swiftwing, crime fighting isn't her biggest battle. Nor is it having to meet the whims of Hollywood star Gwen Knight as her mild-mannered assistant, Ava. It's doing all that, while tracking a giant alien bug, being asked to fake date her famous boss, and realizing that she might be coming down with a pesky case of feelings.

A fun, sweet, sexy lesbian romance about the masks we wear.

THE POWER OF MERCY

(The Superheroine Collection)
Fiona Zedde

ISBN: 978-3-95533-854-1
Length: 113 pages (37,000 words)

To her family, Mai Redstone is weak. When she becomes Mercy, a rooftop-climbing chameleon with at least nine lives, she finds her power. But when Mercy is called in by police to a murder case, her whole world threatens to crumble. The dead man made her childhood a hell. She is torn between giving the murderer a medal and finding the killer for her family. Mercy is a blade that can cut both ways.

CODE OF CONDUCT

Cheyenne Blue

ISBN: 978-3-96324-030-0
Length: 264 pages (91,000 words)

Top ten tennis player Viva Jones had the world at her feet. Then a lineswoman's bad call knocked her out of the US Open, and injury crushed her career. While battling to return to the game, a chance meeting with the same sexy lineswoman forces Viva to rethink the past...and the present. There's just one problem: players and officials can't date.

A lesbian romance about breaking all the rules.

THE MUSIC AND THE MIRROR

Lola Keeley

ISBN: 978-3-96324-014-0
Length: 311 pages (120,000 words)

Anna is the newest member of an elite ballet company. Her first class almost ruins her career before it begins. She must face down jealousy, sabotage, and injury to pour everything into opening night and prove she has what it takes. In the process, Anna discovers that she and the daring, beautiful Victoria have a lot more than ballet in common.

IN FASHION

Jody Klaire

ISBN: 978-3-96324-090-4
Length: 220 pages (68,000 words)

Celebrity Darcy knows all about perfection. She's famous for stripping bare and restyling women on her UK TV show, Style Surgeon. Fans hang off her #EmbraceDesigner tweets and there's no challenge she can't meet. That is, until security guard Kate struts into her changing room. Suddenly Darcy's the one who feels exposed. A lesbian romance about facing and embracing your own unique design.

GETTING BACK

Cindy Rizzo

ISBN: 978-3-95533-395-9
Length: 239 pages (73,000 words)

At her 30th college reunion, Elizabeth must face Ruth, her first love who bowed to family pressure long ago. As they try to reconcile with their past, Elizabeth must decide whether she is more distrustful of Ruth or of herself. Is she headed for another fall or does she want to be the one who walks away this time? It's not easy to know the difference between getting back together and getting back.

FALLING INTO PLACE

Sheryn Munir

ISBN: 978-3-95533-972-2
Length: 228 pages (56,000 words)

Romance isn't for Tara. After a college fling, she vows to never love again—especially since it feels like there's no future for same-sex love in India. Then, one rain-soaked night, a mad decision brings Sameen into her life. She's cute, full of life…and straight. In an instant, everything changes.

HEART'S SURRENDER

Emma Weimann

ISBN: 978-3-95533-183-2
Length: 305 pages (63,000 words)

Neither Samantha Freedman nor Gillian Jennings are looking for a relationship when they begin a no-strings-attached affair. But soon simple attraction turns into something more. What happens when the worlds of a handywoman and a pampered housewife collide? Can nights of hot, erotic fun lead to love, or will these two very different women go their separate ways?

Language of Love
© 2018

"The Friend" © 2018 Lee Winter
"Deck the Halls with Bullets and Holly" © 2018 Alex K. Thorne
"Mask" © 2018 Sheryn Munir
"Love Just Is" © 2018 Jody Klaire
"Grand Market Bliss" © 2018 Fiona Zedde
"Orphans' Christmas" © 2018 Cheyenne Blue
"And The Bells Are Ringing Out" © 2018 Lola Keeley
"Paula Gets a Pony Ranch" © 2018 Patricia Penn
"Four Chanukahs and a Bat Mitzvah" © 2018 Cindy Rizzo
"The Night Before Christmas—a Cumbrian Tale" © 2018 Andrea Bramhall
"It's in the Pudding" © 2012 Emma Weimann

ISBN: 978-3-96324-101-7

Also available as e-book.

Published by Ylva Publishing, legal entity of Ylva Verlag, e.Kfr.

Ylva Verlag, e.Kfr.
Owner: Astrid Ohletz
Am Kirschgarten 2
65830 Kriftel
Germany

www.ylva-publishing.com

First edition: 2018

No part of this book may be reproduced, scanned, or distributed in any printed or electronic form without permission. Please do not participate in or encourage piracy of copyrighted materials in violation of the author's rights. Thank you for respecting the hard work of this author.

This is a work of fiction. Names, characters, places, and incidents either are a product of the author's imagination or are used fictitiously, and any resemblance to locales, events, business establishments, or actual persons—living or dead—is entirely coincidental.

Credits
Edited by Lee Winter, Astrid Ohletz, and Amanda Jean
Cover Design and Print Layout by Streetlight Graphics

www.ingramcontent.com/pod-product-compliance
Lightning Source LLC
Chambersburg PA
CBHW031610240626
47153CB00002B/701